THE
LAND
of the
LIVING

THE
LAND
of the
LIVING

a novel

Timothy Crellin

GREEN WRITERS PRESS | *Brattleboro, Vermont*

Printed in the United States.

10 9 8 7 6 5 4 3 2 1

Green Writers Press is a Vermont-based publisher whose mission is to spread a message of hope and renewal through the words and images we publish. Throughout we will adhere to our commitment to preserving and protecting the natural resources of the earth. To that end, a percentage of our proceeds will be donated to environmental and social-activist groups. Green Writers Press gratefully acknowledges support from individual donors, friends, and readers to help support the environment and our publishing initiative.

GReen
wrITers
press

Giving Voice to Writers & Artists Who Will Make the World a Better Place
Green Writers Press | Brattleboro, Vermont
www.greenwriterspress.com

ISBN: 979-8-9904801-1-7

COVER IMAGE: SHUTTERSTOCK.COM

PRINTED AT KASE PRINTERS, ON FSC-CERTIFIED PAPER AND PRINTED WITH SOY-BASED INK, DEDICATED TO SOUND ENVIRONMENTAL PRACTICES AND MAKING ONGOING EFFORTS TO REDUCE OUR CARBON FOOTPRINT. WITH PAPER AS A CORE PART OF OUR BUSINESS, KASE IS COMMITTED TO IMPLEMENTING POLICIES THAT FACILITATE CONSERVATION AND SUSTAINABLE PRACTICES. KASE SOURCES PRINTING PAPERS FROM RESPONSIBLE MILLS AND DISTRIBUTORS THAT ARE CERTIFIED WITH AT LEAST ONE CERTIFICATION FROM AN INDEPENDENT THIRD PARTY VERIFICATION, SOURCED DIRECTLY FROM RESPONSIBLY MANAGED FORESTS. WE ALSO MAKE ONGOING EFFORTS TO REDUCE OUR CARBON FOOTPRINT, REUSE ENERGY AND RESOURCES, MINIMIZE WASTE DURING THE MANUFACTURING PROCESS, AND RECYCLE 100% OF SCRAPS, TRASH, CARTRIDGES, EQUIPMENT, AND SOLVENTS WHENEVER POSSIBLE. WE ARE A FAMILY-RUN BUSINESS, LOCATED IN HUDSON, NEW HAMPSHIRE.

For Jenny and Adam,
my companions on this journey,
and for my parents, who showed me the way

and

dedicated to the memory of all those courageous women
and men who left Sicily in search of greater economic and
educational opportunities for their children and their children's
children, especially my maternal great-grandparents.

Repeat a prayer also on behalf of
Women who have seen their sons or husbands
Setting forth, and not returning:
Figlia del tuo figlio,
Queen of Heaven.

—T. S. Eliot (from *Four Quartets*)

Si sapu dunni si nasci ma ʻun si sapi unni si mori.
(We know where we were born but we do not know
where we'll die.)

—Sicilian saying

What if I had not believed that I should see the goodness
of the Lord in the land of the living!

—Psalm 27

ABOVE THE TOWN there is a hillside of extraordinary beauty, even for Sicily. The sun arrives early in the morning and lounges about comfortably all day. Wild grasses offer miniature flowers, lavender and yellow, to the sky. Lone cypress trees pierce the ground, as though fixing the unruly terrain to earth. The landscape ripples a time or two before carrying warm, fragrant breezes gently down across meticulously tended orchards of grape vines, olive and citrus trees, and on to the sea.

Long ago an unremembered ancestor, drawn by the sublime peacefulness of the place, chose it as a burial ground. The rich, red-black soil shelters the remains of generations: here an old man who nearly reached one hundred years; there a boy who drowned in the harbor; and, just beyond, a woman who died giving birth to her fourth child. Many of the graves, long since forgotten, have returned to their natural, grassy state. Others, more recent, are marked with whitewashed wooden crosses, and lovingly adorned with roses, hyacinth, and gladiolus.

A young man wades through the knee-high grass, wiping sweat from his forehead with a handkerchief as he reaches the top of the hill. He walks pensively, reverently, to the newest grave, where the soil is freshly dug, untouched even by rain. Flowers cover the site like a blanket. The young man bends to place his own token among the others: a bouquet of white lilies.

"It's me, Nanna" he whispers, "Tommaso," and adds a prayer, asking God to smile upon her, concluding with the Our Father, after which he turns his face to the sun and looks out over the water in the distance, watching lazy clouds drift from west to east, and remembering his grandmother, a woman he had orbited since childhood, held by the gravity of her ceaseless love until her death had left him empty, untethered.

After a time, he readies himself to leave. Kissing the tips of his fingers, he touches the white cross bearing her name. "Goodbye, Nanna." He turns to go . . .

ONE

i.

TOMMASO SPAT INTO THE LOW WAVES that slapped against the stone pier just below his bare feet and raised his head to scan the broad harbor where scores of fishermen should have been at work in their brightly colored boats, cast like confetti across the dark blue waters of the Tyrrhenian. Holding a string loosely in each hand, he controlled the front and back ends of a basketwork fish trap and raged in his mind. He swayed the thing back and forth in the water as his uncle had taught him, aware just behind his nearly blinding bitterness that he could never catch enough fish to support the family with this old-fashioned trap. For a moment he considered abandoning the task and going off down the beach to dig for clams. He spat into the water again. He would die before he'd go to work for the goddamned Mandralisca.

No one had foreseen or prepared for the storm that had destroyed their livelihood. On that morning, two months earlier, a dim, indistinct scarlet sun had risen, and with it a thickness in the air, cooler after a week of miserable heat and humidity. By noon the atmosphere had calmed to a stillness that sent the old men into a panic. At their urging, all of the fishermen scrambled to secure their boats, as they would when the clouds menaced low and heavy with rain.

The storm that befell them by evening struck with a savageness not even the old men could have foreseen, and the boats, along with anything else on the north coast that wasn't tied down, were blown about like children's toys. Some insisted it was the worst storm to strike the Tyrrhenian since the hurricane that shipwrecked the fleet of the Norman conqueror, King Ruggero II, in the twelfth century. His safe landing at Cefalú had led him to build, in thanksgiving, the tremendous cathedral where many desperate families had gone for shelter when the storm hit.

Tommaso's father's two boats were swept from the beach and scuttled, shredded eventually to splinters, leaving the Amorellis with no means of income. Even now, his older brother was in the Mandraliscas' boatyard, sanding or maybe painting. He imagined Enrico Mandralisca's satisfaction watching Calogero toil, having tried for years to buy the Amorellis' boats and hire his father, his brother, and Tommaso as laborers.

He swept the trap through the water with even greater agitation. His brother had called him a stubborn mule, and he had shot back that Calogero had gone to the Mandralisca like a whore.

The midmorning sun drew beads of sweat from his forehead. Pulling off his shirt, he sat down and dropped his feet into the cool water. There was another option. Selling out to the Mandralisca, becoming their boy, was not his only choice. All over Sicily, young men were leaving fishing villages, sulfur mines, salt flats, pastures, and the serfdom of baronial holdings to set out for America. His cousin Carlo, who felt as he did about the Mandralisca and the other rich families, had left two weeks earlier. Why shouldn't he and Calogero follow? *La Merica* was the land of opportunity where they could become rich and then return to shame the Mandralisca, or even better bring the whole family over to share their new life across the ocean.

Spotting a jellyfish floating across the water, carried by a wind-driven current towards the mouth of the fish trap, Tommaso pulled on the front string to allow the blob to pass. Carlo had begged him to come along, but his father would not allow it. And anyway, unlike Carlo, he had a wife to consider. Adventure was fine for a young man on his own, but to ask Angela to leave her family and friends was more than he had a right to expect. She was willing to go, but he carried his own doubts, as well as the fear of asking her to put her love for him and belief in his plan above her loyalty to her mother and sisters.

He stared down at the empty fish trap and saw it as a futile and pathetic attempt to hold on to something that by God's own will was gone. Sighing, he stood and pulled the trap out of the water. Only two hours until dinner. He couldn't go home empty handed.

Furnished with the few items Tommaso's parents had been given years earlier as wedding gifts—the brass trivet on a hook by the scarred pine sideboard, the icon of the Virgin Mary hung above the cast-iron sink, the ceramic vase from Caltanisetta sent by a cousin from the other side of the island—their small house was barely able to contain the tension brought on by these desperate times, tension that tended to peak during family meals. Calogero was working hard for the Mandralisca. Tommaso, it seemed, was busy doing nothing, sitting on the pier or on the beach with his head full of ridiculous dreams of *La Merica*, while their mother, Pina, worked not only to keep the men fed, but to keep peace in the house.

"How's your buddy Enrico today?" Tommaso scoffed as soon as his father had blessed the food, unable to control his emotions after another fruitless morning.

"Tommaso, don't start," Pina intervened. "Don't."

"I'm just asking." He lifted a forkful of rice, mixed with a meager amount of minced shrimp, to his mouth.

"At least I accomplished something today," Calogero answered, tired of his younger brother's self-righteousness. "At least we've got food on the table. No thanks to you."

"Ah, and just what did you accomplish this morning, Geru? Yes, I'm sure you did a fine job helping Enrico get his boats back in the water, months, maybe years before we can hope to. And then what? You'll fish for him? And he'll pay you shit, because he knows you have no other choice, and then maybe . . ."

He broke off as Angela kicked him under the table. He knew she was right. This would not end well. But he couldn't stop. "Maybe one day, in a few years, we'll have our own boat again, and we can start all over. If we don't starve."

Their father was a man who said little. Pina was the authority in the family. He listened, though, and was diminished by the anguish of both of his sons.

"Tommaso, you'll either stop or leave the table," Pina announced, and now there was an edge in her voice. "Don't make me embarrass you in front of your wife."

Getting up from the table, she went to the kitchen and returned with a plate of chicken which she had cooked with wild mushrooms in watered-down wine. They had only two more chickens in the coop behind the house, pecking ravenously at seeds in the dust.

"The storm was no one's fault, Son," Pina began as she returned to her seat. "We're doing what we have to do to survive. That's all. Your brother is doing what he thinks is best, and we've allowed you to do the same. You brought home some very nice squid the other day and we all appreciated that." She forced a smile and tried to sound kind, but her brow was furrowed, and her jaw was tight.

"It's always about surviving, though, isn't it?" Tommaso replied, gripping the edge of the table as though to lift it off the floor. "Even before the storm, we had to work to hold off the Mandralisca, breaking our backs, salting fish for the lean seasons, scratching a few vegetables and fruit out of the garden, paying taxes to the fucking . . ."

"Tommaso!"

"I'm sorry, Mother. Excuse me, Angela. But don't you see? Even after we get our own boat back—and who knows how long that will take—even then we'll still be struggling just to survive. And my children, if God is good enough to give me some, my sons and their sons after them will be caught in the same struggle."

"It was good enough for your grandfather and his father before him. Why shouldn't it be good enough for you?" Calogero sneered.

"Because why should it be good enough? In America . . ."

"Oh, Christ."

"In America, you don't have to settle for that," he insisted, unwilling this time to give over. "In America, you can make money, buy what you need. Buy what you want. And your children can go to school instead of working when they're six years old. Calogero, if we went to America, we could . . ."

"Tommaso, little brother, I've said it to you before," his brother interrupted, pouring wine into his glass. "I wish you could hear me. I'm not going to *La Merica*. It's a lie. *La Merica* is a lie. It's propaganda."

"It's not. It can't be. Let's just try it. Let's go find Carlo. If it doesn't work out, we'll come back and I'll shut up forever." He tried to look his brother in the eye, but Calogero glanced away.

"That's hard to imagine."

Tommaso rolled his eyes. "Come on, Geru. Aren't you at least curious?"

Suddenly, their father sat up straight in his chair and, pushing his plate forward, folded his hands on the table in front of him.

"Tommaso," he said, his tone firm, decisive. "You've been talking about going to America for weeks. Sometimes it seems to me that you're already gone."

He raised his hand in front of him like a priest about to give a benediction.

"I've changed my mind," he said. "Go. You have my permission."

Tommaso stared back at his father, searching his eyes. Realizing he meant what he said, the son was surprised to feel not relief and gratitude but rather an overwhelming sense of loss.

After their wedding, Angela had moved into the Amorellis' home. Tommaso had built a partition, dividing in half the small room above the kitchen he had shared with Calogero for twenty years, leaving just enough room for a narrow bed and some makeshift shelves. Angela hadn't brought many things, hoping one day soon they'd have their own place to live. That hope had died with the storm. Now she went to her parents' home almost daily, carrying clothes and other possessions back and forth. During the day, she helped both her mother and Pina with chores. She also sewed and made the intricate lacework called *puntini*, though there was no market for luxury items.

Tommaso pulled the curtain that closed off their room from his brother's, blew out the lantern, and lay down on the bed next to his wife. His brother, exhausted after a long day of work, had fallen asleep and was snoring.

"We can't live like this forever, Angela," he muttered, folding his hands behind his head and staring up at the ceiling. "We can't even be together like husband and wife in this place. I never wanted you to have to stay here."

Angela turned on her side to face him, putting her hand on his chest. From the light of the moon shining through the window, he could see her face, the warmth of her eyes, the pleasing curve of her cheek, bordered by her hair which melted into the darkness.

"Your father said you could go, love," she reminded him in a low voice. "Isn't that what you want?"

A tremor of shame passed through him. "He was angry. I shouldn't have said the things I said. I don't know the answer. It just seems like if I stay here, sooner or later I'll have to give up and join Calogero, or else try to invent some other way to live. It's got to be better over there."

"I'm scared," she said after a moment, reaching for his hand. "I won't lie. I only know one place—here. *La Merica* is far away. Far away from my family and everything that's familiar. What if we get there and it's not . . . I mean, what if we want to come back and we can't?"

Tommaso tried to think of an answer but failed. She was right. They would be risking everything, counting on rumors and second- or third-hand stories.

"Things will get better here. We just have to be patient. I know it would be hard, but you could go work with your brother for now, and then when . . ."

"No, Angela! I'll never work for them. I'll die first. Geru's going to be their boy for the rest of his life. He and I are different. Don't you understand that?" On the other side of the wall, Calogero coughed, rolled over in his bed and fell silent.

"Are you settled, then?" she asked him. "Have you made your plans? Is that what you think about all day on the pier? I need to know."

"If I were alone . . . I would go. Now. But I can't ask you to go with me . . . unless you . . ."

"Tommaso." She made a fist and tapped him gently on the forehead. "Don't you remember what the priest said at our wedding? Don't you remember our promises to each other? If you think this is best, then . . . I'm ready. Just send for me soon, because I can't be without you for too long."

He turned his face to kiss her. "Thank you," he whispered. "Thank you. All right then, if you're sure, I'll talk to my father about the money tomorrow. They'll see, Angela. As soon as I start sending them envelopes full of cash, they'll see that I was right."

He closed his eyes and tried to stifle his fear—of talking to his father, of going alone to America, of being responsible for their future. He worried that both of his parents would feel the repudiation of their way of life, and the helplessness at not being able to offer their son more. He'd heard their conversations about all of the other neighbors who were gone, and now he'd be joining them, another foolish pilgrim grasping at an illusion.

ii.

The boat, forced out of its gently bobbing slumber and into reverse, protested in a series of guttural groans, each trailing off in a wretched, piercing squeal, and she began to drift sluggishly away from her berth. Long, narrowing streaks of auburn rust dripped down the rotting hull from corroded iron bolts across faded, flaking green paint. Molded, deteriorating ropes and festering nets were piled chaotically on the worn, rutted deck. *The Samantha* had been one of the first steam draggers on the harbor a dozen years earlier, but her condition had declined from neglect and exposure to New England's punishing climate. Plumes of toxic, sooty smoke hiccupped from the stack and tumbled down to the water, floating like ghosts before finally dissipating into the fog. Cursing, the captain wrenched the aged, sputtering craft violently forward. The propeller churned roughly before prodding the boat into motion.

A breeze raw for late May with a spit of drizzle caused Tommaso to blink and wipe his eyes, clearing his vision to look out across the inner harbor. As the vessel steamed with shuddering reluctance away from Fish Pier and towards Rocky Neck, he peered ahead into the ocean's expanding emptiness, the fine spray dampening his hair and the mist clinging to his three days' growth of beard, where it gathered into droplets that slid down his neck to be absorbed by the straw-colored wool sweater his wife had given to him the night before he left. He hadn't seen the open water since the barge carrying him from the liner had entered New York harbor two weeks earlier.

The rocking of this decrepit fishing boat as it met higher surf in the outer harbor was the first familiar sensation he'd known since the day in Naples when he had boarded the ocean liner, the imposing S.S. *Principe di Piemonte*. Closing his eyes to concentrate on reacquainting his body to the sea's rhythmic motion, he filled his lungs with marine air and wondered whether he had spent more of his life on a fishing boat or on solid ground. But fishing at home was an art, a way of life, something that was honored. One's boat was his masterpiece, a matter of pride, even if he wasn't fortunate enough to own one but was instead forced to rent from the rich fishing-boat owners. Still, he took as much pride in the appearance and performance of the rented boat as if it were his own. It never would have occurred to him not to do so, any more than it would occur to him not to be a fisherman, or not to teach his sons to fish, or not to sing while fishing. It was the way. The storm had taken their boats, but they had all been devoured by the sea or crushed against the rocks with fresh paint, carefully scrubbed decks, and nets that were, as always, faultlessly tied.

The *Samantha* scared him, and yet to him her condition seemed to match the rest of his experiences in America so far. Not only were the streets not paved with gold, as he had been promised by the ticket salesman in Palermo when he hesitated before turning over his father's money, but everything here seemed to be dirty, shabby, and in disrepair.

The sky was darkening and the drizzle was thickening into a cold rain. As they passed the squat lighthouse on Ten Pound Island and neared the taller beacon on Eastern Point, the engine coughed and died, sending the choleric captain, shouting, out of the wheelhouse and down the ladder into the hold. Tommaso hugged himself under his black oil-skin poncho. How would the news be received back home if he died on this stinking heap? How would Angela be able to hold her head up in public? How would she face his brother, who swore he would never leave Sicily—who insisted that leaving home was stupid? She would be ruined, squandered, a nineteen-year-old widow in black, her husband lost at sea far away in America, in a place with the unpronounceable name of *Gloucester, Massachusetts.* What a reckless fool he had been, they would whisper behind her back.

And yet, with the engine gasping and rumbling back to life, Tommaso could sense a bit of hope. One day he would captain his own fine boat on this very harbor. Perhaps he would even own one, or more than one, a fleet of handsome vessels, with a tall American son at the helm of each one. Or maybe his sons would do even better: go to school and become doctors, businessmen in expensive suits. Then he would return to Cefalú in triumph. He would drive past the amazed townspeople in the piazza and on to his stubborn brother's house in an automobile, the first ever to be seen on the entire island. Perhaps this was a beginning, humble to say the least, but a beginning, a chance.

He was grateful for the opportunity to ride this mess of a fishing boat. A second cousin of his earned a dollar a day in the textile mill in Lawrence, and a former neighbor was forced to give half of what he earned to the crooked agent who hired him each morning to shovel coal in the rail yard. If there were fish, he would be paid decently. And he knew, in spite of the pitiful limitations of this boat, that he could bring in fish.

Out of nowhere, the captain's face was six inches in front of his own, cracked lips and stained teeth forming the words of a tirade he did not understand. Scorbutic and shriveled, the old man might well have been hired to match the boat. Tobacco-juice spittle began to bombard Tommaso in the face as the captain's rage intensified. And then, abruptly, he was gone, hobbling off toward the stern. Tommaso turned, perplexed, and spotted his cousin laughing at him from the gunwale. It was through Carlo that Tommaso had been directed from New York to Boston, and on to Gloucester and this job. "That's his friendly way of saying it's your turn to stoke the boiler, you dago, good-for-nothing son of a bitch," he explained to Tommaso. "Welcome aboard."

Carlo was nearly half a foot taller, clearly more the man than the still-boyish Tommaso, though they were born only sixteen months apart. His beard was full, unlike his cousin's which grew in patches, and he had thick eyebrows above his olive-colored eyes. He reminded Tomasso of the man with the vegetable cart in their old neighborhood, whose salesman's smile could set anyone at ease.

"Come on, now, cousin," he began, seeing Tommaso's tight-lipped scowl. "It's not so different from home. A perfect harbor for fishing, and look. See the fort on the hill overlooking the harbor and the town? It's just like the old citadel. Look at the village. If you squint, the spire on the town hall looks just like the *duomo*. And Tommaso, come on, fish are fish. It doesn't matter where you are."

"Just squinting won't work, cousin. You can only close your eyes all the way and dream of Cefalú. Besides, idiot, there are two towers on the *duomo*."

"Fine, little guy. Have it your way." It was going to take some work to keep his younger cousin steady. "At least I tried. Now, you better get down below before Captain Sunshine comes looking for you again." Taking his cousin by the back of the neck, he pushed him playfully in the direction of the ladder. "And try not to be so depressing."

Tommaso paused at the top of the ladder. Maybe Geru was right about Carlo. Maybe he saw things that weren't there.

When the *Samantha* returned to Gloucester Harbor twice with impressive hauls, a rumor passed along the pier suggesting that Tommaso and Carlo had a "magic touch." Soon the cousins were offered work on one of the finer boats on the harbor, a newer version of the decaying dragger with mechanical winches and a powerful engine. At the end of the 1912 season, they convinced the owner—a decent enough man who treated his immigrant workers with a measure if not of respect, at least of propriety—to dry-dock his vessel for the offseason. By the time spring arrived they had restored the craft to its original condition—or better, Tomasso thought, admiring the glistening paint on the day the boat was launched and the captain had rewarded them for their long months of labor.

That payday, along with what he could save that season, had brought him to the point where he could send for Angela: forty dollars, plus five to ensure that the money arrived in her hands. He had hoped, imagined, that he might have a suitable home for his bride, and had considered waiting another season to save money to lease one of the small cabins across the road from the inner harbor.

But the talk in the bars of the North End, where they spent an occasional free weekend visiting Carlo's friend Santo, was all about war. All of Europe was unnerved by the crisis in the Balkans, and if war came, an Atlantic crossing would be dangerous if not impossible. In the penciled note he sent with the money, Tommaso told Angela to prepare herself for austere conditions. He assured her, though, that after one more successful fishing season, followed by the restoration of one more boat during the winter months, they could move out of the dingy boarding house attic he shared with Carlo and into a place they could refer to as a home.

Now he paced back and forth across the station platform in Boston as the arrival time for the train from New York came and passed. If all had gone according to plan, Angela would be on this train. If not, he and Carlo would come back the next day, and the next. He looked down the track, hoping to see a wisp of steam, or to hear the long whistle announcing the train's approach. He began to imagine all that could have gone wrong. He recalled each step of his own passage through immigration. His ship had waited tantalizingly outside the Narrows for two days before a barge had come to take the steerage passengers into the harbor. With thousands of immigrants arriving each day, there were frustrating delays at each stage of the procedure. Elbowing his way to the rail as they came into the harbor, he'd taken in the sight of the enormous and ornate registration building, its cupolaed towers rising above the lush, emerald lawn. If they welcomed newcomers in such a beautiful palace, he reasoned, then *La Merica* must be everything he had heard.

Once on the island, he had been awed by the mass of people, most appearing weary and scared, speaking to each other in a dozen languages, wearing the working class and peasant attire of towns and villages across Europe. Was there room for everyone? Would some be sent back? He waited all morning to climb the staircase into the expansive registration room, unaware of the immigration officers scrutinizing the crowd for people who appeared ill, until a companion alerted him to their presence, urging him to stand up straight and look energetic.

From the entrance to the registration room, the wait was three hours more in line before he reached the desk. After his initial interview, he sat with his head back, staring up at the high, vaulted ceiling until he dozed off. An officer woke him for the brief medical examination to determine that he was reasonably healthy and capable of working to support himself. A legal examination followed. He produced his stash of neatly folded lire, which was cursorily deemed adequate by the grayish, corpulent official, who then approved him for immigration.

From there, he had been directed to the exchange window to purchase dollar bills. With these in hand, along with the scrap of paper on which was written, "Boston, Massachusetts" and Carlo's name, he bought his train ticket and was sent out to wait for the ferry across to Hoboken with a yellow card pinned to his jacket indicating his destination. While he waited, he bought a box of food containing strange items he had never seen before: bread made from corn, a plain boiled potato, and pork so salty that he had to eat it with gulps of water. By their relative freshness alone, though, they were by far the best food he had eaten in weeks.

The frenetic train station in New Jersey was the scariest stage of the arrival process for Tommaso, who was reminded of being lost as a small child in the piazza during a festival. He held out the card on his chest towards anyone who looked official. Finally, through the chaos of crying children, anxious mothers, and worried fathers pretending to appear confident, he found the train to Boston, and hours later thanked God when he first saw Carlo at the station, certain that his safe arrival had been a miracle.

Now he recited a prayer to St. Christopher, asking for a second miracle to bring Angela to him. He knew the many opportunities for the devil to cause trouble. Perhaps she had fallen ill on the ship, like so many others, and had been sent back to Sicily by the doctors on Ellis Island. What if she had been robbed on board and was being held in detention on the island, waiting for someone to bring her money to buy a train ticket? Perhaps, in the end, she had changed her mind and stayed home, and the letter she had sent to tell him she wasn't coming had been lost. He would certainly understand that decision. His mind charged ahead until, shaking his head as if to wake from a nightmare, he pushed aside images of disaster.

What would it be like to see Angela? After all, they had lived most of their married life with an ocean between them. How would she react to this "new world," which was nothing like the paradise they had allowed themselves to imagine?

Carlo, who was splayed on a wooden bench smoking a cigarette and trying to warm himself in the midmorning sun, called to Tommaso, "This is not the same sun we have back home." Tommaso wasn't listening. "This sun has no fucking warmth."

At last the train's whistle cut through the distance. Tommaso hurried to the edge of the platform and gazed down the gleaming track as the locomotive came into view, no more than a speck where the two rails appeared to meet nearly a mile away. In the moment, he was conquered by doubt. Why had he brought her to this place? She'd come all this way to be with him. It had all been a mistake. He had nothing to offer her.

Carlo, now standing at his side, saw the panic on his cousin's face. "Knock it off!" he commanded, pounding him on the back in his affectionate way. "She loves you. Why would she come all this way? *Curaggiu*. And smile, you idiot. You want her to see you for the first time looking like that? Come on now." The brakes of the steam locomotive screeched the train to a halt. "Smile."

Finally Tommaso watched Angela step into the doorway of the Pullman. He could see as she glanced about desperately that she was shaken. He called out to her and their eyes met. He felt his heart pounding when she threw herself down the steps of the car into his arms. Carlo pretended to examine the mechanics of the locomotive as the two clung to each other, Tommaso holding her head in his hand and sighing as the sense of security he'd been missing returned.

"Welcome, Angela," Carlo said, smiling, when she finally pulled away from Tommaso. "How was your journey? You must be exhausted."

"I'm more hungry than tired," she replied, greeting Carlo with a kiss on each cheek. "What do they eat in this strange country? I can see it's a problem, as you're a pair of skeletons. Thank God your mothers can't see you. And thank God I got here before it was too late." Angela poked playfully at Tommaso's ribs. He pretended to defend himself before grabbing her in another embrace.

Later in the evening they arrived back in Gloucester after taking Angela to the North End, Boston's Italian quarter, to eat something familiar and hopefully comforting. She was too tired to comment on the accommodations. Tommaso had worked in vain to make them presentable for her arrival. Staring by candlelight at the roofing nails sticking through the boards less than three feet above, he lay awake while his wife slept, holding her in his arms on the canvas cot and going over and over his plans for their lives, the house they would live in, the children, the sons, who would be Americans and grow up to live in a way no one from back home could imagine.

iii.

Moonlight filtered through the gauzy white curtains Angela had made for the front window of the rented cabin. Humming to herself, she stirred a steaming pot on the stove, before opening the fuel door and dropping another piece of scrap lumber taken from the boat yard onto the coals. With their reputations established, Tommaso and Carlo had been able to demand payment as the work on the dry-docked fishing boat progressed this year, rather than waiting until the job was finished. Angela took in laundry and mending from the large homes on the other side of town, rolling the loads back and forth on a wooden cart Tommaso had found for her. Combined, their income was enough to lease the cabin, a bare, single-roomed structure with no amenities save the sunny window and harbor view, and they had even been able to purchase a few items to remind them of home: a tablecloth decorated with sunflowers, a white cotton bedspread, a tin breadbox with lemons painted on the front.

Angela was steadfast in the face of a challenge, more resolute than her husband, and devout in her Catholic faith, determined to succeed in their new life. Although her mother had begged her not go, her father, who bore the humiliation of having four daughters and not a single son, hadn't even bothered to argue. In the end, as one young woman after another followed her man to America, both of her parents had recognized the futility of standing in the way. Faced with the reality of a hard life in Sicily, with the threat of a European war, leaving one's home and family for a far-off land had begun to seem not only reasonable, but logical, even hopeful: a sacrifice one willingly made, a risk optimistically taken for the sake of one's children—and one's children's children.

By late October of 1913, the talk of war in Europe dominated conversation on the docks, on street corners, and in the taverns in Gloucester. Angela worried about her family back at home. Which side would Italy join, and what effect would that choice have on daily life in their hometown? With supper simmering on the wood stove, Angela began to twist a linen bed sheet, wringing out water and bleach. Sicily was probably far enough from where the battles would be. Maybe the powers would make peace before their armies began to march across Europe. She prayed, "*Santa Maria, Matri di Diu . . .*"

She was still worrying about the future when Tommaso arrived home from the boat yard just after eight o'clock. His hair and his clothes, even the fine black hairs on his arms, were specked with sawdust. His left eyelid, the one with the scar above it from a childhood scrape in the schoolyard, always drooped slightly when he was tired. Angela wrinkled her nose as she kissed him.

"Take a bath, love," she suggested. "I heated water for you." He was ever the handsome boy she had fallen for, with the sensitive and gentle eyes. She could see the strain he felt, the pressure to make their life together better, and she knew she would have to temper her doubts and fears for him.

A hard winter passed. Frigid air entered the cabin through the many cracks and holes in the walls and floor, which Tommaso attempted to seal with tar he brought home from work. Angela was shocked by the cold. She would step out into the blowing snow to take the bitter wind as a slap across her cheeks. "You didn't tell me about this," she lamented to her husband again and again, to which he responded lightly, "I was afraid you wouldn't come if I did."

At last spring arrived, the fishing boats once again steamed out of the harbor, and Angela, renewed by the return of light and color, set out to plant a garden. She was beginning to feel settled, having established a home, regular work, and at least a smiling acknowledgment from the priest at St. Anne's, even if they couldn't communicate. She missed her mother and her sisters, wishing she could somehow have even a brief visit with them from time to time, but she had begun to accept America as the only future she would ever know.

Then came a balmy Saturday evening in early July, the air dense with the threat of a storm, when Carlo and Tommaso returned from a trip to the city with a copy of the Italian newspaper. These days they went to the North End for news alone, and not for fun. "I'm sure there'll be war now," Carlo said as they showed Angela the headline: AUSTRIAN ARCHDUKE ASSASSINATED.

Tommaso explained to Angela that Franz Ferdinand's death—murdered with his wife during a state visit to the Serbian capital—meant that Austria would be forced to respond. The only question was what Germany would do next. Having listened to the old men back home discussing politics in the piazza, he and Carlo both understood the tension in Europe, the strained balance of power, and he knew that the assassination could lead to war.

"Some of the boys say they're going to enlist if America enters the war," Carlo ventured, pretending not to notice Tommaso glaring at him. He was eager to enlist, believing the promise of citizenship and maybe even heroism outweighed the risks.

"Well, I know one boy who's not going to be enlisting." She set down the potato she'd been peeling and wiped her hands on her apron. "So why don't you two would-be war heroes put your minds to something else and let the British and the French and the Austrians and the Germans worry about their war."

Carlo shrugged and lit a cigarette, while Tommaso covered a smile with his hand. He loved her for being smart and fiercely protective.

"Don't worry, love," he murmured in Angela's ear, taking her by the waist and pulling her to him. "Let's just wait and see."

For months President Wilson left the war to the European powers, though his intentions were debated at every level of American society. In the winter of 1915, and into the spring before the fishing season commenced, the Germans began using their newly deployed submarines against civilian targets, sinking merchant ships in the English Channel and laying mines in the North Sea. Though Wilson warned the Germans against attacking American ships, Angela worried each time Tommaso's trawler left the harbor. The sinking of the *Lusitania* early in May weighed on her mind throughout the summer.

As another autumn passed, and another winter took hold, the warring powers descended into hellish, intractable battle. The new year brought a further massing of armies on the continent, and in February, the attack on Verdun. Tommaso and his cousin returned from their frequent trips to the city with the latest information on the war, examining the maps in the newspaper and arguing about what might happen in the days and months to come.

Meanwhile, Angela wasn't well, although she insisted it was the cold that made her feel tired and often nauseated. At first,

Tommaso feared that she might have influenza. He suggested they call for a doctor, but Angela refused, reminding him that they had no money.

"Might you be, you know . . ." Tommaso asked one morning, holding her head while she vomited into the basin by the bed. As it turned out, she was. She'd missed her period twice before she'd begun to consider the possibility that she was pregnant. Perhaps, she reflected, she hadn't allowed herself to think about bringing an infant into these uncertain times. Fear tempered her happiness, and she missed her mother more than she had since she left home. Her mother would know what to do, what signs to observe and which remedies would make her feel healthier and strong.

Tommaso was thrilled, believing his American dream was proceeding to its logical next phase. Yet before there was time to celebrate or even begin to prepare for the baby, Angela stumbled home from delivering laundry on a frigid afternoon with knifelike pains in her abdomen. Tommaso came in from the shipyard surprised to find her in bed, blood-stained underclothes soaking in one of her tin wash pails.

"I'm sorry, Tommaso," she whispered, lifting her head from the damp spot on the pillow where she had perspired during a troubled hour of sleep. Dropping to his knees next to the bed, he began to stroke her hair.

"No, my love, no. It's my fault." He kissed her forehead, once again besieged by the same sense of shame and regret that took hold of him when there were no fish to be caught, or when she complained of the bitter cold and he saw that her hands were chapped and raw from scrubbing laundry with bleach, or when he noticed some upper-crust matron in the village looking at him like he was an animal—that feeling that found imagined expression in his brother Calogero's pompous voice: "You never should have left Cefalú."

Despite several days of weakness after she miscarried, Angela was steadfast. Convincing herself that her loss was God's inscrutable will, she carried on valiantly, and they passed a pleasant enough spring, growing more accustomed to their new country. Sometimes, on fine Sundays after Mass, they would walk all the way to Eastern Point to gaze out across the ocean and talk about home, each trying for the other's sake to dilute their sadness with sweet and amusing stories of family and friends.

In mid-September a German U-boat attacked off the island of Nantucket, sinking five merchant vessels. When Carlo and Tommaso told Angela, she was alarmed, shaken, and at the same time relieved that the fishing season would soon be ending. But there was other news.

"We spoke to a man from the army," Tommaso began. "He told us we'll get citizenship. He says we'll be well paid. He also says America will wait until the French and the British have things in hand, and then we'll just go to help clean up. Actually, he says there's a good chance we'll not have to go at all, and we'll still be given citizenship just for enlisting."

"What good will citizenship do you if you're dead?" she asked, and when he didn't reply: "And what good will it do me if I'm left here alone? Didn't I just come all the way here to be with you? You're not going back across that ocean to fight in a war."

"Sweetheart, do you really think they'll let us immigrants fight? We'll be so far behind the lines we won't even hear the guns. Believe me, we'll be cooking and cleaning up after the horses in the cavalry. Then, when it's over, which won't be too long once the states join, I'll come home a citizen and we'll have a new life as Americans." He finished his speech with a triumphant grin.

Angela shook her head and felt the ribbon she had tied her hair back with loosen and slide down the thick braid. "Our life is fine as is. What's wrong with it? Look how far we've come already, without the army or the war."

They stood, silent for a moment, looking at each other across the room.

"The fishing season is over," Carlo offered, believing he was seeing equivocation on her face. "We'll go to a place called Camp Devens, not far from here. We'll be able to come home for weekends. The money's better than what we could make working in the boat yard this winter. With a little luck the war will end soon and we'll be back at work on the boat in the spring."

Angela stayed quiet, looking out the window to avoid eye contact with the two men.

"Our families are suffering at home, Angela," Carlo continued. "Life in Sicily is hard. That's what we heard from a man who arrived last week. He sneaked aboard a cargo ship just to get out. Many more would come, he said, but no more passenger ships will cross. Let us—let Tommaso—do our little part, and we'll all be glad when it's over."

Tommaso and Carlo left for the city soon after Christmas. From there they would be taken to Camp Devens. For months, life for Angela was just as Tommaso had assured her that it would be. On many weekends they came home from the camp. Angela was used to being alone, as she had often been during the days when Tommaso had gone out to Georges Bank fishing. She did her work and visited with acquaintances in Gloucester's small Sicilian community, looking forward to the weekends when Tommaso would be with her to stroll along the beach or to wade laughing into the waves. Tommaso would help her in the garden, and she would prepare his favorite meals for him, and often for Carlo, too. Sometimes Tommaso would arrive on a Friday night with a bottle of wine, purchased in the North End on his way back to town. Then they would light candles and dance to familiar tunes from home that they sang or hummed together, eventually tumbling giddily onto the bed where they would make love and fall asleep wrapped around one another.

One morning, hours before they were due to return to the camp, Angela was making breakfast. "So I was wondering," she began, turning fried eggs onto a plate, "what do you brave soldiers do all week at this important Camp Devens?"

Tommaso had warned Carlo that this question would eventually come and had sworn him to secrecy on the subject of guns, bayonets, ammunition, gas masks, grenades, and even marching, the preparation for battle which consumed most of their time.

"Well, it's not very well organized," Tommaso replied. Though he had rehearsed his response in his head many times, he still felt like a little boy lying to his mother. "Just keeping forty thousand men fed takes a lot of time. Carlo and I have skills, so mostly we've been carpenters, helping to build more barracks for the new recruits who come every day. There's really nothing warlike about it. At all. Most people are saying the war will end without America."

Part of this was true enough. The two cousins had helped to build barracks and to unload supply trains. On most days, though, they were trained for the infantry, acquiring skills they would need to survive trench warfare, training which frightened Tommaso and kept him awake at night in his bunk, imagining what it would be like if he was facing a real enemy. Hiding the truth from Angela made him uncomfortable, but he knew how she worried. "She's like an old grandmother in Cefalú," he told Carlo later, trying to justify his deception.

The possibility that the two men might start and finish their war service at Camp Devens was real, too, notwithstanding the military drills and mustering. As 1917 began, diplomats were working to broker a peace treaty. With winter turning to spring, however, the cousins returned almost weekly with reports of further American and Allied losses at sea. The Germans, in hostile concert with diplomatic pressure from London, were finally forcing Wilson to bring the United States into the war. In May, the first American troops stepped off a landing craft and onto French soil.

As troops left Camp Devens for Europe, Carlo and Tommaso stayed behind. Their talents were needed as the camp prepared for conversion to a hospital and "demobilization center." They spent another Christmas at home, attending Mass at St. Anne's, seated in the back of the nave with other Sicilian families. After the service, Angela slipped a nickel into the box, lit a candle, and knelt before a statue of the Virgin to pray for peace.

Meat was hard to come by, but Carlo had been able to purchase a scrawny chicken from people he knew in the city. Angela stewed it with tomatoes and peppers she had preserved in glass jars, and they presented each other with small gifts. "Maybe by next Christmas," Tommaso smiled, "we'll have something to talk about besides the damned Kaiser."

"Ah, *una brinnisi*!" Carlo cried. "A toast to that!"

Ultimately, however, their good fortune was exhausted, like a last handful of money lost in a bet. One snowy February morning a sergeant woke them early to announce that they should prepare to "ship out." Shivering, Tommaso crawled from his canvas bedroll and looked out the frosted window of the barracks at the snow blowing across the parade grounds. "Carlo, I don't want to go."

"What a strange boy you are, cousin. Always so full of doubts! Remember what you told Angela? They'll never send us Italians into battle. We'll be shoveling snow miles behind the trenches." He flashed the salesman's smile and clapped Tommaso on the back.

"I lied to Angela, cousin. We both lied to her. We Italians will probably be the first they send into battle to waste German bullets on." He felt sick to his stomach.

Carlo would remember these words years later when he learned that Italian soldiers in the United States forces had died in dramatic disproportion to their numbers in the military.

"Listen," Carlo teased, sliding out of bed and pulling on his pants. "If you keep whining like that, I'm going to ask to be switched to a different battalion. Let's just try to think of this as a big adventure, okay? You're going to make me cry with all that other bullshit."

Tommaso rolled his eyes. A few moments later as they made their way to the mess hall for breakfast, Carlo picked up a handful of snow and plopped it onto his cousin's head. Tommaso turned and tackled Carlo at the waist, and they fell laughing into the snow.

The next day the two men secured passes to return to Gloucester once more before being shipped abroad. Tommaso asked Carlo to visit a friend so he could speak to Angela alone. It was evening, and he found her mending by the light of the lantern, the stove stoked to take the chill out of the winter air.

"My love!" she shouted, jumping from her chair to embrace him. She hadn't been expecting him until the following weekend at the earliest. "What a surprise. You scared me." He smiled, unable to think of any words to say. Awkwardly, like a teenager on a first date, he handed her a gold foil-wrapped box of chocolates and she embraced him again, pulling away his scarf to kiss his neck.

"You must be frozen in this weather, and hungry, too," she said, glancing about as though food might appear. "Sit. I'll find something. Where's that silly cousin of yours?"

Then her smile faded as she put all the pieces together in her mind: the unexpected visit, the chocolates, Tommaso's arriving alone. "You're not leaving, are you?" She turned quickly to face him. "Is that what you've come to tell me?"

He shrugged, then nodded, looking down at the wide pine floorboards. "Yes, love. We're being sent to France. But not for long, I'm sure. They . . . they need us to build barracks. Hospitals. Actually, the war may be nearly over by the time we get there."

Glancing up he saw both fear and anger on her face, redness coming to her cheeks and forehead as it did when she was upset, and a lump rose in his throat. He was afraid of going to France, but even more, he didn't want to leave this woman who had been his rock, once again putting an ocean between them.

"I'm sorry, my love. I was hoping . . . Angela, please, try not to worry."

She turned her back to him. "Let me make you something to eat," she said, her voice expressionless.

Later, as they lay in bed together, she moved towards him, pulling herself close against his body. "I am angry, Tommaso. I never wanted you to join this cursed army. I don't want you to go to France. I don't want to be left here. But I love you. You're my husband." She paused, her voice softening. "Just come back safe, please? And don't let Carlo talk you into doing anything stupid."

"Maybe you should come along to keep us out of trouble," Tommaso kidded, stroking her hair. "We could sneak you on board."

"No thank you. I'll leave the war to you men. Just come back in one piece, Tommaso."

"I will, my darling," he promised, kissing her forehead, her nose and then her lips, "and then we'll go on with our lives."

The following day at noontime Angela prepared as large a meal as she could for the two men. Afterwards, they shared the chocolates Tommaso had brought and told stories from home. "Do you remember the time Carlo fell asleep on the bow, and my brother pushed him off into the sea?" They laughed, trying to ward off the now-inevitable parting.

Finally, it was time for the cousins to begin the journey into the city and, from there, back to camp to make final preparations for departure. Angela embraced Carlo. "Watch out for each other. If you hear gunfire, hide." Her voice was tight, pinching off fear and sadness.

"It won't be long, my love," Tommaso whispered, taking her in his arms. "Pray for us." His eyes filled with tears too, when he saw that she was crying.

iv.

The vessel that would take Tommaso and Carlo to Europe was a luxury ocean liner called the *Aquitania*, commandeered and converted for the purpose of carrying American troops to France. The cousins remarked more than once that they were making their second crossing of the Atlantic in much higher style than the first. On deck, a variety of languages could be heard, from Italian to Greek to Polish. As they had discovered at Camp Devens, they were not the only immigrants to see military service as an opportunity for advancement in their new country. The mood was jovial, with singing and laughing late into the evening. They had all heard unsettling details of the brutality of the war as it neared the end of its fourth year, but they felt assured that the mere presence of a fresh army from the United States would bring the enemy to its knees.

Tommaso, however, was tense, to the point that his head ached most of the time. He could not enjoy the practical jokes and friendly competition that took place among the various ethnic groups. Nor could he sleep. Despite Carlo's efforts to calm his cousin, Tommaso was filled with anxiety. Convinced that the *Aquitania* would be sunk by a German U-boat, he alarmed Carlo repeatedly with mistaken sightings of submarines. It was only when the gray outline of the French coastline appeared on the horizon one foggy morning that Tommaso began to believe that they would at least arrive safely.

Yet by the time they stepped off the ship onto French soil, word of the new German offensive on the Western Front had turned Tommaso pale with fear. Freed from the burden of a two-front war by the withdrawal of the Russians from the conflict, the Germans turned all their efforts towards France. The onslaught began on March 21. Within a week, the Germans had recrossed the Somme and were driving the French and British to scrambling retreat. To the frustration of the other Allies, the unseasoned new arrivals from America were not sent into battle by their superiors due to General Pershing's reluctance to commit his troops, numbering eight hundred thousand by mid-June, until there was a full army on the continent under his command. By the most optimistic estimates, that goal would not be achieved until the following year: 1919.

Tommaso allowed himself to be heartened by these rumors as they passed through the barracks where he and Carlo were housed. Later in the month, however, when influenza began its destructive siege, killing more soldiers than were dying in the trenches, Tommaso became convinced that he would get sick and die. He shivered in his bunk, imagining that he was coming down with the virus, blowing his nose repeatedly and trying to come up with a way to escape.

"You're like that nasty old hag who lived in my street back home," Carlo said to him one day after he had voiced his dread yet again, "the one who always swore that a beautiful morning would be ruined by a storm in the afternoon, or that a perfect, ripe fig was probably full of worms. You're making me goddamned crazy."

Tommaso stared back at him vacantly, lost in premonitions of tragedy.

Daily life continued as normally as possible for Angela. She often tried to convince herself that Tommaso was only at sea, fishing, and would amble in at any moment with his sweet smile and his robust appetite. She continued to make her usual rounds of laundry and mending. Her skills as a seamstress, learned from her mother, were becoming well known. She had even been hired to make a wedding dress for the daughter of a prominent merchant in town.

Nearly every day, Angela would include a stop at St. Anne's in her circuit. There she would light a candle, say a rosary and pray for Tommaso's safety. On days when her yearning for him became nearly a physical aching, she would beg the Virgin for his prompt return. Once, as he came out from the sacristy to set the missal for Mass, the priest found her on her knees weeping in front of the marble statue of Mary. Although he didn't speak her language and didn't know the cause of her sorrow, he tried to offer words of comfort. "Trust in God, and He will deliver you," the priest consoled with genuine concern, holding her hand in his. We must have faith—*fides*, faith," he continued, hoping he was making himself understood. Angela smiled shyly.

In late March, she realized again that many weeks had slid by since her last period. Too many weeks. Soon she began to feel nauseated, and she grew unusually tired before she finished her work in the evening. "*Santa Maria,*" she said to herself, making the sign of the cross repeatedly. She recognized the physical signs. She convinced herself to recognize a blessing, a sure sign that God was planning to send Tommaso back to her in time for the birth of their baby.

March 31 was Easter Sunday, a warm and beautiful spring day. "God is stronger than the evil forces of this world," the priest had stated confidently during his homily, after retelling the story of the empty tomb. The Sicilian man who had been in Gloucester the longest translated for the community, which huddled around him in the back pews. "The resurrection of our Lord Jesus Christ from the dead demonstrates beyond a doubt that the power of darkness cannot ultimately prevail over what is right, and good and holy."

Angela left Mass squinting into the brightness of noonday, feeling hopeful that Tommaso would soon return, and that she would place his newborn son in his arms. Perhaps he might even arrive home in time for the baby's birth, she thought, strolling down Main Street, her face turned up to take in the sun. Even if it was a girl, Tommaso would be a devoted and affectionate father. She was sure of it. For the first time in a long while, excitement about the future and the promise of new life allowed her to push aside her worries.

Spring dragged on in France. Reports came daily from the front, along with gossip which passed from company to company, so that Tommaso found it impossible to know what to believe. Four years of war had made a decimating mark on the populations of France and Britain. Their ability to call up new recruits was waning. Pressure on General Pershing and on the American president to send their troops into battle grew. By now, Tommaso and Carlo and their cohort had been trained intensively in the techniques of trench warfare, adding Allied experience to the instruction they had been given at Devens. In May, a rumor began to spread through the camp that Pershing had finally given in to the desperate pleading of the other Allies, and that American divisions would be entering the conflict under Allied command. The rumor was confirmed in late June, when their commanding officer announced at colors that they should prepare to be moved towards the front.

Angela was worried. No word had come from Tommaso since March, not even a postcard. It was late May, and her belly was beginning to grow. In Gloucester, it was difficult to find someone who could explain what was happening abroad in terms she could understand. Tommaso and Carlo had been her source for information about the war. As weeks became months, she grew desperate. What if Tommaso was dead? If not, he surely would have written to her. Perhaps he had tried and the letter hadn't reached her. All she could do was cling to the hope that the war would soon be over.

When she could bear the silence no longer, the terrifying lack of information that set her imagination darkly working, Angela resolved to travel to Boston. Tommaso always claimed it was better there, with more current information available in the city. She would go and make inquiries herself, hoping to return to Gloucester with some idea of where her husband was and when he might be back.

She woke early on a cool Saturday morning. Before boarding the steamship *Cape Ann*, she delivered mending to the Babson house. Taking the coins she was given by the maid in compensation, she walked to the church to light a candle and to leave an offering in the alms box. Someone, as her mother always said, was worse off than she.

The fare to Boston roundtrip was a dollar and a half. She bought her ticket and stepped onto the gangplank, still unaccustomed to the extra weight she was carrying, and climbed the steps to the upper deck of the ship. There was a steady breeze off the water, and when the large, slow-moving clouds eclipsed the sun, she pulled her shawl tight around her shoulders. But it wasn't only the cold that caused her to tremble. She was scared. The ferry could be attacked by a German submarine. She might get lost in Boston. She feared the city, and had gone there only once, aside from when she passed through on the day she arrived from New York. Tommaso and Carlo had brought her to the North End the year before to celebrate her birthday, and she had found it crowded, dirty, and crushing. Even in Sicily she had been to Palermo only a few times, preferring the slower pace and familiarity of her own neighborhood in Cefalú. Though she was confident she could find her way to the North End from the waterfront, Angela didn't know where she would begin to look for the information she was seeking.

By late morning, she was walking down bustling Salem Street, looking in the windows of the shops and trying to protect her belly from fast-moving passersby. The rich, musty aroma of aged cheeses, cured meats, and garlic emanating from a *salumeria* sent a sharp pang of longing for home through her chest. Passing a bakery, she heard someone call her name and, turning, saw Marisa Puliati, a neighbor from Cefalú, coming toward her, arms outstretched. As the two women embraced warmly, kissing each other on each cheek, Angela felt her eyes fill with tears. The sight of a familiar face framed by a brightly-colored scarf from Sicily broke down her loneliness, and she held onto her friend with delight.

"What are you doing here?" Marisa cried, she, too, lifting a tear from the corner of her eye with her finger. "I heard you and Tommaso were living in a fishing village somewhere near here, but I never thought I'd see you."

As they strolled through the neighborhood arm in arm, Angela recounted the story of her trip to America and years in Gloucester.

"I was totally opposed to his joining up from the beginning," she explained, nearing the end of the story, "but he and his cousin, Carlo—you remember Carlo—were convinced that the army was the quickest way to become a citizen, make good money. I'm worried. Lord, do I worry. I haven't heard from him in months."

"Poor thing," Marisa replied, reaching for Angela's hand. "And pregnant, too. Well, we've been here only a few months. Things at home are bad, I'm sorry to say. The war has brought nothing but suffering. We decided to risk the crossing. Would you believe we came on a freight ship? It wasn't fun. Soon we're going to a city called *Lorenzo*, not far from here where there's supposed to be work in a mill that makes cloth. Why don't you come with us, and stay until Tommaso comes back? I'm sure it won't be much longer. We can take care of you."

"I don't know . . . no, I couldn't. I have work to do at home, and I want to be there the moment Tommaso arrives. But you're kind to offer, my friend." She wanted nothing more than to accept the hospitality of a friend from home, but her hope that Tommaso would be returning soon guided her.

Marisa told Angela about the crowd of men who gathered each day to gossip and deliberate in front of the Banca Ettore Forte, and they turned in that direction, stopping to look at fabrics, fresh pasta, coffee beans, and other provisions in the store windows.

At the bank they found the crowd as Marisa had described it: primarily older men, sitting on the curb or on wooden crates or milling about in the street. The two young women stood on the edge of the would-be parliament, listening to the banter. The atmosphere was relaxed. Later in the day the conversation would grow more heated, as prominent speakers joined them to debate the critical subjects of the day, as well as those less critical but entertaining nonetheless.

Finally, Marisa turned to a kind-faced man near them. "My friend's husband left for France several weeks ago," she said. "She's heard no word from him in a long time. She wants to know what's happening over there, and when the war will be over."

"Ah, when the war will be over. The question on everyone's mind," the man replied, his thick eyebrows and heavy jowls bobbing up and down in unison as he spoke. "Well, I'm sorry to say that the situation is not so good. You've surely heard that the Russians are out of the war. A treaty was signed, closing the Eastern Front. The goddamned—excuse me, ladies—the Bolsheviks have no appetite for war."

Attention in the group had now turned to this side conversation, the unusual participation of women worth investigating. A short man with a battered brown hat and intense eyes jumped in when the first man paused for breath. "Now the Germans are throwing everything they've got at the Western Front," he declared. "Mark my words, they'll be in Paris by June. It's a disaster."

Another voice: "The Kaiser won't be happy until he flies his flag in every capital in Europe. He's calling up twelve-year-old boys and putting guns in their hands."

"No, no, idiots. What do you know? The tide has turned on those bastards! The Kaiser will hang."

Now the debate began to pick up, with some arguing that the Germans could not make war forever, and that the momentum would begin to swing to favor the Allies, while others continued to insist that nothing could stop the ruthless Germans with their superior training and advanced weaponry. Unable to keep up with the pace and contradiction of the interchange—the torrent of military terms and geographical locations in a flood of dialects was dizzying—Angela turned to Marisa and repeated that she simply wanted to know whether her husband was safe.

"Please," Marisa broke in again. "If her husband left for France during the winter, where might he be?"

"Probably playing bocce with General Pershing and drinking wine in the French countryside!" a man called out, and everyone laughed. Then the kind-faced man stepped in to explain about the American general's reluctance to let his troops fight, even as the war raged at an impasse.

"So it's likely," he concluded, "that your husband is safe in France, waiting for something to change." Feeling heartened, Angela thanked the man, and the two women walked away. Angela had come to Boston hoping for good news, and she clung to what she had heard as an answer to prayer.

Angela followed Marisa to the market, where she purchased a few items she could not buy in Gloucester, including fennel, pine nuts, and a small bottle of olive oil. There were many things she wanted, but she didn't know how long she would have to live on the money Tommaso and Carlo had left for her.

Finally it was time for her to go to the dock for her boat to Gloucester. Again, the two women embraced. "Take care of yourself, sweetheart," Marisa smiled.

"You too," Angela replied, straining to return the smile. "Hope to see you soon. Come to Gloucester when you can. It will remind you a bit of Cefalú." Reluctantly, Angela turned to go, loneliness welling up again as she faced the trip home to the empty cabin.

By the time Angela stepped off the steamship onto the pier, the sun had set and she was exhausted. Before going home, though, she walked down Pleasant Street to St. Anne's. Partway up the stone steps she paused to collect her strength, surprised again at the amount of energy it took to be pregnant. Inside, she knelt before the altar in the chapel to the right of the high altar. "*O Signuri,*" she began. Normally, she directed her prayers to the Virgin, but tonight she addressed Christ himself. "Lord, please, if not for me, then for the baby. Please, keep Tommaso safe." After she had said the Hail Mary several times, she rose wearily to her feet.

Outside, the wind had brought a change in weather. Rain began to fall, beating on the granite steps. Wrapping the shawl around her head, Angela made her way back to the dark cabin, feeling lonelier than she had ever felt since Tommaso had left her.

The July sun rose white through a haze of suffocating humidity. As the men became dehydrated, their sweat dried, leaving trails of salt on their faces. They marched on, beginning to hear the guns in the distance.

The renewed German offensive on the Western Front had been successful. By mid-July, the enemy had again overrun stretches of eastern France, threatening to recapture Paris. American troops had at last joined the campaign to counter the advance.

On July 18, the balance scale began to waver. The Germans were intercepted, slowed, and then halted, and the newly bolstered Allied forces began for the first time to push their foe back across conquered French territory. Carlo and Tommaso had been assigned to a division whose mission was to chase and harass the Germans as they retreated. Moving east from Paris, their unit followed the advancing front, safely behind the fighting, available if necessary to reinforce the more highly trained troops ahead. Carlo silently hoped they would remain in the rear, far from the action. Tommaso was shaken by the sight of corpses along the road, many mutilated and burned, dismembered by the explosion of artillery shells.

After camping in Château-Thierry, a small town on the Marne, they moved northeast to Fère-en-Tardenois, where they spent a stifling, miserable day burying Allied dead in a scorched field. Tommaso tied a shirt across his nose and mouth against the stench, keeping his eyes fixed on the spade and the dark soil to avoid looking at the mangled bodies. This first bitter taste of war's actuality validated his worst fears. That evening, exhausted and dazed, they received orders: they would march from Fère-en-Tardenois towards Seringes. Prussian Guard troops had retreated to the small village. Clearing them from Seringes was the next task on the way to liberating Reims and expelling the enemy from France.

The march began before dawn and ended at eight o'clock in a rolling field on the edge of the war-torn village. The field had been plowed in the spring for wheat, though planting had been abandoned as the German army approached. Standing on dusty clods between the furrows, the men could hear the battle rise a few hundred yards away, seething at first and then exploding. Smoke billowed from the village. Mustard gas hung in the haze. A light breeze stirred, carrying the toxic odor of burning buildings and human and animal flesh out of the town and across the field. Carlo smoked a cigarette to neutralize the foul reek and talked with a small group of Sicilians, while Tommaso sat in the dirt, staring at the ground between his feet. He pulled the rosary Angela had given him from his pocket, closed his eyes, and began to pray.

From time to time, Carlo glanced at the officers of the detachment, who were studying a map in the half shade of a dying pear tree across the field on the bank of a muddy, trickling rivulet. At about ten o'clock, a sentry came towards them from the direction of the village. He gestured energetically as he reported to the officers, who then quickly issued a call for the troops to fall into formation. The battle in the village was a quagmire. The Prussian Guard was well fortified and the elite Allied troops were outnumbered. Reinforcements were needed immediately to prevent a massacre. As a result, the division was split into five groups, each of which would enter the village from a different point along the southeast side, where they were to fall in behind the troops already in position, take cover, and await further orders.

As they took up their weapons and began to move forward, Carlo glanced at Tommaso, who, with the rosary wrapped through his fingers, was mouthing the words of the prayer. "Just stay with me, cousin," Carlo said, trying to sound reassuring. "It's going to be okay." But he, too, was terrified. This was closer to war—to the basic, brutal act of war, one man trying to kill another—than he had ever imagined being.

Their contingent entered the town, a labyrinthine cluster of low, umber brick-and-stucco buildings with corrugated terra-cotta roofing, patched in places but still collapsed in others from the original German assault. The soldiers crept slowly down the street through smoke so thick they were forced to put on their gas masks. There were no Allied troops to be seen except the bodies of dead soldiers. They could hear the crack of ammunition rounds being fired just ahead. Broken glass crunched under their boots as they came to where the street they had been following emptied into a larger one. They paused for a moment. Carlo stepped away from Tommaso to speak to another soldier. Just then their commanding officer, a broad-shouldered lieutenant, strode through the middle of the group with his arms outstretched. He stopped between Carlo and his cousin. "Everyone in front of me, move south!" he shouted above the sound of a sudden burst of artillery fire. "Everyone behind me, move north! We're going to clear this area building by building. Now get going!"

"Carlo. Carlo!" Tommaso cried out. Carlo turned and came towards him, but the officer blocked his path.

"Where the hell are you going?" he yelled, thrusting his hand in the direction of the departing troops. "I said get going! Do you understand, soldier?"

Carlo hesitated, then pivoted helplessly, and looking over his shoulder saw another man grab Tommaso by the shirt sleeve and pull him in the opposite direction. Tommaso turned back, too, and for an instant the cousins looked each other in the eye. "It's going to be all right!" Carlo hollered. A look of terror hung on his cousin's narrow face like a mask.

Carlo, together with his group of about-fifty other soldiers, proceeded cautiously down the street to the corner and then turned. Suddenly, they were under fire. Men began to fall around him, including the soldier beside Carlo, shot in the stomach. Dropping to the ground he dragged the wounded man behind the ruined building on the corner.

For the next hour, the lieutenant and those who hadn't been shot waited behind the wall. Carlo tended to the injured man until he realized he was dead. Occasionally the lieutenant would stick his gun around the corner, and within seconds, bullets would begin to knock chips of brown brick off the wall at his side. Carlo pressed himself against the building, still shocked by the death of his comrade and frantic with worry for Tommaso. "I can't lose him," he repeated to himself over and over, wishing he could smoke a cigarette to calm himself down. His best hope was that his cousin would keep his head and stay under cover, or that someone would protect him until the battle ended.

Still there was nowhere to go, and Carlo was relieved when the order finally came to drop back, the commanders having decided to bluff: they would pull out to the perimeter of the village, acting as if they were in retreat. When the enemy troops followed, they would be surrounded, and the Allied forces would destroy them.

It was now past noon. When they reached the edge of the town, passing the last row of buildings, Carlo began to look for Tommaso. But he was not to be found, and neither was the rest of his contingent. There was nothing to do but hope that his cousin's group had fallen back to another point on the perimeter of Seringes.

Soon the artillery shells stopped falling and gunfire ceased. An eerie quiet descended on the village, broken only by the awful moaning and cursing of injured and dying men. While the Allied troops waited tensely for further orders, Carlo shared a cigarette with a soldier originally from Messina, who tried to assure him that Tommaso was safe. "Knowing him, he's found a cellar to hide in," he said. "By now he's probably taking a nap with a belly full of wine and cheese." Carlo tried to smile.

Tommaso had begged the commanding officer to allow him to join his cousin, but the man was in no mood to negotiate, and finally told Tommaso to stop complaining and "act like a man." He followed the contingent in a daze, around the edge of the village, across a small square where a group of cats paced anxiously, jumping at the sound of each distant explosion. Without Carlo to steady him, he felt his heart racing and his body trembling. The officer signaled for the men to follow him down a narrow street between boarded-up shops, broken glass from the windows in the apartments above under foot. With every step, he anticipated disaster. At an intersection, the men crawled across the street, Tommaso at the back of the group keeping his head low to the ground and following the feet of the man in front of him. On the other side, the officer, sensing a break in gunfire, stood to walk. Tommaso watched him and tried to stand on wobbling legs. The officer picked up the pace nearly to a jog, shouting for the men to follow him. Again, they approached the end of a block. Tommaso prayed that they would emerge from the city and the ordeal would be over. As if from nowhere, the air filled with bullets, shouting, and smoke. Tommaso froze as the men around him dropped to the ground or began to run in the opposite direction.

Then word came down the line of troops surrounding the village: the Prussian Guard had fallen for the ploy and were advancing west through the village. The Allied troops began to move forward, back into the town, inching down the cobblestone street. The quiet was unbearable. Fifth in line behind his commanding officer, Carlo followed, his heart beating so fast that he was trembling. When they came into a small square, he heard the pop of a rifle being fired and realized that they had surprised a group of Prussian soldiers who had believed that they had the town to themselves.

Leaping through an empty window frame into a house, Carlo knelt below the sill for cover and began to fire. He saw a Prussian soldier trip and fall to the ground. He fired again and again until an enemy soldier spotted his hiding place from across the square and bullets began to whistle through the window frame. Carlo and the other two men who had joined him covered their heads with their arms and ducked down below the opening. He shook his head, unable to believe that he had just killed a man, possibly more than one.

When the enemy gunfire stopped, Carlo scrambled to his knees and peered out the window to see the unflappable lieutenant standing in the square, urgently motioning for the men to follow. There were bodies scattered across the square as though they had been dropped from the sky. There were also wounded men, some half dead, writhing on the stones in seeping puddles of blood, screaming for help.

Carlo climbed through the window and followed the lieutenant to the other side of the square and down a cramped alley. Reaching the other end, the officer took off his helmet, hung it on the end of his gun, and waved it into the street. Silence. He stepped out, and Carlo and the others followed. Carlo's nerves were shattered. He felt his body shaking uncontrollably.

He had taken only a single step into the street when the pop of a rifle sounded. The lieutenant dropped to the ground. Instinctively, Carlo turned back towards the safety of the alley, throwing himself outside the range of a barrage of bullets, only to slump to the ground as he realized he was in pain. His canvas pants were torn open at the calf, and blood was running down into his boot. A bullet had ripped through the side of his leg, exiting just below the knee.

Gunfire continued to crackle in the street just a few feet away. A soldier staggered into the alley grasping his throat and fell dead at Carlo's feet, his face blackened and burned, a gaping hole where his chin had been. Woozy from the pain, Carlo gagged, dry-heaving and spitting mouthfuls of bile into the dust.

As soon as he was able, Carlo began to crawl down the alley back towards the square, dragging his injured leg behind him. He stopped to rest. Tearing cloth from his pants, he made bandages and wrapped his hemorrhaging wound. Another soldier appeared, cursing fiercely, his arm broken and bleeding. Carlo tended to his injury, as well, and together they began to move towards the field where the Allied operation was based, cringing each time a shell crashed into a building near them or thudded to the ground.

The sound of the battle faded as they reached the limits of the town. Everywhere he looked there were dead men. He was exhausted, hungry, in pain, and worried about Tommaso, hoping desperately that he would find his cousin safe.

By seven o'clock, the scorching sun was beginning to set, and quiet had returned to Seringes, as though a costly battle had not just been fought within her walls. The Prussian Guard had been driven from the town and were being chased in retreat by a British column which had arrived late in the day. Carlo's wound had been cleaned and dressed by a medic, who warned that enough muscle damage had been done that he might walk with a limp for the rest of his life. He had also been given something to eat and drink. But Tommaso was still missing, along with hundreds of other men. Using one of the splintered boards that littered the street as a crutch, Carlo hobbled back into the town.

He went first to the place where they had become separated, and then walked in the direction Tommaso's group had followed, only to find that they hadn't gone far. At the end of the street they had encountered a Prussian fortification. Scores of men, many of whom Carlo recognized, were lying dead in the street. And then he saw Tommaso. The group had apparently been slaughtered in the ambush, row after row, as the Prussians opened fire from behind the shuttered windows of a two-story house. Tommaso had been shot through the forehead above the left eye, just below his helmet. He was lying on his back, arms and legs spread. Carlo's eye went to a trickle of dried blood that ran down into Tommaso's sideburn, to his ear, and into a dark pool on the ground. Though he must have died in an instant, his face was twisted in agony.

Carlo sank down beside the body, overcome. He had seen the horror of war. He had killed. He had been shot. And now he had found his beloved cousin, his brother, dead. Taking Tommaso's cold hand in his own, he began to sob.

Almost beyond rational thought, he remembered the first time they had gone out on the *mattanza* together. When Tommaso turned fifteen, their fathers had decided it was time for them to experience the hunt for the enormous bluefin tuna that pass the north coast of Sicily each year. They had gone up the island past Palermo to a trap owned by a distant relative. On the day of the killing, they stood on a boat over the *camera della morte*, where the fish would be taken. The men had begun to raise the net forming the floor of the trap, bringing the fish to the surface to be speared and hauled into the colorful fleet of tuna boats. A rousing song arose, the chant-like song of the fishermen, a call-and-response led by a wiry man with a high, tremulous voice. His biceps strained pulling the ropes, his neck arched and tense as the rhythmic wail rang out: "*Urrá, urrá, urrá!*" Carlo and Tommaso were rapt, thrilled and ready for blood.

As the fish rose, however, the finely woven net had begun to tear. The leader began to shout and gesture wildly for the men to drop the net before the hole grew large enough for the valuable tuna to escape. Such an outcome would have been a disastrous end to a year of preparation. Pulled down by the weight of the tuna, along with the anchors which held the net in place, the apparatus began to drop to the floor of the sea as soon as the men released it. And then, in an instant, Carlo was on his back, shooting across the deck and slamming into the gunwale. One of the ropes was wrapped around his ankle and had pulled his feet out from under him. In another moment, he would have been yanked overboard into a churning pool of enormous fish, where he could have been killed by the thrashing of a single, powerful tail. Tommaso had been the first to move. Pulling out the knife he'd been given for his birthday and diving at his cousin's feet, Tommaso grabbed his ankle and sliced the rope, allowing the net to fall away.

"Do you remember that, cousin?" Carlo whispered through his tears. "You saved my life. But I couldn't save yours." He should have been there. He should have seen the shot fired. He should have followed its trajectory. He should have pulled Tommaso to safety. He should have taken the bullet himself to save his cousin's life. He stared at Tommaso's lifeless face.

Carlo lay down, emptied of his last reserve of energy, and fell asleep on the ground next to Tommaso, his hand resting on his cousin's chest. He only began to stir when he heard the stretcher bearers coming to take his cousin's body for burial. "This one's alive!" one of them shouted, placing his palm on Carlo's forehead. Carlo came fully awake as they were placing Tommaso's stiffened body on the litter.

"What the hell are you doing?" he shouted, reaching for the handle of the litter. "*Firmari! Chistu é me cugnu!*" In his confusion, he cried out in his native language.

"Soldier, you need to get outta here. Where's your division?" the man demanded, and when Carlo did not reply he repeated, "Go, for Chrissake!" They helped Carlo, wincing, to his feet. A nearly full moon had risen with a foggy, pinkish halo surrounding it. Carlo watched, destroyed like the village itself, as they carried Tommaso away.

v.

It was a fair September morning, cool and dry, the kind of morning that made one aware of summer's ending. Outside the cabin, a pair of squirrels chattered in the trees, dropping pieces of acorn husk as they gorged themselves to prepare for the coming of cold and snow. A mild breeze off the water made the curtains in the window dance. Angela sat at the table cleaning a large flounder sent to her by Tommaso's captain who had remembered her each time the boat returned to the harbor throughout the fishing season.

She was thinking of the shy but determined way in which Tommaso had courted her, following her home after Mass and standing in front of her house with a flower or a small gift. She would watch him from the window as he wrestled with his courage, trying to bring himself to walk up to the door. Other times he would wait for her to cross the piazza with her sister or a friend, and then would step out of a doorway and clumsily pretend to be surprised to see her. Charmed by his awkwardness, she had finally decided to make it easier on him by walking right up to him and taking his hand.

Her thoughts were interrupted by a knock at the door. "*Signura!*" The excited voice of the little boy from next door. "*Signura!* There's a soldier coming!" Angela stood up, wiping fish guts on a rag. Her heart began to race as she hurried to the door. It was a soldier, but not Tommaso.

"Are you Mrs. Amorelli?" the young man asked in English, removing his cap. Angela nodded. He had an aristocratic face and posture, with a gentle manner and a soothing voice. "Do you speak English?"

Angela shook her head, raising a hand to steady herself against the wall of the cabin. Her heart continued to pound. She could feel the eyes of the neighbors watching her and the soldier.

"*Allora, mi dispiace,*" he continued in Italian, "I'm sorry. I hope you can understand me. I don't speak Sicilian. I am Lieutenant Rienzo with the United States Army." A second soldier stood behind him, watching.

"Where's Tommaso?" she demanded. "Where's my husband?"

The officer paused, glancing with pity down at her swollen belly. "*Signora,*" he began, "I am most deeply sorry. On behalf of President Wilson and a grateful nation, I wish to extend my sincerest condolences."

Angela began to feel dizzy. She leaned her body up against the cabin, supporting the weight of the baby with her hands. "Where . . . is . . . Tommaso?" she cried.

"I'm sorry, *Signora*. There's no easy way to tell you. Your husband, Tommaso Amorelli, was killed on July 28 . . . at Seringes, east of Paris, France. He was one of many who gave his life for our nation that day. He was buried alongside six thousand others at Fère-en-Tardenois. But he's a hero. The fortunes of war turned against the Germans in those very days. The Allies are going to win, by the grace of God, and your husband will be remembered as one of the heroes of this terrible war."

Angela nearly collapsed as the pain that would stay with her for the rest of her life came over her. "No!" she screamed, stumbling into the cabin with Rienzo following her, trying to offer comfort.

"I'm sorry, *Signora*," he said, "but you must . . . your baby . . ."

"Go!" she shouted. "Please . . . go."

He hesitated, saluted awkwardly, and left.

When the door closed behind him, Angela broke into sobs. She lowered herself onto the bed and wept for more than an hour, trying to believe it was a nightmare. She found herself wanting to die as well, simply to cease to exist. If not for the baby, she felt she would.

And then, her grief gave way to rage. She had begged him not to enlist. She had fought him and his foolish cousin. She had made him promise that he would return to her. What a stupid, cursed idea. All of his empty assurances and meaningless talk about citizenship. Now he would never come back and she wanted to smash something, to break every dish, to tear the curtains from the window, because he had left her alone. The bastard! He had brought her here only to leave her alone to raise his orphaned child. She would never forgive him. Never.

For most of the night Angela lay awake, adrift, until, near dawn, she fell into a restless sleep to dream that she was walking across the piazza in Cefalù. From a darkened doorway, a young man stepped into her path holding a small bouquet of flowers. But it wasn't Tommaso. It was Lieutenant Rienzo.

In the morning, as though in a trance, she walked to a shop on Main Street to buy several yards of black fabric. The sympathetic merchant wouldn't let her pay anything, which brought more tears. After passing by the church to light a candle, struggling as she did so not to curse God, she went back to the cabin. Her face swollen and her eyes bloodshot from crying, she began work on the first of two dresses, one to wear until the baby was born, and one after. There was no body to wash, or wake, or prepare for burial. There were no relatives and friends to feed. None of the ancient rituals of death were possible, other than wearing the widow's attire. And so she worked, an unendurable emptiness holding her in its grip.

The war ended. News of the Armistice signed at Compiègne reached the East Coast late in the afternoon on the eleventh. Elated townspeople celebrated in the taverns in Gloucester until after midnight, spilling out into the streets when the establishments closed. Similar festivities had erupted exactly two months earlier after the Red Sox won their third championship in four years. Angela presumed another similar event was being celebrated until a friend told her that the Germans had surrendered.

She woke early on the morning of the twelfth with pains deep in her abdomen, and with mountains of laundry to collect and wash. It was a chilly November morning, and as she pulled her wooden cart along the dirt road she noted that this was no weather for a baby. When the pains came again, stabbing at her belly, she stopped to brace herself. Turning down Middle Street, she arrived at the back door of the Sargent house, with its white clapboards, dark green shutters, and an assortment of brick chimneys jutting out of the shingled roof. She struggled up the steps. When the maid, a French-Canadian woman with auburn hair and a kind, freckled face, came to the door, Angela was sitting on the steps, clenching her teeth to stifle a moan.

"Oh, *mon Dieu!*" she cried. "Come in. Oh, Jesus, come in!"

She stooped to pull Angela to her feet and helped her with difficulty up the stairs to her own quarters above the kitchen. "Stay here," she told Angela, offering her hand to squeeze as another contraction shook her. "Doctor," she said in English, "I go for doctor."

Soon Angela's contractions came harder and closer together. Sometime later—Angela wasn't sure how much time had elapsed—the maid, whose name was Marie, returned alone. She soothed Angela, holding her hand and speaking encouraging commands in French as each contraction peaked. By the time the doctor arrived three hours later, Angela's waters had ruptured and she was beginning to feel an urge to push. Her body buckled forward, and then back onto the bed as the next wave passed.

"Where's her husband?" the doctor asked Marie. Seeing that she did not understand, he tried in French: "*Où est son homme, son mari?*"

Another contraction. Marie shook her head and mouthed, "*La guerre.*" The doctor raised his eyebrows, and then closed his eyes for a moment. Indeed, he had heard talk in town of the young Sicilian woman in widow's garb, heavy with pregnancy. She was, he thought, the symbol of a world coming apart: crossing an ocean to escape poverty and begin a new life, and now giving birth, alone, her husband killed in a hideous war that, now over, had never seemed to be about anything except mutual destruction. "God help her," he whispered to himself.

He washed his hands in a basin and then reached beneath the sheets, wet with mucus and blood. "Your baby has a fine head of hair," he said, trying to sound cheery, though neither woman understood his words. "Whenever you're ready, push," he coached, placing his hands at the top of his abdomen and thrusting them downward towards his waist to demonstrate. "Push."

Angela grabbed Marie's hand. Bearing down, she began to push, letting go with a scream as the baby's head crowned. Slowly the baby emerged, his blue-gray face coming into view with another forceful push and scream. The doctor took the black-haired head in one large hand, and then turned the infant's body to bring his shoulders and hips through the birth canal, finally lifting him up for Angela to see. "It's a boy," he declared with a triumphant smile. Catching her breath, Angela reached for the baby as Marie wiped the sweat from her forehead, and the doctor placed him into her arms. The baby coughed and let out a cry. Angela used the sheet to wipe his body, a wave of relief passing through her. The baby lowered his head to search hungrily for a nipple. Finding it, he began to nurse and she wrapped the blankets around his tiny body, feeling the wonder of his weight on her for the first time, the way he sunk into her and his heartbeat synced with hers.

"What will you name him?" the doctor inquired after she had birthed the placenta, using her last reserve of energy. Closing her eyes, she let her head drop back into the pillow, the sharpest pains of labor beginning to ebb. She thought about Tommaso boarding the boat in Palermo. It seemed so long ago. He had dreamed of being the father of tall, handsome American sons. She had lost him, but she held in her arms his American son. The baby lifted his head and let out another wail, and then nuzzled into her neck and fell asleep.

"What is his name?" Marie asked. "Son nom?"

"*Si chiama*," Angela murmured, "Vittorio."

In early spring Angela heard from neighbors that Carlo had come back to Gloucester. The nights were still cold, and when she learned that he was sleeping on the beach, she sent for him. She wanted to blame him for Tommaso's death. After all, he'd had much less to leave behind than his cousin and much less to lose. At times during that long winter, she'd blamed herself for her miscarriage, as well. Perhaps if her first child had been born, Tommaso would never have left. Yet when she spoke the truth to herself, she couldn't fault Carlo or the loss of the baby.

Carlo arrived at the cabin with his bedroll and a small knapsack. He was gaunt and seemed diminished, both in appearance and temperament. After Seringes he had spent weeks in an overcrowded military hospital near Paris where his wound had become infected. One night, when he had been delirious with fever, his leg swollen grotesquely, he was told it would be amputated in the morning. The fever broke, however, and the swelling lessened, and after a time he recovered. He eventually sailed back and passed through Camp Devens, where he was surrounded by memories of Tommaso, before being discharged from the Army.

He stepped through the door, staring at his feet to avoid Angela's eyes. She was knitting, the baby asleep in a cradle given to her by Mrs. Sargent. Carlo sat down at the table, shaking his head. "I'm sorry, Angela," he said in a low voice. "I'm sorry . . . I can't talk about it, though. I don't really want to talk at all." Asleep, and often even awake, he was tormented by images, vivid, haunting images of dead soldiers. But more often images of the wounded: burnt, disfigured, blinded, bleeding, shell-shocked, wailing men, their lives forever shadowed by the hideousness of the war.

"It's all right, cousin," Angela answered after a moment. She had many questions, yet she could see that this was not the time to ask them.

Becoming aware of another presence, Carlo stood up, noticed the cradle, and looked down at Vittorio. His back was toward Angela, so it took a moment before she realized that he was weeping.

"You can cry today, Carlo," she said after a few minutes, wiping a tear from the corner of her own eye. "For your cousin, and for his son. Go ahead. But tomorrow, we have to face that this is what God has given us. We have no choice but to go on."

Thus began an unusual companionship that would last nearly fifty years. Carlo built a small room for himself off the side of the cabin. With his pension from the army and the money she was entitled to as a widow, along with her earnings from laundry and his from fishing, they made a life. Carlo never spoke of the war. In fact, he who had been the talker, the quick wit, the back-slapper, now rarely spoke at all. Silently, they carried Tommaso's memory together, doing what had to be done for his son.

Once, and only once, he referred to home. He was minding Vittorio while Angela prepared a meal. Grasping Carlo's fingers, the baby took stiff-legged steps, gurgling happily as they made their way across the wide pine boards of the cabin's floor. The two had taken to each other with playful affection. "Why don't we go back to Cefalú?" Carlo said, as though it was a new thought. Angela paused from stirring a boiling pot on the cast iron stove, and then began to stir again.

"Well," she replied curtly after a moment, "maybe one day we will."

"But . . ." Carlo began.

"But what, Carlo?" she interrupted testily. "We don't have the money to go from here to the other side of the street, so how are we going back to Cefalú?"

"But don't you ever miss it? The beautiful harbor? The way the sun lights up the sea when it rises up over the hill? Don't you miss your family?"

"Carlo, stop." There were many days when she was consumed by a sadness that was almost a physical pain as she imagined strolling the streets, the piazza, the beach, arm in arm with Tommaso, or with one of her sisters or her mother, watching the fishing boats in the warm afternoon sun. Speaking her native language. Seeing the people she had known all her life. Smelling familiar aromas. Being home.

"Anyway, Angela, please . . . forget I mentioned it."

"You have to remember that it wasn't exactly paradise when we left Cefalú." She felt a need to win an argument. "You were one of the first to leave. Don't forget that. And you had good reasons, as I recall . . . good enough to convince Tommaso, and me, too."

Releasing his grip on Carlo's fingers, the baby dropped onto the floor and, finding his toes, giggled as he played with them.

"Maybe someday we'll go back. I can't say. I don't know what God's will is . . . but Tommaso had one dream. Do you remember it?"

Carlo nodded. "Yes, cousin. Of course. How many times did he say it? He wanted to have sons."

"There. American sons. That was his greatest hope. If I go back to Sicily, then Tommaso came here and died for nothing. We have to stay here . . . so that Tommaso can have his American son."

TWO

i.

I N THE DAYS FOLLOWING Vittorio's birth, days when delight and desolation clashed with unyielding intensity, Marie appeared cheerfully at the cabin nearly every morning. She came with bread or biscuits she had baked, or with fresh milk or eggs, sometimes with a full meal for Angela. The language barrier was formidable. Marie's Canadian dialect of French and Angela's Sicilian dialect were incoherent to each other. Carlo was able to help when he was home, as he and Marie both knew many words in English. In his absence, they relied on gestures or drew pictures, sometimes giving up with laughter at their failure to convey a word or idea. Yet despite the difficulty in communication, there was a deep and ineffable bond between the two women, a bond created by Marie's mercy and prompt action on the day of Vittorio's birth, and by the trust Angela had placed so readily in her when she was a stranger. Angela liked Marie, and Marie, who was ten years older and childless, was fond of Angela and devoted to the baby. Though many of her Sicilian acquaintances called on her and offered solace in the form of food, Marie became her closest friend.

Though Angela assured her that she was fine, Marie told her often: "You and the baby can't spend the winter here." Despite

Angela's extensive efforts to make it pleasant, with a flower garden in front and even whitewashed walls inside, the cabin remained lacking, in Marie's view. When she saw Vittorio's nose dripping one February morning and his tiny lungs congested for a third time that winter, she vowed to herself that Angela and the baby would not spend another year in the cabin.

Marie bounced through the door one morning the following autumn, barely suppressing a smile that kept trying to spread across her face. *"J'ai un suprise,"* she declared. Angela glanced at her, not understanding, but noticing the smile. Marie looked to Carlo, who was feeding the baby, now almost a year old, and incessantly hungry. Carlo missed the cue. "Carlo!" Marie prompted.

"My apologies. She says she has a surprise. *Surprisa.*"

"Surprisa," Marie repeated, crossing the room and taking the baby from Carlo. She took his quilt from the cradle and began to wrap it around his plump body. "Come," she ordered, opening the door to leave. Angela put down her sewing and followed. Carlo, by now curious, rose from his stool and stepped out of the cabin behind the two women, pulling the door shut against a cool ocean breeze.

Marie led them up Church Street, nearly passing her own home, and then up the hill until they reached Prospect. Angela walked alongside her, at times falling a half step behind and then jogging a pace to catch up. When Marie occasionally grinned at her she returned a wary smile, not knowing what to expect, or where this unplanned outing might end. Carlo trailed along a few yards back. Turning right at the corner of Prospect, Marie crossed the street and stood in front of a two-story Victorian house, divided into two apartments and set in a row of similar dwellings. The house was bluish-gray, with pure white trim. On either side of the small front porch, window boxes were freshly planted with red and pink geraniums. White lace curtains hung in the windows. *"Içi,"* Marie stated.

When Carlo caught up, Marie began to climb the stairs to the porch, shifting Vittorio to her other hip and motioning for the other two to join her. She handed the baby to Angela, reached into the pocket of her sweater, a plum-colored wool cardigan which Angela had knitted for her over the summer, and produced a key. No longer trying to keep the triumphant smile from her face, she opened the door and, taking Angela's elbow in hand, pulled her into the front room. It was a parlor, furnished with a couch and a chair, and with an ovate braided rug. Marie pressed a light switch, turning on a brass fixture overhead. Then, stepping to the middle of the room with the flair of a confident realtor, she turned to face Angela and Carlo.

"*Vous l'aimez?*" she asked, her face shining with pride. "You love?" With winter coming, she had asked her employer, who owned several houses on Prospect Street, to lease the apartment to her friends at a monthly rate they could afford. Angela was confused.

"It's very nice." Angela replied. "But why are you moving?"

"No." Marie shook her head vigorously. "Vous. You move," she said, pointing first to them, and then to the floor in front of her. The baby had grown heavy in Angela's arms. She set him down, and he began to toddle around the room. "Your house."

Angela heard the words but thought she was misunderstanding her friend. She turned to Carlo. "She says this is your house." Carlo shrugged, raising his eyebrows. "I don't know what she means. She says it's your house."

"Come," Marie said, again taking Angela by the arm. She toured her through the rest of the flat, showing her the bedrooms, the small kitchen with its table and chairs and the freshly painted bathroom. She had cleaned the apartment herself and her husband had painted it. The furniture was collected with the help of Father Shaw, who had appealed to the parishioners at St. Anne's. Marie stopped to demonstrate each light switch for Angela, and to turn the water on and off in the sinks and the tub. "Your house," she insisted again. She took the key from her pocket and placed it in

Angela's hand and closed her friend's fingers around it, hoping this would cement the idea. "You live here now. You, Vittorio, Carlo. You live here now."

Angela shook her head and began to cry. For six years, she had tried to convince herself that the cabin was not so bad, not so cold or unbearably rough—that it was a home. Vittorio pulled at her skirt, wanting to nurse. She lifted him and, sitting down on the couch, opened her blouse. Marie sat down next to her, taking her hand. "Thank you, thank you," Angela repeated through her tears as the baby suckled happily. "I don't know how I found you," she said, "but you are my saint." Carlo translated, and Marie smiled with satisfaction, stroking the hair of her young friend. Angela turned to Carlo, tears shining on her cheeks. "I wish Tommaso could be here to see his son in a real home."

Their possessions were few enough—clothes, cookware, and the few decorative items Angela had collected—that Carlo was able to move them with four trips back and forth using Angela's laundry cart. Marie brought freshly cut hydrangea in a vase for the kitchen table and helped Angela settle in. When Vittorio woke his mother early the next morning, pulling at her nightgown, Angela realized that she had slept untroubled for the first time since Tommaso's departure.

The move to Prospect Street was an improvement in lifestyle for the Amorelli family. But the end of the war and the onset of the decade of the 1920s had brought a backlash against immigrants, especially those with darker skin, and even against families which had given a father or a son to the war effort. Carlo, hurt and angry, explained to Angela the harsh quotas of the 1924 Immigration Act: from the British Isles, sixty-three thousand immigrants would be welcomed annually; from Italy, fewer than four thousand. Even more upsetting to him was the execution of labor organizers Nicola

Sacco and Bartolomeo Vanzetti in Boston, despite obvious gaps in the case against them.

Beyond the headlines, there was fear in the lives of the Italian women, men and even children, recently or not so recently arrived in America, who were building, cleaning, cooking, operating machines in factories, sewing, fishing, farming, and otherwise trying to assimilate, to *be* Americans, and in the process to recreate the nation. Angela, with her unfailing faith and optimism, was confused. Though there were no overt incidents, no crosses burned in front of the house, she could feel the disdain in each back that was turned downtown. She could read the contempt in the face of each neighbor who failed to return her greeting. Worst of all were the whispers among her own people, overheard on one occasion by Carlo, suggesting that her move to Prospect Street was "inviting trouble," and that "some people don't know their place."

Still, Angela was determined. Vittorio was a good boy, with his father's eyes and his mother's thick, dark hair. He was vigorous, curious and animated, in love with the world around him, and as yet mercifully undisturbed by the fact of his father's death. Though God had not made her way easy, Angela believed, the future would surely be better for her son.

Father Shaw, who had been moved on many occasions by the faith of the young widow, approached her after Mass one Sunday morning when Vittorio was five, still wearing his black cassock. He reached down and took her by the hand, hers disappearing inside his. Knowing that she spoke little English, he led her, along with the boy, down the front steps of the church and around the corner to the front of St. Anne's School. He opened the door and held it, motioning for Angela to enter. Smiling, he guided them down the hallway, decorated with children's colorful artwork, to the classroom where the youngest children were taught. He picked up Vittorio by his elbows, swinging the boy he had baptized years before across the room and placing him gently in a small chair behind a matching oak desk. "I want your son to go to our school," he said to Angela. He pointed to the boy. "Vittorio," he said. He motioned around the room. "School, here," he said. "Do you understand?" Angela understood, but she also understood that the school was not free.

"No money," she said in English, shaking her head and rubbing her thumb against her fingers.

"No," Father Shaw, replied, smiling again. "Free. *Gratis.*" He spread his arms, as though he were about to begin to say Mass. Angela desperately wanted to send Vittorio to school. Why else had they come across the ocean if not to create better opportunities for their children? Education was the obvious and necessary beginning. Yet she was reluctant to send him into school as an outsider, to be perhaps the only Sicilian child in a classroom, particularly knowing how the parents of the other children might react to her son's presence. It took two visits to the house, but eventually Father Shaw convinced Angela to send Vittorio to St. Anne's School. Father Shaw was a progressive thinker, with a vision of a school where "all kinds of children" could be educated together, breaking down the barriers of ethnicity, language and even class. Vittorio was to be his test case.

The boy's matriculation was very nearly short lived. On the first day of school Father Shaw was confronted at noon by an agitated kindergarten teacher. Sister Bernadette pursed her lips and shook her finger in the priest's face. The child, she reported, did not speak English. How could she be expected to educate a child with whom she could not communicate at all? In fact, she told the priest, she could not even pronounce his name. After calming the distressed nun and discussing possible solutions beyond removing Vittorio from the school, Father Shaw once again walked up Prospect Street to the Amorelli house.

Seated with Angela and with Carlo, who had returned from a fishing voyage the previous evening, the priest explained the problem, being careful not to make it sound insurmountable. By way of a solution, he requested first that Vittorio stay after school for one hour each day to be tutored in English, and second that Angela come to St. Anne's weekly to study English with one of the high school teachers, so that they could begin to speak English at home. The proposal seemed reasonable to Angela and Carlo. "Then there's just one other thing," Father Shaw concluded. "Sister Bernadette would like to call him Victor, to make it easier for the other children to say his name. It might make him stand out a bit less."

"No." Carlo responded, quickly and sternly. "He has a name. Good name." He then turned to Angela, who was perplexed by Carlo's reaction, and explained the priest's idea. "My nephew will not change his name," he insisted. Carlo had decided soon after Vittorio's birth, with Angela's consent, to consider himself the boy's uncle. "Victor," he spat. "It sounds like someone's choking."

Angela was quiet for a moment. She wanted her son to go to school. She was certain that Tommaso would want it too. "Carlo," she began. "We're in America. The father's right. You're learning English. I should learn English. Vittorio was born here. He's growing up here. He needs an American name." It was a conversation which had been and would be repeated in thousands of households, in dozens of languages, across the United States. Many saw the change with regret, as home drifted further away. Others gave their children "American" names right from the start, to ease their entry and to minimize their different-ness. Either way, the change in language was an experience unifying the diversity of households in which children, in some profound way, differed from their parents; in which children grew up unable to converse with their grandparents; in which children one generation—perhaps only a few years—removed from Cefalú or Palermo, or Belfast or Minsk or Lisbon or Potsdam, would find their ancestral home a foreign place. "I want him to go to school, Carlo," Angela said with conviction, looking from Carlo to Father Shaw. "Let them call him, how do you say it? Victor." She pronounced it "Vee-tore."

Vittorio was seven years old the first time Gloucester's Italian community marched through the streets in celebration of St. Peter, the patron saint of fishermen. A crowd of little boys jogged along behind the men who proudly carried a carved, painted statue of the apostle on their shoulders. At school, Vittorio, now called Victor, spoke English and followed the customs of the American school in what his teachers called an "appropriate" manner. In the streets with his friends, however, he was still Vittorio, or more often Vito, and the boys chattered together and teased each other in the slang of their parents' tongue, interjecting an occasional word or phrase in English, the way a flowing stream splashes up against a stone, gurgles, and then returns to its course.

As the procession moved reverently down Prospect Street, past the Amorellis' flat, Angela's neighbors stood on their front porches to watch. Never had they seen such a spectacle. The statue was preceded by young girls dressed in white with silver tiaras on their heads. The fishermen who carried the saint sang a hymn of praise common in the churches of Southern Italy and Sicily. Occasionally, they would move to the side of the road and lower the platform on which the statue stood, allowing a grandmother or a blushing teenaged girl to attach a dollar bill to St. Peter's satin stole. Despite the staring, headshaking townspeople, despite the sense of unwelcome the Italians had felt at times like a slap, perhaps in defiance, the mood of the crowd was joyful. Arriving at Stage Fort Park, the procession was met by a cheer which rose up from among those who had gathered. Food was brought out in great quantities, and the afternoon passed with children running among the blankets which were spread on the grass where the adults lounged, drinking wine and telling stories, remembering the festivals they had celebrated at home in the "old country."

Late in the day, a dripping and shivering Vittorio, freshly

emerged from the cool water of the harbor, collapsed at his mother's side, ready to fall asleep in the warmth of the descending sun. Angela wrapped his slender, brown body in a towel and pulled him to her side. Stroking his damp hair and speaking softly into his ear, she began to recount her earliest memories of the patronal festivals celebrated in Cefalú. She told him about the days when she had marched as one of the little angels, festooned in lace, leading the way for the Virgin. She described the games the children played, the decorations, the food, and the dances which went on late into the night. "Maybe one day you'll see it for yourself, my son. You'll see how the water sparkles at night in the light of the lanterns, and you'll hear the beautiful music, and smell the cashews roasting in sugar. There's nothing like it, Vito," she murmured, touching his smooth, sun-darkened cheek. The boy had fallen asleep.

Vittorio ambled home from school one day that autumn with a troubled look on his handsome young face. Normally he jumped through the door wide-eyed in the afternoons with facts, songs, jokes, and other news to share with his mother. She would listen to his tales, glancing up at him as she sat pumping her foot back and forth on the treadle of the second-hand sewing machine Carlo had bought for her. He would smile and giggle, relating something amusing that took place during recess, and then turn serious to explain some astounding piece of information he had learned in science class.

On this day he was taciturn. He dropped his books inside the front door and took his place at the table, resting his face on his hand, propped up by his elbow. He pulled off his tie and let it fall to the floor. "Vittorio," Angela exclaimed, stopping her work and getting up from the machine. She was alarmed. "Are you sick, my son? What's wrong?" Placing her hand on his forehead, she sat down next to him. She took his chin in her hand and turned his face to hers. He kept his eyes fixed on the table.

"No, Mamma. I'm not sick."

"What is it, then, son? Are you hungry? Did you eat lunch? Let me make you something to eat." She was still convinced that there was something fundamentally unhealthy about saving the largest meal of the day for evening.

"I'm not hungry, Mamma. I ate." She had begun to move toward the kitchen. Sitting back down, she took his hand in hers. He stared at the table in front of him. Angela was at a loss, wondering what to do or say, when at last Vittorio spoke: "Mamma . . . is Uncle Carlo my father?"

Angela closed her eyes and took a deep breath. Many times she had been conflicted, knowing that this conversation one day would have to take place. Her own grief over Tommaso's death, though, could still feel shockingly raw, even after eight years, causing her to falter in previous attempts to speak to Vittorio about his father. She wanted to impart to her son everything that was good and noble and kind about Tommaso, without passing on the desolation she felt about his death. Her inability to do so with confidence, without breaking down, had held her back and had made this moment long overdue. She flushed with shame that he had to ask.

"No, Vittorio, my love. Uncle Carlo is not your father. Uncle Carlo is . . . was . . . is your father's cousin." The boy turned now to look at his mother, waiting for her to continue. She drew another breath, knowing she should not make him ask the obvious question. She imagined what Tommaso would think of this fine, bright child in his little parochial school uniform. How proud he would have been to find him at the kitchen table doing his homework with determination every evening. What joy he would have derived from showing him off to his friends. How much fun they would have had together, playing on the beach, at the park, in the snow, laughing, wrestling, being father and son. How sure Tommaso would have been that coming to America was the right thing to do. Reaching out, she took Vittorio by the waist and pulled him into her lap. "Your father," she began, "was called Tommaso. He was a wonderful, sweet man." She paused to swallow, in search of a toehold as she clung to her composure. "I'll tell you as much about him as I can remember, my son. I'll tell you stories. I'll tell you everything. I'm sorry I haven't told you already. You can ask as many questions as you want . . . But your father, my little one, your father . . . died . . . before you were born."

She watched his face as he absorbed the words, a cleft forming above his nose. "He died?" He blinked his eyes several times. "Floyd Bishop's father died. He was a fisherman. Floyd says he went out one day and never came back. Did my father die like that?"

Angela sunk her nose into her son's tousled hair and pulled him closer. To her, Tommaso's death was a physical thing, something she felt like one would feel a stomachache, or a burn. She realized that to Vittorio, both his father and death itself were abstract concepts with no actual experience attached to them. So, too, was war. How could she make him understand war, and how a political conflict far away had left him without a father? She had struggled often enough to make sense of it herself, usually failing.

"Your father was a fisherman, but he didn't die at sea. There was a war, Vito. You've heard about the war?"

"Yes, Mamma."

"There was a war across the ocean. Your father and Uncle Carlo decided it was important to fight in the war. To try to stop people from doing bad things." She paused. "This is hard to explain, Vito. I don't understand wars myself."

"The bad people killed him?" She could hear in his voice both horror and fascination.

"An enemy soldier, yes. I don't know if he was a bad person. War is horrible, Vittorio. I'm convinced of that. Ordinary men—fisherman like your father, and carpenters and farmers—are turned into soldiers, and they're forced to try to kill each other. Maybe some of them like doing it. Maybe some of them are evil. I don't know. Your father wasn't evil, but he was ordered to kill people too."

"Did he kill anyone?"

This question had troubled her, and she was afraid it would trouble Vittorio as well, who didn't know what a gentle man his father had been. "I don't know. I can't imagine him killing anyone. I don't know much about what happened to him. Carlo won't . . . he can't talk about it. And maybe it's best to leave it there, Vito, as hard as it is. Your father died in the war. I'm sorry, my love. Now that you know, I want to tell you all about him. Because even though you never knew him, you know him. He's part of you, and no enemy soldier or anyone else can take that away from you." A tear slid down the side of her nose into the boy's hair. "I want to tell you all about him, Vittorio. I'm so glad you asked me today." He turned and pushed his face into his mother's neck and began to weep. He couldn't have said what made him weep, whether it was his father's death or the anguish he heard in his mother's voice. But he held onto her and cried for a long time.

"People are starving to death in the south. Starving to death! And this *cretinu* Mussolini is parading around Rome like he's one of the Caesars." Carlo came home agitated again after spending another Sunday afternoon listening to the men of Gloucester's Sicilian community discuss current events back home. "The *Duce*." Carlo said the word with contempt. "He's banned all other political parties except the Fascists. Can you imagine Italia with only one political party?"

It was a warm day for mid-November. As always, Angela had been busy after Mass preparing Sunday dinner for the family. Marie joined them as she often did when her husband was away. Carlo had brought home a piece of swordfish at the end of the week, which Angela cooked in a sauce of her own tomatoes, grown in pots in their small backyard. Carlo sat, vexed, his fork raised in the air, waiting for a reply.

"Who's Mussolini?" Vittorio asked finally, feeling that someone should say something.

"Mark my words," Carlo went on, ignoring the boy's question, "he's going to bring disgrace on the whole country before he's done." He made a sweeping motion with his fork for emphasis. "The whole country."

"Mussolini is the leader of Italy, Vittorio," Angela explained. "The country we came here from, the country that Sicily is part of."

"You don't like him, Uncle Carlo? He's a bad man?"

"He's a terrible man! A miserable son of a—"

"Carlo, that's enough," Angela interrupted, knowing the crescendo of invective that was about to follow. "You can answer the question without polluting his mind, cousin." Vittorio chuckled, drawing a glare from his mother. He liked it when Carlo touched the edge of what was appropriate.

"I'm sorry," Carlo said, chastened. "Excuse me. Yes, Vito, he's a bad man. He's concerned only with his own power and with keeping the rich happy. People in the south, people in Sicily are poor as Lazarus, and he doesn't care. He can't be bothered. If he thinks all the attention on Rome's ancient glory and the fascist ideal is going to make people forget their empty bellies, I'm sure he's wrong."

There was silence for a moment. Carlo shook his head and stabbed at his pasta. A church bell tolled for five o'clock. "Marie," Angela said then, hoping to change the subject, "would you like more *pisci spata*?" She was working on her English, but words like "swordfish" she was still too self-conscious to attempt.

"Yes, please," Marie replied, taking the cue, "it's good. You are a good cooker." Marie, too, was trying to use English for the benefit of the boy.

"Mamma, why did we come here? Why did we leave Sicily?"

Marie took the bowl of food from her friend and lowered it to the table, catching Angela's eye. Angela cleared her throat.

"Well, son, I should probably have your uncle try to answer that question," she replied, glancing across the table at Carlo. He smirked back. She sighed, exhaling slowly. "The truth is that life was hard back home. And there was not a lot of hope for the future. Life had been hard for generations, and there was no real reason to think anything was going to change. It wasn't awful. We had good times, but it was a struggle. And then people began to leave. Young men began to leave Cefalú to come to this faraway place called America. Some of them came back with fantastic stories about jobs and money and streets paved with gold. More young men and not-so-young men left, and then they sent for their families. Your Uncle Carlo decided to leave. He came here and found work, and then he sent for your father. I came over once Tommaso saved enough money to pay for my passage."

The boy listened intently. "So," she concluded, "we came because we wanted a better life for our children. We wanted you to go to school, and to have opportunities that you wouldn't have had if we'd stayed."

"I am going to school," Vittorio said, trying to make sense of what his mother was saying.

"Yes, you are. And you're a smart boy, and a good boy. Your father would be very proud of you, just like I am, and Uncle Carlo and Aunt Marie are too. One day you'll be rich and successful—a doctor, maybe. And in our old age, Carlo and I will know that we did the right thing." She caught Carlo's eye again. "You come from a beautiful land, Vito. I don't want you ever to be ashamed of anything, even though I know other children have said cruel things to you about being Sicilian." The boy had come home in tears one day after being called a *dago*. "Sicily is the most beautiful place in the world. Maybe one day you'll see it for yourself."

"When I grow up, I'm going to buy a palace for you to live in, and you'll never have to do any sewing or mending, and we'll have someone to do all the cooking and cleaning."

"That's very sweet, Vito. Very thoughtful of you." She leaned over to kiss him on the forehead.

"Eh, what about me?" Marie said with a smile. "Don't forget your Aunt Marie!"

"I'll buy you each a palace," the boy giggled, "and you'll need fancy automobiles to go visit each other."

"I want to live in Beauport," Uncle Carlo announced, joining in the fun. Beauport was the forty-room mansion built on a bluff above Gloucester harbor by millionaire Henry Davis Sleeper.

"Oh, no," Angela retorted. "That's much too small. I could never live in that little shack. I'd be so cramped." They all laughed, continuing to debate the level of grandeur each would need as Marie served a chocolate torte she had baked for the occasion.

Vittorio was two weeks shy of his eleventh birthday the first time Carlo brought him to Boston to meet the Freni family, friends from back home in Cefalú. The anticipation of riding the train was enough to keep him from falling asleep the night before the trip. He and his friends had watched the train roll in and out of Gloucester station enough times over the years to know each conductor and each engineer. They had even been invited to climb aboard and sit behind the controls of the locomotive as it loaded coal and water before the return trip.

When the morning finally arrived, Angela accompanied Carlo and Vittorio to the station, waving as the locomotive chugged away down the track. With each mile that passed, Vittorio's world grew. He sat on the edge of the shiny leather seat staring out the window, amazed by the sight of open fields and other towns and villages. His first glimpse of the city brought him to his feet. "Look! Uncle, look!" he shouted. Carlo was amused by the boy's excitement. It was all he could do, as the train slowed to a stop, to keep Vittorio from knocking other passengers down, holding his hand to restrain him as he made his way to the door and jumped to the platform.

Everything was new, and Vittorio was filled with wonder. The questions came at Carlo faster than he could answer them. Vittorio's senses were overwhelmed by the city's scope and commotion: the tall buildings, the busy streets, the smog. Of everything that he experienced that day, though, the deepest impression on the boy came from the cultural dominance of Italians in the North End. Never had he imagined this phenomenon, having grown up in the minority, the only one in his classroom. To see Italian people everywhere he looked, to hear his language or close approximations of it spoken on every corner, to see the foods he ate in store windows, to blend in instead of standing out, was so unexpected that the boy was shocked into bewildered silence, as though the sky had turned green.

"What's wrong?" Carlo asked, still holding his hand as they stepped into a bar. Carlo always craved his espresso. "Don't you like the city?"

"Where are all the other people?" the boy asked after a moment. "You know, people who aren't . . . like us?" Carlo laughed.

"You mean the Irish, and the Germans and the Poles? They have their own neighborhoods. This is our neighborhood."

Carlo saw friends and caught up on the latest news from Italy. He introduced Vittorio proudly as his nephew, chucking him under the chin and telling everyone that he was a brilliant student in a very fancy school. At Haymarket, they bought artichokes and eggplants, asparagus, zucchini, tangerines and figs, produce Angela longed for but could rarely buy in Gloucester. Vittorio was astounded by the pace of activity: the bartering, the arguing, the jostling as shoppers elbowed their way down the narrow passageway between the vendors' stalls. He laughed, watching the speed with which a bunch of grapes moved in the grocer's hand from pile to scale to bag and across the cart into his own hands.

The man winked and tossed him an apple. *"Mangia!"* he smiled. "That's a gift."

At last it was time to return to the station. They had purchased everything on the list Angela had given them, including several yards of fabric in colors she couldn't find in Gloucester, together with matching spools of thread. Recent years had brought the family relative prosperity, particularly with Angela's work as a seamstress. They were far from well-to-do, but there was money on occasion for items that were not absolutely necessary. Carlo even bought Vittorio a blue jersey like those worn by the Italian soccer team. "When can we come back, Uncle?" the boy asked excitedly, settling into his seat on the train.

"We'll see." He tousled the boy's hair. "Don't forget . . . winter's coming."

Vittorio, lulled by the rhythmic motion, fell asleep on the train leaning against Carlo. Carlo watched out the window as evening fell. He remembered Tommaso at Vittorio's age, equally full of dash and curiosity. He wrapped his arm around the boy and pulled him closer. Shutting his eyes, he pictured his cousin, wishing he could be there to see his son, this boy who was going to enjoy the bounty of the American dream for which his father had given everything.

Two days later, the stock market crashed.

ii.

For Angela and her family, the prosperity of the twenties rapidly eroded, and then faded into memory as though it had never been real, like the flickering images of the first talkies. The Depression led to dwindling dress orders. Before long, the only work she could get was mending, and often her embarrassed clients were unable to pay, promising future compensation that was rarely produced. Most families couldn't afford to buy meat or fish, and the fishing industry in Gloucester suffered, too, lowering Carlo's income as well.

Angela strived to shield Vittorio from the stress of their reduced means, especially when she and Carlo struggled to pay the rent. Vittorio, now sixteen years old, for his part, was happy to have Carlo home more often and to fill up his mother's increasing stretches of unoccupied time. Yet he understood that their problems were growing. Inevitably, financial support for St. Anne's declined as well, and many unemployed fathers were forced to withdraw their children from the school.

Father Shaw came to the house on a humid August afternoon looking damp and grim in his black cassock. He held a starched, white handkerchief with his fingertips and dabbed at his forehead. There were simply no funds available for a scholarship this year, he told a crestfallen Angela. Vittorio would have to take a leave unless Angela could find a way to pay. He promised that as soon as circumstances improved, which, God willing, they certainly would before long, Vittorio's education would remain a priority. He was determined to see the young man graduate from St. Anne's School within the next two years. "I plan to hand him his diploma myself," Father Shaw proclaimed, though his eyes betrayed his doubts.

"When I was sixteen, I was already an experienced fisherman," Carlo said at dinner that evening. Vittorio had not yet decided how he felt about the news. There were aspects of school that he liked, and he knew it was important to his mother. Yet he had long ago tired of feeling like an outsider. Though he felt he was well liked, he had never once been invited to a birthday party, and as a teenager, he knew by instinct that he could not walk any of the girls home from school. "Tomorrow I'll speak to my boss," Carlo continued. "Times are hard, but he owes me. I'm sure he can make room for one more man."

From the beginning, instantly and thoroughly, Vittorio hated fishing. The other men on board laughed as he wretched over the side of the boat into five-foot swells, gasping, gagging, and wiping away snot and tears with the sleeve of his flannel shirt. "It happens to everyone their first time out," Carlo told him, patting him on the back and shooting an angry glance at the amused spectators. "Don't worry. Forget those jerks."

But Vittorio never got used to the sea, never got his "sea legs," as Carlo had promised him he would, and was often sick, unable to keep food in his stomach as long as he was on the boat. He was repulsed by the inescapable and penetrating odor of fish. He was desperate for a bath at all times, disgusted by the way his clothes and hair became after a day or two at sea—damp, smelly, oily, his hair stiff and greasy, his clothes limp and rancid, his skin sticky and foul. The cramped quarters, the stale drinking water, the way his hands ached and bled after pulling at the lines for hours, all of it was offensive to Vittorio. He missed school more than he had anticipated. An unwelcome bitterness began to seep into his mind when he thought about the future, like the stink of mildew and rotting fish. He would return cranky from long, trying days to find his mother still sewing, humming old songs from home, and he knew he could not complain.

For the remainder of that deadening season and the four which followed, Vittorio worked alongside Carlo on the boat. Carlo absorbed unending jibes from the crew as his protégé failed to master the basics. Though he was growing, his shoulders broadening, a mustache filling in with a tuft on his chin, Vittorio's fingers still fumbled over nets and lines. He would stumble, often fall to the deck, when the boat pitched abruptly, while the others stayed on their feet even in the roughest seas. Carlo defended his nephew, telling his coworkers repeatedly that the young man came from a long line of great fishermen, and that he would vindicate himself before long. Because the captain remembered Tommaso, he took pity on Vittorio, and tried to assign him tasks he could manage. Carlo was patient with him, too, only rarely growing frustrated with his ineptitude. Not wanting Angela to worry, he assured her that Vittorio worked hard, and that he was making progress.

In the summer of 1938, Vittorio was approaching his twentieth birthday. He was taller than his father had been, with a broad forehead and bright eyes, his hair combed to the side like Cary Grant. He was coveted by the girls in the North End where he went as often as possible to escape Gloucester. Father Shaw's vision of Vittorio graduating from St. Anne's School had fallen away, and in fact the priest had been transferred to another parish earlier that year. Vittorio resigned himself, sourly, to life as a fisherman. No one said it aloud because it was too obvious and too painful, but this was not what his father and mother had hoped for when they left Sicily.

On the morning of September 21, Carlo and Vittorio rose early, dressed, ate breakfast, and said goodbye to Angela, who was already at work behind her sewing machine. They walked down to the harbor, ready to put out to sea, the now-familiar feeling of dread growling like hunger in Vittorio's stomach. Carlo remarked, with the extra sense of a seasoned fisherman, that the sky was a strange color, and that the breeze was unusually gusty, coming now from the east, now from the south. The captain had been impressed by the same ominous signs, and he sent the men home. "I don't like the way the air feels," he told them. "Let's give it a day."

There was enough left of the ruthless and unforecasted hurricane by the time it reached Gloucester in the early evening to damage nearly every boat in the harbor, and many homes close to the water. Carlo and Vittorio, wearing their foul-weather gear, stood back far enough not to be soaked by the waves which exploded over the sea wall by the pier. Soon the water covered the road to their ankles. The storm was still generating sustained winds of eighty miles an hour, tearing boats from their moorings and hurling them across the inner harbor. The two men squinted into the driving rain and tied the hoods of their parkas tighter around their heads. Carlo was always reluctant to talk about the past, but he was stirred by the sight of the hurricane to tell Vittorio the story of the storm in Sicily which had led to his departure. "We had no time to prepare. None. When the storm hit, we thought about saving the boats, then we worked on saving our houses. Finally we just had to save ourselves. I'll never forget watching your grandfather cry when his boat broke up and sank. Tommaso . . . your father . . . and I, we couldn't console him. It was a disaster." Vittorio usually enjoyed stories about Sicily, but this one made him sad and, combined with the hurricane, made him even more uneasy about the unpredictable ocean.

The newspapers in the following days reported that the powerful storm had killed nearly six hundred people in New England. A massive storm surge had destroyed nine thousand homes and businesses. More than two thousand fishing boats were lost. In Boston, six Italian fishing boats had been out of the harbor on the day of the storm. Most of the thirty fishermen on those crafts made it home, after a terrifying night on the seas. Three fishermen, though, never returned. Reading the article to his mother, Vittorio thought about the morning of the storm, and about how easily he and Carlo could have been at sea when the hurricane struck. He shuddered and crossed himself.

The storm had brought the fishing season to an abrupt and early end. Carlo went to work helping to salvage his employer's boat, which had been dropped with relative gentleness on the beach when the ocean finally receded.

Vittorio, for his part, swore to himself that he would never go to sea again.

Throughout the winter, Vittorio made frequent and extended trips to the city. He convinced his mother that he could make money there, and indeed, teaming up with friends, he brought home cash earned shoveling snow, making deliveries, and doing errands and odd jobs to help Angela with the rent. As spring approached he began to brood about the idea of returning to the fishing boat. He knew he couldn't avoid it, that his mother, and especially Carlo, would never understand if he refused.

On a late afternoon in February, he sat smoking cigarettes and drinking espresso in a bar on Hanover Street with his two closest friends, Paolo and Marcello. Paolo, his friend since childhood, was stocky, resembling a wrestler in a circus, with thick arms and heavy hands. Marcello, the son of a tailor, resembled Vittorio in his slender height and straight jawline, and they often passed themselves off as brothers. "I hated fucking fishing before the storm," Vittorio lamented, "but that hurricane got into my head. I think about getting on that goddamned boat and I want to die. I mean I really want to die."

"Why don't you get a different job?" Paolo asked, trying to be helpful. "Your mother won't care, as long as you're working." Vittorio stayed with Paolo's family in their small third-floor apartment when he was in the city, sharing Paolo's tiny room.

"Have you ever heard of the Depression? It's not like there's people out there begging for the chance to hire you. For example, buddy, you don't have a job." Marcello laughed, and even Paolo smiled. "Anyway, I don't know what I'm gonna do."

"I'll hire you." A voice came from behind Vittorio. Surprised, he turned to see a short, sturdy middle-aged man. He was wearing a black beret above his jowled face. He looked Vittorio over with intense, penetrating eyes. "You look strong. Do you work hard?"

"Yes, I work hard," Vittorio answered defensively, not sure

what to make of the stranger. The man extended his hand, which Vittorio noticed was calloused and rough. Vittorio stood and took it, trying but unable to match the man's forceful grip.

"Name is Murabito. Antonio. You can call me Nino. Sit down. I'll buy you another espresso. Waiter!" Vittorio stepped away from his two friends, glancing back at them with arched eyebrows, and sat down across from Murabito. "I didn't get your name," the man said.

"Amorelli. Vittorio. People call me Vito."

"Where you from?"

"Gloucester."

"No, where are you *from*?" he asked again, gesturing back over his shoulder.

"Oh, Cefalú," Vittorio answered.

"Cefalú. Well, I can't say I ever heard of a stone mason from Cefalú. I thought you people were all fishermen."

"That's right," Vittorio nodded, "but I hate fishing. May God and my father forgive me, but I hate it. I've been working in Gloucester for five years. I want out."

"What do you hate about it?" Murabito asked.

"In a word? Everything. I hate boats and fish and knots. The whole package."

"Interesting." The waiter delivered an espresso, placing it in front of Vittorio, who stirred it self-consciously, waiting for the other man to speak. "Let me see your hands," Murabito said. Vittorio hesitated, then placed them, palms down, on the marble tabletop between them, one on each side of his espresso. Murabito picked them up, inspecting his fingertips as though they were ancient relics. Then he turned them over, running his fingers across Vittorio's palms, noting the calluses, thick from rope and fishing line. Vittorio heard Paolo and Marcello snickering behind him and turned his head to shush them over his shoulder. "*Grazzi*," Murabito said, placing Vittorio's hands back on the table. He nodded, glanced at his hands as though there might be something about them he hadn't noticed before, and then pulled them off the table.

"I come from Adrano . . . near Adrano. Ever heard of it?" Murabito asked. Vittorio shook his head. "Have you heard of Etna? *Mongibello?*"

"Of course. The volcano."

"Right. Murabito. Do you get the meaning?" Vittorio did not. "*Mur abito*. I live on a wall. That's what it means, literally. When you live at the foot of a volcano, you have to live on a wall. You have to keep building walls. We're masons because we had to be to survive, for centuries. So we're the best masons in the world. You see?" Vittorio nodded and smiled. "Now I live *off* of walls." He pretended to move something from one side of the table to the other. "*Capisci*? I make my living building walls, and charging good money for it." He leaned forward and spoke softly and conspiratorially. "The Depression is winding down, Vittorio, my friend. It's winding down, thank the Madonna. The rich are spending money again. So they hire me to build a nice attractive wall in the garden, then I convince them that they need me to do a little landscaping, take care of the lawn, plant a few trees. You see, Vito? Pretty soon, they can't live without me." Murabito leaned back and laughed. "Ever heard of Lincoln? Weston?" Vittorio shook his head. "Rich towns. Rich people. That's right. Rich. Like you and I can't imagine. I've got a good feeling about this summer. There's money to be made out there," he said, leaning toward Vittorio again and rubbing his thumb against his fingers.

Here he paused, and once again examined Vittorio, who was considering Murabito's words, wondering whether this could be the way out of his troubles. "I work hard, son. I'd expect you to work hard, too. I'll teach you what you need to know. I'm more concerned that you'll work."

"You don't need to worry about that, sir. I'll work."

"Well, you look like you've worked before. That's a good sign." A grin spread across his face. "Let's see if I can make a mason out of a fisherman. A *muraturi* out of a *piscaturi.*" Murabito laughed and Vittorio smiled. He was excited by the possibility. Yet as he swallowed his espresso and returned the cup to the saucer, he knew the idea would not be well received at home.

Carlo was stunned, then furious. He had gray streaks in his hair, and lines across his forehead, but his eyes could still be intense and fiery. He refused to look at or speak to Vittorio. Instead, he addressed Angela, speaking about Vittorio as though he were not sitting across the table from him. "He's too good for fishing? This family's been fishing for generations. We're not masons! There are no masons in our family. Are there masons in our family?" He gestured with his fork in Vittorio's direction but continued to look only at Angela. "What would Tommaso say? His own son thinks he's too good for fishing."

"Uncle," Vittorio said calmly, "it's not that I think I'm too good for fishing. It's just, I'm just—you *know*, I'm not good at it. I've been an embarrassment to you for long enough. You think I don't know that they tease you about me? Still, after all these years." Carlo glowered at Vittorio. "I'm not a fisherman, Uncle Carlo."

"He's not a fisherman," Carlo repeated, turning back to Angela and shaking his head. "Vittorio Amorelli, son of Tommaso Amorelli, grandson of Giuseppe Amorelli, is not a fisherman."

Angela had been sitting quietly, listening. She had perceived that he was miserable fishing, but had never addressed him directly about it, partly because she felt badly that there was nothing else to offer him, and because she had not been able to keep him in school. "He's given fishing a good try, Carlo."

"Five years," her son interjected. Carlo was expressionless.

"Vittorio," she continued, "I know you don't want to go back to the fishing boat. I accept your decision. If you want to try something else, I won't stand in your way . . . but tell me, how is this, what do you call it . . . landscaping? How's it going to work? Signuri Murabito . . . he lives in Boston, no?"

"Yes, Mamma." He knew this would be the harder piece for his mother. "And he leaves Boston early in the morning to go to work in the towns outside the city. Where the rich people live."

"So . . ."

"So, I'll have to stay with Paolo's family during the week. I'll come home on Sundays whenever I can." He put his hand on her forearm.

Silence. Angela looked at Carlo. He shrugged, raised his hands in the air in a gesture of indignant surrender, and then looked away.

"You're ready to leave home, my son? All grown, are you?" Angela forced a smile.

"It's just for now, Mamma. You know Paolo's parents. It's not like I'm gonna be with strangers. I'll come home whenever I can . . . I promise. What? You want me to end up a *mammoni*?"

Angela stood up and began to collect the plates, stacking them on the platter that had held the roast pork and potatoes. She gathered the silverware into one hand and then stopped. "You're a man, Vittorio. It's happened too quickly. I wasn't ready. I'll tell you the truth. I wasn't ready. I suppose one day soon you'll come home with a girl to marry. My Lord, Carlo, can you imagine? Me, a grandmother? Does it seem so long ago we were children ourselves?" She carried the load of plates to the kitchen and returned to the table. "Just remember one thing, Vittorio: I'll always be your mother." She touched his cheek, feeling the bristles of his shaven face.

"Okay, Mamma, now don't start," Vittorio said, standing up and wrapping his arms around her. "You make it sound like I'm moving to California. And, by the way, how old were you when you left your mother in Sicily and came to the great USA?"

"Too young," she replied, pulling back, gripping his elbows firmly and looking him in the eye. "I was too young. If you miss me as much as I've missed my mamma, though . . . I guess I'll be satisfied." She smiled, though the old emptiness clutched at her, the melancholy hewn out of all that she had lost. "Now come help your old mother with these dishes."

Antonio Murabito was a decent man. He could be stern, lecturing on the importance of "organization and discipline." He was patient, though, and his eyes exuded a warmth which undercut his efforts to be strict or authoritarian. Before Vittorio began working for him, Nino, with his wife, drove to Gloucester to meet Angela. He had been affected when Vittorio told him the story of his father's death and his mother's struggle to make a life for them. He understood the significance of Vittorio's leaving home.

Nino arrived with his wife, Rosa, who was shy but amiable. She wore her hair brushed back with a pink kerchief, in the old style from home, and a long dress with a silver crucifix around her neck. They brought gifts: a bottle of wine, homemade biscotti, and chocolate. Angela had made stuffed shells, along with baked cod. The meeting was successful, though Carlo excused himself politely enough soon after the Murabitos arrived. He was still angry. Though he could not have said so, he also felt a deep sadness to see the boy grown.

After dinner, when the dessert and sambuca were brought out, conversation inevitably turned to the "old country." Vittorio listened as his mother and the Murabitos shared stories of life in Sicily. Angela and Rosa discovered that they shared having only sisters, no brothers, and laughed at each other's stories of their fathers' trials in houses full of women. "*Una traggedia*, my father used to call it," Angela recounted, pretending to pound her fist on the table as her father had been accustomed to doing. "'Just one son, that's all I asked you for,' he would say to my mother when he went off to work alone, and 'all you gave me was girls and more girls. *Una traggedia.*'" The two women grasped hands across the table and laughed together.

Listening to his mother talk about Sicily, hearing both the joy and the sadness in her voice and seeing the dreamy look and occasional tears in her eyes, Vittorio renewed a promise to himself: one day he would take her back to Cefalú. One day he would walk into the house with the tickets. First-class tickets on a luxury ocean liner, and he would declare: "Mamma, I'm taking you home."

"Don't worry about anything," Nino said on the front porch, kissing Angela on each cheek in parting. "I'll keep a sharp eye on him. And I'll send him home to you as often as I can spare him."

"Let me know if he gives you any problems," Angela teased, reaching up to grasp her son by the ear, "and I'll set him right."

Nino Murabito had emigrated to America with his father at the turn of the century. Together they had worked as bricklayers after finding their way to Boston from New York with the assistance of friends. Living in rooming houses and overcrowded apartments, earning less than a dollar a day, they had struggled through those first years to establish themselves in the New World. For Nino, it was frustrating to watch his father carrying the hod, mixing cement and laying row after monotonous row of bricks, knowing the artistry he was capable of as a stone mason. His father, however, was stoic. In time, they sent for Nino's mother, who crossed with his sister, her husband, and their infant daughter. Through the referrals of acquaintances who worked in construction, Nino and his father eventually were given the opportunity to use their ancestral skills, moonlighting to build a retaining wall on the grounds of an estate on Fisher Hill, to the west of the city in Brookline. The beauty of their work was all the advertising they would need, and before long they had their own business.

The Depression, in just a few years, took away nearly everything that Nino and his father had spent decades developing. By then, Nino's father was in his seventies and unable to work, with arthritis locking his fingers in fists. They let their employees go and Nino returned to bricklaying when he could find it. Rosa, whom he had married not long after his mother and sister arrived, and their two children all left the house each morning, hoping to find work to sustain the family. Having toiled to be able to feed his family the milk and honey of America's promised land, Nino suffered as he slid helplessly back into the same poverty they had known in their earliest days in the United States.

Vittorio Amorelli was Nino's first employee as he set out to rebuild the company in the late thirties. He paid vigilant, even obsessive attention to the state of affairs in the country and hoped that the economy was generating a recovery that could eventually restore all that he had achieved ten years earlier.

Nino's standards were uncompromising, but he was reasonable and a good teacher. In Vittorio he found a willing apprentice, eager to prove to his mother and Carlo that he could succeed, and desperate to stay off a fishing boat. They began working together on a bright, blustery April morning. Nino picked Vittorio up and drove him to a quarry in Quincy to look at stone. He lectured his new pupil on the nature of rock, emphasizing the importance of choosing the correct type for the job at hand. From there, they drove through Chestnut Hill and Brookline, stopping to look at some of the work Nino and his father had done years before.

"Do you see any mortar in that wall?" Nino asked, the two of them standing in front of a four-foot-high, fifty-foot-long stone wall bordering a large colonial revival house on Buckminster Road.

Vittorio knelt down to look carefully between the stones. "No. None," he replied after a moment.

"Do you know what's holding those stones together, Vito? Do you know why this wall will still be here in a hundred years?" Nino asked, placing his hand proudly on the top of the wall. "Placement," he answered himself, not waiting for Vittorio to reply. "Perfection in the way the stones are placed together, working in harmony with the natural force of gravity. This one holds that one in place and together they're supporting this beautiful piece of granite right here. Do you see?" Vittorio nodded. "Here is what you must learn: to take a pile of stones and turn them into a work of art. To place the stones together like this, so that they're so comfortable and happy together, they never want to move." Vittorio smiled, nodding his head vigorously to show that he understood. "They should look like they were placed here by the hand of the Almighty himself."

"To be a great stonemason," he concluded, clapping his hand on Vittorio's shoulder and looking him in the eye, "like any form of art, requires the investment of deep emotion, because you have to be able to feel something. Not only with your hands, but in your soul. You have to go beyond mere thought. Organization and discipline get you started. They support the process like scaffolding. But from there, a deeper sense is called for. How did Michelangelo know what to take away from a block of marble to reveal the magnificence of David? Was it in his head?" He tapped on his temple with his forefinger. "No." He paused, watching Vittorio's face. "I don't expect that to make sense to you right now, Vito. You're probably thinking it sounds ridiculous. But you'll see."

Vittorio took to his new vocation in a way he had never taken to fishing. He was intrigued by the concept of creating something permanent, a work of art, as Nino had described, that would be seen and admired by people now and into the future. At first, Vittorio fetched things for Nino, and then stood watching as Nino built. Nino delivered animated lectures as he worked, emphasizing the importance of a solid, "unshakeable" base, and providing an explanation for the choice of each stone and its positioning in the wall.

Slowly, he began to bring Vittorio into the process. "Now," he would direct, "choose a stone for this spot, and tell me why you've chosen it." Then he would critique the choices his apprentice made. He taught Vittorio how to handle the hammer and chisel and how to trim stones for a tighter fit. He taught him how to square a corner and how to cap a wall with a smooth, even plane.

Finally the day arrived when Nino allowed Vittorio to build a section of wall on his own. They were nearing the completion of a large job: a wall with a sweeping curve, designed to tie the front yard of a grand Chestnut Hill home into the newly terraced flower garden on the south side of the house. Vittorio worked alone for an hour, examining the pile of stones and placing, removing, trimming, and then re-placing each one.

Nino worked several yards down the wall, where it would to taper gently into the lawn. He observed Vittorio as surreptitiously as possible, not wanting to make him more nervous than he already seemed. When he finished, Nino held out his hand for a congratulatory shake. "Excellent!" he shouted. Vittorio beamed. "You're making progress. This is very nice work. Now . . . let me show you what you did wrong." One by one and lecturing as he did so, he removed the stones Vittorio had arranged on the wall until his work was completely undone, the stones lying in a pile at the young man's feet. "Apologies, Vito, but that's how my father taught me. And it worked. I used to get furious with him, so I understand how you feel." He pounded him affectionately on the back.

"I'm not angry, Nino. I understand." Vittorio tried to hide his disappointment.

"Well, you may learn to hate me. Just don't take it the wrong way. I think you've got potential to be a great mason. Now, let's put this back together. Pass me the hammer."

The first time Nino allowed Vittorio's work to stand just as he had done it, uncorrected, he took his apprentice by the arm. "Look at that, Vito. You did it. I couldn't have done too much better myself. You can be proud of your work today."

Vittorio had taken to Nino, accepting his guidance and instruction and even fatherly care, but there was something about Nino that troubled Vittorio, as grateful as he was to be working alongside him. He seemed to carry a degree of shame, or defensiveness, in being Italian, and especially Sicilian. He insisted that they speak English. "We're in America, don't forget," he would say if Vito spoke Sicilian, though he was usually the one who unconsciously lapsed midconversation, retreating into the comfort of their first language. He would comment often on the faults of other Italians, noting that Al Capone had "got what he had coming," and even that Sacco and Vanzetti "should have known better than to associate with a bunch of unionists and anarchists." Mussolini was another common target for Nino's comments. He was convinced that the dictator was going to draw the world's recrimination and bring scorn upon Italians everywhere. He seemed to fear that his employment in certain neighborhoods was tenuous, despite his obvious skills, and that the mistake of some Italian somewhere at any moment could cost him his livelihood.

On a brutally hot July day Vittorio was working alone, repairing an ancient stone wall in the yard of a colonial home in Weston. He was drenched in sweat and tired from lifting the large stones. Finally, he peeled his shirt off, wiped his face and neck with it, and spread it on the grass in the sun to dry.

Suddenly, he heard Nino shouting. His boss had been bidding on another job not far away and had arrived in the truck to eat lunch with Vittorio. "Put your shirt on!" Nino hollered. Vittorio turned, surprised to see the anger on Nino's face as he stormed towards him. Nino snatched the shirt from the grass, balled it up and threw it at Vittorio. "Put on that shirt! Now. What's wrong with you?" he yelled. Vittorio was perplexed. He had seen Nino angry before, but the anger had never been directed at him. "Look at that house," Nino said. Vittorio glanced over his shoulder at the house. "Do you think those people—the people who live in *that* house—want to look out the window and see you out here half-naked like some kind of animal? This isn't the goddamned North End swimming pool. Are you trying to get us fired? You want me never to get another job in this town? Holy Jesus."

Vittorio pulled the shirt over his head and pushed his arms into the sleeves. He didn't know whether to be ashamed or angry. Putting his hands on his hips, he spat into the dust. "I'm sorry, Nino. It's hot. I was just hot," he said, hoping his boss would calm down. He did, then, telling Vittorio not to do it again.

"Go splash cold water on your face with the hose, and then let's eat something."

Vittorio was disturbed by the incident, and by Nino's peculiar attitude. He and his friends sometimes joked about being "wops" or "dagoes," tapping into the ambivalence of first-generation identity, and making light of the anti-Italian sentiment they often heard. He had never, though, known an Italian who seemed so deeply to believe, or at least give power to, those negative messages. He wanted to talk to Carlo when he went to Gloucester that weekend, knowing that Carlo would have something sensible to say about Nino's behavior. He held back from raising the issue, though, not wanting to give Carlo any reason to dislike his employer.

With Vittorio maturing in the trade and contracts backing up, Nino was anxious to expand his business. Once Vittorio was self-sufficient for the most part, able to execute a project once he and Nino had formed a plan for it together, Nino hired two younger men for landscaping. He had acquired a pickup truck and two lawn mowers. Before long there was more work than the two new men could do.

"Next year I'll take on two more masons, and who knows how many landscapers," Nino said to Vittorio in late August. "You see? I told you there was money out here." Vittorio turned a stone over in his hands, examining it carefully.

"You were right, Nino. It's a different world out here." They were in Weston, behind a large house on Church Street. Vittorio was finishing a retaining wall to form a bed for plantings at the edge of a terrace which spread out from grand French doors at the back of the house. He looked out across the lawn and the gardens. "Amazing," he said, shaking his head.

"This is why we came here, Vito. It's the land of opportunity. And you helped me get this all started. I won't forget that. We're in this together. If all goes well, my boy, soon you'll be supervising crews of workers all over the suburbs. We'll be like partners, Vito. Murabito and Amorelli. Then one day, when I'm too old to be out here, you'll take over. You see? You were lucky I overheard your conversation in the bar that day. You didn't even know your whole future was being planned." Vittorio smiled, laying the stone snugly into the spot he had arranged for it.

"Murabito and Amorelli," Vittorio mused. He enjoyed teasing the older man. "You know . . . honestly, Nino . . . I think Amorelli and Murabito has a better sound to it."

"Very funny, Vito. Very funny. Don't get ahead of yourself."

"Okay, *Capu*," Vittorio said, tossing him a stone and grinning. "We'll leave it your way . . . for now."

In September, Carlo tried to hide news of the blitzkrieg invasion of Poland from Angela, knowing that any talk of war would upset her. Marie, unaware that Carlo was shielding her, asked him his opinion one Saturday afternoon in the earliest days of the German aggression, while she and Angela worked canning tomatoes and pickling eggplant.

"War?" Angela cried. "Carlo, why didn't you tell me?" She crossed herself. "Germany, England, and France? Oh, God in heaven."

"It's unfinished business. I'm sorry. I didn't want you to—"

"Where's Vito?" Angela interrupted, standing up after ruminating for a moment on the news.

"He's probably down at the harbor with his friends," Carlo replied. Vittorio had returned home for the weekend earlier in the day. "Why?"

"Why? Because I happen to know that young men sometimes decide that joining the army when wars start is a good idea," she replied sharply.

"Angela—" Carlo began, chastened.

"We're going to sit him down. I'm going to sit him down today, before he gets any stupid ideas about war," she said, cutting him short. "I'm not going to be a fool a second time."

Roosevelt's signing of the Neutrality Act in November was only partially reassuring to Angela, as was Vittorio's insistence that he had no intention of joining the military. She made Marie promise that together they would follow events carefully in the months ahead.

Vittorio, truly, had little interest in the war. He lacked the passion that his father and Carlo had shared for world events. Knowing enough of the story of his father's death, military service did not appeal to him at all. He enjoyed his work and was content spending his leisure time with friends in the North End, or with the family at home in Gloucester.

His mother was still shocked to glance at him when he emerged from his room in the morning and to see a man. She teased him about the hair on his chest and squeezed his thick biceps in mock admiration. "You must have the girls in Boston chasing you down the street," she would say. "When are you going to choose one? I can't take care of you forever."

"Just waiting for the right one, Mamma," he would reply, smiling. "What's the rush? I'm just having fun." Indeed, he and his boys, whom he had taken to calling Bud and Lou after the popular comedians, had plenty of fun, flirting with the girls at the patronal festivals in the streets of the North End during the summer, lingering with them, making promises they did not intend to keep in the secret places where they went to test the limits. These pursuits occupied Vittorio's mind, and to him the war seemed far away.

As Hitler continued to progress across Eastern Europe, winter was coming. Nino purchased a second truck: a 1937 Ford pickup, used, bearing signs of abuse, but containing a strong engine. In order not to lose a season of the year, he was determined to do business plowing snow. "We didn't have to worry about such things at home," he told Vittorio as they surveyed the new vehicle, "but in this crazy country, God buries the world half the year. I can't build a wall under three feet of snow."

The pickup was outfitted with a rudimentary steel rig which could hold a small plow, clutching it on hooks so that it clattered over each bump in the road. The plowing process was arduous, requiring one to get out of the vehicle and jack up the plow at the end of each pass before backing up. Then the plow had to be lowered manually before it could once again be pushed, thudding, with intermittent screeches, across the road.

The first task, however, was for a skeptical Vittorio to learn to drive. The initial attempt ended badly, with Nino shouting commands as the pickup bucked down a back road in Wellesley. "Shift!" he hollered. "Clutch! Push in the clutch!" Vittorio stomped on the pedals and jerked the stick, but the truck seemed to work against him like an opposing wrestler, counteracting his efforts and in the process stalling, backfiring, with gears gnashing and tires howling.

"*Basta*," Vittorio announced finally, exasperated, defeated, as the truck coughed and quit yet again. "Don't you know my people are fishermen? I can't drive a fucking truck."

"Well, you couldn't fish either," Nino quipped, "so you better keep trying."

A few days later when he was willing to try again, and after leaving Nino sitting under an orange-red maple tree so he could concentrate, the young man began to develop a sense of the machine, and his hands and his feet learned to work together with the automobile. He let out a triumphant whoop the first time he made it travel smoothly down the road. By the time the first storm rolled through in early December, dropping half a foot of dense, wet snow, Vittorio was able to follow Nino, driving his truck, out into Brookline to look for work. They began with clients they had served in masonry and landscaping and made further contacts from there. Without traveling far from Boston, they found enough work to occupy them from early in the morning until dark, when most of the snow was cleared.

They were both exhausted from the strain of operating the plow and on the edge of frostbite. Rosa made chicken stew for dinner to warm them. Their layers of wool and canvas, abundant but still inadequate, were laid out to dry by the stove. "It's going to be a long winter, Nino," Vittorio moaned, shivering as he picked up a glass of wine with his still-numb fingers. "I was praying for snow so we could make some money like you said, but now, I don't know . . . I might be asking the Virgin for a little extra sunshine this winter."

Nino was undeterred: "Nonsense. You just keep praying for snow. The streets might not be paved with gold over here, like people used to say, but there might as well be gold under the snow, as long as we keep pushing it out of the way." Vittorio and Rosa rolled their eyes and laughed. They tried not to take him as seriously as he might have liked.

The total snowfall was higher than average that year, and by the time they cleared away the last storm in mid-March, they had done as well or better than they would have building stone walls over the same period. But when the grass first reappeared, poking above the retreating snowbanks for the first time in months, Vittorio was thrilled.

The color green returned with a burst to the gray landscape of New England, the last muddy, slushy miniature glaciers surrendering to the reinvigorated sun. While the new season provided relief to winter-weary populations in the northern hemisphere, it also afforded new opportunities for the Germans. Angela followed the news closely as Hitler attacked in the west, his divisions advancing swiftly into Belgium and Holland. The French, even with British support, couldn't mount an adequate defense. After Dunkirk, the fall of Paris was inevitable. The French, returning to Compiègne, this time in defeat, signed an armistice on June 22.

The papers reported that Hitler was optimistic, convinced that the war would soon be over with only the English remaining to subdue. Angela, for one, hoped he was right. Europe would work out its new order, as foul as it might be, and no Americans would have to cross the ocean to enter the conflict. The specter of her son boarding a ship, looking sharp but scared in his new uniform, began to fade from its central place in her fears.

The participation of the United States as a supplier of war machinery and supplies was stimulating the economy at the same time, and there was no shortage of work for Nino and his growing business. He added workers and Vittorio's responsibilities grew. The two men, despite their sarcastic banter and occasional differences of opinion, made a balanced team. Vittorio was easy where

Nino was uptight, and Nino provided direction where Vittorio could be lackadaisical. Nino felt increasingly confident, throughout that year and their second season of plowing together, that he had chosen well, and that in Vittorio he had found a partner for the long term.

Angela would encourage Carlo to walk down to the café where other Sicilian men gathered to converse, hoping that one day soon he would bring back news that the war was ending. Carlo was not accustomed to women taking such an interest in world affairs, and he shook his head to watch Marie and Angela poring over the newspaper, hoping to discern something from the photographs or the headlines. They were all amazed to learn, in late June, that the Germans had begun an invasion of Russia.

"This proves that he's a madman," Carlo stated. "How many fronts does he expect to keep open at once?"

"It's good news, though, isn't it?" asked Marie. "He'll be beaten in the east, and weakened in the west, no?"

"It'll be to Italy's eternal disgrace that we were with Hitler in this war," Carlo said sadly. "Mussolini is a fool, just another northerner out to screw the south. But now, he's in over his head."

"I have no concern for him. I only worry . . . I'm always worried about when America will join the war," Angela said, looking tired, dark semicircles dipping below her eyes. "Every time you come home with news, Carlo, I ask myself, 'Will this be it? Will Roosevelt send the army now?' What will it take?"

The answer came nearly six months later on December 7 in a place Angela had never heard of. The following day, speaking before Congress, Roosevelt declared war on Japan.

When the first shocking bulletins of the Pearl Harbor attack reached the east coast, midafternoon on the seventh, Angela was frightened. Marie had heard about the catastrophe and had rushed to see Angela as soon as she finished her duties. Both women knew that American neutrality could not survive an act of aggression on this brazen scale.

After dinner, which she couldn't eat, Angela put on her heavy coat, wrapped a shawl over her head and went to Mass at St. Anne's. Special prayers were offered on behalf of those who had been killed in Hawaii. Afterwards, Angela sat in a pew in the side chapel for a long time. She was shaken. Hadn't she sat in this same spot, she thought, begging God to spare the life of her beloved Tommaso? She remembered Tommaso saying goodbye to her for the last time, and she recalled the sight of Lieutenant Rienzo walking nervously toward the cabin. It had been more than twenty-three years since that day. She had lived half her life as a widow, raising her son without a father. She had survived Tommaso's death and persevered for the sake of the boy. And now? Now the boy was twenty-three years old and ripe for harvesting by a nation on the verge of entering another awful war.

Before leaving the church, Angela lit a candle before the statue of the Virgin. "Have mercy on me, Santa Maria. You're a mother. You know. Please, spare him."

iii.

The first time Ellen Lathrop saw Vittorio Amorelli, he was standing in her mother's rose garden, hands in the pockets of his brown overalls, listening to his boss. The garden bordered the mansion's veranda to the south, giving way to a rolling meadow, carefully designed and richly cultivated. The meadow sloped down to wetlands, where a crew of Irish laborers had spent weeks excavating the muck and carting in gravel, sand, and loam to create an artificial pond, just visible from the house and a key element in Mrs. Lathrop's vision when she laid out the plan for her gardens. She was proud to note that the pond, encircled by a cinder path and adorned with an elaborate cedar gazebo, provided a waystation for a community of hooded mergansers during their annual migration, along with a pair each of great blue herons and glossy ibises.

Ellen's mother had for many years engaged a gardener who, under her supervision, tended her flower beds, shrubs, flowering trees, and other plantings. Nino could not forgo the opportunity to hold forth on his favorite subject. "Rosa," he explained, "of the family Rosaceae. God's own masterpiece. Its cultivation is a mystical science." Nino grew them with magnificent success in his own small garden, including several plants which had made the trip from Sicily with his family years earlier: lush climbing vines and robust bushes blanketed in season with an array of colorful blossoms. Vittorio listened with as much attention as he could gather, knowing it was important to Nino, who by now was kneeling, expounding on the proper—or in this case, improper, in his view—application of fertilizer to the particular variety in the Lathrop rose garden. "That's why they look unhappy," he pouted, leaving his bottom lip protruding to emphasize his disapproval.

It was a warm spring day, near noontime, and Ellen, intrigued by Vittorio's handsome face and dark eyes, decided to prepare lemonade for the workers. She watched him, though, for another moment from the kitchen window, pausing from the omelet she had been eating. She liked the way he smiled as he squinted towards the sun, allowing a dimple to dent his cheek.

The spring semester of her junior year at Radcliffe had recently concluded, and Ellen was home in Lincoln for the summer. She had spent the morning playing tennis with old school friends across town. She was athletic: a member of the tennis team at Radcliffe, a strong swimmer, an experienced sailor, and an able equestrian, skills attributable to private lessons and the finest summer camps.

Her father, and her grandfather before him, had rowed at Harvard, and an uncle had been a star football player there, as well.

The Lathrop's never talked about their Mayflower lineage. Ellen's great-great-grandmother was an Allerton. But then it wasn't necessary to discuss it. Mr. Lathrop, Whitney, together with his brother, Calvin, directed the family business, which consisted essentially of managing the family's investments; an old-money fortune that had burgeoned during the second industrial revolution of the Gilded Age. Mrs. Lathrop, Caroline, who came herself from a Social Register family, her father having served in Theodore Roosevelt's cabinet, occupied her time with Garden Club, Junior League, various charitable concerns, and the altar guild at the local Episcopal church, St. Anne's-in-the-Fields. She was also a patron of symphony, dragging her husband to the city for concerts whenever possible.

Among her friends at Radcliffe, Ellen had earned a reputation as the daring one. She was sophisticated, with intelligence backed by experience. She had traveled widely in Europe with her parents before the war and exuded worldly self-confidence in any situation. Admiring adults called it poise. Her friends called it nerve. To a certain degree, she had raised herself, with the assistance of a rather reserved nanny, who saw primarily to her basic needs. She was comfortable with the independence of living away from home in Cambridge, and enjoyed the limited freedom allowed by life in a dorm. If anything, she wanted even more than the dorm authorities allowed. She was the first to smoke cigarettes and led the way for the other young women in sneaking booze, usually a bottle of her father's Scotch or her mother's gin, into the residence hall. She had no interest in finding a husband at Harvard and was anxious to see what life had to offer.

Ellen's immediate attraction to Vittorio was not consciously an act of rebellion, designed to shock her parents. The idea of rebellion did not occur to her, as there was little to rebel against. She had a good enough relationship with her parents, who were summering as usual on the Vineyard. Acts of rebellion would only have called attention to the details of her life, which she was content to keep out of their view. They, in turn, were pleased enough to let Ellen live her life, and they were not at all likely to suspect her of doing anything to embarrass them.

Instead, her attraction to Vittorio that day, as he worked in her mother's splendid yard, was physical. She was not completely inexperienced with men, though for the sake of her reputation had never allowed things to go beyond a certain point. Vittorio's strong features and muscular frame drew her. He reminded her of beautiful men who had whistled at her on the Piazza di Spagna in Rome. He was different from anyone she had met at Harvard. She watched him. He carried himself with an alluring ease, not cocksure and conceited, but rather content and self-possessed. With a long summer in Lincoln stretching ahead of her, she decided that she would have to find some way to amuse herself. Her father had arranged a boring internship for her at a law firm in the city, but that would occupy her only during business hours three days out of the week. She wanted to have fun.

Vittorio was surprised to see a pretty girl in tennis clothes approaching him, carrying a blue-and-white porcelain tray with two crystal glasses of lemonade. In three years of working with Nino, nothing like this had ever happened before. Nino was still talking, not having seen Ellen, grasping a vine from the trellis and explaining to Vittorio the correct way to cut a bud from the plant. "Not like this. Like this," he directed, making scissors with his fingers to demonstrate. Ellen smiled as she crossed the veranda towards the rose garden, her tennis shoes crunching the pebbles with each stride. Her eyes caught the sun, causing Vittorio to note their deep blue sparkle. Her hair seemed golden, nearly white to him, and though she was wearing tennis clothes, he thought she walked with the air of a queen or an actress, maybe Olivia de Haviland. He took note of the light sprinkling of freckles on her nose and shoulders.

"Would either of you like some lemonade?" Ellen asked. "It's awfully warm out here. You must be suffering." She took a glass from the tray and extended it to Vittorio. By now, Nino had turned to see why he had lost his pupil's attention, and from whom this unanticipated and refined voice was coming.

"Thank you," Vittorio answered, returning Ellen's smile and taking the glass from her hand. "That's nice of you."

"And you, sir?" She offered the other glass to Nino. He was uncharacteristically flustered, but realized that it would be impolite to refuse, and he was always careful not to appear impolite under any circumstances.

"Uh, thank you, *signorina*," he said, nearly dropping the glass in the transfer, wanting to be sure not to touch Ellen with his dirty hands.

"Hope you enjoy it," Ellen said, turning back towards the house. "I made it myself." She looked back over her shoulder, catching Vittorio's eye and winking as she walked away. Vittorio watched her. He was used to being liked by girls, even to having them be bold in their approach. He was not sure, though, what to think about this interaction.

She's just being polite, he decided after a moment. Rich people are like that. But then, how to explain the wink and smile?

Nino, watching Vittorio watch Ellen, was not pleased. In his mind, any hint of a romantic connection between one of his employees and the attractive daughter of one of his clients would doom his business. The reprisal, if such a relationship was to be pursued and then, God forbid, exposed, would destroy his name, he was sure, in Lincoln and probably all the surrounding towns. The contracts he secured were based on trust, he felt, and no one would trust him if his men were chasing the daughters of the clientele.

Vittorio turned back to Nino. "I'm sorry, Nino. What were you saying about pruning?"

"Vittorio," he replied, hands on his hips, "I hope you're not thinking what I think you're thinking." Vittorio put on his best confused look.

"What are you talking about, boss?"

"You know what I'm talking about, Vito. Don't give me that innocent crap. I'm talking about her. She's not your type. And believe me, you could never be her type. You just stick to the girls in the North End, okay? There are plenty of them for you."

"Nino," Vittorio scoffed, "your imagination gets away from you. You think I like her, or she likes me? Come on, old man. You're crazy. She was just being nice." Nino rolled his eyes and pursed his lips. "Oh, Nino. Jesus, will you stop worrying? You worry too much. It's not good for you." He gave his boss a pat on the back. "Come on, now. Finish telling me about the roses."

"I think you should invite her out," Marcello offered earnestly. "And just act like it's the most normal thing in the world."

"You're an idiot," Paolo retorted, glaring at him. "The most normal thing in the world that a girl from a rich family in Lincoln, a college girl . . . a tennis-playing college girl from a rich family would want to date this guido? That's normal?"

"I said *act* like it's normal. And this guido, as you well know, has a particular charm with women. So, if a rich, tennis-playing college girl from the suburbs were going to date a guido, it would be *this* guido."

The debate was unfolding in a tavern off Scollay Square, late Friday night. Vittorio was finally close enough to drunk to tell them about Ellen Lathrop's note. The day after he first met her, she again brought lemonade out to the yard where he and Nino were working. Their main task at the Lathrop estate was to rebuild the crumbling colonial-era stone wall which extended the length of the property's frontage on Sandy Pond Road. Vittorio had not seen her coming this time. His back was to the house as he dug out dirt from behind the wall with a spade to free a large, stubborn stone.

"It's another hot one," she had said sympathetically, startling him. This time she had lingered after delivering the cold beverage, which Vittorio gratefully received. "You're doing a beautiful job," she had said. "That's really a kind of art, isn't it?"

"Thank you. That's very kind," Vittorio had replied. "Nino, my boss . . . my partner . . . says it's mostly about organization and discipline. But I find it is, you know, kind of artistic."

"Thank you very much for the lemonade, miss," Nino had cut in, giving Vittorio a stern glance. "I don't mean to be rude, but I'm hoping to finish this part of the wall and begin on those steps before the day's over." With a final exchange of pleasantries, she was gone. At the end of the workday when Vittorio went back to his truck, he found a note.

"I don't know," he said, distracted. He had been staring across the room, smoking a cigarette and sipping at his beer, ignoring his two friends as they debated how he should respond to the extraordinary invitation. "She's beautiful . . . I like her. You should see her. She's just . . ."

"Just what?" Marcello asked, eagerly.

"Anyway," Vittorio continued, refocusing, "I don't know what she wants with me. On the one hand, I don't really need some rich girl playing games with me just because she's bored. On the other hand, it might be kind of fun to play games with a bored rich girl."

"Exactly," said Marcello. "What's the worst that could happen?"

"Juliet's brothers could kill him," offered Paolo, drawing a finger across his thick neck.

"Shut up, Paolo. Jesus Christ. Agree to meet her and act like it's the most normal thing in the world. That's what I say." With that, Marcello leaned back in his chair and crossed his arms on his chest. Paolo looked at him, shaking his head in disbelief.

"Come on, Vito," he reasoned. "There are plenty-a girls around here. You know that. Our kinda girls. You got more girls chasing you than you know what to do with. They're all waiting for you to pick one to marry so they can be your mistress." Vittorio laughed. It was true. He was twenty-three and there was constant gossip about which of the young women in the neighborhood he might choose. "Don't get yourself into a mess with some snobby girl. You and her are from different worlds, Vito. Nothin' good is gonna come of that. Leave it alone. Let her stick with her tight-ass college boys. What if she wants to play tennis? You've never touched a damn tennis racket in your life."

"Paolo, you worry too much," Vittorio concluded after a moment, his eyes clearing, as though a fog had burned off. He slapped his friend on the back. "Hey, our parents came here so we could have a better life, right? It's the land of goddamned opportunity. What faster way to move up in the world than to marry a rich girl? Then her daddy can take me into the family business, and I'll be a fucking millionaire!"

"You're right," Paolo said, knocking himself on the side of the head. "I worry too much. You're right. In fact, why settle for some small-town girl? Why don't you just marry Judy Garland?"

"You two are no help, you know that?" Vittorio said, motioning to the bartender for another round of beer.

"So, what are you gonna do?" Marcello asked.

"I don't know. Maybe I'll go to Mass tomorrow and ask the Virgin what I should do," Vittorio responded, trying to appear serious, to snickers from his friends.

"I guess that would be appropriate," Paolo replied. Vittorio punched him in the arm.

The note from Ellen Lathrop had said, simply, "Do you like to go to movies? Please respond. Ellen. P.S. Do you have a name?" She had written it after delivering lemonade the second time and had dropped it onto the seat of Vittorio's truck later in the day while Nino and Vittorio weren't in sight. She was not overly concerned about appearing too forward. If he found it so, whom would he tell? She did, nevertheless, want to leave him room to consider his response without being scared off. Expecting that he would be surprised to receive her note, she watched out her bathroom window to see the expression on his face when he found it. She wasn't certain, but she thought that he squinted and smiled as he glanced up from her small piece of floral notepaper and looked toward the house. A long moment passed before he started the truck and drove away.

She was disappointed the following Monday morning when the workmen failed to arrive at their usual early hour. Due to begin her internship in the city that day, she didn't know when she might see Vittorio again. Nino had decided to extend the separation that the weekend had afforded by taking Vittorio with him to prepare an estimate for another job. Vittorio pretended not to care when Nino informed him of the plan: "Oh, great. I've been waiting for you to start teaching me about bidding on jobs." He had prepared a response to Ellen's note, though, and he was anxious to deliver it.

On Saturday, he had gone to a stationer's and purchased a gold embossed card with a matching envelope, lined in gold foil. After extensive thought and many trial wordings written out in pencil on scrap paper, he decided, without consulting his friends, on the following message: "Dear Ellen, I do like movies. You, too? Could I take you to see one sometime? P.S. Yes, I do have a name. It's Victor." In his best handwriting, he wrote "Ellen" on the envelope and sealed it. He decided to match her boldness with a direct invitation, which he guessed was what she was hoping he would do.

By Monday night, after another day to reconsider, he was close to changing his mind. Paolo was probably right. He questioned Ellen's motives and recognized the futility of any relationship that might develop between them. But on Tuesday morning his sense of adventure won out, and arriving early at the Lathrop house, he slipped his note into the letterbox next to the front door.

By means of another surreptitious exchange of notes, they agreed to meet. Vittorio was to wait for her outside the building where she worked. He was nervous, not sure how to act, or even what to wear. He knew exactly how to be with girls in the North End. He could charm any girl in the neighborhood. Ellen was different, presenting a different set of challenges which he could not even yet identify. More than once, as their date approached, he asked himself why he was getting so tense. She was just another girl in the important ways, no different than others he had taken out. One afternoon, curious, he left work early and rode the train to Harvard Square. He walked around the Yard, casually observing how the college students dressed, and then went into a clothing store to purchase khaki pants and a plaid oxford cloth shirt with matching socks from a condescending clerk who appeared shocked when Vittorio produced the money to pay. He also bought new shoes and a brown leather belt. He laughed as looked at himself in the mirror, smoothing the unfamiliar fabrics. The girls were supposed to get dressed up for him. What the hell was he doing worrying this much about what to wear on a date?

At the appointed time, he lit a cigarette and leaned up against the granite wall of the office building, waiting for Ellen to appear and hoping no one he knew would see him dressed as a college boy. "Hi!" she called, spotting him as she walked through the door and not hiding her delight that he was actually there. She wore a navy skirt with a ruffled white blouse and a sweater over her shoulders. Her hair was braided and wrapped in a bun, allowing him to see her slender neck and the way her cheekbones curved back below her eyes.

"Hi, to you!" Vittorio responded, pleased that she seemed happy to see him. He dropped his cigarette and ground it under his shoe, smiling despite his determination to remain nonchalant.

"We need to hurry," she said. "The film starts in fifteen minutes. I took the liberty of choosing one. I hope you haven't seen it. It's called Springtime in the Rockies, or something like that. I don't know much about it, but it's meant to be good. Does that sound okay?"

"Perfect."

They were seated in time to watch the newsreel, which showed the Axis advancing: Rommel's relentless march toward the Egyptian border; the fall of the Soviet defenses at Sevastopol; the sinking by the Italians of the British destroyers Airedale, Bedouin, and Oakley. Ellen and Vittorio sat quietly, eyes fixed to the screen, as the booming voice of the narrator recounted the Allied setbacks.

The film itself, a musical comedy, turned out to be an awkward selection. Filmed in Technicolor on location in Lake Louise and starring Betty Grable, it told the story of an on-again, off-again Broadway couple who were constantly trying to "get even" with each other. Betty Grable's character leaves for Lake Louise, where she takes up with a Latin dancer played by Cesar Romero, named "Victor" in the film, by uncomfortable coincidence, in order to make her lover jealous. The lover, played by John Payne, in turn pretends to be in love with Rosita Murphy, his Brazilian secretary, played by Carmen Miranda. In the end, Grable and Payne realize that they're truly meant for each other, and Victor and Rosita, having served their purpose, are cast aside. Vittorio shifted in his seat as the thin plot unfolded.

Afterwards he was quiet, exiting the theater onto the street. "Well, did you like it?" Ellen asked.

"Uh...I guess so. I liked Carmen Miranda singing 'Chattanooga Choo-choo.'"

"Wasn't she great? She stole the show. I like Betty Grable, too."

"She's getting to be a big star," Vittorio said absently, then paused. "Listen," he went on, "that whole thing with Carmen Miranda and Cesar Romero kind of got me thinking. It's just . . . I mean, I don't know why you wanted to go on a date with me, but if it's to make someone else jealous, or to upset your parents or something, then . . . I mean I think you're really nice and everything, but . . ."

Ellen was looking down at the ground between them. They had stopped walking and stood at a corner. She looked Vittorio in the eye. "I was afraid you might be thinking that. I'm sorry. That probably wasn't the best choice of movie. I really apologize. But I'm not trying to make anyone jealous. I'm not seeing anyone at all. And my parents don't pay much attention to whom I date. Actually," she said, reaching out and taking Vittorio's hand, "I wanted to go on a date with you because I think you're handsome. That's what I thought when I looked out the window and saw you working." Vittorio cocked his head to one side and smiled. She tugged on his hand, and they began walking again. "I'm hungry," she said. "Let's go get something to eat." Walking down Boylston Street, Vittorio was aware of people staring at them, heads turning, hushed comments exchanged.

"So, is that man you work with your father?" she asked. She seemed not to be aware of the attention they were drawing. Vittorio was distracted by it, and by the way Ellen didn't seem to notice.

"Nino? Oh no, he's just my boss. My father was a fisherman. I come from a long line of fishermen. But I hated fishing, everything about it. I worked on a boat for five years. Hated it. So I went to work for Nino."

"You like this kind of work better?"

"Much better."

"You said your father was a fisherman. Is he retired?"

Vittorio laughed. "No," he said. "Fishermen don't retire. But my father's dead. He was killed in France during the war."

"Oh, my God, I'm sorry," Ellen said, squeezing his hand.

"Me too," Vittorio replied. "I never met him. He never even knew he was going to be a father. But my mother's very strong. She worked hard . . . did whatever she had to do to raise me."

They stopped in front of a small café to look at the menu in the window, and then went in and sat down at a linen-cloth-covered table in a corner.

"Anyway, what about you?" Vittorio asked after they ordered. Glenn Miller's "Moonlight Serenade" played on a radio behind the counter. Two other couples stepped into the café, laughing boisterously.

"Me? Not much to tell really. It's just what you've seen. I've got a year of college left. I forced my father to get me a job in the city this summer. Mostly I'm just observing . . . watching what lawyers do. I'd like to go to law school, but I haven't raised the idea with my parents yet."

"What's college like?" He liked her voice, the confident tone, just a little deeper than he would have expected, easy and fluid.

They sat talking for two hours, ordering dessert and coffee after their sandwiches and smoking cigarettes. She told him about college, and about some of the places she had been, including Italy. He told her about his shortened education and made her laugh with stories about Carlo and Marie. He even felt comfortable enough to confess the story behind the outfit he was wearing. She blushed, flattered, and told him she didn't care what he wore.

By the time she had to leave to get home, an easy tenderness had begun to grow between them. In front of the café, she again took his hand and kissed him on the cheek. He smiled and leaned forward, kissing her lightly on the lips. She leaned into him and sighed.

"What do we do now?"

"I don't know," he answered.

The summer of 1942 was suffused with increasing uneasiness for Italian Americans. It was a time when gains were measured against growing tension. One could find reason for pride in people who were ascending to fame. The entire country was falling in love with Joe DiMaggio, who, since joining the Yankees in 1936, had led them to five championships in six years. His fifty-six-game hitting streak during the 1941 season had captivated the nation, drawing attention away from the worsening situation in Europe. Joe DiMaggio and his brother Dom, who had joined the Red Sox in 1940, were especially important to Vittorio, as they were the sons of a fisherman from Isola delle Femmine, not far from Palermo. Their older brother, Tom, said to be the best ballplayer in the family, had passed up a professional career to continue fishing with his father in California. Vittorio was exhilarated by the idea that Joe, a Sicilian, could do something quintessentially American better than almost any American.

Another Sicilian had also entered the American mainstream. In the fall of 1941, Fiorello LaGuardia, son of a musician from Foggia, was overwhelmingly reelected, becoming New York's first three-term mayor. Having inherited a city in crisis upon his first election in 1933, he had reached hero status to many for his strong leadership, aggressive reforms, and civic projects such as the Triborough Bridge, which had helped to bring New York out of the Great Depression. Following the heady victory of 1941, LaGuardia had quietly begun to confide to his closest associates his belief that America might at last be open to the idea of an Italian-American president.

The increased visibility of Italians in American society, which brought with it the hope that the immigrant class had finally arrived, was foiled by Italy's role in the European war. In the summer of

1942, it was far from clear that the entrance of the United States into the conflict would happen in time to prevent an Axis triumph. News of Axis victories on many fronts continued to be received by an outraged American public. Inevitably, along with those of Japanese ancestry, Italian-Americans became the objects of suspicion and derision. For those who had been in the country long enough to remember the anti-immigrant sentiment of the 1920s, the wrath brought on by Italy's status as an enemy nation seemed to dampen the progress that had been made since.

Vittorio felt the increasing awkwardness of being Italian in America the second time he met Ellen for a date. He felt as though the atmosphere was thickening, and that drawing breath was becoming more difficult. He stood waiting, realizing when he reached into his pocket for matches to light his cigarette that he was more nervous than the first time, and that his palms were slick with sweat. As much as he wanted to spend more time with Ellen, a sense of dread gripped his stomach when he found her note in the usual place in his truck on Monday: "Same time, same place? -E." After a week of considering the hazards of their relationship, Vittorio dressed in the jeans and white T-shirt he would wear if he were going out with his friends, and walked downtown to meet Ellen, planning to put an end to it.

She greeted him with a kiss, complimenting him on his good looks, and putting him quickly at ease. "I think I've chosen better this week," she announced, taking his hand. "How would you like to see Gary Cooper as Lou Gehrig? *Pride of the Yankees* just opened."

This time, they huddled together in the theater. He put his arm around her, and she leaned into his body. By the end, they were both overcome by emotion, as Cooper's Gehrig was decimated by disease. Ellen pulled a handkerchief from her purse, wiping the tears from her cheek, and then dabbing at the one in the corner of Vittorio's eye.

They emerged from the theater into a warm summer evening, still pressed closely together. "I'm a mess," Ellen said, laughing. Separating from the crowd she pulled a compact out of her purse to check her makeup, using her pinky to clear a black smudge from below her eyelid.

"Such a sad story," Vittorio agreed. "I'm glad I didn't see it with the boys. They would have been on my back for getting misty."

"I think it's sweet," she said, putting her arm around Vittorio's waist and pulling herself closer. He turned his face toward her, and they kissed. Looking past her, he noticed two young men standing at the edge of a shadow across the street. He wasn't certain at first that they were looking at him, but he convinced himself that they were. One seemed to elbow the other in the gut, and they appeared to shake their heads in disgust. He pulled away from her.

"Do you want to go somewhere?" he asked.

"Is something wrong, Victor?" She had noticed the edge in his voice and the abrupt change in his mood.

"Well, let's start walking," he answered, glancing back towards the place where the two young men had been standing, relieved to see that they were gone.

"Okay. Where do you want to go? Shall we go to that same café?"

They turned to go. "What is it, Victor?" she asked. "What happened?"

He continued looking down at the sidewalk. "Doesn't it bother you," he began, "the way people stare at us? Have you noticed it? People don't think we should be together. Some of them actually look angry. . . . Do you know what I mean?"

She stopped walking and took his hand, firmly. "Listen, Victor," she said, sounding businesslike. "I can't worry about strangers on the street. I like you. A lot. Do you know that?" When he still didn't look at her, she stopped and reached for his cheek with her other hand. Her tone softened. "Do you know that?"

"I guess I do know," he said, feeling his face turning red.

"Do you like me, Victor?" she asked.

He laughed, throwing his head back and looking up at the sky. "Yes, Ellen. It's kind of obvious, isn't it?"

She wrapped her arms around him again. "Then let's forget about any ingrate who doesn't think we belong together. What do they know about you or me?"

"Well, Miss Lathrop, that's easy for you to say. You're not the one that's likely to get beat up."

The confident smile disappeared from her face. "Are you really afraid of that?" she asked.

"I'd be a fool not to be. You don't know what Boston is like. People keep to their own kind. They keep to their own neighborhood. That's the way it is. And being Italian these days . . ."

"Jesus, Victor," Ellen said. "I'm sorry." She was immediately conscious of other people walking past them in the street, and she scanned approaching groups nervously. "Why didn't you say something sooner?"

"Honestly . . . I came tonight planning to tell you that maybe we shouldn't see each other anymore. I would hate for you to get caught up in something . . . ugly."

Ellen noticed a dark doorway a few steps away and pulled Vittorio into it. Glancing once more up and down the sidewalk, she turned and kissed him. She squeezed his hands, and reached up, brushing his lips with hers so that a shiver went through her and he sensed her longing.

"That's not an option," she said, pulling away. He could tell she was used to having things the way she wanted them. "So, here are the only options." The businesslike tone returned. He could imagine her as a lawyer. "We can continue meeting in the city and risk an incident. Or, we can start meeting in other places, where there's no danger of being confronted by this nonsense. It seems to me like the second one is the better option. Agreed? So, I'm going to go now. I'll leave you a note. Follow the instructions." She kissed him again. "See you soon, my secret friend." She stepped out of the doorway, turning back only once to wink and blow a kiss.

On Monday morning there was a car in the driveway at the Lathrop's which Vittorio hadn't seen before: a 1941 Cadillac de Luxe Club Coupe in rich, gleaming cobalt. He knew the make and even the model—Series 61—from the advertisements, but he had never seen a real one. Attempting to appear purposeful in his work, he strode down the driveway past the automobile with a tin bucket. After filling the bucket at the faucet below the kitchen window, he walked back towards the car. This time he couldn't resist the vehicle's magnetism and, pausing, peered in through the lowered window to marvel at the opulent, cream-colored leather interior. His head was nearly inside the window when a male voice startled him.

"Do you like it?" Vittorio jerked his head back and turned to see a tall, slender man standing at the back door. He wore Bermuda shorts and a tartan shirt. His thinning brown hair, gray at the temples, was combed straight back with a daub of Brill cream. In the man's narrow, patrician nose and strong chin, he could see the resemblance to Ellen.

"I'm sorry, sir," Vittorio managed to say, flustered. "I was just . . ."

"No, don't apologize," Mr. Lathrop interrupted graciously. "I'd be concerned about a man who could walk past an automobile like that without having a closer look. Best one I've ever owned, and certainly the best looking." Vittorio was silent, not knowing what to say. He passed the bucket to his left hand and looked across the yard toward the pond. More than anything, he wanted to disappear. He had rarely spoken to anyone for whom he worked. He left that to Nino. Interacting with Ellen's father, of all people, made his heart begin to pound in his chest, especially remembering the way she had kissed him.

Finally, Lathrop spoke: "Well, go ahead. Don't let me interrupt you. Open the door so you can see better." He smiled broadly, leaning against the door frame with one hand, arm outstretched, and holding a mug of coffee in the other.

"Thank you, sir. But I should be getting started. My boss . . ."

"You people do nice work," Ellen's father said. "That kind of thing is my wife's bailiwick, but I couldn't help but admire the job you're doing on that wall. I guess it's sort of . . . in your blood, isn't it?" Vittorio was not about to explain the story behind his adopted vocation.

"I guess you could say that, sir."

"Well, keep up the good work," Lathrop called cheerily, turning to enter the house.

"Thank you, sir."

"Oh," he said, looking back at Vittorio through the doorway, "and please do feel at liberty to admire the Cadillac."

Vittorio stood still for a moment, not sure whether it would be rude, following Mr. Lathrop's invitation, to leave without looking at the car. At last he shrugged, turned, and walked quickly down the driveway, swinging the bucket at his side.

Having lost an argument with her mother, Ellen was forced to leave a note for Vittorio on Tuesday morning: "Family obligations on the Vineyard this weekend. Sorry. Next weekend? Missing you. –E." Ellen's aunt and her family were arriving for a visit over Independence Day, and Mrs. Lathrop insisted that Ellen join the family for the weekend. Ellen protested that she had made plans with friends, but to no avail. Her aunt would be expecting to see her, and Caroline was unwilling to disappoint her sister.

The following morning Vittorio was at work joining the wall to a granite light post he and Nino had installed at the edge of the driveway. Ellen was home preparing to leave in the afternoon for the Cape, where they would spend the night with friends in Falmouth before meeting the ferry early Friday. When she saw that Vittorio was working alone, she prepared a glass of iced tea and brought it to him. Not wanting to let another week pass before they spoke, she decided to be direct.

"You got my note?" she asked as Vittorio drank the iced tea. He glanced at the house nervously, afraid they might be under surveillance. Vittorio had seen Mrs. Lathrop earlier inspecting her flower beds and observing her birds through field glasses.

"I did. Thank you."

"I don't want to go, but it's a bit of a family reunion. I was looking forward to seeing you." She hoped this might draw a response confirming his continued interest.

Vittorio smiled. Remembering their kiss in the unlit doorway days earlier, he suppressed an urge to embrace her now. Her hair was pulled back in a ponytail and tied with a pink ribbon. She wore a sundress, a shade lighter than the ribbon, showing her shoulders, strong from swimming and tennis.

"You look very pretty today." Her face reddened.

"You're teasing me," she replied, "because I'm a disaster. Just trying to get ready to go."

"I think you look pretty."

"I better go," she said, still blushing. Their kiss was on her mind too, and she was afraid of what might happen if she stayed there with him. "Can we see each other next week?"

"I'm going to be done here tomorrow," Vittorio answered, gesturing toward the stone pillar. "I don't know where I'll be working next week." Ellen thought for a moment.

"There's a telephone at the law firm. I'll leave the number in your truck before I go today. Call me there on Wednesday. Tell them it's about the Richmond matter."

"The Richmond matter?"

"It's a case I'm working on. Just tell that to the receptionist." Reluctantly, she began walking away. "Goodbye, Victor."

"Thank you for the iced tea," he called after her. "You're very sweet."

☙

Vittorio was nervous about making a telephone call. He had used a phone only a few times before. His mother didn't have one, nor did Paolo's family. The tobacconist on Cross Street had a phone which he allowed neighbors to use for a nickel. Vittorio rehearsed his lines with Paolo, who urged him to try to sound confident and cool, before finally picking up the telephone to give the operator Ellen's number. He turned to face the wall, pretending to read the posted advertisements, hoping other customers in the shop wouldn't overhear his conversation.

"May I speak to Ms. Ellen Lathrop," he said tentatively when the receptionist answered.

"Ellen Lathrop?" The woman seemed not to recognize the name.

"Yes. Ellen Lathrop," Vittorio replied, enunciating carefully.

"Hmm." Vittorio was ready to hang up. "Oh, yes, Ellen. I'm sorry. May I ask who's . . . ?"

"It's about the Richmond matter," Vittorio cut in.

"The Richmond matter. Yes, fine. And your name, sir, so I can tell Miss Lathrop who's calling?"

"Uh, it's, uh, Victor. Victor . . . Richmond." He felt a drop of sweat sliding out of his armpit and down his arm to his elbow.

"Victor Richmond. Thank you, Mr. Richmond. One moment please." Several minutes passed.

"You're gonna have to give me another nickel if you don't hurry up, Vito," the clerk yelled from behind the counter. "I got people waiting for that thing."

"Yeah, yeah—another nickel. I'm almost done. Jesus."

"Victor?" At last Ellen's voice came across the line.

"Ellen," he said, relieved to hear her.

"I'm so glad you got through. Listen, I can't talk. I'm in the middle of observing a meeting. I have an idea for Friday night. Are you free?"

"I think so. For you, I'm sure I could get free."

"Good," she said, almost whispering. "I miss seeing you. So, do you know where Walden Pond is?"

"Yeah. I've driven by it. I know where it is."

"Wonderful. There's a sort of beach off Concord Road, right at the Lincoln-Concord town line. Meet me there at seven o'clock? I'll bring a picnic."

"I'll be there."

"Good, Victor. I've got to go. Goodbye." She hung up.

He turned around. Paolo was still waiting for him. Seeing the smile on Vittorio's face, he cried, "Oh, Lord. He's gone. He's completely gone. We've lost Vito."

Vittorio grabbed him by the arm, and dropping a nickel on the counter, pulled him outside. "Come on, Paolo. You know I don't want this to get around. Help me out, okay? Keep that big mouth shut."

Paolo bit his bottom lip and winked at Vittorio. "I'll keep my mouth shut, Casanova, but it shows. All over your silly, stupid face."

Nino came by late in the afternoon on Friday. Vittorio was working in Lexington, laying a fieldstone walkway to link the front door of a stately Greek Revival with the driveway. For an hour, the two worked together. At such times they fell into their original roles of master and apprentice, with Vittorio assisting Nino, even though he had built two-thirds of the walkway skillfully on his own.

"I'm going to head over and pick up the other two on the way back to town," Nino announced at four-thirty, washing his hands at the spigot between the rhododendrons on the side of the house. "Are you ready to finish up?"

"I'm just gonna stay a few more minutes and square off this section before I quit," Vittorio replied.

"You're a good man, Vito. What would I do without you?"

"Well, boss, if I'm such a good man, would you mind letting me use the truck tonight? I want to take a girl out."

"What kind of a girl?" Nino asked. "I wouldn't want some of those girls you go with in my nice clean truck." Vittorio gave him an ugly look.

"Oh, not the evil eye!" Nino shielded his face with his hands. "All right, all right. Have a good time. I'll see you Monday. You've got another day or so here?"

"A day at most. Thanks, Nino. Kiss Rosa for me."

After Nino was gone, Vittorio went to the truck and pulled a bag, carefully packed early in the morning, from under the seat. The owners of the house were away on vacation and had left the back door open for the workers to use the bathroom. Checking to make sure he was unobserved, Vittorio carried the bag into the house. He left his work boots by the door and climbed the stairs to the bathroom on the second floor. There he bathed, shaved, brushed his teeth twice, and dressed, checking himself in the mirror three or four times. Satisfied, he cleaned the bathroom thoroughly, gathered his belongings, and went back out to the truck.

He arrived at Walden Pond at half past six and parked in the field off the road. Following the path, he made his way down the hill to the pond. The air was still and humid. The flat surface of the water reflected the few high clouds in the sky and the hazy, descending sun. At one end of the packed mudflat a group of teenaged boys sat smoking cigarettes and clowning. They were in swim trunks and had been throwing a football in the shallow water. Vittorio walked down the beach away from them until he found a large, dry rock. He sat and scooped up a handful of pebbles and tossed them one at a time into the pond, disturbing the dusty surface and sending languid ripples across the water.

Ellen arrived, self-assured as ever, vaguely regal, carrying a wicker basket with a folded blanket over her arm. "Victor," she called while still twenty-five yards away. "There you are!"

"Here I am, just enjoying the beautiful evening." She walked unhesitatingly to him and kissed him. "And it just got more beautiful," he added. Ellen wore a peach blouse, Capri pants, and sandals. She was radiant, with a golden suntan acquired while sailing and playing badminton the previous weekend on the island.

"I hope you're hungry," she said. "I brought a feast. Let's follow the trail over here. I know a pretty spot where we can spread the blanket and watch the sunset." He took the basket from her and glanced back to see whether they were being watched. They left the beach, following the path for several minutes until Ellen took his hand. "Now it's this way," she said. They scrambled up a small hill to a clearing. "How's this?"

"Perfect," Vittorio replied, setting down the basket. The sun sparkled orange and red through the trees, casting dappled light onto the ground around them. Ellen spread the blanket on the ground. She sat and motioned for Vittorio to join her.

"So, what's the story with the fellow who came to live out here? I remember hearing something about that," Vittorio said, settling close to Ellen. She put her hand on his knee.

"Thoreau," she answered. "Henry David Thoreau. He built himself a little hut—a cabin, really. Lived out here for a couple of years. He was . . . brilliant. He didn't like the pace of modern society, so he just quit."

"He lived out here all by himself?"

"All by himself. He wanted solitude, so he could think and write, and . . . commune with nature, I guess."

"You'd never catch a Sicilian doing something like that," Vittorio mused, shaking his head.

"Oh no? Why not?"

"First of all, your mother would never let you."

"He was twenty-eight years old!"

"Doesn't matter. His mother still wouldn't have let him. And even if he tried, the family would always be dropping by, bringing food, making sure he wasn't lonely. We don't spend too much time alone."

"Don't you ever want some . . . peace and quiet? Sometimes I just have to be by myself."

"I guess I never really thought about it."

"Well, it's nice to be here with you," she continued after an awkward pause, squeezing his knee. "Let's eat." She began to pull food from the basket: chicken salad sandwiches, potato salad, carrot sticks, chocolate cake, and a bottle of her father's wine. "Open this?" she said, handing him the wine and a corkscrew. "So, how did you get the name Victor?" she asked as she organized the food and Vittorio removed the wax from the top of the bottle. "Were you named for your father?"

"No. His name was Tommaso. Thomas. Traditionally the first son is named for his father's father, so I should have been Giuseppe. But I was born on the day after the war ended so my mother named me Victor. I think she was trying to be optimistic. She only found out a few weeks before I was born that my father was killed in action."

"I can't imagine. All alone in a strange country, with a newborn son."

"Well, she's strong, like I said. What about you?"

"Am I strong?"

"No, who were you named for?" Vittorio said, blushing.

"I knew what you meant." Ellen laughed. "I was named for my aunt, my mother's sister. She's my godmother."

They sat cross-legged facing each other, their knees nearly touching, and then, touching. Ellen told him more about her family as they ate, about her grandparents and her cousins. He was amazed to learn that in her family she was the fifth generation to attend Harvard.

"My mother was hoping I would be the first in my family to finish high school," he said. He told her about starting school speaking no English and the uproar it had caused. He told her about fishing, and about Paolo and Marcello, and festivals in the North End. She told him about summers on the Vineyard, and about prep school. As they talked, the bottom of the sun settled into the trees across the pond, mirrored in orange streaks across the water.

"We don't have too much in common, do we?" Vittorio said after a pause.

"Hmm. Well . . . we're both only-children, right? That's something."

"True."

"Do you want to kiss me?"

Vittorio laughed. Somehow she always made his face turn red. He shook his head in wonder. When had a girl ever made him blush?

"Yes, I have to say, I do," he said, trying to find his relaxed, girl-charming voice.

"So, that's another thing we have in common, then," Ellen said, turning her face towards his. Leaning forward, he kissed her lightly. As they lay back, wrapping their arms around each other, Vittorio sensed that he was the more experienced, and his confidence increased. Slowly, gently, they made love. He watched her eyes and cushioned her head in his hand.

"I don't want to leave you," she whispered later as he put the picnic basket into the backseat of her car. They embraced and held each other sleepily for several moments. It was nearly two o'clock in the morning.

"I don't want to leave you either," he said, kissing her on the forehead.

"I feel like you could disappear, Victor. How would I find you? My parents don't know your parents. We never went to school together. You could just slip back into your world and be gone."

"I'm not like that. Don't worry." He lifted her chin with his finger. They looked each other in the eye, hers questioning, his reassuring, and then he smiled and kissed her.

She eased herself into the car, gripping the steering wheel. He could see that she was trying to steady herself. He felt tender and complete, and at the same time that they had perhaps dangerously broken the laws of nature.

iv.

The glen on the rise above Walden Pond became the sanctuary where they could pretend, implicitly, that the barriers of class and ethnicity didn't exist. Except for the occasional weekend when her presence was demanded for family events, Ellen met Vittorio on the beach at seven o'clock on Friday evenings. She would bring dinner and the two would eat and talk and laugh about the week that had passed until finally they would couple in the dark. Often, they would wrap themselves in the blanket afterwards and sneak, giggling, to the water's edge, where they would leave the blanket and swim together nude.

Both kept the deepening affair secret, even from their closest friends, realizing that it was too dangerous to share. When asked by Paolo and Marcello, Vittorio explained that he had found the rich girl "snobby" after all, and that they had broken it off after two dates. Judging from Vittorio's strange behavior, his indifference towards the girls with whom he normally flirted, his lack of interest in the women who were always ready to go out with him, Paolo and Marcello surmised that Vittorio was keeping something from them. The weak excuses he offered for his absence on Friday nights added to the evidence. When pressed, Vittorio denied it, straight-faced. There were moments, particularly with alcohol softening his resolve, when he wanted to tell them all about his new love: her beauty, her intelligence, her allure, how deeply in love with him she seemed to be. But his fear of their reaction, and particularly the reaction the news would draw when it inevitably leaked out to the neighborhood, was enough to keep him quiet.

Ellen, too, was tempted to disclose her secret to the few friends she saw for tennis or met in the city for lunch, or even to write her Radcliffe roommates with the thrilling story of her summer affair. As time passed, though, she felt an increasing sense that treating it as a scandalizing subject for idle correspondence would cheapen what was, impossibly, becoming a serious relationship.

Ellen and Vittorio did not, for many weeks, discuss the tenuousness of their situation. In the quiet, romantic darkness of a Friday evening by the pond, as they clung to each other, everything seemed possible, especially to Ellen. Vittorio harbored a sense that there was no future for them, no matter how strongly he had begun to long for her during the week between their covert meetings. Ellen's hope was that there might be a way to create an acceptability for the relationship that she could present successfully, a way to convince her parents that a handsome, decent, skilled artisan, the son of a war hero, could make a suitable husband, even if his last name was Amorelli. Or, if nothing else, that true love mattered more than pedigree. This hope insulated her from the idea that the summer might end, and that, as she slipped back into the world of Radcliffe, Vittorio would evaporate from her life like a pool in the desert.

Vittorio leaned against the massive poured-stone base of the dramatic statue. The Lakota chief on horseback, his arms splayed and head thrown back in supplication, towered above him. Vittorio had circled the monument slowly before inclining himself against the pedestal to wait for Ellen.

"Magnificent, isn't he?" She peeked around the corner of the base. She had convinced him to meet her at the Museum of Fine Arts despite his reluctance to be seen together in the city. She argued that it was far enough from his neighborhood, that it was a neutral location, and besides, there was something she wanted him to see.

"What's he doing, praying for rain?" They kissed in greeting.

"Good guess. It's called *Appeal to the Great Spirit*. His tribe has been defeated and he's asking God for help."

"I like it. I've seen that look on my mother's face during Mass . . . probably when she's praying for my soul." They kissed again. She wrapped her arms around his neck.

"You're funny." She smiled. He loved the dimple that formed on the right side of her face when she was happy. "Let's go in. You've really never been here before?"

"To an art museum? I've driven past it a few times."

They paid the entrance fee at the desk and then climbed the stairs to the second floor. The museum's collection of Italian paintings from the Renaissance was displayed in a long, narrow room with a vaulted, wood-paneled ceiling. It was Sunday afternoon, and other patrons lingered about the gallery, discussing the artwork in hushed voices. Ellen took Vittorio's hand and led him toward the first painting along the wall.

"Saint Sebastian," Vittorio stated. The martyred saint, naked but for a cloth around his waist, was depicted with long flowing curls and a halo surrounding his head, and with ten arrows piercing his body. His serene face showed no sign of pain. "Do you know his story? He was shot through with all those arrows, but he actually lived." Vittorio shook his head sympathetically.

Ellen didn't try to hide her astonishment. "How do you know about Saint Sebastian? I thought you didn't go to art museums."

"Catholic school, sweetheart. Ten years. We had to memorize this stuff. This one must be Saint . . . Jerome." He moved to the next canvas: Pinturicchio's *Virgin and Child with Saint Jerome.* "You can tell because he's dressed as a Cardinal. Famous for translating the Bible into Latin."

She was stunned. To her it was art. To him, hagiography.

"Look at this one." Vittorio was enjoying himself as he stepped in front of the Botticelli. "That's John the Baptist. See? He's only a little boy, but he's already dressed for the desert." As they made their way around the gallery, Vittorio identified the figures and scenes in the paintings. When he wasn't sure, they read the descriptions together. They stood for a long time before Daddi's *The Crucifixion*, a graphic panel showing angels in flight collecting the blood that gushed from Christ's pierced side and hands, with Mary Magdalene embracing the foot of the cross.

"My mother would like this one. It matters to her that Christ suffered, that he really felt pain. She says it means God knows how it is for us when we suffer."

"Sounds like she's very religious." Ellen had begun to think more and more about Vittorio's mother, what kind of person she was and what it would be like to meet her.

"That's not even the word for it." They sat down on the bench in the middle of the gallery. "She's more than religious. She goes to Mass practically every day and reads the Bible. I've got dozens of rosaries and little bottles of holy water she gives me to keep me safe. The church is everything to her." He paused and said, as if to himself, "She would die if she knew I was seeing a Protestant girl."

"Excuse me?" She was stung by the offhandedness of his comment. She shook her head as though she had misheard him.

"She would die if she knew I was seeing a Protestant girl. I mean, she'd be surprised if she knew I was seeing a girl who wasn't Sicilian. But I just don't think it would ever cross her mind that I would date someone who wasn't Catholic."

"And why is that?" From her tone, he realized that he had offended her.

"Well, you know . . . that's just kind of the message you get, that Protestants, I don't know, just aren't . . . something."

"So, she wouldn't like that you were seeing me?" Ellen asked, crossing her arms and frowning, the wounded tone still in her voice.

"No, it's not about you. She'd love you. No. Look, forget I said anything. It's got nothing to do with you personally, okay?" He put his hand on her back.

"What if you wanted to marry someone who wasn't Catholic?" The question hung between them for a moment.

"Well," Vittorio began, "I guess she would have a hard time with it." He knew that he wasn't prepared for this conversation and the host of issues it would bring to the surface. "Listen, Ellen, let's not worry about all that stuff today. I didn't mean to hurt your feelings."

"They're not hurt, Victor. It just took me aback, that's all." In light of his words, she wasn't prepared for the conversation either. She regretted raising the topic of marriage, feeling surprisingly exposed. "Let's go."

They squinted as they walked from the dim foyer out into the bright afternoon sun. "Thanks for inviting me to the museum." He kissed her on the side of her forehead.

"I thought you might like to see some art produced by your people," Ellen said, accepting his effort at normalization. "After all, Italy is the home of the Renaissance."

"Oh, those aren't my people," Vittorio said.

"Oh yes, those were Italian paintings. All of them."

"Right. I'm Sicilian. There's a big difference between being Italian and being Sicilian. You should hear my uncle. "Those people don't want nothin' to do with us,' he would say."

"But Sicily is part of Italy, right?" She wondered if Vittorio was teasing her, or trying to hide something.

"Uh, yes and no. Italy's only been a country for about eighty years. Before that, well . . . Uncle Carlo says Sicily is the punching bag of the Mediterranean. It was conquered by every civilization that came along. It's belonged to the Greeks, the Romans, the Normans and the Arabs, the French, the Spanish. Everybody's claimed it and stepped on it. Most people now blame the Italian government for the hard life in Sicily. Carlo says the Northerners complain that the South is deadweight on the country, and people in the South feel like they work to make the North rich. High taxes and all of that. There's a lot of division and . . . bitterness."

"So you don't consider yourself Italian?"

"Well, officially. But not really. It's a long way from where my people come from to the cities where those paintings were done." Ellen began to feel that it had been wrong to bring him to the museum, that he was offended by her unawareness.

"I'm sorry, Victor," she said, "I just thought . . ." She looked down at the ground.

"Shhh." They were still standing on the front steps of the museum. He put a finger to her lips. "I loved the paintings. They reminded me of everything I learned in school. It was great—a great idea." He smiled.

"Are you sure?" she asked, still feeling awkward, frustrated that they were bumping up against their differences for a second time, unable to tune out the annoying static of reality.

"I'm sure. More than anything, I just like being with you." He kissed her on the lips. "Now, you better find your Sicilian boyfriend something decent to eat before I faint on you." She relaxed slightly.

"Do you ever wonder what Sicily is like?" Ellen asked him later as they sat drinking coffee in a pub in Kenmore Square. "Do you think you'll ever go there?"

"My mother talks about it sometimes. About going back. Carlo, not so much. I know they miss it, even after all these years. I would like to see it, though, to see Cefalú, where my parents grew up. I have a lot of relatives that stayed behind too. Aunts and uncles and cousins."

"Wouldn't that be interesting? To meet people you're so closely related to, but you've grown up in a different world? You should go."

"Well, maybe one day, when the war's over. I have this dream of taking my mother back home."

"That's a good dream, Victor. You're a good son. Even if you are seeing a Protestant girl."

"Ciao, Vito." Nino emerged from his truck late one morning. The younger man was working on a polished granite wall along the driveway of a Victorian house in Wayland, newly remodeled by a stockbroker taking advantage of faster cars and New Deal roads to live in the country and work in the city. Vittorio dropped a piece of stone at his feet and took off his gloves, wiping his brow and waving as Nino approached.

"Rosa got a call last night from Mrs. Lathrop, from Sandy Pond Road in Lincoln," Nino reported, after they had said hello and commented on the sweltering heat. Vittorio held his breath, turning away from Nino and picking up his hammer. He didn't say anything, expecting that the downfall had arrived: Ellen's mother had discovered their secret relationship and had called Nino in a fury. He cringed, waiting for death to take him.

"She said she doesn't like the way Giorgio cuts the lawn." He sighed. "I ought to fire that lazy bastard. Anyway, she's having a garden party this weekend. Wants everything perfect. Would you mind finishing up here early and going by there this afternoon to take care of the yard? Do an extra good job. She's an important person. She said three o'clock would be best."

"Sure, Nino." He was breathing again and stifling a smile.

"Do you remember the house?"

"I think so," Vittorio replied. "The one with the big oak tree in front?"

"Isn't that the house where the pretty girl brought you lemonade?" Nino asked, with a sudden note of suspicion.

"Pretty girl?"

"You remember. She came out in tennis clothes and flirted with you."

"She wasn't flirting with me. You were imagining things, Nino. Anyway, that was in Lexington, at the red house with the long, narrow front yard." Vittorio still had not looked at Nino. He was down on his knees pretending to examine stones for the wall.

"If you say so. Anyway, Mrs. Lathrop will be expecting you."

"I'll take care of it, boss. Don't worry."

Four hours later Vittorio pulled the truck off the road onto the shoulder in front of the Lathrop house. Ellen was in the front window, pulling back satin drapes and signaling for him to meet her at the back door. She led him silently up the back stairs to her room where they made love on her bed, sweetly, filled with passion but unhurried, the first time they had ever done so indoors.

Afterwards, they bathed together. She washed his thick, black hair, massaging his scalp with her fingers as he kissed her breasts. He dried her body with a luxurious, velvety towel unlike any he had ever seen. It matched all the others, and the décor of the sizable bathroom, as well.

"You live in a museum," he teased, pointing out her antique tiger-maple bedroom set, along with the flowered, lavender wallpaper and its coordinated curtains, bedspread, pillowcases, and hooked rug.

"It feels like it," Ellen concurred, rolling her eyes. "It's my mother. She likes everything just so. She let me pick the color, when I was about twelve, but she took over from there." Ellen gathered her damp hair with both hands, twisting it into a bun on top of her head, and then letting it fall back onto her bare shoulders.

And then they were on her bed again. She pushed him with playful roughness onto his back.

Each year, the extended Lathrop family spent the first two weeks of September on vacation in the Berkshires, together with a community of families with whom Ellen had grown up. She was reluctant to go, not wanting to be away from Vittorio, whose presence was beginning to feel essential, like air. There was no possibility of argument, however. Her internship had ended, and classes at Radcliffe didn't begin until later in the month.

In Ellen's absence, Vittorio found himself on Friday night at the tavern with Paolo and Marcello, who had cancelled a date with his steady girlfriend, Antonella, when he heard that Vittorio was free for the evening. Vittorio surveyed their familiar haunt with contempt. The stale-sweet odor of spilled beer rose up from the rough-cut pine floorboards to meet a thickening fog of cigarette and cigar smoke. Patrons were scattered at small, dilapidated round tables surrounding the bar, where an elderly, skeletal drunk with a yellowish beard and a sparse scattering of teeth teetered on a stool in his grimy overcoat, haranguing the bored barkeep about the Red Sox—nine games behind the Yanks, twenty-four years since their last championship—and the machinations of the temporarily unemployed James Michael Curley—congressman, mayor, governor—what would he run for next? The same drunk. The same unanswered rant. A sense of disgust rose in Vittorio.

At a table nearby, four men played their same Friday-night poker game, arguing habitually at the end of each hand. Vittorio missed Ellen's skin, her laugh, and the aliveness he felt when he was with her. Trapped in that place, seeing himself reflected in his friends' faces and in the faces of the other people in the tavern, only sharpened the sense that his love affair with Ellen was a fantasy that could never exist in the real world. This was life before Ellen: a hole he would slide back into when he lost his grip on her. Sourly, he swallowed a second shot of grappa.

"We're proud and honored to have you with us tonight, Vito," Paolo declared, his voice ringing with sarcasm.

"Vittorio Amorelli, the amazing, disappearing wop," Marcello added, folding his long fingers together and resting them on the table.

"All right, all right. Back off, hey? I'm not in the best mood tonight." Vittorio signaled to the bartender for another shot of the strong, colorless brandy.

"I can see that, Vito," Paolo replied. "Maybe you ought to slow down, though. I don't feel like carrying you up all those goddamned stairs."

"Order a beer instead," Marcello suggested.

"Fine, order me a fucking espresso, I don't give a shit."

They were quiet for several moments.

"Vito," Paolo began, "you haven't been around much, so Marcello and I haven't had a chance to tell you—"

"Tell me what?"

"We're enlisting!" Marcello interjected. Vittorio narrowed his eyes and flared his nostrils, staring at him as though Marcello were a cockroach crawling across the table.

"I hope you're joking." Vittorio glanced at Paolo, who smiled weakly and shook his head. "I think I will have that other grappa." His sense of irritation sliding towards alarm, he raised his hand for the bartender.

"You should enlist with us, Vito."

"Why the hell would I do that? You two are stupid. What made you think it would be a good idea to join up? Jesus."

"Well, Vito, my friend, have you ever stopped to think what some people might begin to . . . suspect, if you didn't join up? A healthy young man like yourself. An American boy. I mean, you aren't *for* the Fascists, are you?" Paolo raised his eyebrows.

"What are you getting at, Paolo?"

"Have you heard about the Japs out west? Have you heard what they're doing to them? They've packed thousands of them into camps. Not nice camps either."

As news of the camps and their harsh conditions filtered east, rumors in the North End were rampant: Italians would be next. Any young Italian male who didn't enlist would be arrested for being a spy and shot. The only way to protect your family was to enlist.

"It comes down to this, Vito." Paolo grasped his friend's forearm and looked him in the eye. "If you're not against Mussolini, it might start to look like you're for him."

Vittorio shook his head. "You fools have been watching too many movies." He turned to Marcello, hoping to find support, but Marcello's face was equally serious. Vittorio shook his head, bewildered, picked up a cigarette and patted his pockets for matches, all the while mumbling to himself about his friends' lunacy.

"The officer at the recruiting center said that by the time we enlist, go through basic training, and then go somewhere to practice maneuvers, the war'll be over," Paolo said.

"Right. They told my father shit like that too," Vittorio shot back.

"All we're saying is, you should think about it," Marcello said. "You should really think about it."

He did think about it over the next days, turning it over in his mind, wondering whether either the threats or the promises were real, working it through so that his head ached and he felt that he was being torn in two. He felt no desire to enlist. He had no interest in going to war. He wanted to do his job and maybe figure out, against the odds, a way to be with Ellen. What if Paolo and Marcello were wrong, or were exaggerating? He felt pulled by the competing opinions and feelings. But his friends continued to work on him, bringing him newspaper articles and begging him to go with them to speak to the recruiter. They amplified the fear circulating in the community, a fear which was confirmed by his conversations with others in the cafés in the North End over the following days. Italy was an enemy nation. Italians were suspect. No one, he heard people say over and over, was safe.

The next time Vittorio saw each Ellen, she was back at school. He refused to meet her in Harvard Square for the usual reasons. She told him she didn't care who saw them together, but finally agreed that they would meet in the Public Garden near the ticket booth for the Swan Boats. Ellen sat on a park bench tapping her foot and scanning the park for Vittorio's arrival. Sliding across the glassy surface of the pond were the shadows of thin, furrowed clouds and the indistinct reflections of prowling seagulls and frantic pigeons. She felt anxious but resolved. Then she heard his whistle, soft and low, and turned to see him peeking out at her with a giant smile from behind a weeping willow, its leaves tinged with yellow and brown. She kissed him with the ardor of not having seen him in nearly a month. She held his face in her hands.

"I love you," she announced. He laughed and, flopping onto the bench, pulled her into his lap.

"You're crazy! *Pazzu*, my mamma would say. *Pazzu*."

"I'm not, Victor. I mean it. I love you." She took his face in her hands again, and looked into the dark eyes she'd been thinking about and missing. "I want to be with you. I don't want to sneak around anymore. I want us to be together in the light of day. I've thought about it. A lot. I want you to meet my family." She could see from his smile that he wasn't taking her seriously.

"That would be fun," he said with mock enthusiasm. "I can just imagine it: 'Mom, this is my boyfriend, Victor.' 'Hello, Victor.' 'Pleasure to meet you, Mrs. Lathrop.' 'Well, isn't that nice. They're admitting all kinds of people to Harvard now. Or is it MIT? Tell me, is your father a prince . . . or an ambassador?' 'Actually, ma'am, I'm your landscaper's assistant. I met your daughter while spreading shit on your rose bushes.' That's when your father would very politely call the police."

Ellen pursed her lips, frustrated that he was making light of what to her had become deeply serious. "Very funny. Especially since you said your mother would die if she knew you were seeing me. Anyway, Victor, I'm serious about this. Don't you feel the same way? If you don't, please . . . tell me now."

A woman passed the bench, pushing a baby carriage and leading a little girl by the hand. Ellen waited for them to pass, a crowd of pigeons following the girl's bag of popcorn.

"You don't love me, Victor?" Ellen asked.

"Of course I do. You know I do." He kissed her neck.

"Then isn't that the most important thing? Who cares about the rest? Let's get married." He could see that she was sincere, and he was moved, knowing the ramifications for her of what she was suggesting. He paused, trying to keep his emotions in control. He had anticipated that it would be hard to tell her, but he had not expected this declaration of love and commitment, or the fact that she was even more beautiful than he remembered, in her close-fitting sweater and knee-length skirt.

"Well," he said after a moment, "maybe when I get back."

"Get back? Where are you going?"

He squared his shoulders and affected a heroic tone: "I'm going to stop the Nazis from taking over the world."

"What are you talking about, Victor?" She sounded both scared and annoyed, like a child whose older siblings are playing a trick on her.

"I'm going to enlist." The lightness left his voice.

"No, Victor. No." She grabbed the collar of his shirt.

"Paolo and Marcello, they've . . . talked me into it. At first I thought they were nuts, but after a while I guess it started to make sense what they were saying."

"But why? Victor, you can't." She was nearly whispering, her voice choked.

"I guess everyone's scared about what's happening with the Japanese in California . . . and the concentration camps. They think we could be next, or that we're going to be suspected of . . . spying or something if we don't enlist."

"That's ridiculous. You're an American. You were born here."

"So were a lot of Japs they've locked away. It doesn't seem to matter whether you were born here."

"But there must be some other explanation, Victor," she argued, with growing desperation. "They wouldn't just lock people away for no reason. You're a hardworking, honest American citizen."

"People say they've got just about every Jap they can find in the camps now. Who's to say they won't come for us next? I can't risk it. I'm not letting my mother go to jail. If I join up, maybe they'll leave my family alone." He shrugged. She felt tears coming to her eyes.

"I can't stand being away from you, Victor," she said, taking hold of the front of his shirt with both hands. "I want us to be together. I can't think about anything else. I can't pay attention in class, or study at night. I go around and around in my head about how we can be together, how to convince my parents and your mother. I've just started to think that maybe it's possible, somehow, and now you tell me you're leaving."

"Think of this, though, Ellen." He pulled her close. Not wanting to see her upset, he was trying to be hopeful. "Maybe I'll be more acceptable to your family after I serve. Maybe I'll even get a medal or something, and they'll see me as a soldier, a hero, instead of as a mason."

"But what if . . . I mean, your father . . ." She was distraught, shocked, reeling. Sobs were rising from her gut into her chest.

Vittorio cleared his throat and swallowed. "I guess we have to hope for the best."

While he had been unprepared for the intensity of Ellen's reaction, Vittorio knew what to expect from his mother.

The week before All Saints' Day began with favorable news for the Allies. Montgomery had triumphed at El-Alamein, forcing the Germans and the Italians into retreat. At the same time, the American troops on Guadalcanal were clinging to their positions, warding off repeated attempts by the Japanese to dislodge them. Vittorio brought this information as evidence that his military service might be brief when he returned to Gloucester after work on Friday for the weekend's observance.

He also brought a box of marzipan, formed and colorfully decorated to look like apples, pears, bananas, and cherries, purchased in the North End as a gift for Angela, along with a paper cone of chestnuts for Carlo to roast. As had become their tradition, they would mark *I Morti* with a feast, prepared by Angela, to which Marie, her husband, and other friends would be invited. After dinner, the dead would be lovingly recalled. Stories would be told, tears would be shed. Angela would tell of her grandparents, and Carlo would wistfully remember his cherubic younger sister who had died in childhood. Eventually, generally after a long, pensive silence following dessert as everyone watched the candles burn down, Angela would say: "And then there was my dear husband, Tommaso." More stories would be told, more tears shed, more wine consumed.

For years, Vittorio had sat quietly through the annual ritual, feeling an aching, inexpressible emptiness, with no memories of his own to share. He was even quieter this year, with the gravity of his announcement occupying his mind. Claiming fatigue after a long week spent rushing to finish a job before winter, he excused himself and went to his room.

Vittorio joined his mother and Carlo for Mass the next morning. The priest, arrayed in a white-and-gold festival chasuble, extolled the saints who had "entered into light," making a point to name those young men from the parish who had lost their lives since the previous All Saints' Day "opposing the tyrannical forces of darkness which threaten God's creation." Vittorio winced. "There is no doubt," the priest continued, "that they will be numbered among the saints."

They walked home in silence. Twenty-four years after Tommaso's death, Angela and Carlo both continued to be undone by *I Morti*, as though the wound had never healed but still festered beneath the scar, erupting into a boil with the poignancy of the memorial Mass. Angela, removing her black veil, retreated to the numbing routine of the kitchen and began to prepare another large meal, this time to be shared only by the three of them.

Vittorio had intended to raise the subject of his enlistment during dinner, but his determination flagged in the solemn atmosphere. Perhaps the onset of another war had sharpened the pain his mother and Carlo experienced at this time every year. After the meal, Vittorio stepped out to visit with friends.

He returned at twilight, standing in front of the house to finish his cigarette and to review the points he would make as the debate progressed. Angela was sitting in her chair, her embroidery in her lap. She had dozed off, and his entrance startled her.

"Sorry, Mamma," he whispered.

"No, no, it's okay, *figghiu miu*, I'm glad you're home." Carlo was at the table, the edition of *Il Progresso* which Vittorio had brought to him on Friday spread in front him. Vittorio sat down on the sofa, avoiding eye contact with his mother.

"Vito, where are you? I can't find you this weekend." Angela waved her arm as though groping for something in the dark. "What are you so busy thinking about? A girl?"

"No, Mamma." Still, he didn't look at her.

"Then what? Tell me, Vito." He took a deep breath, exhaling slowly and rubbing his hands together. Now he placed them palm up on his lap.

"Paolo and Marcello have decided to enlist." He said it quickly, with no inflection in his voice.

"Paolo and Marcello have decided to enlist." She nodded once, repeated the words deliberately, then paused. "And?"

"They think I should—"

"No."

"But—"

"No."

"Mamma, listen to me." Carlo turned from his newspaper.

"No, Vittorio. I'm not listening to you. You are not going to the war. How could you even . . . did you actually think I would allow that?" she scoffed. "That I would say, Oh great, Vito, good luck to you?" Her face was flushed, her eyes hardened.

"Mamma, listen to me," he insisted again. She folded her arms across her chest, daring him to make his argument. "We're Italians, Mamma. Italy is on the other side in this war. People are saying that if we don't join up, the government will think we're spies. We could be hanged." He was trying to lay out as much of his case as possible before she interrupted again. "Do you know that they're putting all the Japanese into camps? We could be next. What if they came and took you and Carlo away? I have to do this to protect you, to show that we're against Mussolini."

Angela smiled, a familiar, wry smile that had always signaled to Vittorio that he was losing an argument. "If I have to go live in a camp, I'll go live in a camp. We'll all go live in a camp. I've been through worse, Vito. You forget that. And they'll have to hang me before I'll let them hang my only child."

"But Paolo and Marcello—"

"Paolo and Marcello, God bless them, must have mothers that don't love them. Your mother loves you, and so you're not going." She smiled again, triumphant.

"Mamma, I'm twenty-four years old," Vittorio said, falling back on his final and most dangerous point. "I can . . ."

Angela stood up, her embroidery falling to the floor. Her eyes flashed. "I don't care how old you are, Vittorio. I've made this mistake once, and I'm not going to make it again." Her voice was strained as she tried to control her anger. For a long moment, they looked at each other. She turned to Carlo. "Carlo, help me. Say something to this boy. Excuse me, this . . . man."

Carlo looked at her, expressionless. Vittorio knew his uncle wouldn't want him to go. Yet he also knew that Carlo hated Mussolini, and that Carlo believed that stopping the Axis was a cause worth risking one's life to support. He read the ambivalence on Carlo's face as he turned and looked down at his newspaper. Angela grabbed her hair with both hands.

"Aah, men!" Furious, she shouted at the ceiling. Then, a wrath more than twenty years old rose inside of her. Her face bright red, she turned on Carlo: "Do you not remember Tommaso, Carlo? My husband? Your cousin? Your best friend?" She folded her hands and changed her tone to a mocking politeness: "You know, Carlo, you've never really told me exactly what happened to Tommaso. Would you like to now? Would you like to share it with us, with your boy here, who's all ready to follow his father off to war? Tell us, Carlo, was Tommaso blown to pieces?" Now she was yelling again. "How many times was he shot, Carlo? How badly was his body burned?" She paused to punctuate each question.

"Were his brains scattered in the streets? How long did he suffer before he died? Tell us, Carlo!" she screamed. Carlo was unable to speak. "Why don't you tell us, Carlo? Go ahead. Tell Vittorio all about it, about how his father who he never met was killed." Carlo looked at Vittorio, then covered his face with his hand. Vittorio stood up and walked toward the door, shamed by her reaction, confused, lost.

"That's right, Vito. Go for a nice long walk and think it over."

Vittorio pulled the door shut softly behind him.

He heard her in the kitchen when he woke up the following morning. Nino had given him the day off. Families traditionally spent the second of November visiting the cemetery, bringing flowers to the tombs of the deceased. With no cemetery to visit, Vittorio, Angela, and Carlo normally passed the day quietly.

He lay in bed for several minutes, glancing more than once at the sepia photograph of his parents, taken by a photographer in the harbor one summer day the year before his father and Carlo had gone to France. They were holding hands and looked happy, hopeful, and young.

He got out of bed, pulled on his robe, walked out to the other room, and sat down at the table. Angela brought a cup of coffee and placed it in front of him, with extra milk as he liked it. She went back to the kitchen and returned with a plate of fresh rolls she had baked, cut open and buttered. She sat down and pushed them across the table to him. He picked one up and bit into it.

"Vittorio . . . please . . . don't do it." Her voice was choked, hoarse. He looked up at her, noting the creases that had begun in recent years to deepen around her eyes and across her forehead, and the silvery-pearl strands that shined across her dark hair. He nodded slightly. He hated to see his mother angry, not wishing to cause her any more suffering than she had already endured.

"All right, Mamma. I won't."

Marcello and Antonella were married two days before the boyish groom reported to the induction center. After the surprise announcement, their families collaborated with just three days' notice to create a festive celebration. The mothers of the bride and groom, along with a staff of aunts, sisters, and cousins, began cooking immediately, while the two fathers set out to make the other arrangements.

The ceremony took place at Sacred Heart, Antonella's church, on Thursday evening. Father Marino, an ovate man with a thin, nasal voice, presided at the brief rite. Marcello wore a gray flannel suit, purchased at a secondhand shop. The last-minute tailoring was a gift from a family friend with whom Marcello had been serving as an apprentice for two years. The bride's dress, cascading with lace, had been created by committee in a marathon session, replete with temper tantrums, jittery anticipation, and the percussive thud of the sewing machine. Paolo was Marcello's best man, opposite Antonella's sister, the maid of honor. The bridal party drew cheers from the neighbors as they processed down Prince Street and across North Square to the church. A trembling Marcello met the bride at the altar, where he received a double kiss from Antonella's father. Paolo steadied his friend throughout, though he, too, succumbed briefly to emotion when Marcello lifted the veil to greet his new wife.

Afterwards, friends and family gathered in the undercroft, cleared of the desks of the catechetical students and hastily arrayed for the banquet with crepe-paper flowers and brightly colored streamers. The lengthy series of toasts, both solemn and humorous, which accompanied the meal, along with the clanging of glasses urging the newlyweds to kiss, was followed by dancing. The band, consisting of an accordion player, a fiddler, and two cousins on mandolin, swayed them through "Somewhere Over the Rainbow" before breaking into a lively tarantella. The bride and groom were soon joined on the makeshift dance floor by a crowd of well-wishers.

After a tormented sleepless night, Vittorio decided to invite Ellen. In the face of mounting uncertainty—war, the departure and possible loss of friends—he decided to take the risk. The wedding was to be held on his birthday, which he had planned to spend with Ellen. The love she had confessed weeks earlier in the Public Garden emboldened him as well. If she was ready to take this step, why should he stand in the way?

In fact, he was astounded by her grace. Despite the stunned looks on the faces of everyone gathered when he and Ellen were ushered by Antonella's brother down the center aisle to their pew, Ellen glowed. Vittorio was afraid they were drawing more attention than the bride and groom. What he thought was impossible, she accomplished with her charm and ease with people. He was particularly impressed by her manner with Paolo, Marcello and his other friends, to whom she good-naturedly and skillfully gave back in equal measure what she received.

"So *you're* the girl who stole our poor Vito's heart away."

"Yes, and he put up *such* a terrible fight."

Before the cranky church sexton chased the last guests out, well after midnight, Ellen had danced with the fathers of both the bride and groom and had consumed a prodigious quantity of lasagne, veal, roasted eggplant, calamari, wine and cake. Vittorio, surprised by how well her debut had gone, received the compliments of nearly all the men who attended the party.

"You were amazing," he told her afterwards, holding her close and kissing her neck. They stood on the corner waiting for a cab, as they had nowhere to go to be alone and she was already in trouble for missing curfew at the dorm. "Are you sure you're not part Sicilian? A great-great-grandmother or something?"

"Such a beautiful night, and so sad. I got to see who you really are, Vittorio, your real life. I'm in love with all of it—you, them, this place. But I'm hurting for you, my love. Those are your best friends, and . . ."

He held her tighter. "They're my brothers. The only ones I ever had. Marcello is my twin. I don't really know who I am without them." The cab driver pulled up to the curb and honked the horn. "Let's just hope there are lots more nights like that one . . . when the boys get home. Now that you're part of the family."

He walked back to Paolo's apartment considering for the first time that he might have been wrong, that his love for her could be viable in what he had assumed would be a hostile environment.

Early on Saturday morning, just after sunrise, a tearful crowd gathered to see off Paolo and Marcello. Vittorio embraced each of them, unable to speak, and found himself running along behind the automobile Paolo's father had borrowed to deliver them to the induction center downtown, waving with both arms as it turned the corner at the end of Hanover Street and was lost from view. He tried to offer consoling words to Antonella, who sat distraught on the curb with her sisters for more than an hour, still in her bathrobe and slippers, smoking cigarettes and crying.

The thought of spending the weekend alone in the room he shared with Paolo was sadder than he could face. He went to Nino's and borrowed the truck to go home. He arrived in Gloucester, to his mother's delighted surprise, an hour before the mailman slipped the notice from the local draft board through the mail slot. The only piece of mail that day, the envelope hung at the edge of the opening for an instant before floating to the floor.

v.

On the day of Vittorio's physical examination, Angela got up early in the morning and went out, not wanting to watch him walk out the door and into the hands of the military. She felt as though there must be a way to fight against the forces behind her son's conscription, and she was prepared to fight. In Sicily, a bribe could be arranged. A disqualifying health condition could be attested to by a doctor. An untimely death could even be faked, with proper documentation provided. For every loophole she imagined, however, Carlo had an explanation as to why it wouldn't work in the United States. She was prepared to fight, but felt helpless and vulnerable, unable to move against an invisible force she couldn't see or understand.

At quarter to ten, Vittorio left the house and walked slowly down Prospect Street, arriving at City Hall five minutes early for his physical. He sat on a bench and watched a squirrel forage in a trashcan until the bell high up in the clock tower tolled. To Vittorio, it was a forlorn pealing.

Entering the imposing building, he recognized several other young men who stood talking in a group, including two who had been classmates at St. Anne's. He nodded to them, then joined another man, also Sicilian, who leaned up against the marble wall of the foyer alone. Their mothers knew each other and the two had played together on the beach as children during picnics and festivals. Now they exchanged greetings and chatted nervously. Vittorio tried to act nonchalant, as though the appointment was just a formality, but the sense that these people held his future in their hands unsettled him. He felt the sweat in his armpits, and hoped no one would notice.

Amorelli was the first name called on the alphabetical list. His friend patted him on the back. Vittorio shrugged. He had been unable to eat the breakfast Angela had left out for him, and his stomach ached. An older man in a suit and wire-rimmed glasses, seated behind a card table, confirmed his identity. Vittorio handed him the notice that had arrived in the mail. The man examined the letter, then made a mark next to Vittorio's name on the typed list in front of him.

The doctor, wearing an oversized lab coat and carrying a clipboard, led Vittorio into an office which had been converted into an examination room. He was a small, youngish man, the son of the doctor who had assisted Angela at Vittorio's birth, though the two men did not realize this connection. Afflicted by polio as a child, he walked stiffly with a clanking brace on his left leg. He asked Vittorio a series of questions about his health, childhood diseases, and possible exempting conditions. Vittorio answered each with a nod or a shake of the head. After jotting down these responses, the doctor instructed him to undress. Vittorio had little experience with doctors and had not seen one since contracting German measles as an eight-year-old. The nurse at school had attended to a sprained ankle and a badly scraped elbow. Otherwise, his mother always stated that she knew more about her son than any doctor could, and she used her traditional remedies to see him through colds, intestinal viruses, and poison ivy. He found the doctor's cold, dry hands invasive, particularly when he knelt in front of him to inspect his penis for sores and to check for hernias. The examination ended and Vittorio was excused.

"You'll receive a letter regarding your status within a few days," the man at the card table told him when he stepped out of the examination room. Vittorio lit a cigarette and wandered home by way of the harbor, stopping to watch the fishing boat crews in their morning routines. He thought of his mother and her grief, the burden she could never put down. He wondered what it must be like to suffer that kind of loss, to never see the person who had been your life, your future again, and he shuddered, imagining something happening to Ellen. He turned for home, amazed in a new way that his mother had persevered.

The official document arrived on the thirtieth of November. Angela opened the envelope, unfolded the heavy sheet of paper, examined the seal, and then handed it to Carlo to read. He sat down at the dining table and began to scan it, intending to summarize it for her. "Carlo," she said, watching his eyes move across the parchment, "I want to hear the words. Read it to me." Carlo had not entirely mastered the English language in written form, so he proceeded slowly, attempting to wrap his mouth around the formal verbiage. Angela stood behind him looking at the document over his shoulder. She was quiet for a moment when he finished, gazing out the front window at the street where Vittorio had spent innumerable hours playing ball with his friends as a child.

"They make it sound like he committed a crime. 'Willful failure to report subject to imprisonment'?"

"That's just the way they talk," Carlo assured her. "They wouldn't take him if he'd committed a crime. They know he's a good boy."

"How are we going to get the news to him? He's only got ten days." She was attempting to focus on the practicalities, trying to still the combination of anger, fear, and powerlessness that was churning in her stomach. "You'll have to take the train to Boston, Carlo. Can you go this afternoon? Tell him to come home right away."

Carlo reached Paolo's apartment fifteen minutes before Vittorio came back from work. The sun had set and the temperature was taking a wintry plunge. He pulled his overcoat tight around himself and sat down on the stoop. The cold made his leg ache, sending an occasional burst of pain from the site of the old injury up to his hip and lower back. He shuddered to think of Vittorio embroiled in a firefight like the one he had endured in France. Closing his eyes, he saw his cousin's corpse, and shuddered again.

Vittorio was surprised only for a moment to see Carlo, who stood and handed him the envelope. Vittorio took off his gloves and held it in his hands, staring down at it without opening it, as though by not opening it he could keep its grim news trapped inside.

"How long do I have?"

"Ten days . . . until next Thursday. I'm sorry, Vito."

They walked back to Nino's house to tell him the news, and to ask permission to take the truck to Gloucester and the following day off from work. Nino wept. Rosa insisted that they eat before setting out, which they did, with few words.

Few words were spoken in the truck on the way to Gloucester either. Carlo knew that any encouragement or assurance he might offer would be empty. Vittorio told him about his latest project at work as they left the city. After that they passed the miles in silence.

Angela was waiting for them though it was nearly eleven o'clock. For once, she was unoccupied; there was no sewing or knitting on her lap. Instead, she clutched her favorite rosary. She embraced her son, holding him with her face against his chest. Neither of them spoke. Finally, she eased her grip, and stepped back.

"Have you eaten?"

"Yes, Mamma. Rosa cooked."

"Well, you obviously haven't bathed. I'll heat some water."

"How long can you stay?" she asked later, after he had washed and stepped outside to smoke. They sat at the table, eating biscotti and drinking scalded milk. Vittorio saw the weariness in his mother's eyes and knew she hadn't been sleeping.

"Nino said I could have tomorrow. He wants me to finish the work I'm doing in town before I go. I'll come home for the weekend, and then I'll come back to say goodbye." He saw the tears in her eyes. "Mamma, don't worry, I'll—"

"No," she interjected. "No, Vito. Don't make promises. Your father filled my head with guarantees. There are no guarantees. Save the nice words for when you come home."

The next morning he accompanied her to the market, carrying her purchases from the butcher to the produce cart to the bakery, trying with mixed success to keep her entertained and distracted. He told her about work and about the strange ways of rich people. "They have huge houses—mansions—but they don't live in them. They're always off somewhere else." He considered asking her how she would feel if he ever dated a girl who wasn't Sicilian but decided that the timing was wrong. Instead, he told her about the thrill of being at Fenway to see Dom and Joe go head to head.

Passing the newsstand, he saw headlines about the battle of Tassafaronga, when the *Northampton* had been sunk and three other ships badly damaged by the Japanese. For the first time, mortal fear poked at him, causing his gut to clench as he imagined that within weeks or months he might be serving on such a ship. Before, he had been upset mainly by the idea of leaving Ellen and his mother. Now the prospect of his own imminent participation in the war shook him. Angela stopped several paces ahead to see what was delaying him.

"What do the papers say, Vito? Tell me the truth."

"The Allies are making progress." He forced a grin. "They've held Guadalcanal."

"I don't know what that means, Vito, but I'll accept what you say. If it means the war is closer to being over, I'm happy." She was trying, too, to hold a sense of normalcy. She had to remind herself that Vittorio had not chosen this any more than she had, and she didn't want him to feel that he had to take care of her even as he dealt with his own anxiety. But realizing this ideal was exhausting, like trying to get away with an elaborate lie, and it was all she could do to keep from being toppled by anguish.

After dinner, Angela went to her room to rest. They planned a walk on the beach later in the afternoon. Meanwhile, Vittorio sat down at the table to write a note to Ellen.

Ellen was waiting for him in Harvard Square on Tuesday afternoon. He had finished his work for Nino Monday, returning Tuesday morning to rake the worksite and plant grass seed on the front lawn of the house on Clyde Street. Ellen saw the pickup coming towards her on Massachusetts Avenue and began to wave. Vittorio pulled to the curb. He was embarrassed to be coming for her in the truck, in his work clothes, but she climbed across the seat, took his face in her hands, and kissed him.

"Ellen, someone might see us," he objected, pulling back.

"Victor," she sighed. "Jesus, Victor. Look at me. How'm I going to make you understand that I don't care who sees us? It doesn't matter anymore. All that matters now is you coming back to me— soon." Again, she kissed him. "I love you."

They drove across the city to the Arboretum in Jamaica Plain. Ellen had been there with the botany class she took to fulfill her science requirement. Vittorio parked in front of the brick administration building inside the main gate. Arm in arm, they meandered down Meadow Road. Workmen in green uniforms were busy raking the last of the season's leaves into piles. Crisp brown leaves danced across their path on a swirling breeze. Ellen jumped to crunch a huge oak leaf under her foot.

"Last time I was here they were still cleaning up the mess from the hurricane," she remembered, as they turned onto the road which wound to the top of Bussey Hill. "Almost every tree was damaged."

"That was our hurricane," Vittorio said. "I never would have met you if not for that storm. I watched it come across the harbor in Gloucester with my uncle—watched the waves smash into the boats—and I swore I was never going fishing again."

Arriving at the top of the hill, they sat on a bench facing the Blue Hills, cuddling close together against a chilling wind. The sun was surrendering to winter's advancing night sky.

"I don't want you to go, Victor," Ellen said, resting her head against his shoulder. A cashmere scarf, chosen to match her eyes, was wrapped twice around her neck and tucked into the lapel of her trim, camel's hair coat. "I miss you when I don't see you all week. I feel hollowed out. I can't imagine you being thousands of miles away. And I'm going to be sick worrying about you all the time." She paused. "Are you going to miss me, darling?"

He nodded. Looking up, she saw tears in his eyes. "Are you crying, sweetheart?"

"No," he sniffled. "It's just the wind."

"Yes, you are. You're crying. You do love me, don't you?" She laughed, her own throat tightening, and pulled herself closer to Vittorio.

"I do love you. A lot. It's just everything—my mother, and my father's death, and . . ."

"You don't have to explain. There's plenty of good reasons to cry. I cried all day yesterday when I got your letter."

"I just want to stop everything from happening, and I can't." He gave up trying to hold himself together, and he let the words flow. "It reminds me of being on the fishing boat at night, and the waves would be rocking it and I'd be miserable, and desperate for it to stop, desperate to get the hell off, and there was nothing I could do. I'd go up above and watch the waves coming at us, one after another, and I'd curse them, but they'd keep coming just the same."

Another couple arrived, pushing bicycles. They stood at the split rail fence looking at the view for a few moments, at the stars brightening in the gloaming, and then moved on. Vittorio and

Ellen watched them. When they were gone, Ellen, staring off into the distance, spoke through tears: "Victor, I know you can't promise, but promise me anyway. Promise me you'll be okay. Promise me you're going to come back. Please . . ."

Later, they exchanged few words over dinner at Doyle's. Ellen felt an urge to break the heaviness but could think of nothing light to say. They sipped beer and smoked cigarettes, holding hands across the table and leaving their food nearly untouched. On the other side of the room at the bar a group of young men had gathered to say goodbye to a buddy who was also due to leave for the army. They were laughing, growing more raucous the more they drank.

"Let's get out of here," Vittorio said.

He parked the truck on Avon Street, a block from Ellen's dormitory. They kissed and cried, trying several times to say good-bye. Twice, Ellen got out of the truck to go, and then climbed back inside and into his arms. Finally, the third time, she closed the door and began to walk away. She turned at the corner, looking back to wave and to blow a kiss. Vittorio stuck his head out the window. "I love you, Ellen!" he yelled. She blew another kiss and waved, unable to answer.

The following morning Vittorio purchased a suitcase, new socks, underwear, and T-shirts and a pair of wool pants, along with toiletries and a small leather case for them. He laid out his clothes on Paolo's bed and packed the suitcase. Then he drove to Gloucester.

To keep herself occupied, Angela had planned a party in Vittorio's honor. The house was decorated with streamers, and there were fresh flowers on the table. Angela was in the kitchen, rolling out dough for pasta.

"Mamma?"

"O, Vito!" she called from the kitchen.

"What's all this?" He entered the room and hugged her. She was wearing the floral printed apron he had given her for her birthday.

"I invited a few people over to say goodbye."

"Mamma, you didn't need to—"

"Yes, I did. When someone goes on a journey, you give them a big send-off with the best food. That way they'll be sure to come back." She tried to smile, and he was grateful to her.

By six o'clock the house was full of guests: Marie and her husband, the priest from St. Anne's, and Angela's closest friends and their families. Nino and Rosa drove up from the city too. Vittorio received scores of hugs and kisses, and advice from the veterans who had served in the Great War. They instructed him to follow orders and not to volunteer for anything. "Keep your nose clean," counseled one man, "and you won't have any troubles."

At one point, Angela led her son into the kitchen. She placed a rosary in his hand and wrapped his fingers around it. "Keep this with you, Vito. Say your rosary every day, please. Ask God to bring you back safe. I'll be doing the same."

"I know you will, Mamma. You'll probably light enough candles to bring the ships into harbor, too."

"I'll do whatever it takes. Can't let the Madonna forget that I'm waiting for my child to come home." They hugged. "Now, help me fill this last tray of cannoli."

At eleven o'clock, Vittorio announced that he had to leave. He was due at the draft board office at eight o'clock in the morning. After a final round of tearful goodbyes, Angela and Carlo walked him to the truck. Angela kept her composure until Vittorio drove out of sight, then she dissolved. Carlo called for help. He and Nino nearly carried her back inside the house.

The season's first snowflakes drifted to the ground from weighty, ominous clouds. Vittorio said goodbye to Paolo's parents, thanking them for their generous hospitality. He picked up his suitcase and stepped out into the cold, colorless morning. The draft board was located in City Hall on School Street. Crossing Scollay Square, he was filled with nostalgia, remembering the carousing he had done with his friends when there was not much more to worry about than which girl he might take out the next night. He looked over his shoulder towards the old neighborhood, imagining that he might never return to the places and the people who had made up his world. He felt anxious and alone, not knowing where he might be by the end of the day.

The answer came within a few minutes. He turned his induction notice over to the uniformed clerk at the desk, who instructed him to be seated in the waiting room. By the time his name was called, there were more than fifty young men in the room, some in subdued conversation, but most sitting silently. It seemed to Vittorio more like a wake than the beginning of an adventure.

The clerk informed him that he would be sent to Fort Dix in New Jersey for induction into the United States Army. An officer would accompany him, along with his cohort, to the train station. They would be met at the other end of the trip and transported to the fort. Vittorio felt dizzy. He hadn't eaten anything, and for a moment he couldn't focus his eyes. The clerk noticed that his face had turned white.

"Are you all right, young man?"

"I think I just need to sit down." The reality of what was about to happen to him was pressing down.

"Your train leaves at nine-thirty. There's a bathroom over there. Go splash some cold water on your face. We'll call you."

Vittorio gazed at the gray ocean out the window as the train followed the coast across Rhode Island and into Connecticut. The young man sitting next to him had introduced himself and made polite conversation only briefly before pulling a worn, leather-bound Bible from his canvas knapsack. For the rest of the trip, he sat reading intently. Eventually Vittorio fell asleep, using his jacket as a pillow between his head and the window of the Pullman. He surfaced from a dream confused when the conductor announced New Haven, and then drifted back to sleep.

The conductor woke him as the train approached Trenton. "Your stop is next. Good luck to you." It was nearly dark outside when the train pulled into the station. Two uniformed men stood on the platform: one an older man, a sergeant, and the other an enlisted man. Both had crew cuts and wore olive-green uniforms. When Vittorio and the group of inductees were assembled and the train had chugged out of the station on its way south, the sergeant spoke:

"Welcome to New Jersey, gentlemen. I'm Sergeant Williams." Williams had served in the Great War but had contracted pneumonia in France and returned to the States without seeing action. Despite being in his mid-forties, he was one of the first to reenlist in the days after Pearl Harbor. His strong jaw, stubby nose, brawny stature, and strident voice contrasted with gentle, avuncular eyes. "We'll be bringing you to Fort Dix. When we arrive, we'll take you to the barracks and assign your bunks. Then you'll be given supper in the mess hall. Your induction will begin in the morning. Any questions?" There were none. "Then let's move out."

Vittorio's sense of dislocation deepened as the evening progressed. Everything known, everything familiar had been stripped away. There was little interaction among the men in his corner of the barracks. They moved quickly to their bunks as lights-out approached. Because he had slept on the train, he lay awake late into the night. He was hungry, not having been able to eat the unrecognizable brown slop served in the mess hall. He was uncomfortable, lying on a hard, narrow bunk, and he was cold, with only a thin blanket protecting him from the night's chill. Most of all, he was lonely. He had rarely been lonely in his life, and yet the feeling in his stomach was familiar in a vague, remote way. Then he remembered the first day of school at St. Anne's, the first time he had left his mother, thrust into a group of strangers who did not speak his language. Vittorio finally fell asleep, with the image of that scared little boy in his mind.

A lock of his black hair landed with a slight thump on the canvas gown in his lap. "Don't cry, big boy," the barber, a tall, gangly youth with enormous ears—his cheeks ravaged by acne—joked cruelly. "It's always the pretty ones that cry, ain't it?" he said to the other man who was cutting hair. They cackled. Another clump fell. Vittorio picked it up, letting the individual hairs drop between his fingers. He winced as the barber nicked the skin behind his ear with the clippers. He touched the spot reflexively and looked at the blood on his fingertips. "Sorry!" the barber called with cheery insincerity, slapping witch hazel onto Vittorio's tender, razor-burned neck.

The morning had begun early, with another disgusting meal. His hunger won out over his aversion, however, and he spooned the food into his mouth, gulping water after each bite. The new recruits, a group of close to four hundred who had arrived in the preceding twenty-four hours, were lined up and sworn into the United States Army. Then they were issued dog tags, uniforms, gear, and boots, and given instructions on how to keep the items up to Army standards.

The haircut followed. He knew it was coming. To see the hair dropping into his lap, though, and then, worse yet, to see his bald head, cast Vittorio into an even darker mood. He was no longer himself, he thought. In just one day, the Army had taken away his identity, his clothes, his hair, his free will, even his name, preparing him for his role absorbing bullets in a muddy trench somewhere in Europe or on a malaria-infested island in the Pacific. Looking in the mirror he lifted his hand slowly and touched the stubble on his head. He felt an urge to run, to escape. He felt scared, desperate, crazy.

•

Two weeks later, Private Amorelli was a seasoned military man, joining with the others to laugh at the pale, frightened new arrivals. He had made friends, mostly other Southern Italians, and had learned the trick of eating the food without paying attention to it. He had been told that it would probably be months before he shipped out, and most importantly that he would earn ten days' leave after basic training.

On Christmas Day he wrote to his mother and Carlo: "It's all a little disorganized. Most of the time, we're waiting for something to happen. Some of the fellows I arrived with have gone off to basic training, but most of us are still here. It seems like they're not sure what to do with us Italians, where to send us. I've learned to salute and say 'Yessir!' and to shine my boots real well and to shovel coal and mop the floor. Mamma—the food is terrible! I'm dying for your cooking!" And to Ellen: "I can't believe it's been only two weeks since we said goodbye. It feels like a year. I look at your picture a hundred times a day. I'm trying to buck up, but I can't stop missing you. It's worst at night when I'm trying to fall asleep. I hope you haven't forgotten me . . ."

vi.

Ellen climbed the steps to the entrance of the Radcliffe infirmary. She gave her name at the desk and was shown into Dr. Hardy's office. "The doctor will see you momentarily, Miss," she was told. Dr. Hardy's large cherry desk sat at the edge of an Oriental rug in front of a fireplace. Above the mantle, framed documents attested to her education and training as Radcliffe's first female doctor.

Bookshelves lined the wall to the left of her desk. On the right, two windows looked out over Brattle Street. Steam hissed as it escaped from the radiator under one of the windows. Ellen sat in a chair facing the desk and closed her eyes. She was tired. It was Reading Week before the first semester's exams, and she had been studying and fighting the flu. Feeling depleted, she had come to the infirmary earlier in the week.

"Good morning Miss Lathrop." Ellen stood and turned to the door, surprised to see Dean Sherman entering the room behind Dr. Hardy. She had seen the dean most recently at the Christmas dinner, Ellen's final time attending this favorite holiday event. Now Dean Sherman seated herself in the maroon-upholstered armchair to the right of Dr. Hardy's desk, her gray hair pinned up in a bun, a grave look of concern on her face. Dr. Hardy, wearing a long white lab coat over a prim brown dress suit, avoided eye contact with Ellen, sitting down behind the desk and picking up a folder.

"It is still, *Miss* Lathrop, am I correct?" the doctor asked. "With so many young men going off to the war, I understand that a number of our students have recently married." She smiled, weakly.

"Yes. It's still Miss Lathrop."

Dean Sherman and Dr. Hardy looked at each other.

"In that case, Miss Lathrop, I'm afraid what I have to tell you today will not come as good news." The doctor paused, taking off her glasses and looking at Ellen, though Ellen had the sense that she was looking just above her head. "Miss Lathrop, the urine sample we collected indicated that, to use the medical term, you're . . . pregnant."

Ellen closed her eyes. Pregnant. She breathed. Of course she was pregnant. Of course. Somehow she hadn't allowed the thought to enter her consciousness, but now the doctor's words defined the unfamiliar sensations in her body. She was not ill with the flu. She was carrying Victor's baby. Forgetting where she was, ignoring the circumstances, she smiled.

"Miss Lathrop, Dr. Hardy and I anticipated, apparently wrongly, that this news might be upsetting to you. I can assure you that it is profoundly upsetting to me."

Ellen opened her eyes and looked at the dean. Over the years, she had learned to respect and, at times, fear the woman, especially when pushing the limits of prescribed behavior at Radcliffe. Her peers considered the dean's opinion of them to be important, and her good favor was solicited. Ellen looked at her now and felt empty of such concerns.

"Would you like to provide an explanation, Miss Lathrop?" The dean's voice rose, her gray eyes narrowing into a scowl.

"No, Dean Sherman. I would not." She said it without antipathy, only as a matter of fact.

"Miss Lathrop," Dr. Hardy began, sounding sympathetic, "it is our policy to notify the parents of a student in such circumstances . . . an unmarried, pregnant student that is. If it would be helpful, we could invite your parents here and I could—"

"Thank you, Dr. Hardy, that won't be necessary. I'll tell them."

"You can tell them that we will gratefully receive prompt written notification of your withdrawal from Radcliffe," Dean Sherman added, sharply.

"For medical reasons," Dr. Hardy offered.

Ellen nodded. "I'll let them know."

"Ellen, I just don't understand . . ." the dean began, breaking her stern expression. Ellen stood up.

"Thank you, Dr. Hardy," she said. "Goodbye, Dean Sherman."

Leaving the infirmary, she closed her coat against the blustery January morning. She walked down Garden Street toward the Radcliffe quad. Everything was different. In a world that had gone insane, wrenched out of her control, she now had something— something within herself—that made sense. Her connection to Victor was now real, living, irrefutable. Their future together was no longer in doubt.

The completeness and order that Ellen had felt so strongly after leaving the infirmary had frayed by the following morning. She woke, perhaps for the last time, in the dorm room her mother had "helped" her to decorate three-and-a-half years earlier. Salmon-colored curtains hung in the window, blocking the distant winter sun. Her head still on the pillow, comforter pulled to her chin, she looked across the room at the books on her oak bookcase. The thoughts she had held off as she fell asleep the night before began to overrun her defenses: withdrawing from school in shame, leaving her education unfinished, abandoning the pursuit of a law degree and a career as an attorney. Facing her parents. The war and Victor's absence.

She sat up slowly and then stood to reach for her robe, hanging on the closet door. Quickly, however, she sat down again, feeling weak and unsteady on her feet. Janet, her suitemate, knocked on the door. "Ellen!" she called. "Are you coming to breakfast?"

"Hi, Janet. No, I think I'll stay in. I'm not feeling so well." The door opened and Janet's face appeared, her small nose turned up and eyes squinted in a look of curiosity and concern.

"Oh, honey," she said. "You do look a bit peaked." Ellen smiled. "Can I bring you anything? Some oatmeal?"

"No, dear. You're very kind. I think I just need to sleep."

"Are you coming to the study group later in the library?"

"I'll have to see. Don't look so worried. I'm fine . . . really."

She fell asleep again moments after Janet entered the room, kissed her on the forehead, and left. Her sleep was fitful, disturbed by dreams of Dean Sherman, Victor, and her mother. When she woke again, close to noon, she felt stronger, though hungrier than she could ever remember being. Revisiting her list of worries from earlier in the morning, she came to a conclusion: her greatest concern was getting him back alive. She felt that she could confront and overcome the other obstacles that loomed. His safety was the only thing that seemed frighteningly beyond her control.

By evening, she was again resolved, with the shock of being pregnant now more fully integrated into her thinking. She had acquired from a hesitant Dean Sherman—after consultation with President Comstock—permission to take her exams, pending written confirmation that her parents had been apprised of her "situation," and with her promise not to discuss her "condition" with her fellow students. She sat down at her desk to study, a welcome distraction from rehearsing for the conversation with her parents.

The remains of a crackling fire smoldered in the parlor fireplace, casting the faint shadows of finial-topped brass andirons across the white marble hearth. The phonograph ticked softly on the mahogany library table, where it had finished playing Brahms's F-major symphony an hour earlier. Mr. Lathrop sat in his armchair facing the fire, the newspaper folded on his lap. He'd been dozing for nearly an hour, an empty Scotch glass and his pipe on the table beside him. Ellen's mother had been reading on the sofa and, growing drowsy herself, was about to wake her husband to tell him that it was time to retire when Ellen entered the room. She sat down next to her mother on the sofa.

They had conversed politely over dinner, discussing her exam schedule and her parents' travel plans for spring. Ellen's nerve had faltered, and she'd gone up to her room to study after dinner without making her announcement. As she prepared for bed, she realized that she was tired of being anxious, weary from the dread as much as she was from the changes in her body, and decided to confront her parents. Eventually she would have to do it, and the sooner they had the news, she reasoned, the sooner they would come around. Her mother would be stunned, and then furious and hurt. Her father, she expected, would be silent at first, and then after withdrawing, would return to voice his disappointment and to decree a course of action.

"There's . . . something I need to . . . tell you both," she began.

"What is it, Ellen?" her mother said absently, closing her book. "Your father and I were about to go upstairs."

The words "never mind" were on her lips, but she knew there would never be a good time. She swallowed. "Last summer, I met a young man. We've fallen very much in love . . . and we're planning to get married."

"Ellen, that's wonderful!" Her mother was now wide awake, putting her glasses back on and refocusing. She had been uncomfortable with the idea of her daughter graduating from college without an engagement ring, though she had never said so to Ellen. "How exciting. Do we know him? Do we know his parents? Is he at Harvard?" She took Ellen's hand in hers, squeezing it enthusiastically.

"No . . . I don't think you know him or his parents," Ellen replied.

"Where are they from?" her mother asked.

"Uh . . . from the North Shore."

"Ah. Lovely. Hamilton? Marblehead? Where do they summer?"

"Excuse me," her father interjected. "But isn't it traditional for the young man to come speak to the young lady's father about such things, to ask his permission? After all, I only have one daughter." He was smiling, but she knew that he meant it.

"Well, that's not possible right now, Father. I'm sorry. He's been drafted. He's at Fort Dix, waiting to be sent off for basic training."

"Officer training," her father corrected.

"No, I think it's basic training."

"Oh, how awful. Oh, Ellen . . . well, in the meantime," her mother said, "we'll *have* to meet his parents. We'll invite them to church, so they can see where the wedding will be held, and then we'll have them to luncheon."

Ellen smiled to cover her fear, knowing that the conversation-stopper was coming. There was silence for a moment.

"Ellen, I can't believe you didn't tell me," her mother chided, having had a moment to consider the news. "How could you keep such a secret, dear? You're engaged and we haven't even met the young man?"

"I'm sorry, Mother. It's just that you were away over the summer, and then I was back at school, and there was some uncertainty about when he would have to leave for Fort Dix, and then the holidays are always so busy for you . . ."

"What's the boy's name?" her father asked.

"Victor." Before they could ask his last name, she took the initiative: "There's one other thing."

"Yes, dear?" Her mother's mind was rushing: bridal showers, reception halls or whether a tent might fit in the back yard, bridesmaids' dresses, florists and photographers, invitations.

"I'm going to have a baby."

Silence.

"Ellen? I don't understand." Her mother looked confused. She had only been half-listening, but the words made their way into her comprehension.

"I'm going to have a baby," Ellen repeated. She held her breath.

"What?"

"Mother, don't make me keep saying it."

"Ellen, I don't . . . I can't . . ." Ellen turned to her father. He was staring at her. After a moment he shook his head and then stood up and walked across the room and into his study. He didn't slam the door but closed it firmly. She watched him go, and then turned back to her mother, who was beginning to cry.

"How could you do this to us?" she whispered, between sobs.

"I didn't do it to you, Mother. I . . ."

"We'll never be able to show our faces in town again. At the church, at the club . . . the humiliation. This has to be a nightmare." She covered her face with both hands. Ellen felt anger rising at her mother's self-preoccupation: of course she would think it was all about her. She checked the feeling, however, knowing it would only escalate the conflict. Instead, she decided to appeal to any maternal instinct, any compassion her mother might be able to garner.

"Mother, I'm sorry. I would never do anything to hurt you on purpose. I made a mistake. But I need your help. I'm scared . . . and alone. Victor's gone, and I don't know when he'll be back." She wiped a tear that wasn't there from her eye. The ploy worked, at least partially. Her mother stopped crying and took Ellen's hand again. She took a deep breath.

"Well . . . I suppose we're in this together. Ellen, I never imagined that you would . . . oh, dear, what a mess. Does . . . Victor know?"

"No. I've only known for a few days."

Her father emerged from the study, came and stood in front of them. He appeared calm but focused. He squared his shoulders and put his hands on his wide, flat hips.

"When's the baby due?" he demanded.

"I'm not exactly sure. Late spring or early summer?"

"When did the young man leave for Fort Dix?"

"Early December."

"You finish your exams when?"

"The week after next—Tuesday."

Now he spoke to his wife, as though Ellen were not present: "We'll send her to my sister in Philadelphia. That will give us some time. Enlisted men usually get a furlough before they go overseas. If so, they can be quietly married then. We can't tell people she's married if she's not, but once they're married no one needs to know how long they've been married."

"Father," Ellen pleaded. "I'm almost twenty-two years old. You can't—"

"Excuse me, Ellen. Your age is not relevant. The fact is that you're in danger of being an unwed mother, a status that will reflect quite poorly not only on you, but on your mother and me as well." His tone was stern, almost biting. "This is a family matter, a crisis, and we will deal with it as a family."

An hour later she could still hear her parents downstairs "discussing" the situation. They never argued, but the discussion was tense. Her mother objected to Ellen's being sent away.

"Fine. So you're going to have her here, then? You're going to take her to church with you on Sunday like that? Impossible. We'll do it my way, and perhaps we can attach the semblance of respectability to this thing. Best case, she comes back with a husband and a baby, no questions asked. Worst case, she loses the husband, but at least it was a husband she lost."

Ellen wasn't sure whether to be furious at their pragmatic reaction, or relieved that her parents knew and that someone else was worrying about her problems. She felt that she had lost control of everything, that she was a child again, dependent and small. She fell asleep longing for Vittorio.

Ellen returned to her dorm, drained physically and emotionally after her last exam. With her semester completed she now had to pack up her belongings. For nearly two weeks she had kept her secret. Now she would have to tell her friends, at least, that she was leaving school, if not why. She walked slowly up the steps and into the building.

The sight of Vittorio's letter, with the military postmark, elated her at first, then intensified her sadness. She hadn't written to him yet. He didn't know that he was to be the father of her child, or the recrimination he would face from her family, or the weight of her anguish and her shame, or the intensity of her hopes for their future together. To him she was just his long-distance girlfriend from back home. Ellen waited until she was upstairs in her room to open the letter.

"Why haven't you written, my love?" he wrote. "Have you forgotten me already?" She smiled at his description of life in the military. "Now, here's the big news," the letter continued. "They're finally shipping me out to basic training. Rumor is that they're not sending Italians to Europe. I guess they're worried about our loyalty—afraid we won't be willing to kill our *paesani*. So it's off to the Pacific, with a stop along the way in beautiful Wisconsin to learn which end of a gun you don't want to be on." Ellen winced. He was going farther away. She had hoped that if her father sent her to her aunt in Philadelphia, she could sneak away and visit him at Fort Dix. She wanted to tell him in person about the baby. "Leaving in a few days," he concluded. "I miss you like crazy, Ellen. Please write."

She sat down to respond, pulling a piece of stationery and a pen from her desk drawer. Telling him the news and pretending that there was no news both felt too difficult, and after a few minutes of looking at the blank piece of paper, she put it back in the drawer. She looked around the room, trying to decide where to begin. Her father would be sending someone for her belongings the following afternoon. She remembered then that she had yet to inform the tennis coach that she wouldn't be playing on the team. She laughed out loud. That will be the most sensational gossip to hit the college in years. What a catastrophe.

Reaching under her bed with a sigh, she pulled out a suitcase, opened the top drawer of her bureau, and began packing her clothes.

Angela had never heard of Wisconsin. She asked Carlo to show her on a map where her son was going. Carlo brought out the atlas he had proudly bought for Vittorio when he was still in school, when the future seemed to hold better prospects.

"It's far," she concluded after studying the map, seated at the kitchen table.

"Not as far as Japan." Carlo was disturbed to hear that Vittorio would be going to the Pacific. Newspapers reported fierce and brutal fighting in the Far East, along with rumors that prisoners of war were being tortured. He had imagined his cousin's son, the boy he had helped to raise, participating in the liberation of Europe, helping to free Italy from the grip of Mussolini and the Fascists, not crawling through a far-off malarial jungle searching for an invisible enemy.

The papers also carried news of the conference at Casablanca. Roosevelt and Churchill met in North Africa in late January to discuss the next phase of the war, having reached, according to Churchill, "the end of the beginning." At the conference, the Americans advocated a cross-Channel invasion of Europe and sought more resources for the war in the Pacific, while the British argued for a continued focus on the Mediterranean. A secret compromise was eventually reached: the invasion of Sicily, to take place during the summer, with planning for the cross-Channel attack to go on simultaneously.

Operation Husky, code name for the invasion of Sicily, was to be the first joint Anglo-American effort of the war. General Eisenhower was given charge over planning. Ultimately, the Allies hoped to take Italy out of the war, leaving Europe's "soft underbelly" exposed, and forcing the Germans to pull out of Russia in the east to defend themselves in the west.

"We're going to win the war," Carlo assured Angela the following week, after reading of the German defeat at Kursk and the Japanese abandonment of Guadalcanal. "The only question is, how long? Vito will be in basic training for months. I'm going to write and tell him to volunteer for more training after that—maybe to be a mechanic on airplanes or tanks or something—training that takes a long time. I don't want him going anywhere near Japan."

"I don't want him going to Wisconsin," she replied, pronouncing the word as "*Veesconesee.*" She sat across the table from him dicing vegetables for soup. "I thought he was too far away when he was in Boston. I don't understand war, Carlo," she said after a moment, pausing from her work. "There must be millions of mothers all over the world lying awake at night worrying about their sons, who are all off in some awful place you never heard of trying to kill each other." She chopped aggressively through a zucchini. "I never should have let Vito go."

"What choice did you have, Angela?" He glanced up from the newspaper. "The government said he had to go."

"I could have kept him home—hid him under the bed. I don't know. What if I did? What if we all did that? What if every mother just refused to send her son? There can't be a mother on God's earth who wants her son to go to war. What if we all just refused? There wouldn't be any war."

"Don't be silly. There will always be war. It's the way of the world."

"Maybe it's the male way of the world. There would be no war if they put women in charge."

"Okay, Angela. You have my vote," Carlo laughed.

"You laugh, Carlo. I lost my husband. Now my only son is out there somewhere, on his way who knows where."

"But Hitler has to be stopped. You agree with that, right? He's a madman."

"Exactly. Hitler can't invade Poland by himself, right? If every mother in Germany said no, he'd have no army. It's because we all stupidly go along with it when you men make your case, just like I did when you and Tommaso went off to war." She jabbed a finger in his direction.

"Angela, please . . ." He was stung each time she reminded him that she still held him partly responsible for Tommaso's death.

"I'm sorry, Carlo," she continued, "but it's true. You convince us that you're right, but you're not. Hitler took all the sons in Germany away from their mothers and all the husbands away from their wives—who didn't put up a fight—and now he's taking ours and we're not putting up a fight, either. It makes me want to rip my hair out." She grabbed her hair with both hands. "You say there will always be war, Carlo, and maybe that's true. But I pray every morning that we mothers one day smarten up and put an end to it." She stood and carried the vegetables into the kitchen on the cutting board. Carlo rubbed his eyes with his thumb and index finger.

When Angela returned to collect her knife and to wipe the table, he spoke: "You might be right, Angela, for all I know. I'm just sorry—for you and for him and for myself—that Vito had to go."

"I still can't believe he's gone." She shook her head. "It's exactly like the nightmare I've had so many times since the war started, over and over. I see him in his uniform and I call out to him, but he can't hear me. He starts walking away and I try to scream, but I can't, and he just walks off without turning back."

Carlo was watching her closely as she spoke. A shiver went through him. "*Signuri havi pietá*," he whispered. Angela heard him and turning, their eyes met. She nodded once, chewing her lower lip, and then walked into the kitchen to stir the soup.

Vittorio was sure he would freeze to death, that his extremities would be permanently damaged. The morning after his arrival at Camp McCoy, with the temperature at minus twelve, snow piled above his head on either side of the road, he sprinted from the barracks to the dining hall, stumbling through the swinging door, gasping with aching lungs and a burning throat. He had shivered uncontrollably all night in his bunk, trying to keep his bedroll wrapped tight around his body and his head. There always seemed to be a gap, however, allowing the unrelenting icy air to creep in and torment him.

"I've never felt cold like this," he groused at breakfast, gulping a second cup of tepid, bitter-tasting coffee. The temperature in the dining hall was barely above freezing.

"Welcome to northern Wisconsin," the soldier across from him replied sarcastically. He wore a black wool cap, pulled down over his ears, and lined leather gloves. "Don't worry, kid, they'll give you some new gear. You should get some feeling back in your fingers and toes within a coupla weeks." Other men at the table laughed, at least partly in sympathy, remembering their own first morning at McCoy.

"Yeah, in your dick, too!" one of them yelled. More laughter.

"It's all part of the plan, soldier," another man added. "They send you here for a while first so you'll be so relieved when you get to sunny Okinawa, you won't mind all the Japs shooting at you."

Vittorio managed a grin, not wanting to appear unable to handle the ribbing. "At least the food's good," he joked, holding up a spoonful of watery oatmeal.

"I have something important to tell you." He read the sentence from Ellen's letter again and again, studying her elegant handwriting as though it were a code. What could she mean? There was genuine tenderness in the letter. "I miss our nights at Walden Pond," she wrote. "How I wish we could go back to one of those warm summer evenings and stay there, holding onto each other, forever." But there was also an unexpected twist in the postscript: "I'm going to visit my aunt in Philadelphia for a while. Write to me there and tell me when you're coming home. Soon I hope!" Below there was an address on Walnut Street, Society Hill, "c/o Mrs. Cornelia Potter." Vittorio pondered the letter for many days. There wasn't much else to occupy his thoughts, other than how to avoid frostbite, and the letter began to torture him. What was he thinking when he got himself mixed up with a girl named Ellen Lathrop, of the Lathrops of Lincoln, Martha's Vineyard, and Palm Beach? Then, later, he would recall the way she looked at him before they kissed for the last time, her eyes full of sadness and desire, and then he would be certain that she would wait for him.

After a week, he wrote back, describing the "ice age" in which he found himself, and the characters who had become his friends. "I think we'll be better trained for the Alps than the South Pacific," he wrote, "but, so far President Roosevelt hasn't called to ask my opinion." Near the end he mentioned that he was entitled to a ten-day furlough at the end of basic training, mid-May approximately, and that he hoped to make it back east to see his mother, and Ellen too, if possible. "Will you still be in Philadelphia? By the way, what are you doing in Philadelphia?" He closed with, "Missing you, too. A lot. Love, Victor."

I do love her, he thought as he sealed the envelope. Seems stupid at this point, considering who I am and who she is, and the fact that I'm buried in this fucking snow and getting closer every day to the war. But damn it all, I do love her.

Ellen's mother accompanied her to Philadelphia, driven by a chauffeur her father hired. They stopped for a night in New York, staying at the Plaza and spending the following morning shopping for maternity clothes now that they were safely outside the normal circles where they might run into an acquaintance. At her mother's insistence, Ellen was wearing a diamond ring and wedding band on the ring finger of her left hand. "I don't care what people think, Mother," she said curtly.

"Apparently not," her mother replied, in her coldest and most cutting tone. Then softening: "Please, Ellen, just do it for me." They purchased five dresses: two for the cold, and three for warmer weather, when Ellen would be larger.

Ellen was tired by the time they arrived in Philadelphia early in the evening, and went to bed after greeting her aunt. Cornelia was her father's elder sister. She was tall and slender like her brother, with hazel eyes and salt-and-pepper hair which she wore in a French braid down her back, over her cashmere sweater. Her three children were grown. The youngest was finishing medical school at Columbia. Her husband had died of pneumonia four winters earlier. Ellen was fond of her aunt, but in no mood to be fussed over.

"Oh, Ellen, look at you," she said, holding Ellen by the wrists. Ellen's appearance was changing, with a modest but noticeable increase in the size of her stomach.

"I know, Aunt Cornie. I know. Can we talk about it tomorrow? I just want to go to sleep. I'm worn out."

"Of course, dear. Tomorrow I'm taking you to see Dr. Carter, the gentleman who delivered Lily's children, so you can meet him. Lily wants to join us." Ellen looked forward to seeing her cousin. Lily would be the first person with whom she could discuss everything without reservation.

She slept for eleven hours, waking when her mother came into the guest room and opened the curtains. "I guess the trip was too much for you." She crossed her arms and looked down at Ellen, who turned away and pulled bed linens up to her neck.

"No, Mother, I'm fine. I just needed to rest." She didn't want her mother worrying over her. In fact, she was ready for her to go back home, as she caught a note of judgment in everything she said.

Ellen found Dr. Carter likable enough, though she could not imagine him touching her body. He was a bulky, slightly awkward man who moved slowly, as though he had to think out each movement carefully, like someone caught in a patch of thorn bushes. Ellen was appreciative of his compassion, however. He agreed to her request that they meet privately, against the objection of her cadre of advisors—mother, aunt, and cousin—and he listened with empathy to her story. His office was pleasant, with a large window overlooking the green on the hospital campus. The wall behind the doctor's desk was covered with photographs of babies he had delivered, and Ellen's attention was drawn to the collage, so that her sentences trailed off into silence. Dr. Carter noted her distraction and sensed that simply meeting was enough for the day. He suggested that they schedule another appointment at her earliest convenience for an examination. "We'll do everything we can to get your baby off to a good start," he concluded, "even if the circumstances aren't ideal."

Later, Ellen and Lily strolled the cobblestone streets of Society Hill, warmed by the bright sun of an early spring thaw. Ellen had always considered Lily the older sister she'd never had. They looked like sisters, with the same straight hair and lightly freckled noses, though Ellen had passed her cousin in height and now stood nearly two inches taller. She recounted, to Lily's amazement, the story of her relationship with Vittorio.

"At least tell me he's handsome," Lily said when Ellen finished, holding her arm as they stepped around an icy puddle.

"More than handsome. Do you think I'd settle for less?" For the first time she could talk about her love without feeling guarded, defensive, and she wanted her cousin to know everything. "He's got the most luscious hair, and these eyes that just pull you in, and big, calloused hands. I love holding his hand. Mostly, though, he's just very sweet and . . . real. Other boys I've dated at school—they have to tell you where they're from and who their fathers are and where they went to prep school and what clubs they're in. Victor is just . . . Victor. He's a real person. He loves me. He sees me for who I am, not for what assets I might bring to a marriage. He doesn't care about those things."

"How romantic," Lily said dryly. "But let me tell you, darling, romance only takes you so far. Believe me. I've been married seven years already."

"You'd understand if you met him." This was her fear: that no one, not even Lily, would understand.

"I hope to meet him. I really do. Anyway, it's an absolute scandal, my little cousin. And your parents know nothing about him?"

"They know his name is Victor, but I told them he was from the North Shore, so my mother's thinking Essex or Hamilton. She's been pushing for more information, but I just act like I can't talk about it, like it's too painful with him so far away."

"Well, I admire your courage. I don't think I'd be as strong as you seem to be." Ellen wondered whether she truly thought she was strong, or maybe that she just didn't understand the gravity of her situation.

"I just hope it holds out once they meet him and learn the truth. I mean, the truth is that he's a gorgeous, wonderful man. But my mother won't see that. She'll be horrified."

"To say the least."

"Are you horrified, Lily? Do you think badly of me?" Ellen tugged at her cousin's arm, and they stopped walking. "Honestly?"

"Of course not, dear. Actually, on the one hand I'm sort of jealous. Romance, passion with a dark stranger . . . a bit of excitement I have never experienced, and never will."

"And on the other hand?"

"Well, sweetheart, try being objective for a moment."

"Right. Objective. Objectively, he's Italian, he's Catholic, he's not a doctor or a banker, and we're not married, and, objectively, I'm having a baby."

"Well . . ."

"So, you're horrified. At least partly."

"It's just a lot to take in all at once," Lily replied with a kind smile.

"Well, I apologize." She was trying not to be hurt.

"No. Don't apologize," Lily answered, her face growing serious. "If you made a mistake, you made it in the past. Now you go forward for the baby. You're going to have to be strong and keep your head high. Forget about apologies and shame, no matter how your mother looks at you. Yes, I've seen how she looks at you. Forget about what anyone else thinks, even the family. Otherwise you'll go under. That baby is going to need you to be thrilled with its arrival—with the way it looks, with everything it does. That's your only concern from now on, understand? You aren't going to apologize for the baby's life once it's born, so you might as well stop now."

"Oh, Lily. I knew you'd have a good perspective. Thank you. You're right."

"I'll be here, darling. So count on me. As much as you need to." Ellen wrapped her arms around Lily and tipped her head down onto her shoulder. She was grateful to be able to share the burden and not keep all that had taken place to herself.

"This is the first time I haven't felt completely alone since this whole thing started."

"I'm glad." They began walking again, Ellen taking Lily's arm, and for a while they were silent.

Vittorio's letter arrived a week later, after Ellen's mother had returned to Boston. Ellen took it to her room and opened it hurriedly. She read it several times, studying the handwriting as though it might yield clues about his feelings, his whereabouts, the future. She considered how to respond, and decided simply to send a reassuring love note, knowing that by the time he saw her in May, she wouldn't have to explain anything at all.

Vittorio was comforted by Ellen's letters, and yet increasingly curious about the cryptic words in her earlier correspondence. He was desperate for basic training to end, in part because he needed to see Ellen, and in part because he was tired of playing war games in the snow and missed home intensely. His growing concern was how he would explain to his mother the need for a trip to Philadelphia when he likely had only ten days before he would be sent to California. She would not want to share him, even with his friends in the North End.

One morning in late April, with the cold easing and the anticipated furlough approaching, he felt a tap on his shoulder as he was
eating his lunch. He turned to see a soldier he recognized as an
aide to Captain Loring, the commanding officer at Camp McCoy.
"The boss wants to see you."

"Me?" Vittorio held a forkful of reconstituted potato flakes
halfway to his mouth. Captain Loring had no reason to know who
Vittorio was. "What the hell for?"

"I guess you'll find out."

"When?"

"Now. He's waiting for you."

Leaving his lunch unfinished and his jacket on the back of his
chair, Vittorio walked quickly out of the mess hall and across the
parade grounds to the office building, at one point nearly slipping
and falling in the muddy slush. His mind raced: had he done something wrong? Was someone accusing him of something? Then he
remembered that another man's brother had died in France and
the man had been summoned to Captain Loring's office to be
given the news. What if something had happened to his mother?
He ran the last fifty feet and yanked open the door.

"Amorelli, Ma'am," he told the secretary, catching his breath.
"Here to see Captain Loring."

"Yes, go right in. He's expecting you." Vittorio stepped into
the office, a windowless box with unpainted cinderblock walls,
snapped to attention, and saluted. "Private Amorelli reporting,
sir."

"At ease, Private. Thank you for coming right away." Captain
Loring continued examining papers on his desk as he spoke, looking up finally and squinting as he peered at Vittorio. He groped for
a pair of glasses with thick black rims, placing them on his meager
nose and pushing them into place with his index finger. He looked
at Vittorio again for a long, uncomfortable moment, as though
trying to commit his face to memory.

"I understand you're a pretty good soldier, Amorelli."

"Thank you, sir." He felt slight relief.

"They tell me you work hard, that you're respectful, and so forth." Loring looked small, like a little boy playing at his father's desk. Vittorio thought that he seemed out of place in the military.

"Thank you, sir," Vittorio repeated.

"Not all the men are like that, as you've probably noticed."

"Uh . . . yes, sir."

"It's good to see a man taking pride in belonging to the United States Army."

"Thank you, sir." Vittorio had never thought of himself as taking pride in belonging to the Army. He was simply following Carlo's direction to obey orders and keep his nose clean and, of course, organization and discipline had been instilled thoroughly by Nino, useful ideals for military service.

"Tell, me, Amorelli, where's your family from?"

"Near Boston, sir."

"Yes, but, Amorelli—the name, I mean, where are you from?"

"Italy, sir. Sicily to be exact. North coast. Towards Palermo."

"Right. And do you speak Italian, Private?"

"Uh, not exactly, sir." Vittorio was growing more nervous again. He glanced around the room, avoiding the captain's eyes. Why was he asking these questions? Did they suspect him of something? Spying? He knew about spies and their fate. He felt his palms sweating and wiped them on his pants, hoping Loring wouldn't notice.

"You speak only English?" Loring sounded skeptical. Vittorio cleared his throat and told himself to be calm.

"Well, with my family I speak what I guess you call a dialect. The way they speak back in Sicily. It's different than Italian, sir."

"So if you happened to be in Sicily, you could speak to the people in their native language . . . in this dialect?"

"I'm sorry, sir. I'm not trying to be difficult. My uncle tells me that there are many dialects in Sicily, depending on where you are."

"I understand. Tell me, Amorelli, would you say that you could make yourself understood to most people in Sicily, speaking the particular dialect that you speak?"

"Yes, sir," he replied after a moment. "More or less. I know Sicilians from other areas—my boss, for one. He's from the east. We can carry on a conversation without too much trouble."

"Ah, very good. I'm asking you these questions, Private, because I've been ordered by my superiors to locate a few men who are conversant in the . . . let's call it Sicilian language. A lot of Italians are passing through here on their way to the Pacific. I imagine you've probably figured that out by now. But a few are needed for a top-secret mission. I'd like to put you down as the first name on the list."

"Sir?"

"I can't tell you any more about it. As I said, it's top secret. Just be prepared to ship out within a few days. You're a good man, Amorelli. Thank you for volunteering. Dismissed." The captain went back to his papers. Vittorio, stunned, mouth open to speak but not knowing what to say, saluted and turned to leave.

Vittorio walked back across the parade grounds, kicking at clods of slush. He wove his fingers together on top of his head. A top-secret mission. Christ. Where the hell? He tried to calm himself, regretting that he hadn't asked Captain Loring about his promised furlough. A desperate shiver passed through him as Ellen and his mother seemed to slip from his grasp.

Angela and Ellen were both alarmed upon receiving the letters Vittorio wrote to them. "What does he mean by that?" Angela interrupted Carlo as he read.

"I don't know. I hope he didn't volunteer for something," Carlo answered, worried.

Sitting in a rocking chair in her room in Aunt Cornelia's house, Ellen shook her head. "I'm going to be out of touch for a little while," she read aloud to herself. How long is a little while? she wondered, growing increasingly upset. She read on: "It looks like my furlough is off for now. I'm sorry."

She pushed herself up out of the chair, noticing the extra effort it took, and went to the dressing table. Taking a piece of stationery from beneath a stack of books, she began frantically writing, her normally precise penmanship shaken by her panic. "You can't be out of touch,'" she wrote. "We have to talk. It's urgent!" She underlined the word "urgent" twice. "Is there a telephone you can use to call me? Tell whomever you have to tell that it's an emergency."

She sealed the envelope, and descending the stairs, called to her aunt that she was going for a walk. She wanted to post the letter without delay.

"All alone, dear?" Aunt Cornelia called from the parlor.

"Just for a few minutes, Aunt Cornie. I need some fresh air."

For eight days Ellen waited for the postman to arrive, watching from her window for him to turn the corner, and then hurrying to the foyer to meet him at the door. She jumped each evening when the phone rang. It was always her mother or Lily calling to see how she was feeling.

Then one day the postman handed her a small stack of envelopes with his usual smile and tip of his hat. Ellen flipped past two letters addressed to her aunt and then gasped, looking down at her letter to Vittorio with the words "UNDELIVERABLE: RETURN TO SENDER" handwritten in red ink above Vittorio's name, which had a line through it. She stared at the words. It was as if the ground had crumbled away underneath her.

"Are you all right, Miss Ellen?" the postman asked, turning around and seeing the color drain from her face.

"Yes, Mr. Briggs . . . thank you," she responded. "I'm fine."

"Well, then, have a nice—" Ellen closed the heavy oak door before he finished. Dropping her aunt's mail on the table in the front hall, she climbed the stairs to her room.

Later in the afternoon, Aunt Cornelia announced that she was going to her bridge club. After she was gone, Ellen went into the parlor and picked up the telephone. For fifteen minutes a patient operator assisted her in attempting to place the call, until a female voice finally answered.

"Good afternoon. Camp McCoy, US Army."

"Yes, good afternoon." Ellen tried to sound calm, though after the series of false starts with the operator, she was agitated. "I need to speak to Private Victor Amorelli. It's urgent."

"I'm sorry, ma'am. The enlisted men aren't available to speak on the telephone at this time of day," the secretary said politely.

"Please, it's urgent. I'm his wife . . . he's going to be a father, and he doesn't know yet. He wrote that he was leaving Camp McCoy. I must talk to him before he leaves. Please." There was a long pause.

"Let me see if I can locate him, ma'am. I can't promise. He could be anywhere. Can you hold the line?"

"Of course. Thank you." Ellen took a deep breath. With all of her concentration focused on reaching him, she hadn't thought about how she would tell him the news, or about how he might react. She was afraid she might fall apart as soon as she heard his voice. After a few minutes, the secretary came back on the line.

"My apologies, ma'am, I don't think I heard the name right. Could you spell it for me?"

"Yes, it's Victor Amorelli, A-M-O-R-E-L-L-I."

"Thank you. Could you hold the line again?"

"Yes, yes of course I will." Nearly ten minutes passed. Ellen chewed on her fingernails. Her ear became hot and red from the nervous pressure of holding the hard, black receiver against it. Finally, the secretary returned to the telephone.

"I'm sorry, ma'am, there's a bit of confusion. There was a *Vittorio* Amorelli here. Could that be your husband? We don't have any record of a Victor Amorelli." She closed her eyes. Of course he was enlisted under Vittorio, not Victor.

"Yes," she said tentatively, embarrassed. "Yes, that must be him... that is him. He goes by Victor," she added, knowing it would seem strange that she didn't know her husband's real name.

"In that case, Mrs. Amorelli, I'm afraid I have to tell you that your husband is no longer here. He left Camp McCoy."

"What?" She was desperate to hear his voice, and this news brought panic. She could feel her heart racing. "When? Where is he? I have to reach him. Do you have a telephone number where I can reach him? I told you, it's urgent."

"I'm sorry, Mrs. Amorelli, I don't have that information."

"What do you mean, you don't have that information?" She was no longer able to sound polite. "You must have records of where people go when they leave."

"Please try to understand, Mrs. Amorelli. We're in the middle of a war. I can't disclose—"

"I'm his wife!"

"Mrs. Amorelli, I'm under direct orders from our command-ing officer Captain Loring. I wish I could help you . . . honestly, but—"

Ellen slowly lowered the receiver from her ear and placed it on the hanger, holding onto the stand to stabilize herself for a moment.

She was more than six months pregnant. For several weeks she had been able to feel the baby kicking. Back in her room, she sat down on the bed, putting her hands on her stomach, and began to cry. Soon enough the baby would be born, and its father had disappeared. As uncomfortable as her situation had been, she had lived in the faith that he would return, and that they would succeed in making a life together as a family. It would be a difficult road, surely, with plenty of obstacles. But she had never let herself imagine a future without her baby's father.

She tried to clear her mind and regain her composure: He's not dead. He's just . . . somewhere. There's no reason to believe he won't be just fine, she reasoned. She assured herself that he would contact her as soon as he could. But she could not quell a feeling of loneliness, unfamiliar and more intense than she had ever known in her life.

v i i.

Stepping onto the gangway, Vittorio looked down at the menacing water sloshing back and forth between the dock and the ship's enormous hull. He crossed himself, remembering his vow never to go on a boat again. The New York skyline faded from view as darkness fell, and he felt his mother, Carlo, Ellen, everything he knew, fading with it. The familiar and dreaded sensations took hold of his legs and his stomach. Hours later, with the open ocean surrounding him, waves splashing against the liner, he began to vomit into the sea.

On deck the following morning, weakened and dehydrated, he hung onto the railing. Behind every wave he expected to see the periscope of a German submarine. His fears overwhelmed him like a terrifying dream.

The ship was joined by eleven others in a convoy crossing the North Atlantic. Vittorio suffered under overcast skies throughout the nine-day journey, spending as much time as possible on deck. The confined quarters below worsened his seasickness. Only when he stepped onto solid ground at Pier Head in Liverpool did color begin to return to his ashen face. He thought the two enormous bronze cormorants, perched in metallic green atop the twin towers of the Liver Building, looked like vultures ready to swoop down and carry off what was left of him.

Liverpool and the Liverpudlians were fascinating to Vittorio once he recovered. He walked the streets of the city, crossing and recrossing the Mersey River; surveying damage inflicted by ten-pound incendiary bombs dropped by German aircraft two years before; examining the stone works of the unfinished Anglican cathedral, now abandoned, and marveling at the impressive Greco-Roman columns of St. George's Hall, a building grander than any he'd ever seen before. The contrast of ancient and modern throughout the city was striking, made even more dramatic with war's nearness settling like a fog in the streets. He found the atmosphere of war entirely different in England. Here the war was tangible. The demolished buildings and the anxiety on the faces of people in the streets made war into something more than headlines in the newspaper. Vittorio was affected by the sight of a group of wounded soldiers on a hospital terrace, sitting in wooden wheelchairs in bandages and plaster casts, smoking cigarettes and staring blankly at passersby. He cringed.

At night, he experienced the seedy side of Liverpool in the garish light of oil lamps around the Albert Dock. The Pumphouse Inn, a church-like stone pub on the waterfront, was brimming with American GIs. The raucous blaring of big band music drew him in. He joined a group he recognized from the crossing who were trying to flirt with local girls. They mimicked their dense accents and competed for their attention. He observed the banter, half amused, as he sipped at a pint of stout. He wondered why some men seemed to enjoy the military life. Watching them, he sensed that they were only pretending to enjoy it, but actually were as miserable as he was, trying to distract themselves from the disturbing fact that they could be dead within days or weeks.

He still was not sure why he had been sent to Europe, and the uncertainty unnerved him nearly as much as the idea of boarding another ship, as his orders dictated.

"Why don't you write a letter to his mother?"

Ellen lay on her bed, resting her hands atop her large belly. "Oh, there he goes again. It feels like he's going to kick his way right through."

"You're sure it's a *he*?" Lily asked, pulling her chair closer and placing her hand below Ellen's.

"No, he's over here." She grasped Lily's wrist and moved her hand to the left. "Do you feel him?"

"I remember those last weeks before Emma was born," Lily said, smiling. "She never let me sleep. She'd be quiet during the day and then kick me all night."

Ellen dropped her head back onto the pillow. "I think he's going to be strong," she said, mostly to herself, looking up at the ceiling.

"He's going to have to be. Anyway, why don't you write to Victor's mother? Maybe she's had news from him."

"If he can't tell me where he is, then he probably can't tell his mother where he is, either, unless he just doesn't want . . . in any case, what am I going to say? 'Dear Mrs. Amorelli, I'm your son's pregnant Protestant girlfriend. Any idea where he is?' If he survives the war, she'll kill him as soon as he gets home."

"Well, she's going to find out eventually, right?"

"What if she *is* in touch with him somehow? Then she tells him and . . . I just don't want him to find out like that. Braid my hair for me, Lily, so I can try to go to sleep?" Ellen, with effort, sat up and moved to the chair, while her cousin stood and picked up the mother-of-pearl hairbrush from the dressing table. They were silent for a moment as Lily pulled the brush through Ellen's hair.

"I don't think his mother's going to take it well at all," Ellen concluded, "at least from what Victor says about her."

"Well, then you'll be even. Your parents weren't exactly thrilled either."

"Oh, dear cousin. You always know just what to say."

"Just trying to keep you smiling," she offered cheerfully. "There." She tied a bow at the bottom of the braid with a length of burgundy ribbon, and then kissed Ellen on the top of her head. "Now, go to bed. Believe me, you're going to need your rest."

For the invasion of Sicily, Patton's American Seventh Army and Montgomery's British Eighth were combined to form the Fifteenth Army Group. After eleven harrowing travel days by rail, sea, and jeep, Vittorio arrived in Relizane in Algeria, at the headquarters of II Corps on the first of July. Omar Bradley, commander of II Corps, which together with the First Infantry Division formed the Seventh Army, had settled into the dusty town on the edge of the Sahara to prepare for Husky.

Vittorio had ridden the final thirty-five miles south from coastal Mostagamen, host to Patton's command post, with an aide to the general. Patton had already secured two translators, making Vittorio available for Bradley's staff. Vittorio was struck by Relizane's bizarre juxtaposition of desert geography with French civilization. All the signs were written in French, save the word SPEEDY, a code name for II Corps, which had been painted conspicuously around the town. Aside from American soldiers, however, the only people to be seen were Arabs, their skin darker than his own.

Vittorio had received orders to report directly to Bradley. He inquired and was told that Bradley's planning office was in the Ecole des Femmes, a low-slung stucco building with a central courtyard. Vittorio found him there late in the afternoon. Tall and thin, his hair graying on the sides but his eyebrows black in contrast, Bradley stood before the south coast of a large topographical map of Sicily which was balanced on student desks pushed together in the middle of a classroom. He swept his hand across the coastline between Gela and Scoglitti, and then pointed inland towards the gray-green mound representing Etna. "We want most of the force pushing this way, right? With a sweep-around to the west?" Vittorio approached the map from the opposite side of the table, looking for Cefalú on the map. Bradley's aide, Ben Dickson, standing to his right, took notice of him and interrupted Bradley to address him with irritation.

"Soldier? Do you have business here?"

"Yes, sir." Vittorio snapped to attention. "Excuse me, sir. Private Vittorio Amorelli, reporting. I was sent by General Patton . . . as a translator, sir."

Bradley, who had been ignoring him, looked up. "Translator? You speak Italian, soldier?"

"Sicilian, sir. Dialect. Sicilians don't commonly speak . . . proper Italian, sir."

"Right, right. Very good. George said he'd send someone. Very good. Could be handy dealing with the resistance if we find any. Ben, he'll travel with us. I want him on our boat and with our CP on the island. Were you born in Sicily, soldier?"

"No, sir. My parents came from Sicily. From right here. Cefalú."

"Cefalú," Bradley repeated. "Well, if we get there in one piece, son, you can stop and say hello to your cousins." Dickson chortled. "Dismissed." Vittorio saluted, turned and walked through the school back to the street. He covered his face too late to stop a hot, dry gust from blowing sand into his eyes.

In Mostagamen, through rumor in the mess tent, he learned that strong German resistance was expected, as Hitler attempted to protect his ally and his southern flank. "The Krauts have aerodromes all over Sicily," one disgruntled soldier told him, pushing his dinner tray away from him and lighting a cigarette. "They're going to bomb the shit out of us before we cross the goddamned narrows."

Vittorio smiled to himself despite his anxiety. "What a way to visit the old country," he said to himself. That night he wrote to his mother and Carlo: "I can't tell you where I am, but it doesn't really matter. You'd never believe me anyway." He started a note to Ellen, but struggled with what to say, and fell asleep before he could come up with words.

Ellen was awakened after three o'clock on the morning of the fifth by her first strong contraction. She had felt tightening in her lower abdomen throughout the day on the fourth during a holiday picnic at Lily's and later while watching fireworks over the city. Fully awake and tense, she waited for another. Eventually, after two more smaller contractions, she fell back to sleep.

Her aunt woke her at nine o'clock and insisted she get out of bed. "I'm tired, Aunt Cornie," she complained. "Let me stay in bed." She wanted to sleep and somehow delay what she sensed was going to be a process she feared she couldn't endure.

"No, dear. Quite sorry, but you must get up and about. That baby is not going to come with you lying around doing nothing. Let's have breakfast and go for a walk."

Minor contractions, with an occasional strong one, continued throughout the day and into the evening. Her parents had been notified of progress the day before and they arrived as Ellen was going to bed. Her father had not seen her in nearly three months. He wasn't prepared for the sight of his daughter in this "condition," and had to excuse himself after giving her a dry kiss on the cheek.

Her mother sat up with her for an hour, trying to offer comfort. "You're going to be just fine," she said. "You're a strong girl. It'll be over before you know it." Ellen did not find this helpful, and politely suggested that her mother must be exhausted from travel and should go to bed.

"What have you heard from—"

"From Victor?"

"Yes, from the father."

"Nothing else, Mother. I told you, he's involved in some sort of . . . mission—a secret mission." Ellen had convinced herself that this must be true.

"So he still knows nothing about the baby?" Her mother had suspicions about Vittorio's disappearance.

"There's no way he could, Mother. I never wrote him about it, and I couldn't reach him by telephone."

"I see," she replied, with a nod that Ellen found condescending.

"Please, Mother. This is hard enough as it is. Victor will be here as soon as he can."

"Of course he will, dear." Ellen's last reserve of patience was taken away by her most painful contraction so far. She clenched her fists until it passed. Then she attempted a smile.

"Goodnight, Mother."

By midafternoon on the following day, her contractions were doubling Ellen over in pain. "You'll know you're really in labor when your toes start to curl," Lily had told her.

"My toes are curling," she cried, bracing herself with both hands on the table in the parlor.

"I'll get the car," her father said, nervously patting his pockets for the keys. Ellen and her mother rode with her father in the Cadillac, with her aunt and Lily leading the way in Cornelia's Buick. They turned into the semicircular drive and stopped at the main entrance to the Pine Building, a stately federal-period edifice, part of the original Pennsylvania Hospital complex.

Lily had phoned Dr. Carter from the house and he met them at the reception desk. "The time's come, has it?" he asked, taking

Ellen by the arm. He tended to finish each remark with a question. She was breathing hard, recovering from a strong wave which had struck as she was climbing the steps. She nodded. A nurse arrived with a wheelchair and Dr. Carter eased Ellen into it. "Let's get you something to take the edge off that pain."

With the help of ether, Ellen slept between contractions as several hours passed. Dr. Carter examined her cervix twice, announcing that dilation was progressing, but that her water had not yet ruptured.

As the first hint of dawn appeared at the window, Ellen hollered in pain, waking her mother, who had fallen asleep in a chair. Fluid leaked onto the bed as the contraction subsided. "Nurse!" Ellen yelled. "Mother, get the nurse. Get Dr. Carter!"

The doctor arrived moments later from his office, where he too had fallen asleep. "It's about time, isn't it? I think the ether slowed you down a bit, but at least you've rested, have you?" After washing his hands, he stepped to the foot of the delivery table to examine Ellen. "Oh, my," he exclaimed. "A full head of hair."

Ellen cried out as another contraction rocked her. The ether had worn off, and she had declined an additional dose. She wanted to keep her head clear. "Ready to push, are you, Ellen?" the doctor asked.

She drew a deep breath, steeling herself for the onset of the next contraction. "I think so," she whispered. Her mother stood by, holding her hand and wiping sweat from her forehead.

"Good girl," the doctor said. "We'll go slow, okay? As the next contraction is peaking, I want you to push." Fifteen minutes later, the baby crowned. Thick black hair appeared between Ellen's legs. "One more good push, Ellen, when you're ready." Ellen clenched her teeth and grabbed the side rails of the bed and, closing her eyes and emitting a long, low grunt, she pushed the baby's head into Dr. Carter's hands.

"Good," he coaxed. "Wonderful! Here we go—one more good push. Yes . . . and it's . . . a boy, isn't it?" Ellen, exhausted, opened her eyes and saw her son in the doctor's hands. Tears ran down her face as she gasped for breath.

"Oh . . . oh," she cried, "I knew it." The nurse assisted Dr. Carter in attending to the baby. After a moment the doctor announced that he was breathing on his own, just as the baby let out his first wail. The nurse cut the umbilical cord and wiped amniotic fluid, mucous and blood from his body. Wrapping him in a pale blue blanket, she held him as the doctor coached Ellen through the delivery of the placenta. Finally, she placed him in Ellen's arms.

"Hello, my Thomas," Ellen said through her tears. "Hello, my son." She kissed his face and touched his nose gently with her finger. "I can't believe you're finally here," she murmured. For several minutes, she gazed into his eyes. In her relief at his safe delivery, Ellen stroked his hair and imagined Vittorio's reaction when he learned that his son had been named according to the Sicilian tradition. Then, sensing her mother's silence, she looked up to see pallid horror on her face, as though Ellen held not a baby but some grotesque and repugnant creature.

"Dear God, Ellen," she said in a hushed tone. "Please don't tell me . . . is his father a . . . Negro?" Ellen turned back to the baby. His skin was brown, and his eyes, like his hair, were nearly black.

"No, Mother," she murmured, kissing the baby again on his forehead.

"I'm going to get your father," she announced, hastily leaving the delivery room.

Before her parents returned, the nurse informed Ellen that she was going to take the baby to the nursery.

"No, thank you," Ellen replied. "I'd like to keep him here with me."

"Oh, no, ma'am," the nurse insisted, "you need to rest. We'll take good care of him." She smiled reassuringly, reaching to take the baby from Ellen. Ellen pulled him closer.

"No, thank you. He's going to stay here with me."

"You must understand," the nurse said, bewildered. "It's hospital policy. After the baby's born we—"

"If you need to send the doctor back in, so be it. Thomas is going to stay here with me." Ellen had a visceral feeling that if she let the baby go, she would never see him again: either a mistake would be made, because Thomas looked like Vittorio and not at all like her: or, more likely, she feared that her parents were scheming to send him to an orphanage or an adoption agency. In either case, without the baby, she felt that she would come apart. Thomas's life depended on hers—and hers, from now on, would depend on him.

The nurse stared for a moment, and Ellen met her gaze. Finally, she left the room.

Hours later, after she had been transferred to a room on the maternity ward and had been assisted in initiating nursing, after Lily and Aunt Cornelia and her parents had arrived to see the baby; after the awkward silence in the room when Lily had said, "Isn't he beautiful?" Ellen fell asleep, still holding—clutching—Thomas in her arms. Lily and Aunt Cornelia eventually left, promising to come back later. Her parents were speculating unhappily as to the origin of the infant's coloring and features when a nurse entered the room. She was a short, older woman wearing a yellow cardigan sweater over her white uniform.

"Are you the grandparents?" she asked.

"Uh, yes," Ellen's father replied, as ill at ease as ever with that designation.

"I'm sorry to intrude. Good to see her resting. She had a long night of it. I just need some information for the child's birth certificate." She held out a clipboard and a pen, which Mr. Lathrop took from her. He began to complete the form, using block letters. In the space for the child's surname, her father wrote: LATHROP. For father's name, he hesitated for a moment, then wrote: UNKNOWN. Hoping she wouldn't read it and ask questions, he handed the clipboard and pen back to the nurse without meeting her eye.

"Thank you, sir," she said, glancing at the form, "and congratulations." Nodding at Ellen's mother, she turned and left.

The day after his son was born, Vittorio passed within seventy miles of the island where his parents had been born. He was with Bradley's staff aboard the Ancon, a ten-thousand-ton converted luxury ocean liner being used as a command vessel. Vittorio's seasickness was tempered with land constantly in view, as the ninety-six-ship convoy skirted the African shoreline for four days from Oran, past Bizerte and Cape Bon. But his stomach began to roil with the increased tension aboard ship in the narrows, where Bradley expected an air attack by German bombers flying out of Sicily. He watched the sky, expecting to see the planes at any moment. Turning to continue along the coastline towards Tripoli, he was relieved when the convoy sailed beyond the threat, at least temporarily.

Vittorio was nearly thrown from his bunk at dawn on July 9 when powerful winds began to rock the Ancon. The gale grew stronger throughout the day, sending Vittorio to the deck where he was not alone in being sick. He even spotted Bradley holding the rail, his face greenish, and overheard him wondering aloud to Dickson whether the landing could go forward in bad weather. By nightfall the convoy had reversed direction and, keeping the island of Malta starboard, had steamed into the Gulf of Gela, where it joined two other naval groups to form a massive attack force. The winds abated in the Gulf, though large swells kept the Ancon rolling, to Vittorio's continued discomfort. As sick as he was from the surf, and as afraid as he was in the face of the attack and expected counterattack, Vittorio was mesmerized by the idea of stepping onto Sicilian soil. This was never how he could have imagined it, yet here he was. He could see lights along the shoreline in the distance.

Bradley was ready to follow the initial landings ashore by mid-morning the next day. Though the air drops had bordered on disaster, with most missing their targets and scores of soldiers landing behind enemy lines, the beachhead had been secured, and troops were advancing slowly inland. Vittorio boarded a landing craft that trailed one carrying Bradley. He could feel his heart racing as the boat approached the coast. Trying to suppress a smile, he jumped over the bow onto the beach, his shiny black boots splashing into a receding wave. Oblivious for a moment to the chaos around him—men shouting and running, leaping off boats, dragging equipment behind them, the sound of gunfire just beyond the trees—he thought of his mother and Carlo, bending over to grab a handful of pebbled sand: home. His feet were standing on his parents' homeland, and he was breathing the air of this place he'd been hearing of for as long as he could remember. He was home.

II Corps established a command post in Scoglitti, not much more than a shack under the shelter of trees. Vittorio sat smoking outside on a flat rock, listening to guns thundering and shells pounding in the distance. Occasionally, a blast would shake the ground under him, rattling and disturbing him until his head began to ache. The town of Gela, to the north, was being shelled by US 1 Division along with the Rangers, against strong resistance from a German panzer unit, while the 45th, the other component of II Corps, was attempting to move toward the interior of the island from the southern side of Scoglitti. Waiting for instructions, Vittorio tried to sleep in a ruined, roofless house, waking often to the sound of small-arms fire.

Late in the afternoon of the eleventh he was called to serve as a translator for the first time. A small contingent of Sicilian troops had given up as the Allies moved inland and, rather than retreat and be shot by the Germans, they had walked into

Scoglitti holding strips of white cloth over their heads. Military police gathered them into the tiny piazza at the center of town. "Tell them to sit down facing that wall," Dickson ordered Vittorio, pointing to the stone façade of an abandoned church. By now there were more than two hundred of the disheveled soldiers, most of them too weary to know whether to be relieved or scared. "Tell them they're now prisoners of war. We'll get them food eventually. In the meantime, tell them not to move." Many of the men gaped at Vittorio in his United States Army uniform as he moved among them speaking their language, or at least a version of it they could understand. For his part, Vittorio was taken aback by the condition of these men, defeated and desperate as they seemed, and he pondered how the war, a conflict in which they were almost incidental players, had come to them and torn their lives apart.

"Where are you from?" one filthy, exhausted-looking man asked him. An affliction of flies swarmed about his head, though he seemed not to notice, making no effort to wave them off.

"*L'America,*" Vittorio replied. The man stared.

"But you're Sicilian?"

"*Sí.*" Vittorio took a step to continue down the line of prisoners.

"You came here to kill your own people?" the man said angrily to Vittorio's back, the image of comrades falling dead around him at the hands of the Americans earlier in the day filling his mind. Vittorio turned.

"I'm not killing anyone, am I? If you're lucky, I'll save your ass."

"I just saved my own ass, cousin," he spat back. "Best you can do is get me something to eat."

Prisoners of war, and not the Resistance, became Vittorio's main concern. A week after the landings, the number of Italians surrendering to II Corps had become overwhelming. The Germans were pulling back to defend Messina, leaving most of Sicily in the hands of Italian troops, many of them Sicilian, who had no desire to fight.

With another group of unarmed men waving white rags approaching, Omar Bradley decided to act on his instinct. By now, he was keeping Vittorio close by. "Private," he said solemnly, "tell them to go home."

"Excuse me, sir?" Vittorio replied, surprised by this direction.

"Tell any of the locals they can go home. I ain't packing these poor fools off to camps in America while their wives and children starve to death. Who the hell is going to tend these crops? All this wheat has to be harvested. Tell 'em to leave their guns and go home, Private."

The next day in Caltanissetta, a shabby market town that had sustained extensive damage over the previous four days leading up to its fall, Vittorio went with Colonel Dickson in search of the bishop. Dickson parked the dusty jeep in the yard of the bishop's residence, a stone building attached to the back of the baroque cathedral, San Sebastiano, scattering a small flock of scraggly, unfed chickens. Dickson pushed the wooden door open after no one answered his knock.

"Anyone here?" Vittorio called. No response. He followed the colonel from room to room, through the dining room and kitchen, a parlor, and back into the dim foyer. Dickson stopped and knocked on a closed door, paused, and then opened it. Behind a desk, the bishop sat praying. He was a small man, the second son of one of Caltanissetta's important families, with delicate hands and a conical head, covered by his scarlet skull cap. His prayer book was open on the desk in front of him. A photograph of Pope Pius the Twelfth hung on the wall behind. The droning of a pair of large black flies accompanied the bishop's devotional whisperings. There was no indication that he was aware of their presence.

"Your eminence?" Vittorio ventured respectfully after Dickson elbowed him. As if waking from a trance, the bishop looked up and began to speak.

"I'm not a Fascist," he began, his hands still folded together. "I've never been a Fascist. I denounce Mussolini and all that he stands for. Please, in the name of God . . ." He appeared calm, though Vittorio sensed his fear. Dickson raised his hand and the bishop fell silent.

"Go ahead, Private."

"Please, don't be scared." Vittorio took a step forward. "We're not here to hurt anyone. We need your help." The bishop relaxed slightly, dropping back from the edge of his armchair. "We don't want to take any prisoners who live here. We just want them to go home. We need you to help us spread the word. If they desert, we won't take them prisoner . . . as long as they give us their guns and go back to their homes. Tell them to go home and get ready for the harvest."

Similar exchanges were repeated with clergy and local officials as Vittorio followed the advancing II Corps towards Enna. In fighting for Enna, however, II Corps came up against fierce, fortified German defenders. Vittorio was stalled with the rear guard for three days while the battle for the hilltop city raged. He wandered through nearby villages, drawing in the touch of light on the vineyards in the morning, the oranges and yellows of the low stuccoed houses, the browns of their terracotta roofs, the beauty of the rolling hills and soft, hazy sky. He was aware, studying one of Bradley's maps, that he was only thirty miles from Cefalú. He imagined going there and wondered how he would be received. What would they say to him when they discovered his identity? Though he had steeled himself since boyhood to the pang of unformed feelings about his father, he thought of him now. Perhaps the invasion was the beginning of a new day for Sicily. Perhaps life there would improve after liberation, and young men would not think to leave in search of a better life for their children, as his father had. Perhaps he was honoring his father's memory by making some small contribution to the coming of that new day. Perhaps his father would be proud of him. Maybe the cousins, aunts and uncles and grandparents who had been left behind— people he had never met but felt like he knew from the stories his mother told—maybe they would be grateful. He wondered for a moment whether anyone in the army would find him if he disappeared and stole off to Cefalú.

After Enna fell, II Corps was again moving forward, pushing east to harass the Germans in their retreat. On July 24, the day before Mussolini was forced from power, Vittorio rode through Enna in a jeep with Aaron, an affable, square-jawed former-high-school linebacker from Iowa who had been with Bradley since the beginning of the Tunisian campaign. They drove east up Via Roma, across Piazza Garibaldi and into Piazza Mazzini, passing the cathedral. Sacred Enna, Sicily's center, where Ceres had been honored for centuries, reeked now not with the fragrance of incense and grain sacrifices, but with the stinging odor of sulfur, gunpowder, and death. Vittorio was not so much inured to the miserable wake of war and its sensory assault as he was unable to absorb any more. He did not ignore the bodies in the streets, soldiers from both sides, civilians, animals, the homes and shops which smoldered, the smashed windows, roofs, carts, automobiles, furniture. He did not ignore them. He simply couldn't see them, or his brain could no longer process the data arriving from his eyes, nose, and ears. He concentrated on the landmarks, impressed by the enormous Castello di Lombardia, with its six towers rising above, drawing his attention up and away from the wreckage all around. "I guess we're not the first ones to conquer this little hill," Aaron joked, impressed by the bulky ramparts of the fort.

They descended from the hilltop down a rocky road toward the gray-green valley. The mid-July sun blazed overhead, causing Vittorio to squint. Mount Etna was visible through the haze, though it seemed impossibly large, as though it could not fit on the island, but somehow floated above, both ethereal and ominous. They passed spent, shabbily-clad villagers on foot heading in the other direction up the steep road, phoenix-like, to discover what was left of their lives in town as they and their ancestors had done in the smoldering aftermath of Greek, Roman, Arab, Norman, and Bourbon conflagrations which scorched their history and seared their collective memory.

Sliding around a steep, tight switchback, they encountered a boy leading a goat. He was leading the goat not because the goat could give milk any longer or because it had enough flesh left on its beleaguered, emaciated bones for a meal, or because he had anything to feed the wretched beast once they reached home, but because the boy didn't know what else to do. His clothes were torn and dirty. Clinging to the top of his head was the tattered remnant of a hat. The animal stood in the center of the road. The boy was attempting to pull him to the side, out of the way, but the goat, who was nearly as tall as the boy, would not be moved. His hooves were planted in the dust. With eyes rolled back, ears pressed down, he jerked his head mutinously in the opposite direction.

Aaron shifted to slow the vehicle, sending the gears whirring, stopped with a skid and gave a short, throaty beep on the horn. The boy looked at them, shrugged, and began yanking harder on the rope, finally putting it over his shoulder, turning his back to the goat and straining with all his power to walk forward. The goat did not budge. Aaron and Vittorio hollered encouragements to the boy, and to the goat, above the rumbling idle of the jeep's engine.

"Well, the Krauts ain't stoppin' us," Aaron quipped eventually, "so I guess we can't let a little feller with a sad lookin' goat slow us down either." Waving to the boy, he shifted the jeep into gear and turned to pass by on the shoulder of the road. Gravel crunched under the vehicle's thick tires.

For an instant, Vittorio was aware of the blast, the noise, and the flash of light as the German mine, planted the previous morning by an eighteen-year-old boy from Herzberg, exploded under the front, right wheel of the jeep. He was aware of his body being thrown violently upwards. He was aware of fire below him.

Falling, he crashed against the jagged embankment, the impact slamming the life out of him. He was half buried by the rust-colored rubble, which, having been sent skyward, now rained back to earth along with pieces of the jeep.

The echo of the blast pulsed and faded across the primeval, indolent heart of Sicily.

THREE

i.

"I DIDN'T THINK IT COULD GET ANY WORSE." Whitney Lathrop sat on the edge of the bed in his sister's guest room holding his Scotch glass. The ice cubes had melted in the heat of a steamy July evening, and he swirled the water in the bottom of the glass absently. He shook his head in disgust. "But it just did."

The morning after Thomas was born, Ellen, with little left to hide, had given them a more complete recounting of her relationship with Vittorio. She assured them, trying not to sound defiant, that when Vittorio returned, he would marry her, and that they would live a decent and respectable life together.

"I just can't believe she was sneaking around with that . . . with a brick layer, or a—what did she call him? A 'stone mason landscaper' . . . person." Caroline was lying on the bed in her nightgown, her hands pressed against the sides of her head as though trying to prevent it from coming apart. "And that baby. Our grandson, for God's sake. He doesn't look anything like her. He's dark and . . . he doesn't look like he belongs with us. I'm just completely . . . sick. How could she do this to us?"

Whitney got up from the bed, crossed the room to the dresser where the maid had left a cut-glass ice bucket and refilled his glass with ice and Scotch. For a moment he stared at the wall, then turned. "I think I saw the boy one day. He was lurking around my car. I tried to talk to him, but I couldn't get anything out of him. I didn't think he spoke English. He took off down the driveway like I was pointing a gun at him. No wonder he didn't want to talk to me. He was—"

"Oh, Whit, stop." She flinched, propping herself on her elbows. "Please . . . I don't want to think about it." He nodded in glum assent, lifting his glass to his lips.

"So, what do we do now?" Caroline sighed, falling back into the pillow and examining her fingernails.

"I don't know. Imagine that? I really don't know. When's the last time I was at a complete goddamned loss?" He exhaled with what was almost a laugh. "October of twenty-nine, maybe, but this seems worse somehow." There was silence between them for a time, the only sound the ice cubes rattling in Whitney's drink and a moth beating its wings against the screen in the window.

Then Caroline sat up on the bed with a start. "You wouldn't cut her off, Whit? You're not thinking of . . . disowning her?"

"Children have certainly been disowned for less, dear."

"Yes, but she *is* our only child. I know this is a terrible mess, but we can't—"

"You're awfully tenderhearted all of a sudden, Caroline, everything considered."

"I'm sure I'm as upset, as . . . hurt as you are, but one must begin to think about . . . acceptance and, I suppose, the future, as it were. I just keep wondering what . . . how we're going to tell people."

"We'll tell them she eloped and then . . . oh, I don't know. Christ. I'm growing quite tired of thinking about it." He took a sip of Scotch and held it in his mouth for a moment before swallowing. He sat down on the bed. "Were we such terrible parents? Did I . . . did we . . . do something wrong? To think that she would—"

"Don't say it. Please. I told you it just makes me . . . sick."

"Well, we trusted her. Too damn much. Obviously that was a mistake. And now she's ruined her life." He glanced at his wife and noticed tears gathering in her eyes. "Oh, Caroline. Please don't start up again." He went into the bathroom and ran cold water over a washcloth, wrung it out and brought it to her. "Let me pour you a drink. What do you want, bourbon?"

"No. Nothing, thank you. I'm exhausted. Whit, when can we go home? I want to sleep in my own bed. I want to work in the garden and do normal things." She dabbed at her eyes with the washcloth.

"I'll talk to my sister tomorrow. I think we should leave Ellen here until we figure out where the hell the father is. At that point, we can make some kind of decision."

"Are you going to tell Ellen that?" Caroline asked, reaching for her brush.

"She'll be fine with it. She has Lily. She's better off here until we have something worked out."

After a moment of staring vacantly at a watercolor picture of daffodils her sister-in-law had purchased from the artist in Paris years before, Caroline shook her head slowly. "I can't believe I'm a grandmother. I never actually thought about it. If I had, maybe I could have imagined what it would be like, for my child to have a child. But I never could have come up with this." Once again, she dabbed at the tears in her eyes. She sighed, reached for her brush on the bedside table, and began to brush her hair.

Ellen pushed the navy-blue pram Lily had given her down the brick pathway across Washington Square to her usual bench in the shade beneath an umbrella-like maple tree. Thomas had fallen asleep during the stroll from her aunt's house. She pulled the cotton blanket away from his sweaty neck and settled down on the bench to read. Lily had encouraged her to read *To the Lighthouse*, but she had found Mr. Ramsay so hateful that she couldn't get through the first few chapters. She left the book in the basket under the pram and instead of reading allowed her mind to wander into the same labyrinth which entrapped her every day.

The baby was a month old and still nothing from Vittorio. Her frustration at the uncertainty was increasing, along with her fear, causing her to question her sanity as the dilemma worked itself like a disease into every moment of her consciousness and her dreams as well, which were troubled by memory and disturbing scenarios of the future. How could she think, or plan, or make sense of what was happening to her without knowing where he was? Dead? Alive? Alive and not intending ever to see her again? She missed him, their closeness, their conversations, their intimacy. Now that she'd been forced to tell her parents the truth about him, being completely exposed, it seemed too cruel not to be able to be with him.

The baby whimpered in his sleep. He would wake soon, hungry. She pulled the cover further over the pram to block the rays of sun which filtered through the tree as a light breeze swayed the boughs above them. Surveying the park, she saw the now-familiar league of mothers and children, some in groups where the women chatted as the children chased each other among their skirts and around the trees, others pushing their carriages up and down the pathways in the hope of prompting a nap. How unexpected to be among this sector of society as one of them. She had always imagined, since childhood, something different. Law school. A career. She had imagined something else for herself in reaction to this very phenomenon: women passing their days in the park bored while their babies slept, their children toddled about, and their husbands worked and played golf.

She wondered what Vittorio would want for her if they were together. Would he encourage her to go to law school? What would he expect from her? Would he want her to be like his mother? She frowned. They hadn't even had the chance to discuss those things.

Where could he possibly be? If she didn't have this living, breathing child in front of her, she might doubt that Vittorio had ever existed, might begin to suspect that the summer affair had been an elaborate trick her mind had played on her.

He'll be back, she concluded, just as Thomas began to stir again. The love she felt for the baby gave her strength and even hope when she was depressed, pulled her back from the edge of emotional collapse. He has to come back. He'll come back with a perfectly reasonable explanation, he'll be thrilled to meet his sweet little son, and we'll work the rest of this out. It has to happen that way. God, please . . . it has to happen that way.

In September, Caroline convinced her husband to write to Henry Cabot Lodge. Ellen remained in Philadelphia, daily growing more distressed. Caroline was concerned. Her sense of maternal obligation was beginning to override her fear of revealing Ellen's shameful secret to their friends.

Henry Cabot Lodge was a family acquaintance. He had followed Whitney at Middlesex and Harvard. They had many common friends, their families having moved in the same business and social circles for generations. Whitney had supported Lodge's senate campaign in 1936, and his reelection a year ago. Anxious for some resolution to Ellen's predicament, Caroline prevailed upon Whitney to contact the senator.

"My sincerest apologies for bothering you on such a trivial matter," his letter began. "You may remember my daughter, Ellen. I believe you met most recently at Sam Gardiner's wedding in Newport a few years ago. In any case, while at Radcliffe Ellen befriended a young man by the name of Vittorio Amorelli. They continued to correspond periodically after the young man was drafted. He went to Fort Dix and then to Fort McCoy in Wisconsin.

She hasn't heard from him in some time and has grown concerned. If it's not too much trouble, she would be most grateful, and I on her behalf, to know what has become of her friend."

"I suppose I should prepare myself to suffer further indignities such as this one," he complained to his wife before taking the letter to be cabled to Lodge in Washington. "Lodge will see right through this. He's a smart man. But it doesn't matter, does it? It's only a matter of time before everyone knows."

Senator Lodge responded within the week that of course he remembered Ellen, whom he described as "radiant," and that he had assigned the matter to a member of his staff.

Late in the month a letter on Lodge's Senate stationery arrived in the mail. "Sadly," he wrote, "the young man was killed in action in Sicily in August. He was serving O. Bradley as a translator during the invasion. A mine exploded under the vehicle in which he was riding somewhere near Enna. I'm afraid that's all I know. No word on where he is to be interred. My condolences to Ellen on the loss of her friend—another one of our fallen young heroes. Let us pray that there shan't be very many more."

Caroline wept when her husband read the letter to her, placing her hand on her chest and avoiding her husband's eyes. "Why are you crying, dear?" Whitney asked, surprised at her reaction. "It certainly simplifies things, doesn't it? I'm sorry for the boy and his family, but—"

"It's going to kill Ellen. She was living for him to come back. She thought they could . . . oh, poor Ellen." She covered her face.

"Well, maybe she should have thought before she—"

"Whitney, don't be an ass. Whether we like it or not, she was in love. I believe she really was in love with him. What a tragedy. Any way you choose to look at it, it's a terrible tragedy." She sighed. "Can we bring her home now? She's been at your sister's long enough. She's not Cornelia's responsibility. She's ours. We'll have to go to Philadelphia to tell her, and then we'll bring her back with us."

"And what do we tell people about the child? Are you ready to face that matter?"

"I really don't care anymore. Tell them what you want." She waved her hand in dismissal. "Either they'll come to support her, or they won't, and then we'll know who our friends are. She's our daughter, Whit. It's time for us to be the parents she needs. I'm certainly not proud of what she did, but we're going to hold our heads up and go forward."

Late at night, with the baby sleeping in his cradle between feedings, Ellen often could not hold off the nightmare: he was dead. She imagined that she could overcome any other scenario. If Vittorio was alive, somewhere, she knew she could eventually reach him and remind him of his love for her, convince him to return, and show him the way to a life together with their son. Even if he had found someone else or had been badly wounded.

But if he was dead . . .

She would turn on the light, put on her bathrobe, and sit in the rocking chair looking at the baby. The resemblance to his father was undeniable: his coloring, his straight forehead above the same black eyes, his hair and the slightest dent in his chin. She would smile, envisioning the two of them playing ball, walking in the park, building a snowman, reading a book, taking a nap. But if he was dead . . . how could she raise Thomas alone?

If he was dead, how would she know? How would she find out? No notification would be sent to her. No one would come to tell her. One especially difficult night, the first cool evening of the season, she resolved to go to the offices of the *Philadelphia Enquirer* to ask for assistance. There must be a listing of war casualties they would allow her to review. But the following morning the plan seemed overly morbid, and she abandoned it. She would remain focused on the idea that he was alive and unable to communicate with her for official reasons, as he had explained in his last letter months earlier.

She first learned of her parents' impending visit to Philadelphia from Cornelia at breakfast one morning in early October. "Why are they coming?" Ellen asked, half-interested, looking at the headlines in the paper as she nursed Thomas: the new Italian government was preparing to declare war on Germany; the Phillies' season was over after their ninetieth loss.

"Maybe they want to see their grandson," Cornelia offered.

"I doubt it." Ellen yawned. She was still in her nightgown, robe, and slippers, which she often wore until lunchtime. She rarely went to the park anymore, finding it too depressing to be around so many women who had husbands. Cornelia placed a cup of tea in front of her with lemon as she liked it. "They didn't seem so excited about him the last time they saw him."

"Now, Ellen—"

"Well, it's true, Aunt Cornie. There's no point in pretending. You should've seen their faces that first day in the hospital. They were outwardly appalled." She squeezed the slice of lemon into her tea with one hand. "So, really . . . why are they coming?"

"Sweetheart, people change their minds, don't they? They've had some time to think about it. They adore you, after all, and . . . "

Ellen admired her aunt's ability to identify the positive, even when it didn't exist.

"All right, then. I guess we'll just see."

"Give them a chance, Ellen. Everybody deserves a chance. You musn't forget how . . ."

"*Shocking* this all is for them. I know. Believe me, I know." She put the baby, dressed in a yellow-and-green-striped bunting, on her shoulder and began patting him on the back. "I'm fairly sure I won't be allowed to forget just how shocking it all is. Ever."

Cornelia crossed the room and stood behind her niece, stroking her hair. "Try to give them a chance, dear. You might need them one day."

Ellen's first instinct was that she would show them nothing. She would not allow them to see her crumple. She would not award them any vindication, no matter how carefully disguised, in their judgment of what she had done. She cleared her throat and asked to see Lodge's letter. They were sitting in the parlor. Cornelia had taken Thomas out in the pram, at Whitney's request, so they could have a chance to talk. Whitney and Caroline sat stiffly together on the sofa across from Ellen, who was in an armchair by the piano.

"I'm sorry, Ellen," her mother began. "Even though I wasn't . . . truly, I never . . ."

Ellen scanned the letter, ignoring her mother. "May I keep this?" she asked her father. She was struggling to contain all that was threatening to tear her apart, glancing anxiously at the door. They seemed sympathetic, but she imagined them receiving the senator's letter with a degree of relief.

"Yes, of course," her father replied. "I hope you understand that I only wrote to Senator Lodge with your best interests—"

"Thank you, Father." She was nearly whispering. She nodded her head and forced a terse smile. Then she stood, keeping her eyes on the door, crossed the room, pulled the door open and shut it softly behind her. Clutching the letter, she climbed the stairs to her room. She had shown them nothing, even as her soul and spirit were being crushed.

Sitting on the bed she reread Lodge's words: "killed in action in Sicily in August." He'd been dead for more than two months. She began to cry, scalding tears dropping from her eyes. He saw Sicily before he died.

Her grief unwrapped itself in layers: the human tragedy of a son who never knew his father, killed in his parents' homeland, leaving his twice-afflicted mother. Her own loss, the loss of her Victor—the one person whom she felt had truly loved her. The future heartbreak of her son, who would grow up without his father, their existences overlapping by only a few weeks, thousands of miles apart. The stark, colorless truth of her own situation, and the prospect of having to rely on her parents for everything.

Later she explained to a friend that in that moment a part of her had not so much died as been stunted forever in its growth—the part of her that could love, trust, feel pleasure, the part that Vittorio had awakened in her and that now would be frozen. She would never be the same.

Her mother knocked on the door and entered the room. Ellen wiped her eyes with the sleeve of her sweater and composed herself. Caroline sat down next to her on the bed, tentatively wrapping an arm around her daughter's waist. Ellen closed her eyes. She wanted to be alone. She needed to gather herself before Thomas returned. Somehow she had to go on being his mother, being strong for him despite the fact that she saw Vittorio every time she looked at him.

"Ellen, darling." Ellen kept her eyes closed, wishing her mother wouldn't speak. "I know I haven't always been the best—"

"Mother, really," Ellen jumped in. "You don't have to do this. It's not about us—you and me or you and me and Father. I just need a few minutes, okay? I'll be fine."

"I want you to listen for a moment, dear. Then I'll go. I know this is an awful time, unspeakably so. I just want to offer one small bit of assurance to you. I know I haven't always been the best mother, and that I've not . . . reacted well to the baby and all that's happened. I'm sure an apology probably won't mean much to you now." She pulled her daughter closer in an unfamiliar but tender gesture, reaching beyond the formality that had kept them at a distance. "But I want you to know that your father and I will do whatever you need us to do, from now on. We want you and Thomas to come home to our house. Nothing else matters now. Who even knows what tomorrow will bring—the war, it's all madness. You need us. You may not be happy about that Ellen, but you need us, and we want to take care of you and the baby."

Ellen wept as her mother spoke. She realized how alone she had felt since Thomas's birth, since Vittorio left, since—maybe always, except for when she was pulled close against Vittorio's bare chest. She was moved by her mother's sincerity and concern, but the tears came because she knew that her mother could never soften the grim aloneness that she now felt destined to inhabit like a prison for the rest of her life.

Lily and Aunt Cornelia saw them off on a cool, sunless morning. Ellen sat in the back of the Cadillac with Thomas wrapped in a blanket, sleeping in her arms. She turned to wave out the back window as her father pulled the car out of the driveway and onto the road. Her aunt and cousin blew kisses.

They were silent for most of the long ride. Thomas woke and nursed every two hours. In between, Ellen rested, having been unable to sleep at night, forlorn and shaken. Each of them tried, unsuccessfully, to think of ways to begin a conversation. There did not seem to be anything that would not be difficult, painful to discuss, or else so trivial as to be awkward, contrived. Ellen wondered when they would be able to talk again, how it would happen. She was aware that in many ways a new relationship would have to be formed, completely different than ever before. It would require a new vocabulary, new gestures and tones, different ways of looking at each other. She was no longer their independent, highly successful daughter with a promising future, about to go out into the world on her own. She was now an unmarried mother, disgraced, not even widowed officially, and dependent on them for everything. She shuddered.

It was evening when they arrived home in Lincoln. Ellen carried Thomas up to her room and, laying him on the bed, began to unpack her suitcases. Her mother entered the room with her father, who carried the last of her belongings from the trunk of the car.

"There, that's everything. Now, we have something to show you," her father announced, smiling. She noted that it was the first time he had smiled at her since before she told them she was pregnant. They led her, her mother taking her hand, to the next room, formerly a small spare bedroom, which they had remade as a nursery. A new furniture set, maple crib, changing table, and bureau were set neatly about the room, which had been painted a pale blue. There was also a rocking chair with a needlepoint cushion with butterflies, which Ellen recognized from the attic as the one her mother had used in Ellen's infancy. The crib was made up with sheets and a blanket of royal blue which matched the curtains on the single window. A smiling stuffed bear with a red bowtie lounged in the crib below a cheerful mobile which dangled brightly painted animal figurines: kittens, bunnies and ducklings.

Taking each by the arm, Ellen kissed her parents on the cheek, feeling visible to them in a way she rarely had. "I do understand how hard this is," she said. "Thank you. It's lovely. Just perfect."

Thomas was christened privately at St. Anne's-in-the-Fields on a Saturday afternoon during Advent. Lily and her husband, Philip, drove up from Philadelphia to serve as godparents. Their children stayed with Cornelia. When Ellen tried to hand Thomas to the priest for the baptism, the baby, normally placid—in fact nearly imperturbable so that Ellen often worried that on some level he intuited her grief and was quiet so as not to bother her—began to scream and thrash about in the white dress his grandmother had purchased for him, his tiny hands clenched into fists, his face turning crimson. The priest, a kind, elderly man who assisted the rector with such rites, was untroubled by the outburst, and allowed Ellen to hold the baby as he administered the water and then the chrism to his forehead.

Whitney thanked the priest in the narthex after the service. "Under the circumstances, I appreciate your willingness to do this," he stated, not looking at the man.

"There are no circumstances, Mr. Lathrop," the priest replied. "He's a child of God, just like the rest of us. I only hope we can all see it that way as he grows up."

"I'm trying," Whitney wanted to say, but he simply shook the priest's hand and walked away.

Ellen excused herself from dinner that evening, citing the baby's newly runny nose. Lily had suggested earlier in the day that they leave Thomas with Caroline and go into the city to see a movie. Ellen still hadn't left the baby for any long period of time, though, and wasn't ready to do so. More than that, however, she was tired and sad. She'd been struggling to be stoic, to convince her parents, and herself, that she was strong, and most importantly, not to show Thomas her sorrow. Yet the baptism was another reminder of Vittorio's absence and, though she had smiled through it, she was in pain.

"I'm afraid going out in the city doesn't sound like much fun, sweetheart," she had apologized to Lily. "It's not you. I just can't think about having fun yet. Not sure when I ever will. I feel like I need to sleep. I sleep almost as much as he does."

"Ellen, dear, don't be angry with me for saying this, but . . . as they say, you have the whole rest of your life ahead of you. You can't . . ."

"Do I? The whole rest of my life? I have the whole rest of the baby's life ahead of me. I think mine's essentially over, Lily." Since the shock of Vittorio's death, she'd been fixated on how he had described his mother's widowhood: stark, endless, draped in black.

"Honey, you're being melodramatic." Lily touched her cheek, pushing her head to the side slightly, reprovingly.

Ellen managed a fleeting smile. "Maybe I just need a little more time," she said.

ii.

The story Whitney Lathrop circulated through his business contacts was that Ellen had eloped in the days before her beau was to leave for officer training. The young gentleman had died heroically, leaving Ellen and the baby he sadly never met. Lathrop was uncertain that people believed the story. Ultimately he felt a respectable marriage was the only cover which, over time, might stomp out any smoldering whispers about his daughter and his grandson. Shortly after D-Day, when Thomas was a toddler and Whitney felt that enough time had passed, he invited a young acquaintance to lunch.

Edmond Wellington was the son of a business associate of Whitney's. He was a lawyer in the firm his grandfather had founded—Wellington, Devon and Fiske—and he was a widower. Wellington lived on Chestnut Street on Beacon Hill in a brick townhouse graciously decorated by his cherished wife, Celeste. The night Celeste died Edmond returned to the house alone. Early that morning, as her contractions intensified, she had begun to swell with edema. He rushed her to Women's Lying-In Hospital across town. The baby was stillborn, and Celeste succumbed shortly after, dying in his arms. He stood at the door of the nursery for nearly an hour, surveying the room his wife had prepared with care and her usual tasteful eye for detail. Then he pulled the door closed, never to open it again. The maid inquired about the room only once, asking if he wouldn't like for her to dispose of the articles in the nursery and return it to its previous form, a guest bedroom. Edmond shook his head and dismissed her, later leaving her a note instructing her to dust and clean the room as necessary when he was not at home, and not to speak of it again.

Whitney knew of the hardship that had befallen Edmond through the senior Mr. Wellington. Two years had passed since Celeste's death and Whitney, recognizing in the young attorney the qualities of a fine prospective son-in-law, asked his secretary to arrange a lunch.

He arrived at Locke-Ober early and, saluting the staff and dropping his hat on the bronze statue of *Gloria Victis,* took his normal place in the dining room with his back to the mahogany bar.

Edmond arrived promptly at their appointed time. Unsure about the reason for the meeting, he had inquired about Lathrop to his father, who told him only that Lathrop was a good person to know and that he should meet with him. Edmond was fashionably dressed in a gray suit with a sharp tie, his straw-colored hair brushed neatly to the side. He carried himself with confidence and poise, yet Whitney could see the melancholy like a shadow around his eyes, just like he saw it each day in Ellen's face. On first sight, he was heartened by the possibility of a match.

After rising to greet him and thank Edmond for coming, Whitney invited him to sit. Over lunch, Lathrop led Edmond in conversation, beginning with an explanation of his connection to Edmond's father, continuing through a discussion of Edmond's work in patent law, the state of the economy, the direction of the war following the D-Day landings and the German introduction of the flying bomb. Edmond found him interesting, perhaps a bit obsequious, but likable enough. He waited with curiosity for a point to emerge. At last, over coffee, Lathrop came to his purpose in asking for Edmond's time.

"Please understand my complete sympathy with you in the wake of the terrible tragedy you've suffered. Being a husband and a father myself, I can only imagine what a difficult time this has been for you. If I'm out of line here, please don't hesitate to say so." Edmond was watching him closely.

"No, sir. Please, continue," he answered, stirring his coffee. "You're a perfect gentleman, just as my father told me you were." Lathrop nodded gratefully.

"I have a daughter, Edmond, who, like you, has endured a tremendous heartbreak. Her fiancé was killed in the line of duty overseas, following the invasion of Sicily last summer." He knew he had to come closer to the truth here than he had with his colleagues.

"I'm very sorry." Lathrop noted the young man's sincerity.

"We all are. Thank you. I understand that this is delicate, of course. I also know what a fine young man you are."

"I appreciate your saying so."

"Edmond, would you be interested . . . willing, to join my wife and Ellen and me perhaps for tennis and lunch sometime?"

Edmond grinned, the broad smile he'd been known for earlier in life. "Aha! Well, I knew there had to be some reason for your wanting to see me, sir, but that's a curveball I didn't expect."

"I apologize, Edmond. As I said, it's quite delicate—even more so than meets the eye. I should tell you, before you answer, that there's a child involved." Edmond raised his eyebrows and tilted his head. "Ellen," he continued, trying unsuccessfully to keep his face from flushing, "has a son. He was born last summer . . . nearly a year ago. He's a lovely boy. Thomas, he's called. But, as you can see, the situation is a bit . . . complicated."

Edmond smiled again and took a sip of coffee. "Intriguing," he said after a moment. His instinct was to deflect, and politely refuse, but somehow Lathrop's earnest approach was drawing him in.

"So you'll come?"

"Why not?" He placed his cup back on the saucer. "I really hadn't planned on pursuing anything like this, much to my mother's great unhappiness. She thinks I should . . . well, anyway, why not? By the way, does Ellen know that you're out matchmaking on her behalf?"

"No. And that might be our greatest obstacle." Subtly Lathrop shifted to the first-person plural, as though they were now co-conspirators. "I'm hoping that if we keep it informal, and she meets you casually, she might—"

"So I'm meant to charm her?"

"Well . . ."

"I can't promise anything, Mr. Lathrop. Honestly, I'm quite rusty in that area. Rusty might not even be the word. But, I'm flattered to be asked." He paused, stifling a sudden feeling of self-doubt: perhaps it was a bad idea and he had said yes too quickly. "It would be hard to say no. So, I guess I can afford a game of tennis and lunch."

Whitney extended his hand across the table. "Thank you. You're every bit as noble as I've heard. Now, if I can just convince my daughter . . ."

Janet, Ellen's former roommate from Radcliffe, was the first of her friends who dared to visit. Janet had married in the spring—an MIT man she met at a dance senior year. His poor eyesight had kept him out of the military but, determined to aid the war effort, he was working for the Navy in a laboratory. Ellen was surprised at first to see her friend dressed in the style of a suburban housewife and with an enormous diamond ring, all grown up and no longer her daring partner in college adventures—but she was happy nonetheless for the company.

Nervous, not knowing what to say, Janet began by apologizing. "Ellen, I'm so sorry I haven't—"

"No apology needed, dear, really." She missed her friends, and felt that her path had diverged to the point that it was no longer connected to her old life. Janet was trying to cross a nearly unbridgeable gap. Ellen was grateful for the effort. "You've done more than most, just by writing from time to time, and you're the first to venture out to see us, so . . ." They were sitting on the terrace. Thomas was standing, holding onto Ellen's chair and bouncing up and down, singing quietly to himself. He wore khaki shorts and a bright red polo shirt and was barefoot.

"He's absolutely gorgeous, Ellen," Janet gushed, extending the word gorgeous. "Look at those eyes. His father must have been . . . I can't believe you kept him secret all that time, never brought him around to meet us."

"Yes, well, my turn to apologize, I suppose." Ellen looked out across the lawn towards the pond where her mother was discussing with the gardener the state of lilac bushes damaged during the winter. She wished it could be possible to chat idly and not broach the painful topic of her relationship with Vittorio.

"So . . . how are people taking it?"

"Ah, you should see. I'm the Hester Prynne of Lincoln. It's quite the scandal, as you can imagine. I try not to pay attention to the staring, though. I just go about my way, pushing him in his carriage." In truth, the staring bothered her and kept her close to home most of the time.

"But you said in your letter that your parents were telling people you had eloped and so forth."

"They are, or were. I don't know who believes it. Probably no one if they put the pieces together. Anyway, the latest is that they—my parents—have arranged a blind date for me." Thomas let go of the chair and sat down on the ground, letting out an attention-seeking yelp. Ellen leaned down to pick him up, settling him onto her lap and covering the top of his head with kisses. "This boy is the angel of my life, I have to say. I don't know that I would've made it without him. I think I need him more than he needs me sometimes." She wrapped her arms around him and pulled him close to her body. He cooed and gurgled.

"I'm glad you two have each other," Janet said, reaching out to stroke the baby's cheek with her finger and then letting her hand rest on Ellen's forearm for a moment. "So, what about this date?"

"Oh, he's a lawyer. Sounds nice enough." Ellen shrugged, embarrassed to disclose that she had to rely on her parents to find a date, something that would have seemed impossible in their Radcliffe days. "My father knows his father. You know how it works. I'm just surprised they were able to find someone willing to meet me, considering everything. We'll see. I really don't think I'm ready for anything like that, but . . . it's important to my parents. Anyway, I'm trying not to think about it too much." She shifted Thomas forward onto her knee and bounced him up and down gently. "But enough about all that. Tell me some news. Gossip!"

Thomas fell asleep in her arms as they talked. The maid brought them crabmeat-and-watercress sandwiches for lunch. For the first time in as long as she could remember, Ellen laughed, recalling their escapades from college days.

"Ellen," Janet suggested at one point, "we should arrange to go out some night, just like old times. Wouldn't that be fun? Can you leave the baby with your parents, or a babysitter?"

"I don't think so, dear, much as I might like to. I've only left him for very short stretches with my mother or my cousin. My parents have been encouraging me. They even offered to hire a nanny so I could do something during the day—take a class or two. But I don't have any desire to leave him, honestly. I can't think of anything else I'd really care to be doing right now." She shifted Thomas from one side to the other gently, so as not to wake him, and brushed his forelock to the side. "I'm not ready to face the world just yet." She was aware that she repeated those words in nearly every conversation she had.

The now-familiar loneliness returned later in the day when Janet said goodbye. Ellen had enjoyed the visit, yet the divide between her new life and her old life appeared wider than ever. She felt sure it could not be crossed.

The doubles match narrowed to singles. Ellen's mother claimed fatigue after a respectable few minutes. Her father, showing off the grass court—his pride—which balanced Caroline's gardens on the other side of the house, volleyed at the net in front of Ellen until he sensed the time was right to leave them.

"I must go check on your mother and lunch," he explained, patting his forehead with a white towel and screwing his racket into its wooden frame. "You two enjoy yourselves." Ellen smirked at his transparency. Matilda, the maid, and not her mother, would be preparing lunch. Her parents would be busy watching furtively from the window.

She watched her father walk away across the lawn, imagining how relieved her parents would be to find a husband for her, though she knew they would miss the baby. Her parents had become attached to Thomas to an extent that surprised them as much as it did her. As grandparents, they were able to find pleasure in his daily discoveries and achievements differently than they had been able to do with Ellen in the midst of the occupations and commitments of their earlier lives. In the process they had grown closer to Ellen as well—closer than they had been in years—enough so that Ellen, looking across the net at Edmond, was willing to consider the possibility that they had, at least in part, her best interests in mind.

She served the ball, which Edmond skillfully returned to her backhand. The ball traveled back and forth across the net three more times before Ellen hit a passing shot that Edmond could not reach but which sailed half a foot beyond the baseline. He's a good tennis player, she thought, and I suppose rather dashing in his tennis clothes. Nice straight teeth. Sandy hair. The blue eyes. Narrow nose. Just the type I might have ended up with in the first place.

She bounced the ball against the ground with her racket and glanced again at Edmond. She sighed: resignation. Victor was never coming back. She was furious at him for that and felt an urge she knew was irrational to hurt him, to hurt his memory. And she felt a duty to her parents. They had, in the end, supported her through this time, and Edmond was everything they would want in a son-in-law. It would merely be a surrender to the way of the world. If it wasn't Edmond, eventually it would have to be someone like him.

"Your ad," she called across the net, and then served. Edmond's return was short. She punched it as it came off the ground, lobbing it toward the back of the opposite court, and hurried to the net to volley. Edmond stepped back with agility, circling to his forehand, and sent the ball past her outstretched racket and down the sideline for a winner.

"Game. Nice shot." Ellen smiled, applauding with her hand and the head of her racket.

"Lucky," he answered, smiling back. He was taken with her, surprisingly so. She was lovely: strong, confident, and pretty. He had decided to think of Whitney Lathrop's unsolicited and unexpected invitation as a sign that it was time to emerge from his long period of mourning. In the few weeks since their lunch, he had reassessed his life, both the fact of Celeste's death and the reality of the decades that lay ahead of him, and had come to the Lathrop's house open to a new possibility.

He had tried to hide his reaction to Thomas. Ellen saw it on his face from the corner of her eye only because she instinctively watched for it with everyone who met Thomas. No one would ever mistake the boy for his son, he considered as they switched ends of the court. There would always be plenty of explaining to do. But on balance they might make an interesting family. Everyone had scars, and he'd always wanted a family. He had given up on the idea after Celeste's death, but now, unexpectedly . . .

Stuffing a ball into his pocket, he served across the net to Ellen. She hit a hard shot directly back to him, which he miss-hit defensively, sending the ball into the net.

"I guess I should stick to serving to your backhand," he said admiringly, walking to the net to pick up the ball. "Your father said you were on the team at Radcliffe."

"He managed to work that into the conversation, did he?" She laughed, rolling her eyes. "Yes, it's true. I haven't played much since, though. I play with him once in a while when my mother won't, or when he and his friends need a fourth for doubles."

"Well, I guess I'm fortunate then—to catch you when you're out of practice, that is. Wouldn't want to see that forehand when you're at your best."

"You're very kind." He was still standing at the net, showing no signs of returning to position at the service line, and so she walked closer. "Listen, Edmond," she said, looking down at the ground, "I'm not sure what else my father told you to get you to agree to this, but now you've met Thomas and I'm sure you can see that there's a story there, and . . . I don't like feeling like . . . a charity case or something. So if . . ."

"Hold on. Stop. Excuse me, but you're about to insult me, and I won't have that. And, by the way, you're hardly a charity case." She blushed, surprising herself. "Look, Miss Lathrop, if we're going to be candid, my life hasn't turned out exactly as I might have planned it either. There's a story there too." Ellen frowned empathetically. She knew the story. It was a large part of the reason she'd agreed to meet him—their shared experience of tragedy, which few of their peers could understand. "I wasn't looking for dates before your father called, believe me. After he invited me to meet you, I thought about it and just decided to be open to . . . I don't know, to living again, or . . . I'm not making any sense, which isn't good for a lawyer." Their eyes met. Ellen saw the sadness in his, and he the shame in hers. "You don't need to protect me, if that's what you're trying to do."

"Fair enough," Ellen said and nodded after a moment. "Fair enough. I believe it's your serve?" She turned on her heel and walked back across the court.

Lunch was less awkward than either of them had anticipated. Edmond was careful to avoid mentioning the war, but the four of them, with Thomas chattering in his highchair, conversed with ease about the upcoming election, Roosevelt's health, Edmond's practice, and the spectacular fall foliage. Afterwards, at her mother's urging, Ellen walked him to his car.

"Shall we put ourselves through this wretched ordeal again sometime?" he asked, turning to face her and catching her eye with a wink.

Ellen extended her hand for him to shake. She appreciated that he could make light of the situation. "Why not? Doesn't look like either of us has too much left to lose."

"Well said. Now, do I have to schedule through your father, or do you think we can take it from here?"

"Very funny. I'll wait to hear from you."

The courtship lasted a year. Edmond became a regular visitor at the Lathrop home: tennis, Sunday dinners, walks in the woods. He and Ellen were comfortable around each other. They had everything in common by way of upbringing and could enjoy each other's company without feeling like it was work. Edmond grew fond of Thomas and the boy began to look forward to his visits. "Edman" was among his first words. Ellen appreciated the way he would get down on the floor and play with Thomas, patiently showing interest in whatever attracted the child's attention. He seemed able to interact with Thomas as a person, separate from the context of being a man dating his mother.

Occasionally, reluctantly, Ellen would leave Thomas with her parents and she and Edmond would drive to the city for an evening out, dinner and a movie or a show, even dancing. Time and again on such occasions they expressed to each other their amazement at finding themselves having fun.

Caroline and Whitney were thrilled by the developing relationship: the promise of an end to Ellen's grief and the dawning of an acceptable resolution to their nightmare.

There were times, though, when memories threatened to bring down any potential there may have been. They seemed to Ellen like aftershocks from an earthquake that shakes whatever remains stable and upright. She strained to steady herself when she felt a sudden, visceral urge to end the relationship. As time progressed, though, she began to accept the idea that she was not betraying Vittorio or dishonoring her love for him, but rather pursuing the best possible life for his son. The boy needed a father. Edmond was a suitable candidate.

He proposed Labor Day weekend. The war had ended three weeks earlier, bringing an atmosphere of relief and hope. The future no longer had to be spoken of in the conditional. Edmond had accompanied the Lathrops to Martha's Vineyard for the holiday. A tropical storm at sea brought gray skies and light rain, chasing sunbathers and children from South Beach. Edmond and Ellen strolled down the shore alone, arm in arm in their rainslickers. Edmond felt himself trembling. He was nervous, and at one point nearly lost his resolve. The relationship had moved slowly. He'd been patient, gentlemanly, taking his cues from her. Yet maybe it was still too soon, he reasoned. He didn't want to scare her away, or to discover unhappily, embarrassingly, that he was miles ahead of her.

She leaned into him as they walked. Wrapping his arm around her, he turned to watch her gazing out at the dark waves battering the beach. She seemed to love him. She seemed to be more relaxed, more at ease than when they had met. She seemed happier—happy to be with him, and less distracted by sadness. He, too, felt much differently about life—less burdened, more positive. Perhaps they had helped each other heal, moving out of bad times into better.

"Ellen, I want to ask you a question," he said at last, his voice shaking almost imperceptibly with the sound of the wind. He stopped walking and took her in his arms.

"What is it, dear?"

"I've been thinking a lot about . . . us and the past year and . . . the future. I think we're good for each other, Ellen. I know you're good for me, and I hope I'm good for you. We've both been through a lot, but I think we've been better since we've known each other. I feel very strongly that . . ." He paused, then, feeling foolish, dispensed with the speech. Reaching into the pocket of his raincoat, he produced a ring, a large diamond solitaire set on a platinum band. "Ellen, will you marry me?"

"Oh, Edmond. Wow." She wasn't truly surprised, though seeing the ring and hearing the words waylaid her briefly. He was watching her face and read the reaction as negative.

"I'm sorry," he stammered, uncharacteristically flustered. "I didn't mean to . . . I mean, you don't have to answer. Maybe you need some time to think and I shouldn't have—"

"It's okay. Shh." She placed a finger over his lips. "Yes. The answer is yes."

"It is?"

"Of course it is, silly. Don't look so shocked." She took his hand. "You've been so good to me and to Thomas. You've won our hearts, which wasn't so easy. I will marry you, Edmond. The answer's yes."

"Ha! Ellen. I can't tell you how—relieved I am. I was afraid you weren't . . ." He stopped and shook his head, seeing in her eyes a brightness that seemed truly to be delight. For a moment he thought of Celeste and the night he had proposed to her. "I wasn't sure I could ever feel this way again. You've given that back to me. I feel very happy right now." He took her hand in his and pushed the ring onto her finger.

"It's beautiful, darling," Ellen whispered, inspecting her outstretched hand. "Absolutely beautiful. Thank you. It's perfect." She lifted her face and kissed him. "Now, we have to go back and tell everyone!"

"Your father already knows. I spoke to him last night after dinner and he gave me his blessing."

"Aren't you sneaky?" she chided, poking him in the stomach. He opened his arms and they embraced, her head resting on his shoulder. "I never would have believed this a year ago," she murmured.

The Wellingtons, Edmond's parents, were swayed from their half-hearted opposition to the engagement without difficulty. While not anxious to associate their family name with a scandal, they were won over by Ellen and even by her young son, who was sweet and well-mannered if rather shy. She was from an excellent family, well brought up. Considering the pain their son had endured, they could not stand between him and happiness.

Ellen and Edmond were married in a subdued ceremony, attended by family only at St. Anne's on a bright Saturday morning the following May. Ellen, with Lily standing beside her, wore a simple but elegant gown, tinted the lightest possible shade of mauve. She carried daffodils and tulips from her mother's garden. Edmond's brother Jay stood with him as the priest, the same man who had baptized Thomas, presided. Thomas, in a blue suit, led by his grandfather, brought forward the rings. He was nearly three years old. Though he didn't understand the meaning of the occasion, the words the priest spoke, the fancy clothes, the tears—he was pleased as always to see his mother and Edmond together.

Whitney offered a toast to open a celebratory luncheon back at the Lathrop house, which had been decorated with flowers and lanterns for the occasion, congratulating himself on his own good taste in choosing a son-in-law. Everyone gathered agreed that they were a handsome, well-matched couple, and they were showered with good wishes.

Theirs may not have been the great, passionate romance each had known with another before, but it somehow made sense. They'd been raised in the same milieu. They shared the experience of loss and brokenheartedness. They had become friends. Perhaps it was more mathematics than chemistry: the three of them added together equaled a family. And simply through stability, normalcy, comfortableness, they found together a measure of restoration.

Edmond agreed to sell the townhouse on Beacon Hill. The lingering presence of Celeste—it was her home—combined with its proximity to the North End and places Ellen associated with Vittorio . . . Ellen couldn't imagine living there, and, in fact, had never even been to see it.

In its place they bought a gabled brick house on peaceful Tyler Street in Belmont, halfway up Belmont Hill above Edmond's ancestral homestead, the Wellington Farm, established by his forebear Roger Wellington, Belmont's original settler, in the 1630s. There was plenty of room and a nice yard for Thomas and his friends to play.

Ellen and Edmond's honeymoon was four days at his parents' summer estate in Chatham. Ellen had agreed to the plan, knowing that it was important to her new husband, but uncomfortable with leaving Thomas for so long. The following weekend they moved into their new home. The house had been decorated and furnished under the direction of Caroline, with input from Ellen and Edmond's mother, Adele. Mrs. Lathrop's gardener had tended to the grounds, neglected in recent years by the previous occupants, revitalizing the flower beds and grooming the overgrown shrubs.

Caroline, Whitney, and Matilda gathered to see Ellen and Thomas off late in the day on Saturday. Edmond put Ellen's last suitcase into the trunk of his car. Thomas had woken from his nap and was clinging to Ellen's neck. Ellen was surprised to see the emotion on the faces of both of her parents.

"Come on, you three," she quipped, including the maid who was sniffling into a handkerchief. "Don't start with that. We're just down the road. We'll be over all the time. And you know where to find us." With his usual quiet aplomb Thomas endured a round of effusive kisses and hugs before settling into his mother's lap in the backseat of the car. Ellen opened the window to wave as they drove away.

The week of Thomas's third birthday they received the official document in the mail: the adoption was complete. Thomas, son of Vittorio Amorelli, was now Thomas Lathrop Wellington.

iii.

More easily than Ellen might have anticipated, they settled into family life. Edmond accustomed himself to the daily commute into the city. Ellen hired a maid and a gardener. They joined the Belmont Country Club and All Saints' Church.

They learned to ignore the poorly disguised stares and awkward comments when they were out together in public. Not only did Thomas look nothing like Edmond, but it was even hard to imagine that the toddler could be Ellen's son. Ellen knew that the whispers would never completely stop, but instead would continue subtly, like mice scuttling through the walls of a house. The story was too good for even a restrained gossip to forgo.

She managed to make friends with a few other young mothers in the neighborhood. Each of them politely pretended not to notice the color of Thomas's hair, skin and eyes. Eventually, however, once the friendship was established, none could resist: "Is it true what people say about his father?" "You don't have to answer if you don't want to, but why does Thomas look so . . . different?" "Not that it's any of my business, Ellen, but . . ." She rarely provided enough of an answer to satisfy the inquisitor; never told the whole story, or the whole truth. Edmond brushed aside similar questions, declaring to his friends or colleagues that Ellen was entitled to her privacy.

His parents made every effort to insulate Thomas from the secret of his identity and his ethnic difference. He didn't know that he was Sicilian, or that Edmond wasn't his father, or that there was anything scandalous about his paternity. With the war over and the economy charging forward, he enjoyed, like other children of his class, a privileged childhood. He learned to swim, to play tennis, to ride a horse, to play the piano, even to speak French. But Ellen observed him as he grew, daily seeing in his eyes a look that she knew would lead him one day to a Rubicon. He was overall a reserved boy, pensive at times, though never exactly brooding. He enjoyed his activities and his friends. Ellen sensed, though, that something was restrained, held back.

Thomas was six when his younger sister Ashley was born. Ellen had been reluctant to have another child, knowing that a sibling, or half-sibling, would bear out her son's unformed sense of differentness. For a while Edmond had agreed, more than anything out of fear that he would lose Ellen as he had lost Celeste. The question wouldn't go away, however, and finally Ellen agreed.

Sometime after two o'clock in the morning on the baby's first night home from the hospital, Thomas was awakened by her crying. He wandered into the nursery, peeking over the edge of the crib as his mother changed Ashley's diaper. "Is this going to happen every night?" he asked sleepily.

"I know she doesn't seem like much fun now," Ellen said, "but someday I think you two will have fun together." Eventually, he would come to appreciate having a sister, another presence in the house, and one of the only people with whom he could be comfortable without being guarded. Her first word was 'Tom,' she took her first steps holding on to his hands, and she always insisted that he read her a story before bed. Thomas sometimes pretended to be annoyed, but he accepted her affection and felt responsible for her as they grew up.

One afternoon not long after Ashley's birth, Thomas ambled into the house after school and sat down at the kitchen table. The baby was sleeping in Ellen's arms and Ellen was reviewing the shopping list with Molly, the maid. She stopped mid-sentence, recognizing immediately that Thomas was presenting more than his usual reserve. He scowled down at the cookies and milk Molly had set in front of him.

"Hi, Tom," Ellen said gently. "Gee, you look a little blue. Everything okay?" Thomas scratched his head behind his ear and poked at a cookie with his finger.

"How come Ashley doesn't look like me?" he growled after a moment. He was right: Ashley's wispy hair was blond, with perhaps a touch of auburn. Her forehead was broad like Edmond's and, like his, her eyes were blue. Her nose was Ellen's, as were her lips and chin. Her skin was pale with bluish veins showing through around her temples. Ellen tensed, sensing accusation in his voice, and then a billow of sadness filled her. She had hoped for his sake for more time, for a longer period of innocence, a greater reprieve.

"Molly . . ." she managed to say after a moment. Molly had been frozen by Thomas's question. She too had wondered when the boy would begin to ask about his origins.

"I'll take the baby." Ellen stood to lay Ashley in Molly's arms, breathed, and then pulled her chair next to Thomas.

"So what's this all about, Tom?"

"How come I have dark hair and black eyes, and Ashley doesn't?" Ellen brushed his hair back from his forehead, noting a salty, dried path of tears on his face. She felt like crying herself.

"Tell me why you're asking, sweetheart." Thomas looked down, tracing the lines on his palm with the forefinger of his other hand. He swallowed, and then swallowed again.

"You can tell me, honey," Ellen assured him, putting an arm around his shoulders. The afternoon sun emerged from behind a cloud, shining through the window over the sink and illuminating Thomas's face.

"Geoffrey Hunt said his mommy said that Daddy isn't my real daddy." Ellen closed her eyes. Geoffrey's mother Linda had been a classmate at Radcliffe. They did not socialize in the same group and Ellen had never paid much attention to her. "Geoffrey said that's why I don't look like my daddy."

"Oh, Tom. I'm so sorry Geoffrey said that to you." She stroked his head.

"Is it true?"

"Well . . . being someone's daddy is about more than just looking like someone." She paused, choosing her words. "You had another daddy, but he couldn't be with us." The words she was choosing grieved her sharply, revising history so that Vittorio barely existed, but she thought it was the best answer she could give. "Daddy is your real daddy, and he's been your real daddy since you were a baby. He loves you so much. He loves you as much as any daddy could love a son. People might say strange things to you sometimes, like Geoffrey did, but I want you to remember that you belong to me and Daddy, and you always will, and Ashley is your own baby sister, and always will be. Do you understand?"

"Do I look like my other daddy? My first daddy?"

"Yes, you do. You look a lot like him."

"Why couldn't he be with us?" His voice was thin and tight, insistent.

Ellen smiled. No wonder she had dreaded this day for years. She debated with herself for a moment. Would it be better or worse if he knew his father was dead? He would be sad to think of his father as dead, but likely angry to think that his father was somewhere in the world and not in his life.

"Your daddy had to go away, Tom, before you were born, and he wasn't able to come back." She cringed inwardly, but plowed forward, before he could ask why again. "The most important thing to remember is that Daddy is your daddy. He is a wonderful daddy, and he has known you almost your whole life. He'll always be here to take care of you and to help you grow up to be a man." She watched his face as the information registered in his mind. There would be time to tell him more, when he was ready, she thought, biting her lip. This was best for now. She was afraid of her own feelings and how much they could still swell within her.

"Do you want me to call Geoffrey Hunt's mother and talk to her about this?"

Thomas nodded. She kissed the top of his head. "Consider it done. Now, let's clean up your face and go get that baby sister of yours. We just have time for a walk before Daddy gets home. Eat your cookies, quick, quick."

She tried to convince herself in the days and then months following that Thomas was not more reticent and remote than he had been before.

Though there was no one in his life who could have told him so, Thomas was made in the image of his grandfather, Tommaso. His hair, the shimmering blackness of coal, gathered to form ringlets above his ears and at the nape of his neck if he went too long without a haircut. His eyes were equally dark, the pupils indistinguishable from the iris except in the brightest light, when they took on a gold-cinnamon hue. His face was Amorelli: broad through the forehead, narrowing across high cheekbones down to a slightly jutting chin. His neck was long and slender, with an

Adam's apple that became prominent after puberty. And, like his grandfather, he had a strong, lean body and the innate sense of balance of fishing people.

He grew accustomed to the comments, both those about adoption which they encountered as a family, to which Edmond was particularly sensitive, and those from other children based in natural curiosity. Later, as the comments from his peers took on a tone of derision and even cruelty, he inured himself by withdrawing as much as possible from social interaction.

His teachers reported that he was a good student, focused, independent and bright. They joined his parents in encouraging him to be more outgoing, to try to make friends. He felt that he could not. He didn't seem unhappy, at least not evidently, just quiet, reserved, shielded. He was never sullen. He rarely complained about anything and was generally kind to his sister. With the approach of adolescence, though, Thomas more and more took on the label he would carry throughout his youth: loner. He ate his lunch alone and often brought a book to read at recess, not far from the watch of the teacher who would be available to interfere with anyone who might take aim to amuse others at his expense. After school, he completed his homework neatly and efficiently without pressure from Ellen, and then read, or went off alone to explore the wooded acres below the house.

His single interest which unavoidably involved other people was the church. All Saints' Church was a long wooden building with a low gothic tower, a handsome New England structure where Belmont's upper-class, low-church citizens went to worship. Early on, Thomas expressed both a fascination with and an uncharacteristic ease in church, based less in spirituality than in a love for the liturgy and music. Father Young, who was sympathetic to the boy's plight, fostered this connection. Thomas became an acolyte, serving proudly in his cassock and cotta, and assisted the ushers on Sundays when he was not assigned to the altar. Avoiding Sunday school, he was content to sit through the service with Edmond and his mother, following the sermon as best he could and singing the hymns softly to himself with pleasure.

Eventually, the rector convinced Thomas to participate in the Confirmation program. Thomas beamed on the day when Bishop Nash laid large, heavy hands on the boy's head. The bishop smiled with a warmth that cut through to Thomas. He decided, secretly, that he would grow up to be a priest.

"St. Paul's was the best thing that ever happened to me," Edmond argued.

"No."

"Ellen, you're not being reasonable," said Edmond. Thomas was twelve, a decision was imminent, and Edmond was campaigning for boarding school. "He loves to learn. He's a natural student. He'll be challenged. It's the finest prep school in the country."

"That's not why you want to send him there." She was sorting through the mail inattentively.

"What are you trying to imply, dear? That I don't want my son around? Ellen, please . . ."

"Look, Edmond, you've been wonderful with him all along—more than I ever could have hoped for. I know you want what's best for him. I'm just not comfortable sending him away from home."

"I'm telling you, Ellen, maybe a female can't understand, but it was the best thing that ever happened to me. I learned to be independent, to take care of myself. I mean, maybe that's part of the problem—he's too tied to you."

"Not being independent is hardly his problem, dear. If he were any more independent he'd just float off the surface of the earth into space."

"Ellen, I just feel that going away from here, a new beginning, a . . . fresh context might help him overcome his . . . situation."

"Oh, Edmond, good God." Ellen dropped the mail on the table. "You make it sound like he has a disease. He's not handicapped. Just because his father wasn't a WASP."

"That's not called for," Edmond shot back.

"I'm sorry. Okay? The fact is that I'm not willing to send him off into an environment which may or may not be welcoming of him, and where I can't see how it's affecting him every day. It's hard enough for me to guess what he's thinking and feeling when I do see him every day. I'm not putting down St. Paul's, Edmond. I know you love the school. I just want to keep him closer for as long as I possibly can. There's a perfectly good school a five minutes' walk from here. Belmont Hill may not have the tradition of St. Paul's, but it's got a fine reputation." She paused. "I need your support here, Edmond. He looks to you, and I want him to know that you want him around too." Edmond had been standing, hands on hips, watching her speak, occasionally rubbing his forehead with his fingertips. Now he threw his hands up in the air.

"So, after all this time, you're saying that he's your son, and you're going to make the decisions."

"If you want to look at it that way, that's your choice. I feel strongly that sending him to St. Paul's would be a mistake. Period."

In the autumn of 1955, Thomas enrolled at the Belmont Hill School.

'Tomato' (as in Tom-ato), was the nickname a clever fellow student gave him. He hated it, as he hated anything that called attention to his ethnicity. He was the only one with Southern-European heritage in his class of forty-six boys, and the only one with black hair and olive complexion; a Wellington among Cornwalls, Thayers, Wadsworths, Livingstons and Peabodys, yet clearly disparate. Disappointingly, he was not a satisfying or entertaining object of mockery. Too diffident to respond in anger, he simply shrugged off the remarks his classmates made.

Over time, Thomas accumulated respect in the principal way respect was gained at Belmont Hill: through athletics. Though football and hockey were the only paths to true heroism, Thomas proved himself on the soccer field, where he was a fleet and agile right wing, and on the tennis court, where Edmond's rigorous lessons bore fruit. He was a less successful wrestler, primarily because he was repelled by the inescapable physical contact with another human being. Midmatch he would become nauseated and would often vomit following his almost inevitable loss.

Proof that his contributions as an athlete were recognized was that his teammates began to defend him, standing up to opposing players who, particularly in a losing cause on the soccer field, would call him "guido," or "wop," or even "spic" or "wetback."

Yet he remained friendless, largely due to his unwillingness to respond to any overtures of friendship. He distrusted the motivations of others and preferred to keep to himself, a practice that led to his appearing on the superlatives page of the senior yearbook as the shyest. Edmond and Ellen encouraged, even cajoled him to join Lyceum, the debating club, or the science club, or to join the staff of the school newspaper, *The Panel*. He wasn't willing.

"I see there's a social next weekend with Windsor," Ellen said to him one evening at dinner. "Have you thought about going?"

"I haven't, Mother," he said. "It's not really my type of thing." He found the question irritating, as it seemed she had no understanding of his existence, his fear that no one would want to dance with him and he would feel foolish and exposed.

Thomas dedicated himself to his studies and excelled academically. He was always happy to stay home with Ashley, playing games or listening to her favorite shows on the radio, *Cisco the Kid* and *Round the Bend*. And he maintained his commitment to the church. Eventually he graduated from service as an acolyte and was trained to assist the priest at the monthly Eucharist, bearing the chalice in his black cassock and surplice.

His parents despaired over him to a degree, wishing they could in some way draw him out, imbue him with confidence or at least encourage him to be slightly more outgoing. He assured them, repeatedly, that he was fine, promising them that he was not unhappy even when he was, hoping they would stop "making a fuss." They made appointments with Mr. Hamilton, the headmaster of Belmont Hill, Mr. Densmore, head of the lower school, and later Mr. Jenney, who oversaw the upper school. They too assured the distressed parents that Thomas, while quieter than most, was not exhibiting any troubling behaviors, and that he must be allowed to find his way.

During the fall of Thomas's senior year, it came to Ellen's attention that the art teacher, Arturo Castiglione, had recently traveled to Naples for a family reunion. Ellen quietly made an appointment to see him. Though rumors abounded, she had never been direct with Mr. Hamilton or anyone else in Thomas's schooling about the boy's paternity. Sensing Castiglione's compassionate spirit, and imploring his discretion, she disclosed to him the secret history.

"Mrs. Wellington, I do appreciate your trust, and I'm quite moved by your story and by your concern for Thomas." Castiglione was nearing retirement. His round face was framed by gray curls. Wearing an argyle sweater under his tweed coat, he leaned back in the chair in his office, surrounded by the paintings and sketches a generation of students had given him. "Of course, I always imagined that he was Italian—somehow. I have to say, this information might have been useful to us earlier. I certainly have a much better understanding . . ."

"*Now* you have a much better understanding. If I had told you at the beginning, I was concerned that people might treat him as though he weren't . . . normal. Edmond and I have always wanted that for him more than anything—that in spite of everything, he might feel like a normal boy. Being from a different ethnic group, being born out of wedlock, having his father die—we didn't want him to be . . . branded by all of that."

"I see. So, why are you telling me now, just a few months before graduation?"

Ellen sighed. Thomas was nearly eighteen, about to graduate and go on into adulthood. Though in some ways she did not feel as though she had ever had him completely, that she had ever been as deeply connected to him as she imagined other parents were with their children, she was preparing to lose him. At this transition in his life and in hers, she was questioning herself, wondering if her decisions, heavily influenced by Edmond, had been right for him. There had been benefits in trying to give him a "normal" life, but there had been drawbacks as well. Had she raised him falsely somehow, denying him something greater than she'd been able to give him? She sometimes remembered the community around Vittorio in Gloucester and the North End, and despaired that her son missed out on that connection. What kind of damage had she done? Was her son broken?

She hadn't taken off her cashmere coat when she came inside, chilled as she was by the damp, early March weather. Now she wrapped it more tightly around herself, sinking deeper into the chair.

"I was hoping you might be willing to talk to him," she said. Castiglione smiled. "Mr. Castiglione, I honestly don't know what he thinks—about being Italian, about being different. He doesn't talk to me or to Edmond. He just says he's fine. Always, fine. We just don't know how to talk to him about it, and I thought maybe— since you're . . . I mean, what do I know about being Italian?" She laughed nervously and shrugged. "Maybe he would open up to you, and . . . I don't know." She folded her hands together as though she were begging.

Castiglione was silent for several moments, watching Ellen's face. She had recently turned forty, and as she smiled there were thin lines running away from her eyes. It occurred to him that if he were to paint her, he would struggle to convey both her beauty and her deep regret, which, though she attempted to hide it, was like blood seeping through a bandage. It was carried in every muscle on her face, in the way she held her shoulders hunched slightly forward as though she were about to do something but couldn't figure out how to begin.

"Mrs. Wellington, I don't pretend to be a counselor. There are others on the staff here at Belmont Hill who are surely better equipped to help with this than I. Again, I appreciate your trust, but . . ."

"Please, sir." Feeling her throat tighten, she swallowed. "Mr. Castiglione, I'm afraid I've made some mistakes. I need your help. It can't be anyone else. It has to be you, because you're . . ."

"Italian."

"Don't you see? He needs someone who could understand."

He nodded. "Okay, Mrs. Wellington. This is what I'm willing to do—more than anything because I feel badly for the boy. Tell him that we've had this conversation, and that I'm available to him. Tell him I'd be glad to speak with him, on his terms. It has to be on his terms."

Mr. Castiglione waited through the remainder of the semester, but Thomas never came to see him. At first, he wondered if Ellen had ever told Thomas about their conversation. But after a while he felt sure that the young man was avoiding him.

Along with nine other members of the class of 1961, Thomas was admitted to Harvard. He appeared in the Belmont Hill yearbook in a jacket with the school seal on the chest pocket and a narrow tie, as was the style that year. His hair was cut short and combed back in a slight wave with Brill cream. He smiled slightly, at the corner of his lips, only because the photographer had insisted.

All four of his grandparents joined Edmond, Ellen, and Ashley at graduation, listening to an address by Dr. Ell, Chancellor of Northeastern University, and applauding proudly as Thomas received his diploma from Mr. Hamilton. Afterwards, they went to lunch at the country club.

A month later, he turned eighteen. To comply with the law, Edmond took him to the town hall in Belmont to register for the draft.

iv.

Ellen held back her tears until she and Edmond left Thomas's room and began walking down the two flights of stairs back to Harvard Yard. She had helped him unpack his two suitcases into half the closet and a bureau and had made his bed. His room was on the side of Straus overlooking the Square, his window divided by mullions into twenty-four small panes through which one could see crowds of people moving slowly through the overcast, muggy afternoon. Ellen held him at the door for longer than was comfortable, especially considering the heat. Edmond gave him a strong handshake and clapped him on the back. Thomas smiled. As always, he didn't want his mother to worry. "I'm just a couple miles down the road, Mother," he assured her. "I'll see you in a few weeks."

His roommate, a cellist from Newport who had been to Exeter, arrived shortly after. Taylor Bowen was tall and angular. Thomas thought he looked like a stork or a flamingo when he played his cello, which he did in the room on weekends when the music department was closed. As a fallback to music, he planned to study chemistry, possibly for premed. He kept to himself, spending his time practicing or studying, on occasion drinking gin from a crystal glass and playing cribbage with a friend from Exeter who was equally introverted. Bowen seemed to find it distasteful to have Thomas as a roommate. There were few in a class of 1,091 men who were not patently Anglo-Saxon. That he had drawn one of the few as a roommate was a bother. As confusing as it was that Thomas had the proper pedigree despite his Mediterranean appearance, Bowen was never curious enough to ask about his roommate's background. The two rarely entered into conversation but, rather, existed in the same confines nearly heedless of the other.

Thomas would have preferred to remain as anonymous to all of his peers as he was to his roommate, pursuing his education with a minimum of social awkwardness. He didn't like the second glances and dreaded being questioned. Quickly identifying the places in the dormitory where people congregated, he avoided them. To reach his room, however, he had to walk past the third-floor common room. The night before classes began, returning from dinner he was confronted by a group of classmates who lounged in the room drinking beer and smoking.

"So, what's your story, Tommy, or Tom, or, what do they call you?" The questioner, Brook Fairfield, was tall and broad shouldered, with nearly white platinum hair slicked down. He leaned back on two legs of a chair, balancing a bottle of beer with one hand on his abdomen. His tone was not wholly cordial, putting Thomas on guard.

"Tom will do." Thomas stood in the doorway, hoping to be gone as quickly as he could escape without appearing rude, or fearful, or anything else that would draw attention to him in the future.

"Where you from?"

"Belmont."

"Belmont . . . ?"

"Massachusetts. Just up the road."

"Really?" Fairfield asked in mock surprise, raising his eyebrows. "You look more like you might be from Belmont-ay, if there is such a place." The others laughed. "Are you sure you're not from Greece, or Spain or something? Mexico?"

"I heard he was Italian." With nine of his Belmont Hill classmates at Harvard, it was inevitable that rumors would be carried along, in this case by a cleft-chinned fellow Thomas recognized from high school soccer games.

"Italian! Shit. Better look out, boys." Fairfield threw his arms up in the air as though he were being held up at gun point, spilling his beer in the process. "We're living with a mafioso! A real live gangster. Cosa nostra, is it?" Several members of the group shrank back in their chairs in pretend fear, and then sniggered. "You boys better sleep with one eye open." Derisive laughter. Fairfield paused for comic effect. "So tell me, Tommy, are you a made man?"

"Hey, lay off, Fairfield!" A chubby rugby player in wrinkled khakis and a plaid oxford-cloth shirt was laughing so hard he could barely speak. "Who you think you are, Bobby Fucking Kennedy?" The group exploded, throwing their heads back and slapping their knees.

"You're funny," Thomas replied dryly to Fairfield when the hysteria died down. "And original, too."

"Seriously, though," Fairfield continued. He wasn't through with Thomas, especially as his audience was enjoying the show. "I didn't know there were a whole lot of *Eye-talians* in Belmont. And your last name is Wellington. What are you, adopted or something?"

"Something like that."

"Hmmm. I know." Fairfield tapped his forehead. "Your . . . poppa . . . made it big in what? Olive oil? Running numbers and maybe . . . breaking a few legs on the side? And you moved on out to the burbs to try to live like rich folks. Come on, what's your real name, 'Patriarca'?" This brought another loud burst of laughter from around the room.

"Look, drop it, okay," Thomas said, trying to sound calm, but failing. His eyes flashed. He had hoped college would be different and was annoyed to discover that it wasn't. Instead, there was a more sophisticated version of the same ignorance that had given him the name "Tomato" in high school, fueled by the Kevauver Commission and popular stereotypes of Italian Americans. He lashed back: "We can't all be fresh off the Mayflower, can we?"

"Ooh! There it is boys—did you see that?" Fairfield pointed, leaning further back away from Thomas. "Look at his eyes? Do you see that notorious *Eye-talian* temper? Oh, crap. I'm about to shit my pants." Then to Thomas disdainfully: "It's okay, Guido, I was just kidding. Jesus Christ, I don't wanna wake up in cement boots at the bottom of the Charles." More chuckles.

Thomas turned and walked out of the room. Not long afterwards, he began initiating rumors of his own when asked as he often was about his ethnicity: that he was descended from a brother of King Victor Emmanuel who had left Italy after unification; that his father had met his mother, the daughter of a Roman nobleman, while serving in the diplomatic corps; that he was Caruso's nephew. He created these autobiographies partly for amusement, but even more to obscure as much as possible the truth of his heritage.

Running became Thomas's passion and escape. Coach Munro, having recruited a right wing from Choate, cut Thomas from the soccer team after a day of tryouts. "I like your speed, though, son," he offered. "Speak to Coach McCurdy on the cross-country team. Tell him I recommended you."

McCurdy allowed Thomas to practice with the team, and eventually he earned a starting spot. He discovered that he loved to run more than he had ever loved team sports, more than anything he could remember doing. After classes the coach would put the team through a workout: two or three miles to warm up, sprints, the steps of the stadium, timed splits on the track. Thomas would then eat, usually alone with a book in the dining room of Straus, study, and then slip out late to run along the river. He was not the fastest on the team at the shorter distances, the distances at which the team competed. When McCurdy took them out for longer conditioning runs, however, seven and eight miles, Thomas would begin to pull away from the lead runners over the final miles. In the spring, McCurdy, who coached both teams, offered him a place on the track team.

Thomas spent much of the summer running, often twice a day on the Vineyard and at home in Belmont. With pressure from Edmond and his mother, he was leaning towards studying government and proceeding on to law school. When he wasn't running or chauffeuring Ashley from one social engagement to another in Ellen's car, he was reading. Edmond had recommended Lerner's *The Mind and Faith of Justice Holmes.* Thomas found it dry. The law didn't interest him particularly, but he knew it was important to his parents. His mother wanted him to fulfill her abandoned dream of going to law school, and Edmond was eager to shepherd him into the legal profession in Boston. Instead, he discovered Hesse, reading and then rereading *Siddhartha* and *Narcissus and Goldmund,* which he found fascinating but also mystifying, as though there was a deeper meaning he could not quite uncover.

He continued, privately, to be interested in religion, and in the idea of the priesthood. Running along the river he had many times seen monks in black habits coming and going from a cloister not far from Harvard Square. The chapel had a simple façade, adorned with a round window featuring the symbols of the evangelists: an eagle, a lion, a bull, and an angel. An arc of stone stairs led to heavy wooden doors at the entrance. Next to the chapel was the monastery itself, a large building with windows on the upper floors looking out from the monks' cells onto the cloister garden and the river beyond. A stone bell tower rose above the enclave. Intrigued by the religious life after reading *Narcissus and Goldmund*, he grew curious about what took place inside.

One afternoon early in the fall semester of his sophomore year, Thomas strolled down Memorial Drive toward the monastery.

Pulling open the door by a large wrought-iron ring, he stepped into a cramped, square vestibule. From there it was through another imposing set of wooden doors into the chapel. Inside, his eyes adjusted to the dim lighting which emanated from narrow, arched stained-glass windows glowing high above, just below the dark, paneled ceiling. The unfamiliar odor of incense tickled Thomas's nose as he inspected the chapel in wonder. A sign in the vestibule had identified the cloister as belonging to an Episcopal order of men. Thomas hadn't been aware that such orders existed, or that the Episcopal Church found expression in this unusual manner.

He walked to the closed gate of a high iron fence which separated the rear of the chapel from the area where the monks sat during their daily liturgies. From a side door, a monk scurried out with a burning taper. He took no notice of Thomas at first, but after lighting the candles on the altar, he turned and saw him. Smiling, the monk started down the nave towards Thomas. He was no taller than a child, completely bald and bent slightly forward at the waist. Thomas imagined that he must be ninety years old at least. Reaching Thomas, he spoke with a clear, even voice. "Would you care to join us for evening prayer?"

Thomas didn't know how to respond to this odd invitation. He was not even sure what constituted evening prayer. Out of the corner of his eye he spotted three and then four other monks entering the chapel. One appeared to be Thomas's age, possibly younger. "Uh, thank you, no . . . really, I must be going." The monk pulled a key from beneath his habit, unlocked the gate and pulled it open. Thomas took a step back. "I have to go," he whispered.

"I understand," the monk replied, grinning cheerfully. "You're always welcome. Come in and pray anytime or join us on Sunday. We worship at nine o'clock." Thomas turned and fled.

On Sunday he was back. Something about the space drew him in despite the strangeness. He took a seat outside the iron fence, where a scattering of congregants awaited the beginning of the service. Presently, he realized that a large number of monks—perhaps twenty, men of all ages—were bowed, silently praying before the altar of repose in the Our Lady Chapel adjoining the sanctuary.

At precisely nine o'clock, a small bell rang. Those assembled stood and began to sing: "Praise my soul the king of heaven, to his feet thy tribute bring." Thomas picked up a hymnal, noting the number on the hymn board, opened the book and joined in singing: "Ransomed, healed, restored, forgiven, ever more his praises sing."

A moment later he was amazed to see the procession coming towards him from the sacristy. The thurifer was followed by an acolyte, a deacon, a subdeacon, and then a priest, the father superior. The rest of the monks fell in behind, two by two. The clergy were vested in green and gold, the superior in an ornate chasuble and cope. Crossing in front of the small congregation, the monks stepped through the gate and filed towards the altar, the brothers taking their places in the wooden stalls on each side of the nave. Thomas was enthralled. Never had he imagined that something like this spectacle he was witnessing existed. At times nearly choking on the cloud of incense which was refreshed after the passing of the peace for the Eucharist, Thomas watched the Mass unfold in disbelief. The entire service was chanted, in part by the schola of monks who sang the psalm in a pure harmony that Thomas found both beautiful and evocative. The father superior, administering the sacrament, looked into Thomas's eyes with an openness and intensity that Thomas could not meet, causing him to look down at his hands after only an instant.

While the final hymn was being sung, the monks processed back the way they had entered, exiting through a small door next to the side altar—except for one. A tall, thin man, almost gaunt, with flat cheeks, gray-green eyes and fine brown hair, stepped out of the procession as it passed Thomas and the other congregants in the back of the chapel. When the hymn was over, he opened his hands in a gesture of invitation: "We would be so pleased if you would join us in the crypt below for refreshments." He motioned to an archway to the left of the iron fence and, grasping Thomas firmly by the elbow, began to lead him towards the passageway.

"I'm Brother Andrew," the monk said, releasing Thomas's elbow and offering his long, slender hand. Thomas took it, and the monk held Thomas's hand in a powerful grip, shaking it once slightly as they walked down a winding staircase to the crypt.

"I'm Thomas."

"Ah, Thomas. Welcome. I don't think I've ever seen you here before." Thomas looked at Brother Andrew. He could not determine his age. At first he thought the monk might be youngish, forty or forty-five. Now, standing in brighter lighting in the crypt, he wondered if he might not be much older. There were only hints of silver in his hair and only slight wrinkles on his forehead and around his eyes, but his eyes themselves looked as though they could belong to someone a hundred years old, someone who had spent a lifetime traveling the world, accumulating wisdom and knowledge.

"I peeked in during the week one day, and then—"

"Well, I'm so glad you came back. You're at Harvard?" The monk tilted his head to the side as he spoke. Thomas shifted on his feet. Somehow he had the sense that he mattered to this man in a way that was unnerving. He had always been apprehensive around strangers, reluctant to divulge any personal information. This monk seemed genuinely to care, though, as if the answer to his question, *You're at Harvard?* was of critical importance.

"Yes, sir. I'm a sophomore." Before Brother Andrew could ask his next question, the father superior, relieved of his liturgical finery and now dressed in his black habit, approached, extending a cup of apple cider to Thomas.

"Welcome, welcome, friend. Here you are—the best the season has to offer. Enjoy. This one's on the house." He and Brother Andrew laughed, and Thomas smiled. Squat and ursine, the superior had seemed earnest and devout during his sermon, which touched on the healing of a blind man and the piety of the order's founder, Richard Meux Benson. Now he was quite jolly, with an impish way of raising one eyebrow as he spoke. His chin came nearly to a point; with ample cheeks, small ears, and a pointed tuft of hair above his tapering forehead, his face was diamond-shaped.

"Father, I present Thomas . . ."

"Wellington," Thomas said, shaking the superior's hand.

"Thomas Wellington. He's a sophomore at that big school back there."

"Thomas," the superior repeated. "The twin. Doubting Thomas. Are you a twin . . . or a doubter, Thomas?"

"Uh, well, I . . ."

"He's teasing you, Thomas," Brother Andrew warned, patting Thomas on the shoulder.

"You know, I've always felt that poor Thomas has been treated unfairly by history," the superior began, "by exegetes and preachers alike. He's seen as a negative example, and yet—"

"Now Father," Brother Andrew interrupted, "you've already had your sermon for today. I was just getting to know a bit more about our guest."

Later, Thomas walked out of the monastery into bright sunshine, back on the steps facing the river as though he had just returned from time travel. A most singular experience the morning had been, not only because of the strange and unexpected customs of the monastery, but because of his conversation with the intense but genuine Brother Andrew, which had continued for more than a half hour. Thomas could not ever remember being so forthcoming with a new acquaintance, or maybe with anyone. Without disclosing information other than basic facts, he had allowed himself to be seen, to be engaged by another human being in a manner that he strictly avoided under all other circumstances.

He became a regular visitor at the monastery.

"Maybe I should become a monk," he mused to Brother Andrew one morning in February when a snowstorm had kept all but a few people from joining the monks for Mass. Thomas, dressed in a turtleneck, a heavy cable-knit sweater, wool pants and boots, had been invited to lunch in the refectory following the service. He couldn't look at Brother Andrew, sitting across the table from him, as he said it. Instead, he looked down, twisting his napkin around his fingers. A slight smile appeared at the corners of his mouth. He and Brother Andrew had become friends over the months since their first meeting.

Brother Andrew gazed at him, steadfast, focused, his brow furrowed. "I can't tell if you're serious," he replied after a moment. "*Are* you serious?" Thomas shrugged.

"I don't know. Maybe. I used to think I wanted to be a priest, but . . . too much public speaking. There's something about this place, though. I don't really know what it is."

The monk rested his chin on his fist and waited for Thomas to continue. Comfortable with silence, he was patient, waiting for answers, which was part of the reason Thomas told him so much: he left room for it.

"So," Thomas said, "what do you have to do? I mean, how does it work?"

"Well, if you're really interested, Thomas, I'd propose that we make an appointment to sit down and talk it through. How does that sound?"

"I'll think about it," he answered, daring to look Brother Andrew in the eye for the first time.

Later in the spring Thomas approached the monk again. As he had considered the idea more seriously, joining the monastery had begun to seem less peculiar. What would he be leaving behind? He was a good student, but his studies did not excite him. He did not feel any inner drive to be a lawyer. He had no social life. At least in the monastery there might be a sense of acceptance, belonging, an absence of prejudice that would help him find peace.

"I think I'm ready to have that appointment we talked about a while ago," he said, noticing that his palms were sweating.

"That will be fine, Thomas," Brother Andrew replied. He pulled a small appointment book and a pencil from behind his scapular and suggested an early afternoon the following week.

"Perfect," Thomas said. "I'll be there."

They met in a small room in the guest house, furnished with two caned chairs, an Oriental carpet, and a prayer desk with a Bible and well-worn prayer book on it. An icon of the Good Shepherd and a photograph of Father Benson hung on the wall. The stone-framed window looked out on the garden where forsythia were in bloom, sheltered from Memorial Drive by a high wall. Thomas had been shown to the room by the dour, sleepy-looking monk who answered the door. Brother Andrew arrived a few minutes later, settling into his chair and fixing Thomas with his customary soul-revealing gaze.

"Thomas. It's good of you to come. Are you well?"

"I am, Brother Andrew. Thanks. And you?"

"I'm well." Silence. Brother Andrew as usual, allowed silence to stand. Thomas looked around the room self-consciously, hoping the monk would say something. Finally he did: "Thomas, you've become quite a fixture around here." Another silence. This time Thomas felt that he was supposed to speak.

"Yes. I like it here. Everybody's been really nice to me. The liturgy is so . . . interesting and beautiful. And, I don't know, I guess I just don't notice people staring at me in here as much."

"People stare at you?"

"Always."

"Why do you think that is?"

"Because I don't look like everyone else. I stand out."

"In what way?"

Thomas grimaced. Was the monk being coy, playing a game with him?

"You can see," he answered, pulling up his sleeve to show the skin on his arms, and then touching his hair at the temple. "I'm different. I don't look like anyone in my family. I don't look like anyone I've ever gone to school or to church with."

"And you find that upsetting."

"Wouldn't you?"

"I don't know. Try walking around Harvard Square in a habit sometime." Thomas caught the monk's eye briefly, then looked away, feeling his face turn red. "Well, I'm glad you enjoy being here," Brother Andrew said, "that you feel comfortable. We're glad to have you. Now, if I remember correctly, you wanted to talk to me about the religious life. You were wondering if you might have a vocation."

"That's right."

"Tell me more." Brother Andrew leaned forward.

"Well, I . . . uh . . . I like it here, and I thought maybe . . ."

"You're always welcome here, Thomas. You can visit whenever you want. It's a bit different when you can't leave. What makes you think you want to live in this odd way that we live?"

Thomas had anticipated this question. "I like to be alone. Like everyone says about me: I'm a loner."

"And you think that's what being a monk is about?"

"Isn't it? I mean, partly at least?"

"No. We're together a lot, to pray four times a day, to eat, to work, for recreation, to talk about our common life. But one does have to be comfortable being quiet and being alone sometimes. Do you understand the vows that we take, Thomas?"

"Poverty, celibacy, and obedience?"

"That's right. What do you think it would be hardest for you to leave behind if you were to take those vows?" Thomas considered the question for a moment, looking out the window and watching a pair of ducks descending to land on the river.

"Uh, well, would I still be able to run?"

"To run?"

"Yes, I think I've mentioned before, I like to run. I'm on the cross-country team and the track team. It's really what I love to do the most."

"Tell me more."

"Well, I run every afternoon at practice. Then I go back to the house, eat, study. Then at night, usually late, I go out and run again—eight, ten miles, sometimes more."

"Where do you run?"

"Usually up the river. Sometimes I just get lost. Newton, Watertown, Mt. Auburn Cemetery. I just keep running till I find my way back."

"Interesting."

Thomas smiled uneasily. "Why?"

"Well, that's a lot of running. Do you ever wonder . . ."

"What I'm running away from? That's what my mother always asks. You know, I guess maybe you can't understand if . . . have you ever done sports?"

"I know how to swim. I was on a swim team once. A long time ago."

Thomas took a deep breath and exhaled slowly though his nose, knitting his brow as he tried to decide how much to say. "You're going to think I'm crazy, Brother Andrew. I've never really tried to explain this to anyone. The thing is that inside I don't . . . feel things that much. I see other people feeling happy or sad or in love or whatever it is, and I just don't know . . . what that's like. I guess I would say that I feel sort of . . . numb all the time. But when I run, especially for a long time, I can feel something. I can feel my body. I feel like I'm actually in my body. Sometimes I just feel tired, or sore. At least that's something. But other times part of me just lets go and . . . I don't want to sound grandiose, but it's like . . . freeing, I guess. I'll be running and I'll be having a great run and then, often it's when I run fast up a hill and come over the top and all of a sudden I feel . . . filled up, and I get tears in my eyes." Thomas realized that he'd been talking for a relatively long time. He stopped and looked at Brother Andrew, who was peering at him even more ardently than usual, his chin resting on his fist. "You're thinking I'm nuts, right?"

"It wouldn't be for me to say that, Thomas."

"You think it's strange, though."

"Are you worried about what I think?"

"Maybe." Thomas began to feel like he'd revealed too much. Suddenly, he wanted to leave. He glanced at the door and considered escaping through it.

"Do you have any idea why it might be so hard for you to feel things, Thomas?"

There was silence between them for a time. Thomas adjusted his watch band and then wiped the crystal with his thumb.

"Do you ever feel things about God?" the monk asked finally, when it appeared to him that Thomas couldn't answer the previous question.

Thomas cleared his throat, increasingly concerned that the interview was not going well. "I guess I . . . think a lot of things about God. I'm not sure if I . . . feel things. Maybe when I get that freedom kind of feeling when I'm running, maybe that has something to do with God."

Brother Andrew, sensing that Thomas was out of his depth, changed the subject. They discussed the details of the religious life, and the novitiate. "A formal visit, where the aspirant comes and spends some time—a few days or a week—living among us, trying us out—that would be the next step." Thomas nodded. "However," Brother Andrew continued after a moment, sitting up straight in his chair and then pausing for what seemed a long time to Thomas, "I'm not sure that's advisable at this point."

"What do you mean?"

"I'm not sure that you're ready for something like that right now."

"You're turning me down?" He had expected Brother Andrew to be pleased, enthusiastic, and as these words sunk in, Thomas felt belittled and hurt.

"I'm not turning you down, Thomas. Understand, I've been at this a long time. The religious life isn't for everyone."

"Can you tell me what your hesitation is?"

"Of course. I don't want to make you feel defensive, but I don't think we'd be doing you any favors to proceed right now. Thomas, in my opinion, to make a commitment such as the one we make in the religious life, to be able to take these vows and keep them for life, requires, more than anything, self-awareness, self-knowledge. Do you know what I mean by that?"

"You don't think I'm self-aware?" He was not used to being denied and he wasn't liking it.

"I think you're very bright. I think you have a good heart. Most people, though, don't have to run themselves into the ground to be able to access their emotions. To live the monastic life, you have to know who you are, what you feel. You have to have a good sense of where God is for you before you can make a commitment like this. You can't come here to hide, Thomas, from the things out there that are painful or frightening or confusing. It just won't work—for you, or for us."

"You think there's something wrong with me."

"I don't at all. I just think, at least for right now, that there's a sort of . . . well, let me put it this way: I experience you on some level as though . . . as though part of you is missing, or at least, I can't find it. Does that make any sense?" Thomas drew back with a slight jerk, as though he'd been stung by a bee. "Thomas, I would never say this to upset you, or to hurt you. I respect you enough to tell you the truth. Why can't you feel anything, Thomas? Where's the rest of you?"

"I have to go." He stood up quickly, so that his chair skidded away from him and clattered against the wall behind.

"Wait. Thomas. Stay for a minute."

"I don't know what you're talking about. I have to go. I'm sorry I wasted your time."

"Thomas—"

He was gone.

He stayed away from the monastery. Though he tried to clear them from his memory, the monk's words bothered him, echoing in his head until, at last, still not entirely comprehending, he began to grope forward, like someone trying to find the doorknob to leave a lightless room.

v.

Thomas was more withdrawn than usual over the summer, sleeping or reading during the day when he wasn't teaching private tennis lessons at the club, a job Edmond had strongly encouraged him to take, or going out at night to run. His mother would hear him coming in at two, even three o'clock, in the morning. Once on the

Vineyard he had found her sitting at the table in her robe drinking a cup of tea when he came in after three, drenched in sweat. He had run fourteen miles, up the shore road to Oak Bluffs and back, a favorite route as he loved to look out into the night across Nantucket Sound.

"Mother, you scared me," he exclaimed, closing the door softly and turning to find her in the weak light coming from the next room. "What are you doing up?"

"Are you all right, Thomas? I'm concerned about you."

He opened a cabinet, pulled out a hand towel and wiped his face, his neck and then his arms and chest. "I'm all right, Mother. Just on a funny schedule this summer. Don't worry."

"A funny schedule so that you never see your family or anyone else? I have to stay up until three a.m. to catch a glimpse of you?"

"I'm sorry. I'm just needing some room. That's all it is." He hung the towel over his shoulder, went to the fridge and retrieved a pitcher of water, a glass from the cabinet by the sink, and then sat down at the table across from her.

"Your sister misses you, too. She came into my room the other night and cried. She said you haven't played croquet or ridden bicycles with her all summer, or taken her into town for ice cream like you used to even once. She treasures that time with you, and she feels the absence of it—of you."

"If you're trying to make me feel guilty, it's working," he said flatly.

"I don't want you to feel guilty, Tom. I just want to understand what's going on."

"Things are different now, Mother. We were kids. I had time for croquet and ice cream. I'm an adult now. I'm working, and—"

"I don't think that's it, actually. If it was important to you, you'd make time for it. I think it's something else." She searched his face. "Can I help?"

He paused, thinking for a moment about whether he had the words to share what he had been feeling, and how she might react if he did. "I don't know yet," he said finally. "Maybe. Thank you. I guess I'm just sort of . . . finding myself, as they say. Trying, anyway." He was still perspiring, so he dabbed again at his forehead with the towel.

She paused, absorbing his words, aware of all that finding himself might mean. "Thomas, I'm sorry. I owe you an apology. A big one." She reached across the table and touched his hand. "I think perhaps I should have . . ."

"It's okay, Mother. Stop, please. I know you always did what you thought was best for me. I'm not angry, just . . . confused, really. Sometimes it seems like I'm always trying to be someone I'm not, and then at the same time it seems like I'm not being something that I am, even though I'm not sure what that is. I know that can't possibly make any sense to you."

"No, I think I'm following you." He watched her face for signs that she understood, and was unconvinced.

Thomas was home in Belmont to celebrate Ashley's birthday. "Thank you for coming, Tommy!" She greeted him with a hug, the only one who was allowed to call him Tommy.

"Would I miss your birthday?" He picked her up and swung her around. "Oh my, I'm not gonna be able to do that for much longer."

"It's too quiet here when you're gone. I have no one to bother. And Mother and Daddy pay too much attention to me. It's annoying." She put her hands on her hips and pouted.

"I'll tell you what. I have some work to do. Why don't you bring your dolls into my room and play with them while I study like you used to do. And you can ask me a thousand questions so I won't be able to get anything done."

"Dolls? Really, Tommy. I don't play with dolls anymore." She punched him lightly in the stomach. "Let's go for a walk instead." He left his bag by the door, and took his sister by the arm.

.

Later in the day, his mother asked Thomas to find his old tennis racket, as Ashley had outgrown hers. In the attic, Thomas searched with a flashlight for his camp trunk, filled with sports equipment from his childhood and high school. On a shelf above the trunk, he noticed a bundle of letters tied together with string. Curious, he flipped through them, not recognizing the handwriting and taking note of a military stamp. He closed the trunk, untied the string and sat down. In the top left corner he saw the sender's name: Amorelli. Sliding the top letter out of the envelope, he unfolded it and began to read.

"So, Tom, what courses are you taking?" Edmond asked that evening as they sat down to dinner, unfolding his napkin and draping it over his lap. "It's your big junior year." The semester had begun a month earlier. He looked down at his dinner, avoiding eye contact with Edmond. Edmond had grown impatient with Thomas's sullenness. The distance between them had grown, and he blamed Thomas for it. He had always worked to have a good relationship with the boy, and he seemed to get less and less in return.

"So?" Edmond prompted.

"Uh, the usual stuff, I guess," Thomas replied, taking up his fork.

"Well, it's been a long time since I was at Harvard. So come on, out with it. What does *the usual stuff* mean for a junior at Harvard these days?"

"Uh, let's see. I'm taking Biology 140—that's genetics—to finish my science requirement. I'm taking Math 103—Intro to Higher Geometry. Same reason—math requirement. Also, History 132— History of Europe, 1750 to 1914."

Silence. Edmond waited for him to continue.

"That's it?" he asked finally, surprised. "All that money we're paying and you're only taking three classes?"

"Edmond, could you pass the gravy?" His mother was trying to come to his rescue. "Honey, sorry to interrupt, but what time are the people coming about the gutters?"

"Just a minute, dear." The attempt wasn't going to work. "Genetics, geometry, history of Europe. You must be taking at least one other." Thomas put down his fork and swallowed, realizing there was no way to avoid the truth.

"I'm also taking Italian A. Elementary Italian."

"Italian? I see." He had picked up his wine class. He drank from it and then put it back down on the table. "Why Italian, Tom?"

"I just thought it would be interesting to learn Italian. It's a beautiful language," Thomas replied. Edmond stared at him, surprised, disapproving.

"Honey," Ellen intervened, "leave him be. He's exploring something. Try to understand. Would you like another glass of wine? How's the roast?"

"What's he exploring?"

"He's interested in his . . . roots."

"In his roots?"

"What are you talking about?" Ashley asked her mother, lost and increasingly unhappy that the conversation was focusing on her brother during her birthday dinner.

"I'll explain later," Ellen whispered.

"He's exploring his roots by studying Italian? Those aren't his roots, Ellen. They're his . . . genes, I suppose. That's about it, if you see the distinction." Edmond's voice was tight. His jaw was set. His face looked as though he was struggling to hold back an explosion within himself.

"You two are talking about me and I'm sitting right here," Thomas interjected, wanting to diffuse the tension. "Look, Dad, don't take it personally, okay? You're my father. You're the only father I've ever known. You've always been great. I just thought it would be interesting to learn the language my ancestors spoke. I'll probably just take a semester or two, just to try it out."

"I'm not sure that's the best use of your education, son. What about your prelaw program? I didn't even know they taught Italian at Harvard."

"I'm using my education just fine, Dad. I'm a straight-A student. You know that, right? I know it's kind of a lark. It's just something I wanted to try. I've had more than enough Latin to fill the language requirement. So, I just thought—"

"You just thought—?"

"Yes. I did." Thomas met his stare so that finally Edmond looked to Ellen, frustrated, who shrugged and smiled innocently.

In fact, he loved the class. The teacher, Professor Della Terza, was serious and exacting. He made his students repeat words and phrases again and again, alone in front of the entire class, until their pronunciation met his uncompromising standards. The class met every day, first thing in the morning. Thomas never missed a session. Della Terza assigned several pages of *"compiti scritti"* each night and administered a test every Friday. Beneath the A on Thomas's final exam for the first semester, the professor had written: *"Bravo! Hai un senso naturale della lingua. Molto bene, Tommaso."*

Zeph Stewart, master of Lowell house and professor of classics, on learning of Thomas's delight in studying Italian, encouraged him to consider classics as a possible concentration. In addition to the second semester of Italian, in the spring Thomas enrolled in Dr. Gruen's class, *The Age of Cicero.*

At night, alone, running along the river, he sensed an awakening within himself.

Thomas took to walking through the streets of the North End, inhaling the aromas, listening to the language in its various regional adaptations, hearing the music, tasting the food: pastries, pizza, cheeses, pasta, olives. He looked at the pictures of Italy—Naples, Palermo, Rome, Catania—that hung on the walls and in the windows of every *salumeria*, restaurant, *caffè*, and barbershop.

Delight and sadness wove themselves together: delight in experiencing real, tangible elements of his paternal heritage; sadness at lacking a connection to it, an entry point, not able to be part of it. Here, too, he was an outsider, an observer of a way of life that was not his—visible, tactile, but maddeningly unreachable, in some indefinable way just beyond the ends of his fingertips.

Further, to his dismay, he occasionally caught people staring at him, though physically he felt less out of place or odd than ever in his life. He assumed it was his attire that drew the second glance, and for younger people it was. He looked genuinely as though he were Southern Italian, but dressed like someone who might live on Beacon Hill. To a number of older people, though, his face was familiar, one they swore they'd seen somewhere before, impossibly long ago, or in a dream.

Thomas walked slowly along the sidewalk across the street from the house, until finally, his nerve slipping away, he continued down the street without stopping. Turning onto Federal Street and then past the shops on Main, he cut back up Washington to pass by, again without stopping. Before trying a third time, he went into an Italian ice cream parlor, bought a Coke and sipped it, sitting on the stool at the counter and looking at the photographs on the wall of Rocky Marciano, Carmen Basilio, Roy Campanella, the DiMaggio brothers and other Italian-American sports heroes. Taking a deep breath, he laughed at himself. This is ridiculous, he thought. I can do this.

Returning to the house, to the bottom of the steps in front, he drew another full breath. He adjusted his Harvard tie, carefully knotted earlier in the day, and straightened his blue blazer. Out of the corner of his eye he noticed a young girl in a grimy yellow dress on the stoop of the house next door. She was staring at him and picking her nose. When she saw that Thomas had spotted her, she crossed her eyes and stuck her tongue out at him. Thomas pretended he hadn't seen her. Then, quickly, before he could stop himself, he walked up the stairs and rang the bell. His heart thudded in his chest.

An hour seemed to pass, though it was less than a minute. He thought about fleeing, glancing around to see how he could escape and noticing that the little girl was still watching him suspiciously. Maybe if he were to disappear, whoever answered the door would assume that the child had been playing a trick. A lock clicked sharply, and a woman opened the door. She was not elderly, but past late middle age, smaller than he had imagined, with gray hair pulled back into a bun. She wore a flowered housedress and slippers. The woman, who was expecting to find a salesman—of vacuum cleaners or aluminum siding or life insurance—looked up at Thomas and, registering his face, drew back a step.

"Are you Angela Amorelli?" he asked politely.

"Yes," she replied, startled, still peering into his face. "Who are you?"

"My name is Thomas Wellington. May I speak with you for a moment?" She hesitated, then stepped aside, motioning for him to enter and directing him toward an armchair. He sat down stiffly and looked around the room, which was neatly kept, not a sign of dust or a cobweb to be seen, or a pillow out of place on the sofa. There were pictures on one wall which drew his attention. He scanned them, seeing for the first time what he guessed was his father's face. He had prepared himself for this moment for weeks, but now that it was happening, he trembled, knowing already that a threshold had been crossed. He tried to avoid looking at Angela for as long as possible, but when he did he saw that there were tears on her cheeks.

"I'm sorry," he blurted, putting his hand on his chest. "I don't mean to upset you. I'm sorry."

"No, it's all right," she said. She had by now, over the course of the decades since her arrival in the United States, learned to speak English with a lightly accented fluency. "It's only that you remind me so much of my husband. It's incredible. You have his eyes somehow, and his nose. You could be him . . . many years ago." She shook her head, as if trying to wake up, pulled a tissue from her sleeve and wiped another tear as it rolled out of the corner of her eye. "It's not possible."

"Well, actually it *is* possible," Thomas began, clearing his throat. "There's a reason for why I look like him . . . and that's why I've come. Won't you please sit down?" Angela lowered herself onto the sofa across the room. "This may be shocking to you, and I'm sorry, again." He paused. Angela gazed at him. "You see . . . well, I don't know how to say this . . . and I know it will be hard—really hard to believe, it's just that . . . well . . . I'm your grandson." He watched the idea register on her face, a look of bewilderment, denial, shock. "Yes, it's true. Your son Victor, your son Vittorio, was . . . my father." He sat on the edge of the chair, gripping the arm rest with his left hand, and his own knee with his right. He watched Angela's face now, as she struggled to make sense of his words.

"Carlo!" Angela shouted, abruptly in dialect. "Carlo! Come! I'm losing my mind! Carlo!"

Presently, Thomas heard a screen door open and close from further inside the house. A moment later an older man limped into the room from the back porch where he had been tending his canaries, a hobby he had adopted after retirement. "Oh, Cousin, what's the yelling?" the man demanded, irritated at being disturbed. Then he saw Thomas sitting in the armchair and he stopped short. He looked from Thomas to Angela, and then back. "Who is *this*? My God, he looks like Tommaso."

"It's not possible," Angela whispered through her tears. "It's just not possible."

Not moving her eyes from Thomas, as though in a trance, she got up from the sofa and crossed the room. As she approached, Thomas stood. She reached out and took his hand from where it hung at his side, holding it in front of her, between them. He looked down at her hands, noticing the way arthritis had swollen and gnarled her fingers. Releasing his hand, she moved up to his face. At first she poked at his cheeks, as if to ensure that he was real, and not a phantom, and then she cupped his chin in her hand. Thomas's lip quivered. She wrapped her arms around him. He reached to pull her close to him. They held each other, her head turned to the side and pressed against his chest.

"I must sit down," Angela said then, after a moment, pulling back and holding Thomas's elbows. "I still don't understand." She sank into the couch, and Thomas sat down next to her. Remembering his manners, he sprung up again, extending a hand to the dumb-founded Carlo. "I'm sorry, sir. My name is Thomas. I know this is hard to believe, but I'm your grandson." Carlo shook his head, ignoring Thomas's hand.

"Now how is that possible?" he shot back. "Who are you? What's going on here, Angela? Her son died in the war. There are no grandchildren. I have no grandson. Angela, what is this?"

"I don't know, Carlo. I don't know. But look. Santa Maria, it has to be true. Look at him."

"I can explain," Thomas said, sitting down next to his grand-mother, hoping his words could calm her. "At least in part. Honestly, I don't know the whole story. My mother never told me. She doesn't even know I'm here." He took a deep breath. "I gather that my father, your son, and my mother met somewhere, I'm not sure how . . . in 1942. They had a . . . love affair, and then, I'm guessing, my father went away to the war. I don't know if he ever knew that my mother was . . . going to have a baby." Angela looked shocked. Carlo less so. Still, he was unconvinced.

"Why should we believe this? Does he have any proof?"

"Look at him, Carlo. Do you need proof?"

"Where's your mother from?" Carlo asked, crossing his arms, stern, recalcitrant.

"She grew up in Lincoln. West of Boston." Angela watched Carlo's face.

"I do remember something about Vito bringing an American girl to a wedding that fall before he left," he allowed, softening slightly.

"Maybe you know, then." Thomas was eager for information. "How would they have met?"

"Vittorio was working for a mason—a stone mason," Carlo explained. "Maybe they met while he was working. They worked in places like Lincoln. I don't know where else he could have met her." Angela was following the conversation in amazement. She wiped her cheeks with the palms of her hands.

"I don't believe this is happening," she murmured to herself. "My grandson. *Miu niputi?*"

"Why have you come now?" Carlo asked. He remained suspicious, though he knew the longer he looked at Thomas that there was no way to deny the young man's story.

"I don't know exactly. A couple of years after my mother—Ellen, her name is—found out that my father had died, she got married. I was raised by the man she married. He adopted me. She never told me much about my real father . . . almost nothing. I always felt like I wasn't supposed to ask. Most of what I know, even his name, I found out from reading some old letters of hers I came across in the attic not long ago. She only told me a few months ago that he had died in the war. Is this his picture?" he asked, pointing to a photograph in a brass frame on a table next to the sofa. Angela nodded. Thomas examined it, then cleared his throat. "For some reason recently I've been feeling like I needed to know more. When I looked you up," he turned to Angela, "and discovered you were still here, I realized I had to come see you."

Angela touched his face again. "Look at you," she said. "Handsome, just like my Tommaso. *Beddu.* And, just like him, too skinny. I'm going to make you something to eat."

"One thing I don't understand," Thomas said, pausing to collect himself and reconcile what he had just heard with the history he had pieced together from clues. "Who is your Tommaso?"

"My husband. Your . . . grandfather."

"But isn't this . . ." He motioned in the direction of Carlo.

"Oh, no, no. This is your grandfather's cousin, Carlo. Your grandfather was . . . he died in the Great War, in France. Carlo was there too. He came back after the war, and we've just been looking after each other since then."

"My grandfather was killed in the first war?" Thomas asked. Angela nodded somberly. He shook his head, stunned.

Marie, responding to Angela's breathless phone call, arrived minutes later. She, too, crumpled into tears upon seeing Thomas. She was near eighty now, though Thomas would have guessed that she was younger. She moved with lightness and energy. Her face was full and robust. "How can this be happening?" she asked Angela repeatedly.

"Only God knows," Angela replied, throwing her hands in the air. "Only he could have a plan like this."

Thomas told them about his upbringing and his schooling as Angela cooked, with Marie's help. He told them he was studying Italian, and they compelled him to speak.

"Very nice Italian," Carlo deemed. "Very proper," he said, "like they speak up in Bologna." Thomas wasn't sure what he meant, but he smiled, sensing that Carlo was proud.

They sat down at the table to eat. "I have so many questions," Thomas said, after Angela had given thanks. They talked for hours over dinner and then back in the living room. Thomas took off his blazer and loosened his tie, sinking into the couch next to his grandmother.

"And then the telegram arrived," Angela said eventually, remembering the awful day. It had grown dark outside, the June sunlight finally fading behind the house. "When your grandfather died, they sent someone to tell me. When your father died, they just sent a telegram. I have it. I'll show you. 'We regret to inform you' and so on. The ladies from town came. They brought me a gold star to hang in the window. They told me he was a hero. He died for an important cause, they said. I never hung the star in the window. I have the medals they sent too. Purple Heart, Bronze Star. They're in a drawer somewhere. You can have them if you want them. They mean nothing to me." She paused. Thomas looked down at his glass of *grappa*. He was trying to be polite—and manly, for Carlo's benefit—but he couldn't drink it. The clear, tasteless liquid burned his throat. Looking up, he noticed that Angela was staring at him. He smiled and put his arm around her.

"Often, since your father died," she continued softly, "I've wondered why I'm alive, why I'm in this country, why I keep breathing, why I wake up in the morning. Many times I've prayed to the Virgin in church, asking her to tell me. She would understand, I always thought, because she lost her son, too. But she never gave me an answer. Never. Now," she touched his face with her fingertips, "now I know. This is my answer. All this time I've been waiting for today, waiting for you to knock on my door, and I never knew it." She shivered. "God is mysterious."

That night Thomas slept comfortably in his father's bed, the first person to sleep there since Vittorio left more than twenty years before.

He woke in the morning with a feeling of peace that was unfamiliar. His father's room was small, no more than a large closet. The twin bed fit perfectly into one end of the room, below the only window. A bureau filled one side. The other side was open, the floor covered by an oval braided rug, green and tan. Along with the rest of the apartment, the room was just as it had been when Vittorio went away. Years earlier, after the war, the landlord had insisted on updating the kitchen and the bathroom, installing modern appliances and fixtures. Angela had seen no need for it but had acquiesced. She had changed nothing herself, other than to replace curtains when they became faded. There had never been much money. Now that Angela could no longer sew because of arthritis and Carlo was too old to work on the boat, they subsisted on the modest monthly pension each received from the Army. Any time there was a little extra, Angela tucked it into an envelope which she kept inside the cover of her Bible.

Thomas took his father's robe from the back of the door, put it on and walked into the kitchen. Angela was pressing his shirt. She had already washed his clothes and ironed his pants.

"Oh, you didn't need to do that," Thomas said when he realized what she was doing. "I could have—"

"I'm very happy to do it," Angela interrupted, smiling. "You don't know how happy. Now have some breakfast."

"Thank you, Grandmother," Thomas said, sitting down at the kitchen table.

"You should call me 'Nanna,'" she said, "like they say back home." He watched her go to the kitchen and return with rolls she had baked, along with butter and jam, and coffee. He thought she was beautiful, dignified and graceful. Her eyes were full of vitality and genuineness. Placing the meal in front of him, she rested her hand on his shoulder tenderly, familiarly.

"I had to peek into the room this morning to see if you were really there. When I first woke up, I was sure I'd dreamed the whole thing."

Thomas smiled up at her. "I can see how you might think that. I hope this isn't all too much of a shock. Maybe I should have called first or written."

"I never would have believed you over the telephone. You did the right thing. As soon as I saw your handsome face," she said and tousled his hair, "I knew. I knew."

Carlo returned from his morning walk, carrying two newspapers. He took his place at the table. Angela joined them after serving his breakfast. "When will you be back, Tomuzzu? You have to come back soon."

"I'll be back, I promise." A sense of contentment came over him. "I'm on summer vacation from school. Just teaching a few tennis lessons at the club, and I have to go to the Vineyard for a couple of family events. But otherwise I'm free. I'll come see you. I've missed enough time already. I don't want to miss any more." Angela beamed, like a child, showing her teeth, and then covered her mouth out of shyness.

When he was gone, Angela poured herself a cup of coffee and sat down across the table from Carlo, who was engrossed in his second paper. "I'm awfully confused, Carlo. Awfully confused." She held her cup in both hands and watched the steam rise and swirl from the hot liquid. She had long ago learned not to wait for a response from Carlo. She knew he was listening, in his own way. "My son committed a mortal sin. It upsets me to find out about it after all these years. I've always prayed for his soul, but now . . ." She trailed off, wondering how she could determine the number of rosaries she should say on her son's behalf without divulging the specifics of his transgression to the priest. "But," she went on after a moment, "I have a grandson. A wonderful grandson who looks just like my Tommaso. And Tommaso, my Tommaso, has a grandson who goes to college—to Harvard. Can you believe that? Can you imagine what he would say?"

Carlo yawned. "The boy took sort of a shortcut, didn't he? On the way to Harvard and the American dream?" He said this without looking up, out of the side of his mouth.

"What do you mean by that, Carlo?" Angela did not like his tone.

"He got there in spite of being Sicilian." Now Carlo lowered the paper and looked at Angela as he spoke. "His . . . *parents* . . . denied him his birthright. Thomas Wellington." Carlo curled his lip. "Thomas Wellington can go to Harvard. Of course he goes to Harvard. Tommaso Amorelli? I doubt it. He's teaching tennis at *the* club and going to *the* Vineyard. His mother comes from money, and she married money. All Vittorio provided was . . . "

"Carlo. *Basta.*" She brought her hand down on the table, causing her cup to bounce on the saucer. "I don't believe it. You've gotten cynical and cranky in your old age. I can't change the past, Carlo. Who knows what might have happened if Vittorio lived. But he didn't. And that's my grandson. He's mine. Blood is blood. I claim him as my own. Why do you think he came here after all this time? Why do you think he went to the trouble of coming to find me? He wants his real family. The years that have passed don't mean anything. He came because he wanted to know. He needed to know. Money can't buy him that. Money means nothing. He's mine, now, Carlo. Did you see his face when he left? He called me 'Nanna.' He's ours. And you better treat him that way, or you'll have to deal with me." She got up from the table and stomped out of the room. "And he said he was an A student at Harvard too, Carlo," she called a minute later from the kitchen. "He earned those A's. He's smart—just like his father. I know how you feel about rich people," she continued, returning to the doorway, "but you're going to have to make an exception this time. He's ours, Carlo."

Carlo chuckled softly and tipped his head back in resignation. "*Va bonu,* Angela. Okay. He does look like my cousin. There's no denying it."

vi.

Thomas began to make frequent visits to Gloucester. He told no one. Whenever Edmond, Ellen and Ashley were away, which was often during the summer months due to vacation time and social obligations, he took the family's second car and drove to see his grandmother and Carlo, arriving on Friday evening or Saturday morning. He would accompany Angela, carrying her bags as she did her shopping. She would cook, and they'd spend hours talking. His father was the most common topic, though they talked too about his grandfather and about life in Sicily. Angela wanted to know everything about his life as well, and Thomas told her all about his family and his upbringing in Belmont. He found it easier to talk to Angela than to anyone else he had ever known. He felt entirely accepted by her, as though she would be pleased with him no matter what he said or did.

With Carlo, he discussed history and politics, though he had never been particularly attuned to such issues. He had observed conversations between his parents, who generally disagreed. He had joined his mother in supporting Kennedy, against Edmond's wishes, and had been affected by the young president's death, more for the human drama than the political impact. Most recently, Ellen had been working to convince Edmond to vote for Johnson, arguing that Goldwater was too conservative, even for him. Thomas remained a mildly interested spectator, lacking a sense of immediacy or connection.

He was fascinated by Carlo's passion for current events. Reticent on most other topics, politics brought out a hidden energy in

Carlo, who, in his later years, reflecting on a bifurcated life in Sicily and then in the working class of the United States, had located himself further and further to the left. Though he stopped short of calling himself a socialist, he was sympathetic to the sentiments at the root of socialism. "The working class has always broken its back to make others rich. It's crazy. I did it, too—like a fool—in Sicily and here. If someone ever rises up to lead workers and wakes them up to the truth, I can't see how he'll be stopped." Thomas was shocked. He'd been educated to equate socialism with communism, and to think of communism as an evil force. Carlo's novel perspective drew him in, engaging him and giving him a new lens to view ideas which had previously seemed remote, out of range, or out of focus. Occasionally he would ask a question to prompt the old man, who would clap his hands together and say "Aha! Very interesting" and plunge into his answer.

After a few visits, Carlo abandoned his reservations and decided that Thomas was all right, despite the trappings he carried from the world where he was raised. He was quiet and respectful. He seemed intelligent. Most importantly, though, Carlo could see that Thomas and his grandmother were quickly becoming devoted to each other. He recognized the significance of this new and entirely unforeseeable relationship for Angela. It was as though she had won a massive windfall in a lottery she didn't even know she had entered. In this boy, her son's son, with an uncanny likeness to her husband, there was the potential for closure which had never existed before. He alone was the salve that could heal her still-open wounds and bring her happiness, recompense, in her later years.

One Saturday morning near the end of July, the skies low and dark with thunder sounding across the water, Carlo took Thomas down to the docks. "Your grandfather was a fisherman—a damn good one—and his father before him, back as many generations as anyone can remember." They stood at the end of Fish Pier looking out over the inner harbor. "But your father never took to it . . . strangest thing." As they strolled about the pier, Carlo pointed out some of the older boats, as well as the new vessels. "Your grand-father and I started out on boats like that one," he said, indicating an old steam dragger that had been refitted with a gasoline engine. "Later, after . . . well, I worked on a couple of lobster boats. It wasn't exciting, but the work was steady and I just got to be too old for adventure. Without Tommaso too, it just . . ." Thomas observed the sadness in Carlo's eyes, heard it in his voice. The old man turned away to look out at the storm approaching across the open ocean in the distance, then said words Thomas later understood as a kind of apology: "It didn't work out the way it was supposed to, Tomuzzu. What else can I say?"

They planned a trip to Boston. Carlo offered to take him there just as Thomas was gathering the courage to ask. He went to Gloucester on Friday afternoon and left with Carlo early Saturday morning. Angela, as usual, had no interest in visiting the city—less, even, if possible, than she had had in her younger years.

The sun shimmered through a thick haze. Carlo rolled down the window and took off his black fisherman's cap, wiping his brow with the back of his hand. "Gonna be warm."

They parked near Haymarket and Carlo began the tour there, leading Thomas into the slow-moving congestion of shoppers who pushed past each other down the narrow aisles, fruit and vegetable stands on one side, fresh seafood storefronts and butcher shops on the other. "Your father used to love the market," Carlo smiled, wist-ful, remembering Vittorio's face as a child. "He was a charmer—made friends with all the vendors. That boy ate more free fruit. I remember one day I was having a smoke with a friend—right over there. All of a sudden Vito stumbles out of the crowd carrying a watermelon half as big as he was. 'Look what Mario gave me!' he kept shouting. He was so proud. You would've thought the thing was made of gold."

From there they walked under the highway to Maria's pastry shop for coffee and a brioche, and then up to Hanover Street. Carlo was the most animated Thomas had seen. He pointed out stores and restaurants, telling humorous, melancholic stories about each, one anecdote after another, as though they'd been stored under pressure for years. Sometimes he would get confused, mixing Vittorio and Tommaso in his recollection of events. He would stop, rub his temple with his forefinger, and then correct himself: "No, it was your father—he was the one who threw up—right here on this spot after smoking a cheap cigar." Thomas was rapt, absorbing the atmosphere and following Carlo's narration intently, wanting to burn every detail into his memory.

Reaching the end of Hanover Street, they turned onto Commercial, and then again onto Salem. Carlo stopped in front of a tailor shop. "Here. Now, your father had two buddies. You remember—I told you about them. The three of them were always together. Paolo, Marcello and Vito. If you found one of them, you found all three. Paolo and Marcello enlisted right before your father was drafted. Paolo . . . didn't make it. He was killed in the Philippines. Japanese machine gunner. Marcello never saw any action. He had good skills as a tailor which he learned here working as an apprentice. Made himself useful—fitting uniforms for officers, mostly—and he came home in one piece. After the war he took over the business. Best tailor in town. He even worked for the Kennedys." The door to the shop was propped open with a bucket full of sand and cigarette butts. A fan buzzed on high speed in the doorway. Carlo stepped around it and into the shop with Thomas following.

Marcello, bald with close-cropped black hair around the sides of his head, wearing rust-colored pants and a white shirt opened halfway down, an apron around his waist, knelt on the floor marking the pants of a customer with chalk. "Don't you think that's a bit short?" Carlo asked, teasing.

"*Salve*, Carlo!" Marcello shouted, turning and recognizing the voice before he saw the face. He stood up and opened his arms, welcoming Carlo with an embrace and a kiss on each cheek. "Excuse me," he said to the customer, who appeared annoyed at the interruption, "this is my old friend." Then to Carlo, "How are you? And how's Angela? How long has it been? My God, you look good. You never change." He had noticed Thomas, but imagined, in his oxford shirt, dress khakis, and loafers, that the young man was another customer. Thomas looked around the shop. It was small and cramped, but brightly lit and neatly organized. Clothes were piled next to the sewing machine, the sleeve of a suit coat halfway to being expertly shortened under the needle. The wooden mannequin in the front window was dressed in a sharp black tuxedo with a satiny red bow tie and matching cummerbund.

"Fine, fine," Carlo answered when Marcello finally gave him the chance. "*Tuttu beni.* Yes, the years go by. Listen, I want you to meet someone. This is Thomas." Thomas was still in the doorway, and with bright sunlight behind him, Marcello couldn't make out his face in detail. He took two steps forward and extended a hand.

"Marcello," he said, grasping Thomas's hand. "My pleasure."

"Marcello, I haven't got all day," the by-now-aggravated customer put in, hands on his hips.

"Excuse me," Marcello said to Thomas. "Just a moment." He knelt and deftly finished marking the pants. "Okay, sir. You're all set. They'll be ready Wednesday." The man went behind a curtain to change. Marcello bounced up and rejoined Thomas and Carlo.

"So, what can I do for you, Thomas? Any friend of Carlo's . . ." Leaning to one side, he glanced behind the young man to see where he had left the clothes that needed tailoring.

"Marcello, I know this is gonna be hard to believe," Carlo cautioned. "There's no way for me really to prepare you. So . . . I'll just say it. Thomas here is Vito's son." Marcello looked at him, squinting, then shook his head, turning to Carlo as though he had said something crazy. "Vito's son? Vito didn't have any . . ." He trailed off, mystified.

"Do you remember Ellen," Carlo went on, "the girl Vito brought to your wedding?"

"Of course I do. God, she was a beauty. We were all knocked stupid. I'll never forget seeing her in the church that day and thinking what a son of a gun Vito was. But . . ."

"Ellen is Thomas's mother. When Vito left, she was . . ."

Marcello's eyes opened wide. He looked at Thomas again, craning his neck forward, then leaned back against the counter, grabbing the cash register for support. His jaw dropped open, and he shook his head again.

"But how . . . when?"

"He showed up at our door a couple of months back. He did some detective work, and . . . and here he is." Carlo swung his hand towards Thomas like a master of ceremonies bringing the next performer on stage. Thomas smiled sheepishly. Marcello rushed forward and wrapped Thomas in a tight embrace, kissing him on both cheeks. He was overcome with emotion, and couldn't speak, hugging Thomas a second time, and then kissing his cheeks again. Thomas felt Marcello's tears on his face.

The customer emerged from behind the curtain and tossed his suit on the counter. Looking up, he saw Marcello embracing the young man. He hurried past them out into the street.

"Let's go." Marcello said, releasing Thomas and composing himself. "I'm closing the shop." He rushed behind the counter and picked up the telephone, dialing quickly. "Antonella! I'm bringing company for dinner. I've got a big surprise. Really big. You won't believe it. We'll be there in ten minutes." He hung up the phone, pulled off his apron and reaching behind Thomas, flipped the sign in the window so it said "Closed." "*Iamu!*" he shouted. "Let's go."

The family occupied the same small apartment on Hull Street around the corner from the shop where Marcello's parents had lived along with two other families when they first emigrated from

Sicily. Up three flights from the street and in the back of a building dating from the early nineteenth century, the apartment was a collection of cramped, low-ceilinged rooms.

Thomas stood in the narrow hallway blushing as Marcello, excited and panting after having raced up the stairs, recounted the implausible story for a stunned Antonella, whose emotions culminated with sobs, rushing up from deep within.

Later, over a huge meal with food being carried course by course from the kitchen by Marcello's daughter, Tina, the oldest of their three children, Marcello entertained them with stories about Vittorio and the old days. Thomas was fascinated as his father's world began to take shape before him. What had been, for his whole life, a complete and impenetrable mystery—as unknowable to him as the origin of man—was being disclosed in detail in the very environment in which his father's life had occurred. His father was a "ladies' man," a Romeo, according to Marcello. He was good looking. He had a great wit and a sharp tongue. He knew everyone in the neighborhood and was popular with the entire community. He loved cars and could identify every make and model. He adored his mother and dreamed of taking her home to Sicily.

As Marcello went on, with occasional corrections and additions from Antonella, who, her work in the kitchen finally finished, had joined them at the table, Thomas wished he had brought a pen and paper. He thought of asking for one but, already self-conscious of the way he was dressed and the way he spoke, he didn't want to appear to be any more of an outsider, there on some kind of sociological research. It's a world I've never known, he thought at one point, amazed. But these complete strangers are my people.

Nino and Rosa were expecting them, Carlo having called ahead out of fear that the surprise would be too overwhelming for the elderly couple. Nino had finally retired a few years earlier, selling the business, along with his good name and reputation, to one of the young men who had been his apprentice. Later he regretted doing so, though it had given him financial security, because the new owner had taken the business in the direction of driveway paving, leaving behind artisanship in favor of a higher profit margin. "I would have worked until the day I died if I had known he would do that," Nino often griped. He and Rosa had left the North End and purchased a small cape house on a short, dead-end road in West Roxbury, a "respectable" neighborhood, according to Nino.

When Carlo and Thomas arrived, Nino was in the front yard tending to a holly bush. The desire for a garden had been the primary motivation for the move out of the city. In front of the house, on each side of the door, Nino had built raised beds a foot high, bordered by his perfectly squared stone walls. He had filled the beds with shrubs: holly and rhododendrons, azaleas and bayberry, surrounded like islands in a lush sea of pachysandra. At the far end of each bed he had left room for a rose arbor, each one heavy with vines and blossoms. He had painted the house himself, a pale yellow, at Rosa's request—it had always been her favorite color—with white shutters.

Nino looked up as Thomas pulled the car into the driveway. He was down on one knee, examining the diseased leaves on a smattering of the holly's branches, a tin watering can at his side. The afternoon heat pressed down. Nino stood, removed his cap and wiped his forehead with a handkerchief.

Carlo emerged from the car first and crossed the well-tended lawn to greet Nino. Angela and Rosa had exchanged holiday cards over the years, but the two men had not seen each other in more than a decade. "Well, *amicu miu*," Carlo sighed, still grasping Nino's hand, "I guess there was a reason he gave up fishing and went to work for you. I didn't understand it at the time, but . . . life is strange, eh?"

Thomas waited, leaning against the car, watching yet another person who knew and loved his father absorbing the jolt of his own existence. "So." Nino said. "This is the boy. *Ncridíbili.*" Thomas extended his hand politely as Nino approached. The old man ignored it and grabbed him, clutching him in a tight embrace. He was significantly shorter, his head pressed against Thomas's chest. Thomas was still trying to get used to these effusive hugs and kisses. "Unbelievable," Nino repeated, releasing Thomas and stepping back a pace. Then he reached out and took Thomas's cheek in his hand, calloused and rough from decades of labor. "Your father," he said, "was like a son to me." Unable to continue, he turned to Carlo helplessly. Carlo smiled and nodded his head sympathetically, raising his hands palm upwards and bobbing them up and down in a gesture which meant, "What is there to say?"

"Rosa!" Nino called in the direction of the house after a moment. "Rosa, come." An older woman appeared at the door, pushing open the screen and stepping out onto the brick steps. She was small and frail and moved tentatively. In recent years she had grown forgetful. Nino cared for her lovingly and grieved at every sign of her gradual deterioration. "Come here, my love." Carefully negotiating the two steps, she obeyed. "You remember Carlo," he told her. She seemed to, and responded warmly when Carlo hugged and kissed her. "And this—this is Thomas. Remember now, I told you about Thomas. He's the son of Vittorio Amorelli. Remember Vito? You remember Vito." Rosa tilted her head to the side and peered at him, her eyes vague, as though waiting for something to materialize in front of her. Before long she surrendered, and, smiling sweetly, turned to her husband for help.

"It's all right, dear. He's a friend. A good friend."

"It's very nice to meet you," Rosa intoned. Her accent was much stronger than Nino's. In recent years, with her memory disintegrating, she spoke primarily in the language of her youth. "Ask them if they'll come in and eat," she said to Nino.

"In a few minutes, my love," Nino replied. "I want to show them my garden first. Why don't you go inside and get things ready."

"Please don't do anything special for us," Carlo called after her. "We've eaten already once."

Nino led them around the side of the house to the backyard, where he had transformed his quarter acre into a small but productive farm. The proud farmer walked them up and down his straight, even rows, showing off tomatoes, eggplants, cucumbers, a variety of lettuces and cabbage, zucchini and *cucuzza*, string beans, cantaloupe, basil, oregano, and garlic. There was enough that Nino was able to share generously with his neighbors, who would find brown bags stuffed with produce on their steps, so that after a season or two they began to think of him as a benign curiosity rather than a harbinger of the neighborhood's ruination, as they had originally suspected. In the part of the garden farthest from the house, covered with netting to keep the birds away, grape vines cascaded from the trellises Nino had built. Each year, using his bathtub and his bare feet as a press, he produced an average of twenty bottles of strong, musty wine, along with a few more of equally potent grape juice.

"Doesn't look to me like you've retired at all," Carlo joked. Nino smiled, satisfied, imperial.

"Keeps me from getting old," he replied. "Now come, sit." Behind the house there was a small patio, set back just far enough to leave room for another tier of rose beds. Carlo and Thomas sat on wooden benches around a picnic table. Nino went into the house and came back with a tray bearing a bottle of wine, three glasses, and a plate of *salame* and cheese.

"I've been searching through the *munnizza* in my brain since Carlo called," Nino said to Thomas once he had poured the wine and seated himself. "I believe I came across something about the girl I'm guessing is your mother. I remember only because it was so strange. There were always plenty of girls after your father—Italian girls. But this one . . . we were out maybe to Lincoln, or Weston. Really, I don't know. I just remember a beautiful girl bringing us a cold drink and flirting with Vito. I was suspicious of something for a while, but Vito promised me and I believed him. He swore I was crazy. Maybe that was . . . your mother?"

"She was from Lincoln," Thomas confirmed. "A big old house with a meadow and a small pond out back. I don't know if it was there back then, but there's a little gazebo on the edge of the pond." Nino squinted, frustrated, trying to recall an image.

"It may be . . . yes, I remember something. She was so pretty, though—the girl—and I couldn't believe she was trying to play around with my apprentice. Handsome as he was, it just didn't seem . . . and yet, here we are. Twenty years later the truth comes out. I still can't quite believe it. Anyhow," he clapped Thomas on the shoulder, "tell me some things about you."

They stayed through the evening. Periodically, Nino would go into the house and return with another plate of food: marinated artichokes and grilled eggplant, ripe tomatoes with basil and mozzarella, sardines with olive paste and bread. Thomas, wanting to be polite, tried to keep eating, though he couldn't remember ever being so full, having consumed a huge meal with Marcello and his family only hours before. He felt almost as though he was falling, sinking into something, being absorbed, and it felt right.

Occasionally, recalling events from the past, the two older men would slip unintentionally from English into dialect. Thomas listened with amazement. He assumed they were speaking Italian, but he couldn't decipher a word. Finally, he decided to ask.

"I know my Italian isn't very good—yet," he began, "but I've been studying a couple of semesters now. I have to tell you, though, I don't understand anything you're saying." The two men chuckled.

"I should've explained this to you by now," Carlo apologized. "You're studying Italian. In Sicily, we don't speak Italian. I mean, some people do—the nobility, I suppose, and government officials. But the people—we have our own language. You're learning the Italian of the north, of Bologna, of Firenze. Nothing wrong with it. It's just not the language your ancestors spoke, that we speak." Thomas was silent, pondering Carlo's words, and the conversation drifted on to other topics: politics, the weather, Angela and memories of the old days when Vittorio was alive and the future seemed to hold different possibilities.

Thomas was tired and overloaded, his thinking clouded by the events of the day and the wine, which hadn't seemed strong at first, but was now bending his thoughts into confounding shapes. Where does this go from here? he wondered, as Carlo and Nino chatted on. He followed a firefly with his bleary eyes as it circled, glowing, above his head. He remembered Brother Andrew's diagnosis. It's one thing to find the other half, he considered, and another to figure out how to make something whole of two pieces.

He began to think about his grandmother. She had welcomed him with warmth and affection. He might have expected that she would, if he had been able to imagine her reaction beyond the initial shock. He hadn't played the thing out as far as the actual relationship that might develop. As awkward as he felt, she had never made him feel like an outsider. Everyone else he had met too, after recovering from the surprise, had been gracious and accepting. The only division, he considered, was within him, of his own creation.

But no. Impossible. They're kind, but they must think I'm a spoiled rich boy. They're probably expecting I'll eventually get over this . . . phase, and disappear. Lincoln and Harvard and all the rest. He let his head flop back and looked up at the sky illuminated by heat lightning. Maybe I should. Maybe I don't belong here—could never belong. I'm an imposter. Again, however, he was visited by the image of his grandmother, and he knew that he could never turn away from her.

In September Thomas returned to school for his senior year. Having decided on classics as a concentration, he was formulating an idea for his thesis. He wanted to examine Shakespeare's *Julius Caesar*, and compare it to archeological data and other historical sources about Rome in the year 44 BC, a subject which would bring together his linguistic studies with his increasing interest in Italy. Meanwhile, he was facing pressure from his parents—subtle from his mother, overt from Edmond—to apply to law school.

His mother knocked on his bedroom door midmorning on the Saturday of Columbus Day weekend. Ellen had requested that he spend the holiday at home, as they had seen each other infrequently over the summer.

She opened the door and stuck her head into the room, hesitant as she had become in his nearly adult presence. Thomas was half awake, having stayed up late studying. "Wake up, wake up," Ellen called. "We're meant to play doubles with Dad and Ashley this morning. Did you forget? We've got a court at the club at ten thirty."

Thomas rolled over. Ellen opened the door all the way and stepped into the room. He looked at her, squinting to focus his eyes. She was wearing her tennis clothes: white pleated skirt, white shirt, hair held in a ponytail by a white ribbon. "Good morning, you," she said cheerfully.

"Good morning, Mother."

She folded her arms across her chest and leaned up against his bureau, just inside the door, absorbing his coolness.

"Do you want to play tennis with us? I suppose you don't have to if you'd rather not."

"Sure, of course. I'll get up. I'm sorry. I was up late working."

Ellen tried to decide if she should say something else. He seemed to be slipping further away. She looked around the room.

His desk was covered with books: a stack taken from the library for research on his thesis, his Italian dictionary and grammar opened as he had left them when he grew drowsy the night before. His clothes shrouded the desk chair, topped by his letter jacket. A pang, sharp, sad, went through her as she remembered choosing the wallpaper for his room when he was a little boy. It depicted antique cars, and she had matched the paint for the trim to the blue in the print and the curtains to the red. Glancing down at the top of his bureau she noticed the wallet she had given him for Christmas the year before now softened from use, and next to it the gold watch that was his graduation gift from Belmont Hill. Then she spotted a set of rosary beads, lying on top of a scattering of coins. The beads were imitation pearls, the chain tarnished plated silver. The medallion closing the loop and holding the single strand that ended with the cross was stamped with an image of the Pietá. Surprised, she picked it up.

"What's this?"

"It's a rosary," Thomas replied, yawning, watching her.

"A rosary?"

"Yeah, a rosary." Ellen raised her eyebrows. "It's just a rosary," Thomas repeated. "You act like it's a roach clip or something."

"What's a roach clip?"

"Never mind."

"Where'd you get a rosary?"

Thomas propped his two pillows up against the headboard and sat up. Apparently, the moment had arrived. "From my grandmother," he said expressionless, looking his mother in the eye. Each time he went to Gloucester, Angela sent him home with a rosary, or a vial of holy water from Lourdes, or a prayer card, some religious object meant to keep him safe until his next visit.

"Your grandmother?" She laughed. "Your grandmother's an Episcopalian. I hardly think she would have a rosary. You're teasing. Do they use them at that monastery you visit?"

"My grandmother gave it to me." He was set to enjoy this moment of power. Ellen looked at him.

"Your grandmother." Thomas nodded. "Grandma Caroline?" she offered skeptically. Thomas shook his head, keeping his eyes fixed on her face. He could see that she was flustered, that the idea was beginning to form in her mind. "Not Grandmother Wellington." Thomas shook his head again. Her face flushed. She walked across the room and sat down at the foot of the bed, unconscious of the fact that she was still holding the rosary beads in her hand. "I don't understand."

"My grandmother. Angela. Angela Amorelli. My father's mother. My grandmother."

"You've seen her?" Observing her shock, Thomas nodded, a thin smile on his face. He could see that she was floundering, dumbstruck. "How? How did you find her? I . . . I . . ."

"I found some letters of yours. In the attic. I was up there looking for my old tennis racquet for Ashley. A couple of them were from my father. There was only one Amorelli listed in Gloucester, still living at the return address on the envelope. It wasn't hard." Anger flashed in his eyes.

"Oh, Thomas." Ellen was staggered. She was beginning to grasp the implications. There was silence between them for several moments—charged, heavy, broken only when Edmond shouted up the stairs.

"Are you two coming? We've got a ten-thirty! Ellen! Did you wake Thomas?"

Ellen cleared her throat. "He's up, dear. We're just talking. We'll be right along."

"We don't want to be late," Edmond answered. "You know how they get." Ellen looked at Thomas. She saw the defiance on his face. She wanted to flee. He looked too recalcitrant and too much like his father. She feared what he might unleash upon her: guilt, blame, hate. She called down to her husband. "Edmond, why don't you and Ash go on ahead? Tom and I will be along in a few minutes."

There was a pause, and then a muffled answer—"Fine"—and the sound of his footsteps retreating. She hesitated for a time, her face towards the door as though she might say something else to Edmond, even though both of them knew she was simply trying to gather herself. Finally she turned back to her son.

"Well, I have to say, I'm—"

"Shocked?"

"That's about right. Is that what you want? Is that what you were hoping for? Yes. I'm shocked. I don't even know what to say." She folded her arms across her chest as though trying to protect herself, or hold herself together. "How is she? She must have been shocked herself to see you. Did she even know?"

"Haven't you ever wondered about that, Mother? No. She didn't know. She didn't know I existed."

"You're angry," she said, trying not to sound defensive.

"I shouldn't be?"

"Tom, you have to understand what it was like to be twenty-one with a baby out of wedlock whose father was not only . . . unacceptable to my family, but also, as it turned out, dead."

"I'm sure it wasn't easy, Mother," Thomas shot back, her defensiveness only making him angrier. "But it doesn't change the fact that I've had a grandmother living *forty miles* from here my whole life and I never knew it. A grandmother who could have helped me understand why I'm different than everyone else in this . . . world you brought me up in. Who could have given me some connection to my father." He was nearly shouting, years of suppressed, muddled emotion finding voice. "How could you let that happen? Do you know, do you have any idea how much it would have meant to her, these past twenty-one years? This person whose life has been a series of tragedies? Who lost her husband and then her son?"

"Thomas, I understand that you're upset, but I don't like your tone. Don't yell at me. And for God's sake, try to have a little compassion." She paused and softened her tone. "Honestly, Tom, your father came into and went out of my life so fast. Afterwards it just never seemed real. If I didn't have you, if I didn't look at you and see him, I'd be sure it was all a dream. I loved him, you know. I wanted to get married." She smiled for an instant, wistful. "I didn't care what my parents would say. When you were born, I named you Thomas, after your grandfather—your father's father. Victor told me that was the tradition, and I imagined how pleased he'd be when he came home. But when he died, Thomas, I had to go on—for your sake, if for nothing else. I did the best I could. I did what I thought was right for you. I'm sorry if I . . . compromised you, if you feel like I did the wrong thing. But try to understand the position I was in."

"You could have helped me find her, Mother. A long time ago. I've felt like a freak my whole life. Do you realize that? I've never known who the hell I am." He'd never said those words to anyone, and they hung in the air between them, weighted and condemnatory.

"I'm sorry, Thomas. What do you want me to say? I apologize." She crossed her arms and shrugged. "I don't expect you to be . . . grateful for what I tried to do, for the choices I made so that you could have a stable home and a . . . normal life. But it would be nice if you could try to have a bit of empathy. I hope maybe someday you will."

Thomas looked out the window. Edmond was backing the car out of the driveway with Ashley in the passenger seat. Yellow-red leaves detached from the maple tree in the yard and floated to the ground on a slight breeze. Tears began to drop from his eyes and down his face. He brushed them away, embarrassed.

"I hear what you're saying. I just can't help being angry and . . . sad. Angela—my grandmother—she's beautiful. Getting to know her has unlocked something. All this emotion I never felt before. I never got to know my father, and I missed knowing her—knowing my family." He choked back a sob. "And always feeling like I didn't belong here—in this family, in this town, in these schools I've gone to, in the country club, at church, but not really knowing exactly why. And now, finally, discovering why. It's all kind of crashed in on me." He wiped more tears from his face with the bed sheet. "You know what gets me most though? The assumption you made, and I imagine anybody else in your position might have made, that it's better to be a rich kid from Lincoln or Belmont than a poor kid from an immigrant family of fishermen. You saved me from that, right? You gave me a stable, normal life.

And you know what? She's so proud that I go to Harvard. It's like the sacrifices she made are all worth it now." He pulled the sheet up to his face and wiped his eyes. "I don't even know what I'm saying. But I'm starting to believe that this isn't better than that, despite how it looks or what we have that they don't have. I was thinking the other day, what if your parents had kicked you out, and what if you'd gone and found Angela? She would've taken us in. Of course she would have, and we would've had a very different life. I can't help wondering what it might have been like."

Ellen pursed her lips. "I'm not sure she would have been so excited. Victor said she would have died if she'd known he was seeing a Protestant girl. If the Protestant girl showed up on her doorstep with a baby, well . . ."

"You know what I mean, Mother. I feel like I've missed out on something, that's all. And it's a relief to know. You hid the truth from me, and as solid as your reasons might have been or seemed, it was pretty damn confusing. Now I know."

She looked down at her feet. "I'm sorry, Tom. I'm sorry you feel that way. And I'm glad you know the truth. I guess it's a relief for me too. I should've told you before." She looked up at him. "We're going to need to think about your father—about Edmond. This isn't going to be easy."

"You see? That's what I'm talking about." He hit the bed with his hand. "You've always been more worried about how he might feel than you have about me. That's why you never told me. You were concerned about him. I spent my whole life feeling like an aberration because you didn't want to upset Edmond."

"It was never that simple. Yes, Edmond deserves some consideration. He thinks of you as his son. He's always loved you like any father would love a son. Of course he wasn't thrilled about the fact that I had a child out of wedlock before I married him. But he made his peace with it. He's been great about it—always. He opened his heart to you from the beginning, and I'm grateful to him." She was struggling, exposed and afraid of where they were heading. "But to suggest that I . . . balanced that, that I put his feelings before what's best for you—no. I did what I thought was right. You've made it clear, now, that I did the wrong thing, and I've apologized, and I will again if you need me to. Maybe you won't be able to forgive me, and I'll have to live with that. But your father—Edmond—is not to blame."

Thomas flopped back onto his pillows and stared up at the ceiling. "Okay. Fine. Let's go play tennis. I'll behave. When I get back to school, I'll write Father a letter so he can have some time to come to terms with it before I see him again. But he's going to have to deal with it because there's no turning back." He swung his feet over the edge of the bed and stood up. "Angela's part of my life now."

As predicted, Edmond did not receive the news well. He was angry, first with Ellen for not telling him as soon as she knew. "What does this woman have to do with him?" he demanded, once he had castigated her for holding the secret. "You never knew her. He's never met her before. She never even knew he'd been born. Why did he feel he needed to . . . Christ, I've given him everything he could want. Everything. My family—the Wellingtons—they've all treated him like one of their own. Now, out of nowhere, he goes off and finds these . . . people." He pulled at his tie and paced in the living room as he spoke, using the clipped, sharp tone he often took on in court. Ellen sat on the sofa in front of the bay window, trying to remain composed. She had wondered more than once in the intervening days whether she would be able to hold her family together.

"Try to understand, Edmond," she began, when he finally paused, ready for some kind of response or mitigating explanation. He had succeeded in removing his tie and began to wind it around his hand like a bandage. Ellen spoke slowly and carefully: "I think it's been hard, painful, for Thomas, growing up . . . different. We've done a good job—a wonderful job, I think, you especially, of not making him feel different, of making him feel like he belonged. But he knew. He knew as a small child, I imagine. We hoped he wouldn't if we just pretended it wasn't there, but he did. Now he needs to make sense of it, sweetheart. Learning Italian was a step. I had hoped it was going to be enough. Apparently it wasn't. Meeting her, knowing her, has been very important for him. And now I think we have to let him do what he needs to do. If we try to stop him, we're just going to drive him away."

"Drive him away? Ellen, I . . ."

"Edmond, let me finish. I've had more time to think about this than you have. I don't want to put him in a position of having to choose. Ironically, I was very nearly in that position once, but for the war, and it wasn't comfortable. I think that if we support him, if we don't get too upset about it, he'll come around. He'll do what he needs to do, and then he'll be okay. He's not rejecting you. He's not rejecting us." She wasn't sure this was true, even as she said it, and doubt showed on her face despite her efforts. "He's just . . . finding himself." Edmond unwound the tie from his hand, holding it by one end and letting the other drop to the floor. He shook his head to express disbelief. On his forehead a vein protruded pur- plish and thudding.

"So, what the hell am I supposed to say to him?"

"You're going to write him back and tell him that while this is difficult for you, you understand, and that you hope it leads him to find some peace. And, finally, that you're going to be there for him, no matter what."

Edmond's eyes narrowed into a scowl and he shrugged. "That's asking a lot, Ellen. Doesn't he realize that he's had every advantage, every privilege in the world? No, he's too busy feeling cheated because he missed out on something. And you want me to feel sorry for him, with his romantic little fantasy? That's asking a lot."

"Maybe so, dear," Ellen replied, using her last reserve of equanimity. "But I don't want to lose him."

Despite Edmond's effort to follow Ellen's direction, to be sympathetic and supportive, Thanksgiving was tense, and Christmas even more so. Thomas spent most of the long Thanksgiving weekend in his room studying and finishing his law school applications, emerging when summoned for meals. He even told Ashley he was too busy when she knocked on his door and asked if she could study with him. He tried for his mother's sake to act as though nothing had changed, and also because while he had steeled himself for open conflict with Edmond, he hoped to avoid it, viewing it as an unwinnable battle. Edmond, too, wishing to placate Ellen, participated in the pretense. The subject of Thomas's newly found grandmother was never discussed openly. Both men knew that something unnamed but real had come between them, or, perhaps, that which had always hung between them—that Edmond was not his biological father, that Ellen had loved someone else, that Edmond's own first child had died along with his beloved Celeste, that he loved Thomas and yet the boy's existence embodied Ellen's shame and made his own pain inescapable—had finally begun to manifest itself.

Thanksgiving dinner, because it was an even-numbered year, was spent at the Lathrop's in Lincoln. No one else in the family knew that Thomas had found his grandmother, so an extra effort was made to keep the appearance of normalcy. Thomas answered questions about his thesis and about his law school plans. He hoped to remain at Harvard, he told them, though he was considering Yale, Georgetown, and the University of Pennsylvania. He hadn't told even his mother that if he was rejected from Harvard he would not leave the Boston area for another school, nor that he was considering pursuing a degree in classics rather than law school.

Both Edmond and his mother watched him as the meal progressed. Ellen was amazed by the extent to which he seemed "grown up." He had always been mature in his own way, never a silly, irresponsible type, but now he was clearly a man. Any boyishness in his eyes and cheeks had fallen away, leaving a narrow face with strong features: a prominent nose; a strong chin; dark, hard eyes; thick black eyebrows; cheek bones that jutted out directly below his eyes, giving his cheeks an almost sunken look. "It doesn't help that he runs so much," Ellen had said to her mother. "There can't be an extra ounce on his body." The thought occurred to her over dessert that he was now the age she had been when he was born. Half a lifetime had passed. When she was his age, briefly, before Vittorio and pregnancy and marriage, everything had seemed within reach, achievable. Now Thomas was nearly gone, out into the world, and Ashley would go soon enough too, and then what? What of the dreams she had held, the things she had wanted which she had put aside for them?

Warily, meanwhile, Edmond eyed him, wondering what Thomas was thinking. Like Ellen, he was scared to lose him, worried more than anything about how Ellen would react if they were to become estranged. But he could not keep himself from being infuriated, feeling that Thomas was indeed rejecting him and all that he had provided. Thomas had experienced a need to find something that he apparently felt was missing in his life, and Edmond could not help but take that personally.

As far as Edmond could observe, Thomas did not offer any signs of hostility. He seemed perhaps more distant than usual, though he engaged politely in conversation. Distance with Thomas was relative, of course. He had always kept himself apart, as though no matter how close he was physically, the narrowest of chasms remained opened to an unfathomable depth, and he kept himself safely on the other side.

At Christmas, the smoldering tension finally flared openly. Thomas informed his mother, in a letter which she received a day before he arrived home for the holiday, that he wished to spend Christmas dinner with his grandmother in Gloucester. He would spend Christmas Eve, as always, at home with the family, and Christmas morning as well. Then, early in the afternoon, he would leave. She should have seen it coming, she realized once she read the words, written in Thomas's neat cursive on his stationery. Of course he would want to spend Christmas with her.

Edmond was more bewildered than angry. "I can't believe this is happening," he complained. "He's going to leave his family on Christmas day." As the day drew near, Ellen, recognizing her place in the middle, as a kind of fulcrum bearing the shifting load of opposing forces, worked with both of them separately in hopes of avoiding ugliness. Above all, she felt she needed to preserve Christmas for Ashley, who was confused and upset by the disturbance in their family life. "Is Tommy going to open my gift before he goes?" she had asked tearfully. With the help of her mother, Ashley had chosen a set of Harvard cufflinks to give to her brother. Ellen held her and tried to explain that Thomas was doing fine, and would be back to normal soon. She didn't know what else to say.

Ellen secured Thomas's agreement to attend Christmas Eve service with the family, followed by dinner. Edmond agreed, in principle, to be magnanimous when Thomas left on Christmas day, though he cautioned that he could not promise. In fact, after the presents had been opened and brunch had been eaten, when Thomas went upstairs to pack his bag, Edmond went into his study and closed the door. Ellen insisted that Thomas knock on the door and say good-bye before he left. Thomas, losing patience with Edmond's sensitivities, did not knock, but opened the door and said, "Goodbye. I'm going now." Edmond was sitting at his desk, his back to Thomas.

"Good-bye, Tom," he said. "I'd prefer that you didn't go. You've hurt me."

Thomas sighed. "I haven't hurt you, Edmond. Try to—"

"Edmond?" He turned around in his chair to face Thomas.

"Look, she's my grandmother. I know that's not very convenient, but it's true. She wants to see her only grandchild on Christmas. At this point in her life, I don't think I can deny her that just because it might upset you. I'm sorry, but that's the decision I had to make." Their eyes met for a moment, before Edmond turned back to his desk. Thomas walked out of the room, pulling the door closed behind him.

Angela had been cooking all day, filling the house with mingling aromas: stewed octopus, pork roast, tortellini soup. The panettone was in the oven when Thomas arrived. His grandmother was overjoyed to see him. She had doubted, up to the moment when she heard Carlo greeting him at the door, that he would come, fearing his other family would prevail upon him to stay home. He was pleased to see her as well, and even more pleased by how happy she was, and by the efforts she had made to create a festive evening for him. He loved the traditions from "the old country" she introduced.

After dinner he was moved to receive from Angela, knowing the pain she had endured with her arthritis, a crewneck sweater she had knit for him in rich crimson merino wool, along with a photograph in a silver frame of three-year-old Vittorio sitting on her lap on a bench down in the harbor. He thanked her with a kiss on each cheek, and then, grinning with proud excitement as though he had made it himself, he gave her a string of pearls and matching bracelet he had carefully selected. For Carlo, he had chosen an elegant silver watch with a black leather band.

At one point, late in the evening when small glasses of sambuca had been consumed, he thought of his mother, Edmond, and Ashley with a pang of regret. He pictured them sitting around the table eating Christmas dinner without him. Maybe he had hurt them, he considered, breaking their long-standing family tradition. Or, he thought, maybe this is just what it is to be me for now.

v i i .

Grandmother Lathrop, dressed in a short-sleeve blouse, pleated Bermuda shorts, a straw hat, and her leather work gloves, greeted them from the porch where she had been overseeing a crew from the landscaping company. She had chosen local flora—begonia, trumpet vine, yellow jasmine, scarlet hibiscus, and of course, orchids—for the gardens surrounding the new Palm Beach house, where they would winter now that Whitney was in "semi-retirement." Proudly she had laid out the design herself and, with the project nearly complete, was delighted to have the opportunity to show off the grounds to Ellen and Edmond and the kids.

The car had barely stopped when Ashley threw the door open and ran to embrace her grandmother. Thomas stepped from the car, a white limousine which had been sent to collect them from the airport, and examined the spread: a boxy, pale peach stucco mansion with a wing of guestrooms on either side. Looking through large front windows across the open living room and out French doors at the back, he could see the patio and the swimming pool and, beyond, a sandy white beach and the ocean, turquoise and sparkling in the late-afternoon sun. He wondered why his grandparents needed a six-bedroom house when they would never have more than a few guests, and he imagined what Carlo might say about the place. Palm trees cast exotic shadows on the perfect lawn. A classical-style fountain trickled at the center of the circular drive, which was paved with octagonal blocks of sandstone.

His spring break had begun, and he was not looking forward to spending the first half of it here. He had convinced his mother to allow him to leave midweek so he could spend time with Angela. To avoid strife, Edmond had been told that he was going home to finish his thesis. Also to avoid strife, Edmond had accepted Ellen's false explanation. In truth, a draft of the paper had already been submitted and Thomas was awaiting comments from his advisor, Dr. Gruen. Harvard Law School had admitted him two weeks earlier, and he had filed his intention to matriculate. Gruen, however, was still working to convince him to apply to the graduate school in classics.

Thomas passed much of the time in Palm Beach in seclusion in his suite, which included a spacious bedroom with an ocean view and a private bath, trying to decipher Manzoni's *I Promessi Sposi* for his modern Italian literature class. He played tennis with his sister, who, he noted from across the net, was vindication for the Lathrop genes: blond and fair, strong and lithe like her mother, mildly tomboyish, with Ellen's facial features. She was a good tennis player and even more a good sport. "Who taught you to serve like that?" he called across the net, after allowing the ball to pass under his racket as an ace. "You did, dummy!" she shouted back.

Each day he went out to run barefoot on the beach, periodically diving into the surf to escape the already balmy April heat. His grandfather took him for a ride one afternoon in his new Cadillac up the coast to Jupiter, and then inland to see the citrus groves. Along the way he explained to Thomas how the futures market functions using oranges as an example, and boasted about some of his contacts in corporate law in Boston, which might prove useful to him in his future career.

A special dinner was prepared on the last evening, complete with champagne and Thomas's favorite chocolate cake, to celebrate his law school acceptance. Edmond drove him to the airport the following morning. They had stilted conversation about first-year professors at the law school and the chances that Tony Conigliaro had recovered enough from his broken arm to help the Sox. They parted with a handshake at the gate.

Returning to Belmont from Logan to repack his suitcase with clothes more suitable for the North Shore of Massachusetts in early April, he drove to Gloucester. He sensed that Angela was always at least mildly surprised when he actually showed up, as though she still could not fully believe that he existed, or that he would choose to be with her. His relationship with his grandmother had continued to deepen as they spent more time together, and he loved being in her presence. She was genuine and she was wise. She was warm and showed her affection for him easily. Settling into his tiny room, he marveled at the extent to which he felt at home there: relaxed, enfolded, much more so than he had been in his luxurious accommodations in Florida.

The morning after his arrival, he woke early, dressed, and slipped out quietly to run. The cross-country team, with his help, had won the Ivy title. Thomas was hoping Coach McCurdy would give him a spot on the four-by-four hundred relay team when the track season began after spring break, so he was working on his speed at shorter distance.

He ran past the harbor and then down to Eastern Point towards the sun, which was appearing on the horizon first as a brightening glow, then a sliver of white fire. After warming up he alternated sprints with his three-mile cross-country-race tempo. The clear, cool air felt good in his throat and in his lungs, and he ran faster, with an easy looseness. Reaching the Point he stopped to stretch, then looked out across the opaque, gently rolling waves, squinting into the sun, remembering how different the water had looked in Florida. Same ocean, other life.

Heading back, he stuck to a steady pace, concentrating on extending his stride as his coach had instructed him. Rounding

Smith's Cove, he spotted lobster and fishing boats under sail, leaving the inner harbor. At the corner of Parker Street he slowed, jogged a few paces, and then stopped. Changing course, drawn by something unformed in his mind, he walked down onto Fish Pier. Though it was not yet seven o'clock, there was a rush of activity. Boats were being prepared for the day's outing. He walked along the pier, nodding in greeting at a man he recognized as a friend of Carlo's. He stopped to watch another man shaking out nets on a dragger, an updated version of the one his grandfather had worked when he first arrived in America. He noted the man's skill as he managed the huge net, pulling here and twisting there so that it was taken up in a perfect roll by the clinking winch above.

On another nearby boat, two older Sicilian men, both wearing black caps and gray wool sweaters, chatted and laughed, cigarettes bobbing on their lower lips. One of the men, the taller of the two, hosed down the deck, water sloshing over his high green rubber boots, as the other man, stocky and powerful, loaded bait from the pier. The one who was hosing down the deck looked up and saw Thomas. His name was Giuseppe Conti, legatee of a long line of Conti fisherman from the village of Pozzillo on Sicily's Ionian coast. He was known in the harbor as "The Tenor" because he often sang while he worked. Puccini was his favorite and he claimed that he would have been performing in Carnegie Hall if his parents had been able to send him to school. He had been preparing to open his mouth in song when he spotted Thomas.

"Ay, *giuvinottu!*" he called. "You're Carlo's boy, right? Vito's son?"

"Hi, yes," Thomas answered, happy to be identified that way. The other man, his face worn and drawn from years on the sea, a patchy beard covering concave cheeks, paused with a wooden crate in his gloved hands and turned to size up Thomas.

"Couldn't mistake him for anybody else, could you?"

"He's an Amorelli. No question. We knew your grandfather, may he rest in peace. *He* was a fisherman, in the truest sense. He could pull those fish like he had special powers or something—like Christ himself, filling Saint Peter's nets. We were just boys when he went away, but he was a legend." It was customary to speak of the honored dead in shades of hyperbole. He pulled on his cigarette, tilted his large head back, and released a cloud of smoke through his nose. "Your father, on the other hand, well . . ."

Thomas smiled. "Yeah, I guess he never really took to it."

"No." The man put down the hose and signaled for Thomas to turn off the water from the spigot close to where he stood checking his pulse, on the dock. Taking another long drag, he blew a series of smoke rings which hung together and sank towards the deck. Then he looked back at Thomas. "So what about you?"

"Me?"

"Yeah. What about you? You know anything about fishing?"

"Uh, well . . . not really. I mean, not much more than Carlo's told me. Stories mostly."

"Oh, that's right. You're in college. Harvard? Carlo was bragging about you. Well, stick with that, my boy. Stick with that. Right, Santo?" The other man nodded. He too was taking a cigarette break.

"Stay in school, son. You're better off," Santo concurred.

The Tenor tossed his cigarette butt into the water and picked up the hose. "But, if you ever get tired of all them books, come see us. If you're cut from the same cloth as your grandfather, we could use ya."

Thomas smiled. He was beginning to shiver, his sweat drying in the cool breeze. The sun was not yet high enough to warm him. He saluted the two men and walked away down the pier.

Angela had rolls and coffee waiting for him when he finished bathing and getting dressed. Carlo was immersed in the paper and grumbling in low, disparaging tones about two-month-old Operation Rolling Thunder, the bombing of North Vietnam, which he was convinced would eventually and cataclysmically draw China and the Soviets into the conflict.

"Carlo, I met a couple of friends of yours down at the pier this morning. They were on the *Josephine*. One of them was called Santo. I didn't get the other man's name, but I think he's the one who sings."

"On the Josephine?" Carlo glanced up from the paper. "Must have been Santo and Giuseppe. What were you doing down there?"

"I was just out running and I decided to walk down the pier, just to look at the boats."

"I've known those two clowns forever," Carlo mumbled, fading out of the conversation and sliding back into the news.

"They asked me if I knew anything about fishing," Thomas said casually, holding up his coffee cup for his grandmother, who refilled it. Carlo snorted.

"Did you tell 'em you're gonna be a lawyer?"

"No. Actually, I was thinking I might like to learn a little bit, though . . . about fishing, since it's how you and my grandfather and I guess all my ancestors made a living."

Carlo looked at him, squinting slightly to read his face. Angela, who had been on her way back to the kitchen, stopped and turned reflexively, as though she had just heard a loud and unexpected noise.

"Well, if you want, I could take you down there some day and show you around."

"You've done that already, Uncle," Thomas replied. "I mean really learn. I want to experience it." Carlo laid his newspaper down on the table and folded his hands on top of it.

"What do you have in mind?"

"Well, I don't really have any plans for the summer . . . nothing I've committed to. Do you think you could get me a job? I've got almost four months between graduation and the beginning of school in the fall."

Carlo turned his head and met Angela's eye. She raised her eyebrows and shrugged, which he took to mean that she didn't oppose the idea. He turned back and examined Thomas's face for another moment. It really was uncanny, troubling in a certain way, how much he looked like his grandfather.

"I suppose I could talk to some people. They usually hire extra men for the summer." He smiled and reached across the table to grab Thomas by the forearm. "You're a strong young fellow. Hopefully with a sturdier stomach than your father. Let me see what I can do."

Spring break ended on Palm Sunday. Thomas went to church with Angela as he had done several times when he was visiting her. By now, Thomas's story had circulated through the community, and the whispers—*pittigulizzi*—Angela called them—had at last begun to subside. Through it all, Angela had held her head up, especially when walking down the aisle to receive communion. She ordered Thomas to do the same. "Somehow," she told him, "even though I might not be wise enough to understand it, this is part of God's plan."

Carlo and Angela settled self-consciously into folding chairs under an oak tree in front of the vast, imposing steps of Widener Library. Thousands of people were flooding into the quadrangle, transformed into its annual manifestation as the Tercentenary Theatre, site of the commencement ceremony. Angela was overwhelmed by the crowd of well-wishers dressed in fancy clothes. She was wearing the long black dress she wore to church, Carlo a blue suit they had found for him in a secondhand store. Patiently, she searched the face of each woman who seemed to be the right age, wondering if she could be Ellen.

At once the bells in the tower above Memorial Church began to toll, and the ceremony began. Hoping to pick out Thomas in the parade of graduates, Angela and Carlo stood on their toes as the undergraduate procession entered from the far side of University Hall and crossed thirty rows in front of them. Carlo thought he saw him at one point, but the young man he spotted wasn't wearing the magna cum laude adornment on his robe that Thomas had told them he would have by virtue of his thesis.

Throughout the program, Angela thought of Tommaso and of what this day would have meant to him. Having a grandson graduate with honors from Harvard, she decided, would have been more than her husband could have imagined, like space travel or television: the pageantry and tradition of the event, the speeches, the music, especially the band's triumphant fanfare as President Pusey approached the dais, academic robes and the rousing cheers of the crowd. He would have been astounded.

They stood with the rest of the boundless congregation for the singing of the Harvard Hymn, which marked the end of the ceremony. From the surrounding neighborhood, bells began to peal in all the churches. Angela took Carlo's arm. As Thomas had directed them in preparation, moving slowly with the departing spectators draining from the yard as they had flooded it, they followed the path around to the back of the library and through the gate at Wigglesworth onto Massachusetts Avenue. Angela held tightly to Carlo, terrified of becoming separated and lost in the throng. They crossed the street and walked a block towards the Square to the corner of Holyoke Street where they were to meet Thomas.

Moments later he emerged from the crowd, flushed, carrying his mortarboard in one hand and waving energetically with the other. He had worried that they wouldn't be there, though he had begged them to come, and so he was delighted to see them. At the same time his heartbeat quickened, aware that now the collision of the two previously separate pieces of his fractured existence was about to occur. Carlo congratulated him and kissed him on each cheek. Angela pulled him close, whispering, "If only your grandfather and your father could have been here" into his ear.

"Now it's off to Lowell to pick up that piece of paper and make the whole thing official," he announced, taking each of them by the arm and leading them down Holyoke in the direction of his house, where his degree would be conferred.

They passed through the entryway and out into the larger of the two interior courtyards of Lowell House. Craning his neck, Thomas began to look for his mother and the rest of the family, still holding firmly to his grandmother and Carlo.

Ellen spotted him first. She too was nervous. She had cringed initially when Thomas told her that he intended to invite Angela to his graduation. While she felt personally ready to meet Angela, who had lived in her imagination for more than half her life like a specter, not evil but frightening nonetheless, she knew that for Edmond and his parents and for her own parents as well, the encounter would be awkward, or worse. She watched for a moment before signaling to him or indicating to the others that she had seen him. Carlo: she had pictured him still young, the way he had appeared in an old photograph Vittorio kept in his wallet, her imagination unable to add thirty years. She noted his limp, which had grown more pronounced in recent years. His suit, too, was remarkable for the fact that it did not fit properly. It was made for a shorter, broader man and had lapels that were no longer in style. In his face she saw the look of someone straining to appear comfortable in a strange setting, like someone in a police lineup trying too hard to appear innocent. And then, Angela: she was smaller than Ellen had imagined, stooped slightly by osteoporosis. She held Thomas's arm, and though she also seemed bewildered and out of place, she looked up lovingly at her grandson from time to time. As they came closer, Ellen could see the intense, searching darkness of her eyes, and she felt instantly laid bare.

Thomas caught sight of his mother. She was standing behind a chair at one of the round tables where luncheon would be served momentarily in advance of the degree ceremony. Her dress was lavender, matching the bow on her pillbox hat. Her shoes, belt, and pocketbook were white patent leather. Edmond was to her left, and Ashley to her right. The Lathrops and the Wellingtons were around the table as well, seated, except for Whitney Lathrop who stood reminiscing with a former classmate. Their eyes met, and Ellen widened hers, raising her eyebrows as if to say, "Here we go." They were ten paces apart when Ellen began walking towards them. Reaching them, she put a hand on the nape of Thomas's neck and kissed him on the cheek. "Congratulations, Tom," she said. "We're so proud of you."

"Thank you, Mother," he replied, then cleared his throat once, twice. "Mother," he croaked, "this is my grandmother, Angela Amorelli." Ellen turned to face Angela. She met the older woman's gaze for as long as she could bear, and then looked back to Thomas. Angela's hand shook as she reached for Ellen's, and then she took the other as well. Ellen felt her eyes pulled back to Angela's, which glistened.

At last, Angela spoke: "You are my daughter," she said, her voice wavering. "You're the mother of my grandson. You are my daughter." Though she had struggled to make sense of her relationship to Ellen, and had even wondered what kind of "girl" she could be in light of her status as an unwed mother, she had arrived at this conclusion out of her love for Thomas. She leaned forward, inclining her face and pulling Ellen down slightly by the hands to kiss her on each cheek. Ellen, sensing that her own composure was about to give way under the weight of the moment and not wanting that to happen in front of Edmond, Ashley, and the family, gathered herself and found her most gracious hostess inflection.

"Well," she smiled, mustering confidence from deep inside, "I am so pleased to meet you. Of course I heard *all* about you from . . . your son, and now . . . well, Tom just raves about you. We're all so glad you could be here today. And you must be Carlo." She breathed and smiled. She was going to survive. The hardest moment had passed. Carlo took her by the elbows and kissed both sides of her face, saying nothing.

Thomas took a deep breath, exhaling slowly. Now, for him, the worst part. He took his grandmother's hand and led her to the table. Ellen gestured to Carlo to follow. A few steps from the table Thomas released her hand and began to make his way around, accepting the congratulations of Edmond and his grandfathers with a handshake, and of Ashley and his grandmothers with a kiss on the cheek. Few words were spoken as everyone waited for what would come next. Arriving back to where he had started, Thomas stood at Angela's side. He swallowed, sensing that all of the moisture in his mouth had dried up, even as sweat sprung from his forehead, his hands, and his armpits. "Everyone, I want you to meet my grandmother, Mrs. Angela Amorelli." Angela smiled and bowed slightly, folding her hands together as though at prayer.

"And this is Carlo," Ellen announced from behind Thomas. For a few seconds, nothing happened. They had all been primed for this moment by Ellen ahead of time. Now that it had arrived, though, they were dumbstruck. Edmond was the first to move, prompted by a glare from his wife, extending a hand to Angela.

"It's a pleasure to meet you, Mrs. Amorelli, and you too, sir." He forced a smile, his mouth jutting upwards unnaturally at the corners. "Please, come join us." Thomas and Ellen then led Angela and Carlo around the table for each clumsy, formal introduction.

Over luncheon the depth of conversation did not plumb far beyond "What a lovely ceremony" and "The weather couldn't be better, could it?" and so forth. There was simply nothing within anyone's knowledge or experience that would indicate how to act in such a peculiar situation. Except that Ellen and Angela, seated side by side, began to talk to each other in soft voices that no one else could hear above the din of the hundreds of conversations around them. Thomas was on the other side of his grandmother and could only make out that they seemed to be talking about what a fine young man he was. At one point Ashley came and stood behind him, putting her hands on his shoulders and whispering in his ear: "How do you think it's going?" "We might just get through it," he told her. Angela was too shy to eat, despite Ellen's urging.

She knew there was a correct way to do so, but she didn't know what it was. Carlo, for his part, hungry after a long morning, did his best to follow along with what the others were doing, choosing utensils and using his napkin accordingly.

Eventually, Thomas had to leave the table to participate in the diploma ceremony, and all conversation ceased—though the Lathrops and the Wellingtons continued to exchange glances, communicating their discomfort. There was polite applause at the table when Thomas's name was called. Carlo, realizing that he was clapping more spiritedly than anyone else, immediately stopped and shoved his hands into his pockets.

Thomas received another round of congratulations when he returned to the table after the ceremony, brandishing his degree proudly. Soon after, people began to excuse themselves: Edmond and the grandfathers were off to join the processional with their respective classes for the Annual Meeting of the Harvard Alumni Association, to be held back in the Tercentenary Theatre, at which United Nations Ambassador Adlai Stevenson was to speak. The grandmothers had plans for tea with an old friend of Mrs. Lathrop who lived on Brattle Street. Ashley was to go with them. After stilted goodbyes had been exchanged, Ellen, Thomas, Carlo and Angela found themselves alone.

"Thank you, Mother," Thomas said to Ellen, placing a hand tenderly on her shoulder. She nodded, accepting his appreciation for what she had engineered.

"I can see why you're so devoted to her," she said under her breath so that only he could hear. His eyes filled with tears. Turning his back to the others, he brushed them away with the palms of his hands quickly, embarrassed, and cleared his throat.

"Now," he said, particularly to Carlo, "shall we go hear Stevenson?"

The ambassador, bedecked in the scarlet and cerise robe of Oxford with an Oxford don's hat, stepped to the podium at half past two. Carlo listened skeptically as Stevenson discussed the role of the United States and the United Nations in both preserving peace and confronting the threat of Communism. "In Asia, too," Stevenson stated, partway through the speech, "I do not believe our aims are false. The right we seek to defend is the right of people, be it in Korea or South Vietnam, not to have their future decided by violence. I do not believe this right can be secured by retreat. Retreat leads to retreat, just as aggression leads to aggression in this still-primitive international community." Carlo scoffed, elbowing Thomas and shaking his head.

"Not to have their future decided by violence?" he whispered. "What does he call Operation Rolling Thunder?" Thomas nodded in support. He still did not generally engage in political conversation with Carlo, feeling that his opinions were vague, caught somewhere between Edmond's Republican values, his mother's Democratic liberalism, and Carlo's intense leftist ideas—which made sense, though they were difficult to square with anything he had heard before. At Harvard, Thomas had joined no associations other than the two athletic teams and the Classics Club, and was as unlikely to attend the anti-war protests that had been taking place on campus as he was to participate in the small-but-vocal Goldwater rallies the year before.

Edmond met them in the Square after the program ended. He too had been skeptical of the speech for different reasons, having little faith in the international community, the rise of which Stevenson identified as the means to long-term world stability. Thomas, knowing that Edmond and Carlo would be at odds, prayed that they wouldn't discuss Stevenson's remarks.

The final event of the day was to be dinner. Ellen had proposed a party at home, and the Lathrops had offered to throw one in his honor in Lincoln. Thomas had politely declined both. Instead, the five of them boarded the Red Line and crossed the river into Boston to have dinner in the North End. Edmond had hoped to excuse himself, but Ellen had insisted he come, knowing it was important to Thomas.

The maître d' at The European was expecting them. A slender older man with silver hair, he welcomed them graciously, uniformed in his starched white tuxedo shirt, black vest and bowtie. Thomas had called ahead to reserve a table and to arrange payment so that the bill wouldn't be brought to the table. He wanted to avoid any awkwardness around who would pay, knowing there would be enough awkwardness already.

Antipasti, followed by large, square pizzas still bubbling with sauce, cheese, artichoke hearts, sausage, peppers, and anchovies, along with pitchers of beer began to arrive at the table, which was large enough to seat a dozen people or more. Just after the food was served, Marcello and Antonella and two of their children emerged from the dark, smoky hallway into the room. Nino and Rosa were right behind them. Paolo's parents came a few minutes later. There were effusive hugs and kisses all around, congratulatory for Thomas, welcoming of Ellen. Nino greeted Ellen with tears.

"How could I ever forget this face? You were a vision, prettier than any flower in your mother's beautiful garden, bringing us lemonade. And what a fool I was. Of course Vito was crazy for you." He grinned, wrapping an arm around her shoulder. "Well, better late than never. You're part of the family now."

Ellen kept an eye on Thomas throughout the evening. He seemed relaxed, at home in his own body in a way she had never seen before. He was laughing, animated, telling stories. At one point he even pulled Angela to her feet and danced with her, spinning her around to the cheers of the crowd. Ellen tried, briefly, to convince herself that he was caught up in the celebration, unburdened, happy to be done with school, to have his thesis finished, to have his law school acceptance. She knew, though, that those things had little to do with his transformation. Yes, it was a transformation. He was becoming himself, the self they had raised him not to be.

The festivities eventually moved on to Caffé Pompeii, where they continued until well after midnight, though without Ellen and Edmond, who, against the clamorous urging of the other members of the party, hailed a cab in front of the restaurant to go home.

The following morning Thomas woke groggily in his bed in Gloucester. He began to open the cards he had received at the party in the North End, embarrassed to discover that each one contained crisp, new ten- and twenty-dollar bills.

viii.

Carlo, remembering Vittorio's struggles—the terrible, pathetic image of him green and retching over the side of the boat—and wanting a good start for Thomas, suggested that he begin on a lobster boat. But Thomas dreamed of nothing less than working on a dragger like his grandfather.

Except for the fact that they both pulled cone-shaped nets across the bottom of the sea to trap fish, the *Barbara Jean* was far removed from the *Samantha* and the other vessels on which Tommaso and Carlo had worked. At a thousand tons and sixty-five feet, with a powerful diesel engine and a wet-fish factory on board, the *Barbara Jean* took a crew of eight men to sea for four days. The old beam trawl, which had held nets open with large timbers, had been replaced by the otter trawl, with two large boards flaring the net apart as they were pulled through the water. Aft of the *Barbara Jean*'s bow-front wheelhouse, with its band of square windows giving the captain a panorama of the water, a mast shaped like an inverted A braced a crane with a power block. Around the base were winches and drums for hauling and storing the nets and lines.

The boat itself was squat, growing slightly wider from the gunnels, before tapering down to the water line, so that it sat on the water like a duck. The wheelhouse was white, the hull blue, a deep shade that appeared black on stormy days.

Thomas had given the same reasoning in convincing his grandmother and Carlo to support his summer job as he had given his mother, and through her, Edmond: it was just for the summer. Before going off to law school and then inexorably into a career, he wanted a glimpse of this life that had sustained, sometimes barely, his forbears. He was pursuing, he told them, a brief taste of his grandfather's life experience, however modern technology might have modified it. Carlo and Angela had made him promise he would go to school in the fall. His grandfather would not have permitted him to forfeit that opportunity for the arduous, unreliable vocation of a fisherman. His mother, appreciating to the extent she could the way her son was changing, the aliveness that seemed to be breaking forth in him, was easy enough to sway. "You worked hard in school, Tom," she acknowledged, "and law school is no walk in the park. If that's how you want to spend the summer, it's fine with me." Edmond, when Ellen told him the news, just shrugged, defeated, and walked out of the room.

For his part, Thomas was scared. In truth, he had never done a strenuous day's work in his life. He was worried that he might not be capable of all that was demanded, afraid that he would fail and embarrass Carlo, that he would be exposed as a pampered rich boy, too coddled and precious to be able to perform as his ancestors had.

Angela and Carlo came down to the pier to see him off on his first day. A warm breeze fluttered Angela's crocheted shawl. The morning had begun cloudy and cool, but the sun was dissolving the clouds, and summer warmth and humidity were setting in.

"Keep an eye on what they're doing, boy," Carlo counseled, taking Thomas by the arm and leading him a few steps away, out of his grandmother's hearing. Carlo wasn't sure it was possible to learn the trade starting so late in life. In Sicily, boys learned to fish as they learned to walk, knowing the sea as well as they knew land. "You're the new man. They'll give you all the shit work. Do it well and don't complain. Stay outta the way when they're setting the net and when they're hauling in, but keep your eye on what they're doing. Nobody's going to stop to explain it to you." This was at least the fifth time Carlo had given him these instructions in the previous days, which only contributed to his apprehension. On Thomas's mind, too, was his father's failure as a fisherman. He wanted to prove he could do it—to Carlo, to the community of Sicilian fishermen in Gloucester who knew his family, and to himself. He kissed Carlo and his grandmother and boarded the trawler, turning as he stepped on deck to wave once more.

Four days later he returned, exhausted. He stumbled off the boat onto solid ground as though drunk, and collapsed abruptly, his legs folding beneath him. "Here you go, College, have a square," one of his more sympathetic crewmates said, following him onto the pier and offering him a cigarette. Thomas declined, suspecting that the one he had smoked at the beginning of the trip, the first one he had ever smoked in his life, had contributed to the sour stomach that had afflicted him throughout. The crewmate, Robert, who they called "Shark" because of his teeth, a tall, powerful man with a coarse beard who seemed more a lumberjack than a fisherman, grinned down at him, his top incisors protruding onto his lower lip. "Don't worry, champ. You'll get used to it."

He staggered home from the pier in a daze. He had never been so tired, or so dirty. His face had never shown four days' growth of beard. His hands were swollen, with oozing, broken blisters across his palms, his fingers nearly frostbitten. One of his "shit" jobs was to operate the ice machine and to shovel crushed ice across the catch in the damp, cave-like hold. Famished and dehydrated, dizzy, he had been unable to eat or drink much once the boat reached deeper waters and began to roll with the heavier surf. Sleep had been fragmented, a few minutes or an hour at a time. He had endured a good amount of ribbing. The crew called him "College," or "Harvard," and seemed amused by his struggle.

Later, though, after he had bathed and eaten the dinner Angela had prepared specially to welcome him home, the discouragement he carried off the boat began to lighten. After all, he had not vomited even once, and he had been able to complete every task he'd been given. His body ached, but it was the kind of aching he could tolerate, that he found satisfying like after a long, hard run. Over dinner, and then afterwards, sitting in the living room, he asked Carlo question after question about fishing, questions he hadn't known enough to ask before.

"In my day, fishing was an art," Carlo grumbled. "You had to feel it, feel the signs Mother Nature was giving you. Now it's all about sonar and power winches, boats the size of battleships. I wish you could've gone out once or twice with your grandfather and me. We could've shown you how to fish."

"I think the captain likes me," Thomas said proudly, holding a biscotti in one hand and a warm cup of chamomile tea, which his grandmother had made to soothe his stomach, in the other. "He invited me into the wheelhouse at one point and even let me take the helm for a few minutes while we were dragging." The captain, Elio Geraci, was an old friend of Carlo's. He had never learned much English, spending most of his life on the water with others who spoke his or some other related Sicilian dialect. He was plump, round everywhere except for his long, pointed nose. His rheumy eyes scanned the sea incessantly, and, in truth, he relied more on his innate, unteachable instincts than on the sonar to find shoals of cod, haddock and flounder. Thomas was intrigued by him, part of the reason why, despite the challenges of the first trip, he began to look forward to the next one.

By mid-July, his sixth voyage on the *Barbara Jean*, Thomas was moving deftly about the boat. His novice's chores had become second nature, and he was beginning to learn new aspects of the trade: working the trawl and sorting and processing the catch.

With no trouble at all, he was able to eat on board, and even fell asleep in seconds when given the opportunity. The smell of fish no longer tormented him; he barely noticed it. Having survived a severe thunderstorm and some strong gales, he felt that he was prepared for anything that might happen. He was stronger too, his upper-body muscles adding bulk and tone with the hard work. At the end of a trip he was always tired—happy to see Angela, have a good meal and fall into bed. Two days later, though, he would be ready to go back to work. He liked being on the water, out of sight of land, disentangled from the world. Especially after two or three days at sea, he didn't appear different in any way from the rest of the crew, a fact which satisfied him immensely.

His crewmates still referred to him by his nicknames, but they'd grown less suspicious of his motivations in dabbling in their profession and were impressed by his willingness to work hard at the jobs no one else wanted to do. They even invited him to join them at night in the bars when they were in Gloucester. Occasionally, he did go down to Main Street to have a beer with Robert and other new friends. When he appeared, sheepishly, the Shark would smile his sharp-toothed smile and clap a weighty arm around his shoulder, announcing to those assembled: "Here's the best-educated deck hand in all of Gloucester. Let's have one over here for Mr. Harvard—on me!" Thomas enjoyed being part of the crowd and eventually began to feel at ease, sitting on his barstool and listening, mostly, as the others told stories about fishing, cars and girls.

Because he was different—a new face, shy, a bit mysterious— he began to attract the attention of some of the women who congregated in the bars with the fishermen. Unaware of this phenomenon until Robert and the others started teasing him about it, he was immediately uncomfortable. He had never had a girlfriend. In his other world, a girlfriend had seemed unattainable. He no more expected to be able to go on a date with a girl than he did to wake up one morning with blond hair and blue eyes. He didn't even consider it. In fact, he had contemplated a life of celibacy in the monastery without any clear understanding or experience of what he would be giving up.

And yet, he had been raised to be polite. When Andrea asked him on a date—Andrea, the daughter of an affable fisherman Vittorio had played with as a child and worked with as an adult—he said yes. The date was a disaster. He was too nervous to make conversation, too intimidated to notice that she was pretty, with large, dark eyes and a warm, easy smile. She found him strange and boring and was as happy to end the evening after an awkward dinner as he was relieved.

Linda, whose family owned a produce store in town, was more aggressive and less fazed by his social ineptitude. She provided all the conversation, filling any silence he left with more information than he could take in about her family, friends, enemies, favorite music, movies, recent trip to New York, and so forth. He drove her home after dinner, planning a quick escape. Parked in front of her house, however, to his horror she kissed him, leaning over and placing her hand on his leg appallingly close to his crotch. He was stunned, especially because, in his view, the date had not gone particularly well. They hadn't connected on any level. Thomas pulled back reflexively, as though her lips had burned his mouth, which he could not stop himself from wiping on his shirtsleeve where it left a brown-pink lipstick smudge. "What?" Linda said, both defensive and accusing, settling back into the passenger seat and rolling her eyes. "You don't like girls, or something?"

"No, I just . . . I'm sorry. I . . ." he stammered. She glanced at him disdainfully, raising one eyebrow.

"Forget about it," she mumbled. "I'll see ya." She slammed the car door behind her and walked toward the house without looking back.

There were no more dates. On the boat, or in a crowd in a bar, he could almost imagine fitting in. He knew he didn't entirely, but he could pretend. Alone, on a date with a woman who might want something from him that he didn't know how to give, he felt like an oddity. More than anything, he wanted to exist plausibly in this environment. Dating only reminded him of how different he was, providing a foil for all the non-Sicilian-fisherman aspects of his history and personality.

He was confused, though, as well. He wanted to be in this world, to figure out who he was. And yet he had absorbed, in his upbringing, the sense that girls like Linda were sleazy, tacky, not good enough for people like him. Her makeup, overdone, and her perfume, too sharp and sweet, the way she dressed and talked, her hairstyle—none of it fit the concept of "attractive" that had subconsciously been inculcated. Even afterwards, he could not put words to the sense of repulsion he had felt when she tried to kiss him. Instead, he felt angry: at her for setting back his quest and reminding him of what he wasn't, and then at himself for being such a snob and a prude.

No more dates. Maybe someday, he thought. Not now.

After a day off at home when the August mugginess was smothering even along the coast, late, after Angela had gone to bed and hours before he was to board the *Barbara Jean* for another trip to sea, Thomas drove to Cambridge. He parked on the edge of Cambridge Common and crossed Massachusetts Avenue. The midnight air was cooling down to a breathable temperature.

Bearing to the right, he walked slowly around to the front of Austin Hall, the building where he was to begin studying law in less than a month. He continued on around the building and into the quad in front of Langdell Hall, named for the school's first dean, Christopher Columbus Langdell. Thomas had been on the law school campus several times, but somehow at night Langdell seemed even more hulking and fortresslike than it did during the day. Massive columns separated by impressive leaded-glass windows formed the long, formidable façade. The building was mismatched with the other nondescript buildings on the quad, like a grotesquely overdeveloped muscleman in a crowd of school children. Thomas sat down on the steps in front of the main entrance. He pulled a handkerchief from his pocket and wiped the sweat from his forehead. He'd been trying to imagine what it was going to be like to go back to school, to undertake this daunting new endeavor, for which he felt little inner motivation. Driving in to see the school, he had hoped, might help him to steel himself, to make sense of what was about to happen.

Now, sitting on the steps, hugging his knees, all the old distressing feelings began to rise up in him. He recalled, too, the day nearly a year earlier when he had come to the law school for an interview. Standing out most in his mind from the brief tour he had been given were the looks of discouragement, frustration, and exhaustion on the faces of the students. *They all seem miserable,* he thought at the time. Of course, the word that trickled down to undergrads was about the "pressure." The saying went: "The first year they scare you to death, the second year they work you to death, the third year they bore you to death." None of it sounded appealing to Thomas.

The longer he sat surveying the campus, the more morose he became. He was going to law school to please Edmond, who hoped he'd become more like a Wellington and less like Vittorio Amorelli's bastard son; and to please his mother, who wanted to go to law school herself but couldn't—because of him; and to please Angela and Carlo, who wanted him to do it because maybe, finally, it would validate the sacrifices they made. If he succeeded, if he made something of himself, then maybe it would have been worth his grandfather's life, and his father's life, and everything else they had been through. They'd be devastated, he knew, if he ended up just a fisherman. He knew this was true of his grandmother, and Carlo too, though Carlo would never admit it. He ran his fingers through his hair—one hand, and then the other—and then shook his head. He lay back on the concrete steps, folding his hands together under his head and stared up at the stars, shimmering vaguely through the haze and the city lights.

An hour later he woke, troubled, from a dream he couldn't remember. After a moment of figuring out where he was, his mind cleared. "I'm not going," he thought. "I'm not doing it." He sat up, his heart beating rapidly. "I'm not going," he called out to the empty quad. His voice caromed off the buildings and echoed back to him. "You have to love the law," the admissions officer had told him. "I don't give a shit about the law!" he shouted now. "I never wanted to do this." He stood up. "I'm not going. I'm not going," he repeated, mantra-like. "I'm not going?" He thought about Edmond and his mother, and his stomach tightened. There would be a battle. He thought about his grandmother and Carlo, and felt sad. He didn't want to disappoint them, to take away the hope he had only recently restored to them. But he also did not want his time with them to end, with his life swallowed up whole by the demands of law school. "I'm . . . not . . . going."

Later, he would remember this moment on the steps in front of Langdell Hall as the second of three turning points in his life, three times when an equal and opposite force rose to overpower the inertia of his existence. The first had been when the monk had diagnosed his halfness. The third would come when Angela sent him away.

Ellen made Edmond a stronger-than-usual gin and tonic when he came home from the office. "They granted Thomas's request for a deferral at the law school. He can start next fall instead." With more time to reflect, Thomas had moderated his impulse, deciding this approach, to defer for a year, was both safer and more likely to gain his parents' approval.

"What?" Edmond had finished his drink and was sitting in his chair in the living room, irritated, distracted, watching Walter

Cronkite, *The Wall Street Journal* folded in his lap. He had driven home in heavy traffic through a forceful late-day thunderstorm. Cronkite's coverage of Dr. King's latest actions in the wake of the Watts riots was only making him more cross.

"Thomas has been granted a deferral."

"A deferral? For what? What are you talking about?" She had his full attention.

Ellen had positioned herself behind him, with her back to him. She was arranging flowers, which she had purchased so that she could have her back to him busily doing something. Edmond turned in his chair. "I'm waiting," he prompted.

"Uh, well," she answered, trying to sound relaxed, "I guess he was feeling like he was just starting to learn about . . . the work he's doing, and, he just wanted to have a chance to pursue it to the point where he had sort of mastered it, and . . . oh, I don't know, dear. He's having some fun, that's all. He wants a break from school."

"We're cutting him off." Edmond's face reddened. "That's it. We're cutting him off!"

"Edmond, stop yelling," Ellen pled. "Ashley will hear you. She's upstairs." She wiped her hands on a dishtowel and turned to face him, hands on her hips. "We're not cutting him off," she insisted, still attempting to sound unperturbed. "He's our son. In any case, we can't *cut him off*, as you say, Edmond. He doesn't really need us anymore. He's an adult. He has full control of the trust my parents set up for him. We'll lose him if we try to cut him off any other way."

"You're always so damned afraid of losing him. He doesn't seem so concerned about losing you. I'm done, Ellen. I am finished!" He was shouting again.

"Edmond, stop it. I do not understand why you react like this. Why do you take it so personally? He's never said an unkind word to you."

"Oh no? Have you noticed that after twenty years he's taken to calling me *Edmond* instead of *Dad*? Are you telling me that's just a coincidence? When he refers to *his father* these days, have you noticed that he's not talking about me? Last time he was home, I heard him describe me to someone he was talking to on the telephone as his *stepfather*."

"Okay, dear. I can understand how that would be upsetting to you, though I don't believe he intends it in a negative way. He would never mean to hurt you."

"Oh, fine, Ellen. And when he comes home to tell us that he's changing his name to Amorini or whatever the hell it is, you're going to tell me not to let that bother me either, right?"

She crossed the room, turned off the television and sat down opposite him on the sofa. "Edmond, I think we have to face the fact that we might have done him a disservice in not telling him more . . . and earlier. I think he suffered . . . a lot . . . not being able to explain to himself or to his peers, to other people, why he doesn't look like us or anyone else in his life. We never talked about it very much—did we, you and I? We just . . . hoped he wouldn't notice. It seems kind of ridiculous now." She smiled sadly. "Now it's all new, and he's a grown man, and I think he just has to go and . . . explore it."

"So he's going to be a fisherman. Instead of a lawyer. And we sent him to Belmont Hill and Harvard for that?" He grabbed at his already-loosened tie, pulling it further down his neck, then crossed his arms on his chest. The newspaper slipped off his lap and fell to the floor.

"He's not going to be a fisherman instead of a lawyer. He's loving the fishing. It means something to him that I don't think we can understand. He wants a little more time. It's only been a couple of months. He's been a good son. You know he has. Honors at Harvard. Star of the cross-country team. Give him a year to do this, dear. Otherwise he'll always wonder. I just know he'll be bitter if we try to force him to start law school now when it's not what he wants to do. He'll be miserable, and he'll blame us."

"You worry too damned much about how he feels."

"And you worry too much about what people will say. You're going to be embarrassed if he puts off school. What will you tell your friends?" She paused, taking a moment to convince herself that it was time to say what had gone unsaid for too long. "You know, I think part of why you're so angry—out of proportion to the situation, talking about disowning him for God's sake—is that you're mad at me for the mistake I made. We've never talked much about that either. You've always been wonderful and accepting, but your reaction to this whole thing—to his finding his other family—makes me think that you've always been a little embarrassed or ashamed, and that we've never dealt with your anger at me."

"That's ridiculous."

"Is it?"

"I knew what I was getting myself into."

"I'm not sure you did. I'm not sure I did. Obviously, there was some place—seems like a big place in retrospect—where we weren't able to deal with it between ourselves, or else we wouldn't have conspired to hide the truth from him."

"Conspired? What the hell are you talking about? I treated that boy like my own son, and now he's throwing it all in my face, and I think I have a right to be angry about that. As far as the rest of this . . . *psychology* you're putting forth, I think it's crap." His eyes glinted, fiery, menacing. They looked at each other in silence for a moment. Ellen heard Ashley in the hallway upstairs and worried that she had overheard the entire exchange. She lowered her voice.

"Fine, Edmond. Forget it. The bottom line is this: he's twenty-two years old. He's a man. He's making his own decisions now. I had a good talk with him about school. I challenged him some, and it's clear that he's thought it through. I think we have to support him."

"Support him? I can't even look at him. I don't know what to say to him. How'm I supposed to support him?"

"Why don't you try asking him what it's like working on a fishing boat?"

"Very funny." He reached down and snapped up the newspaper from where it had landed between his feet.

"I'm serious, dear. Reach out to him a little bit. It'll make it much easier when this is all done and he's found what he needs to find and made peace with it, for him to come back."

Edmond got up out of his chair. "I've given him everything, and now he's chasing a ghost." He shook his head and walked out of the room.

"Edmond, where are you going? Stay here and finish this," Ellen entreated.

"It is finished. I'm finished," she heard him say as he ascended the stairs.

The following day she wrote to Thomas: "Your father is very upset about your deferral. He'll get over it, but we're going to need a little time. Maybe it's best you not come out for Labor Day."

Following his mother's direction, Thomas didn't go with the family to the Vineyard for the holiday, but instead stayed in Gloucester. In a conciliatory letter to Edmond, composed on Monday night after Angela had gone to bed, he explained his reasons for seeking a deferral, asking Edmond to understand. Two weeks passed before he realized that there would be no response. He stayed away from Belmont for several months, at first to give Edmond time, and then because of Carlo's illness.

Thomas revealed his concern to his grandmother at breakfast before leaving for the harbor on a gloomy morning in October. As usual at that time of year, Angela's mind was occupied by memories of Lieutenant Rienzo coming to tell her that Tommaso was dead, and of her son's birth. The cooler air, the shorter days, the leaves changing colors, the flowers and vegetables in the garden going to seed: everything around her contributed to the atmosphere, to the re-presentation of her grief. Distracted and morose, she had been vaguely aware that Carlo was not looking well. Thomas's words alarmed her.

"Sometimes I hear him get up three or four times during the night to use the bathroom. He picks at his food. Have you noticed? And his limp seems worse than usual. He looks sort of . . . gray and . . . smaller. I'm thinking about making him an appointment with a doctor."

Angela poured coffee into his cup, and then into her own. "He won't go," she stated, matter of factly. "He hasn't been to a doctor since he left the army. I tried to get him to go once when his gout was bad, and another time when he had a cough that I was sure would kill him. He won't go."

Later in the week, when Thomas had returned from a drizzly, cold fishing trip with a health problem of his own in the form of an acute cold, the three were around the table finishing supper. Carlo pushed his chair back from the table and rose to his feet with evident strain, grabbing onto the edge of the table for stability and clenching his teeth.

"What's wrong with you?" Angela asked in the accusative, annoyed tone that somehow conveyed love and concern.

"Nothing," he mumbled, turning his back to her to hide the pain on his face. "Just a little sore."

"Where are you sore?"

"I don't know. My back and sort of right here," he answered, pressing his hands into his hips.

"Uncle," Thomas rasped with what was left of his voice, "I'm going to call the doctor about my cold. I think it might be bronchitis. Why don't you come with me to see him? He's a good doctor. Nanna says you haven't had a checkup in a while."

"That's a good idea, *Cucinu*. Go to the doctor with Vito." She often mistakenly called him Vito. She tried not to think of Thomas as a God-given replacement, as a kind of restoration or requital for her dead son, but these things played in her subconscious.

"I'm not going to the doctor with Vito, or Tomuzzu, or anyone else," he barked. "I've made it this far without a damned doctor."

"I'm just a little worried about you," Thomas ventured. "You look a bit . . . tired. Let Dr. Reeves have a quick look at you. It'll only take a few minutes."

"Don't you two start ganging up on me. What's Dr. Reeves going to tell me? That I'm an old man. I already know that. Jesus Christ, that's the only thing I know anymore. No doctor for me. No thank you." He shuffled tenderly out of the room.

A week later he relented, privately to Thomas, not wanting to upset Angela. Pain in his hips, pain when he tried, often unsuccessfully, to urinate, tinges of blood when he did force out a squirt of pee—together the symptoms had begun to frighten him.

"All right, all right, I'll go see your damned doctor," he told Thomas, which Thomas found surprising, as he had not mentioned the doctor again since their conversation a week earlier. "Just don't tell your grandmother."

Dr. Reeves, a tall, still-strong looking, silver-haired older man who had captained the crew team at Harvard during Edmond's father's era, after asking only a few questions, referred Carlo to a specialist at Massachusetts General Hospital. Reeves had been family doctor to the Wellingtons for years. He was a kind gentleman who spoke softly, arms across his broad chest. "I'd like to have a colleague of mine examine you, sir. I'm concerned, from what you tell me, about your prostate."

Carlo turned to Thomas. "What did he say? What the hell is a prostate?"

"Your prostate is a gland about this size." The doctor made a circle with his forefinger and thumb. "It's located below your bladder. It generates the fluid in semen."

"This is why I don't go to the doctor," Carlo mumbled to Thomas.

The doctor's secretary typed a letter for them on crisp, ivory-colored stationery while they waited in the small, brightly lit reception room. Carlo grumbled to himself about doctors and prostates while Thomas tapped his foot nervously and stared at a photograph on the wall of the doctor standing on the bank of a white-water river in his wading boots, fly-fishing vest and hat, holding a foot-long trout.

At first Carlo refused to see Dr. Cunningham, arguing that one doctor every fifty years was enough. But after two more nights of frequent, agonizing trips to the bathroom, he again acquiesced. They told Angela they were going into the city to see Nino and Rosa, news which sent her into the kitchen to prepare a basket of food. They planned, after the appointment, to deliver the basket to the Murabitos, afraid Angela would somehow find out that they had lied.

The appointment nearly ended abruptly when Dr. Cunningham explained the process he would use to examine Carlo's prostate. Carlo stood up and began to walk towards the door. Thomas stepped into his path. "Please. For me and Nanna."

Carlo threw his hands in the air in powerless outrage. "You want me to let him stick his finger up my ass for you and Angela? And I'm the sick one?"

Finally, after a lengthy negotiation which included an oath by Thomas that he would never tell anyone about the rectal exam, Dr. Cunningham went ahead with the procedure. Thomas sat in the waiting room, tense, until the doctor came out to speak to him.

"I don't like the condition of his prostate at all," the doctor told him somberly. Cunningham was a smaller man, about his mother's age, Thomas guessed, with a straight forelock which he pushed back from his face at the end of each sentence. He wore wire-rimmed glasses and a fresh, white lab coat over his brown tweed suit. His manner was reserved and formal. Noticing his short, stubby fingers, Thomas winced to think of what had just taken place in the examining room. "It's significantly enlarged, with a number of nodules. No wonder at all he's experiencing such acute symptoms. I'm afraid the cancer may be quite advanced. I'd suggest we do further labs right away."

"Cancer?" He had feared something serious was wrong, but hearing the word was a blow he hadn't anticipated.

"Yes. I'm sorry. Cancer of the prostate. Unfortunately it often metastasizes to the bones, the kidneys, and eventually the liver. We need to determine quickly whether it's gone beyond the prostate. Then you'll have to decide as a family on a course of treatment. We can certainly try radiation and chemical therapies, though if it's moved as far as stage four, well . . . then I'd encourage you to consider palliative care and try to make the most of the time he has left."

Thomas's felt a cold sweat on his forehead, and he began to feel dizzy, as though he might faint. In that moment, he realized how much he had grown to love his grandmother and Carlo. Losing Carlo would mean losing half of his connection to something he knew he couldn't have on his own. He sat down, gripping the arm of the waiting room chair. Dr. Cunningham lowered himself into the chair next to his.

"I know this is difficult to hear," he said.

"I'm not sure I followed the whole thing. Metastasize and . . . chemical therapies," Thomas managed to reply, looking down at his hands, trying to focus his eyes and stop his head from spinning.

"I apologize. Perhaps that's too much information to begin with. Why don't we go back in and see if we can't encourage him to agree to some biopsies."

"The doctor thinks it may be treatable," Thomas offered hopefully. "Radiation and chemotherapy. They can do miracles these days." The hollowness of his words was amplified by the fact that Carlo seemed not to hear them. He was staring out the car window, wan and fragile, using his overcoat as a blanket, his eyes fixed on a point in the distance. For a time Thomas tried to figure out what Carlo was watching, but it didn't seem to be anything visible, tangible, earthly. Several minutes passed in silence. Thomas could think of nothing to say. Instead, he was beginning to worry about what they were going to tell Angela. Then, Carlo spoke, responding as though a significant interval—more than ten minutes—had not passed.

"No, no, Tomuzzu. No radiation for me. No chemicotherapy, or how you say it."

"But, Uncle, Dr. Cunningham said . . ."

"I've lived a long life, *Niputi*," the old fisherman interrupted. "You must remember that. Dr. Cunningham's job is to keep me from dying. That's the problem with doctors—one of the problems. There are many problems with them. You know, I never imagined I would live this long, Tomuzzu. Never. It's funny, really, a sad kind of joke, that God would waste a long life on someone like me." He continued to face out the window as he spoke, staring far off. "After your grandfather died, I came back, back to America, to apologize to your grandmother. Otherwise, I would have been happy to die in France and be buried with Tommaso. But I had to apologize to Angela. I needed to do that, and then I didn't really care what happened to me. When I got back to Gloucester, I couldn't face her. I was so angry that God had taken my cousin instead of me, and so angry at myself for letting it happen. I was going to leave, but there was nowhere to go. I couldn't go back to Sicily like that. It was too pathetic. I thought maybe I'd go into the city and drink myself to death as fast as possible. Before I could do that, your grandmother heard that I was in town, and she sent someone to get me. I was sleeping in a shack on the beach. When I went and found her in the cabin with your father . . . I'll never forget that moment. I thought maybe there was a reason for me to continue to live after all, a purpose, something I could do that would be good and useful. And, I'm happy I lived long enough to know you." He turned his face from the window for the first time, briefly, to look at Thomas, and then turned back. Thomas tried to swallow. "And now . . . now I'm old. I've had my life. Dr. Cunningham might want to fight. That's what they do. Otherwise, they fail. But I just don't have that kind of fight in me, Tomuzzu. Not anymore."

Thomas wanted to object. He wanted to counter what Carlo was saying. He wanted to tell him to stop talking like that, to cheer up, to be optimistic. Instead, he was quiet. Two miles passed, and then another. He glanced at Carlo and saw that the old man's eyes were heavy with sleep. "Uncle," he whispered. "I'm glad you lived long enough for us to meet too. Thank you for taking such good care of Angela and my father when he was a child. I don't know where they would have been without you."

Carlo smiled, reaching out to pat Thomas on the arm. A minute later he was asleep, his head resting against the window.

Arriving in Gloucester, Thomas helped Carlo from the car, dreading the impending and unavoidable confrontation with his grandmother and the truth.

"What are you two up to?" she asked, once the two men were seated at the table for dinner. "You're sneaking around like a couple of thieves. One of you tell me what's going on."

Thomas looked at Carlo, who indicated—jutting his chin up slightly and hunching his shoulders—that Thomas should speak.

"I convinced Carlo to see a doctor." He looked down at his bowl of pasta to avoid Angela's prosecutorial eyes.

"A doctor. Well, Carlo. A doctor? After all these years? That's an accomplishment, Tomuzzu." Thomas wasn't sure if she was being sarcastic. "Why I wasn't invited to join you . . . well, never mind. I realized long ago that I would never understand how a man's brain works. Or doesn't work. So, tell me then, what did the doctor have to say? Our old Carlo hasn't been himself, has he?"

"He has cancer. Prostate cancer." Thomas glanced up to see the reaction on his grandmother's face. She was standing, as she often did while they ate, having already eaten in the kitchen. She looked at Thomas, and then at Carlo, who continued eating as though the conversation was not taking place. In her hands she held a cut-glass pitcher of water, a birthday gift many years earlier from Marie. She was about to water her plants. Instead, she put the pitcher down on the table and dried her hands on her apron.

"I don't know what that means," she said to Thomas. And then, after a moment, to Carlo: "*Cancru?*"

Carlo nodded without looking up. Carlo and Thomas waited. After a moment she crossed herself, then picked up the pitcher of water and carried it into the kitchen.

Carlo died early in the new year, on a cold, clear morning. Three inches of powdery snow had fallen silently during the night before the little storm meandered out to sea. Thomas had tried to convince Angela to call an ambulance the evening before. Carlo's ankles were swollen and his fingernails were a sickly bluish. His throat gurgled as though he needed to clear it but lacked the strength, and his chest rattled with each shallow breath. His face was gray and drawn. He had not been awake all day. Sepsis was rapidly poisoning him, seizing whatever life remained.

"I think we should take him to the hospital. Something's wrong," Thomas whisepered.

"No. Nothing's wrong." She rested her hand on his arm. "There's nothing they can do for him at the hospital. There's nothing anyone can do for him now except God Himself. It won't be long now." She had placed an icon of the Madonna on the table next to his bed. She lit a candle in front of the icon and then, carefully, wrapped a rosary around Carlo's hands, which were together on his laboring chest.

Thomas fell asleep in a chair next to the bed. Angela woke him and sent him to bed at midnight. She woke him again shortly after dawn. "Come say goodbye," she whispered.

There was an excruciating lapse between each breath now. His frame rose and fell erratically with each one. They said the rosary together. They would say it again after he died, before the coroner arrived.

Carlo held on until midmorning. Thomas was sure each breath was his last, and then his gaunt chest, wrapped in his bathrobe and buried in blankets, would rise scantly once again. Marie came with food, but no one ate. She hugged Thomas, and then spoke something in a hushed tone in Carlo's ear. She was elderly herself, but still moved with the energy of someone much younger. Thomas heard her a short time later cleaning the already-spotless kitchen.

Nino called to find out how things were. Thomas and Angela each spoke to him briefly, promising to call if there was any news.

Then there was silence.

Ellen came to the funeral, which was held in the chapel at St. Anne's in Gloucester. Nino and Rosa came, and Marie, and a few of the old fishermen. Thomas and Father Marzani had planned the service the previous afternoon in the priest's study. Nino read the twenty-third Psalm in Italian from his own tattered family Bible. The priest read from the Gospel of Matthew: the story of the calling of the fishermen, Andrew and Peter, James and John.

After Father Marzani's homily, Thomas spoke, standing at the lectern dressed in a black suit, his hair combed neatly to the side. "Carlo was my grandfather's best friend, more like a brother than a cousin. He was my father's father, the closest he ever had to one, and a good one at that. I called him *Uncle*, but he was more like a grandfather to me, and more than a grandfather: a friend, a teacher. I only regret that circumstances didn't allow us more time." Ellen listened to her son's words. She hardly recognized him. He looked the same, but seemed another person, a stranger who reminded her of her son. She imagined, as he spoke, how different her life might have been if Vittorio had lived, if they had married and she had lived this life instead of the other. So much to be lost, or gained, or both. Could she have managed it? Would she have liked it? Would they have accepted her, Protestant upper-class girl that she was? What would Vittorio have expected of a wife? Would she have suffocated under his expectation? Had she really, as things turned out, lived any bigger, any more expansive or liberated a life in Belmont? It wasn't the one she had once envisioned. Things happen for a reason, she told herself, thinking especially of Ashley, whom she adored. Maybe. Or maybe they just happen.

Thomas concluded his remarks, thanking everyone for coming, for their prayers and support, and inviting them back to the house for dinner. He returned to his pew and took his seat between Ellen and Angela, who was wearing a new mourning dress and veil Thomas had insisted she allow him to buy for her. An initial tear opened the way for sobs, which he attempted to stifle by pressing his handkerchief against his mouth. Later, after the committal at the cemetery, walking back to the car, Ellen told him she couldn't ever remember seeing him cry like that, not even when he was a child.

"I don't think I've ever felt so sad," he replied. "I don't think I've ever felt so . . . anything. I can't explain it, except I guess to say that it hurts, and I can tell that it hurts."

ix.

The man grunted as he knelt, shouldered his bag, and stood. He reached up and pulled his hat down lower on his forehead. His thin face, always clean shaven, had the worn, leathered skin of one who has made a long living out of doors. When he smiled, a starburst of creases shone from the edges of his eyes and the corners of his mouth and his spare lips all but disappeared. Trim, his uniform size hadn't changed in more than thirty years of service. He had missed few days of work over those decades, other than a week to bury his son.

A blustery March wind opposed him as he strained to open the door. He stepped out into a thin mist; any colder and it would have been snow flurries. As always, he was thinking about David Junior. Day and night his mind was filled with memories of his boy and the man he had become. Four months had passed since his death, but the pain had scarcely abated.

D.J., as he was known, had joined the Marines with his father's blessing three years earlier after graduating from high school. At that time, the word Vietnam was unfamiliar to most people in the United States. David Warren was proud that his son had chosen a military career, and that his hard work and dedication in the Marines were being rewarded with advancement. He was not alarmed when he received his son's letter informing his parents that his unit was leaving for a tour of duty in the Far East.

Three hundred five United States servicemen were killed in November of 1965 in the battle of the Ia Drang Valley. David Junior was among them, the first of Belmont's sons to be killed in Vietnam. A dozen more would follow.

Warren pulled his hat lower still to block the mist from his face. He took off his glasses, unzipped his coat and dried the lenses on his sweater. Replacing them on his wet face and zipping his coat up around his neck, he crossed the street and began to climb the hill. He felt sick to his stomach, as he did whenever there were induction notices in the bag to be delivered. When his son arrived in Vietnam, there were 75,000 US troops on the ground. By the end of 1966, there would be 385,000, with more on the way to meet Westmoreland's growing demands. In 1966, 382,010 young men were inducted, the largest number since Korea, and the highest annual total during the Vietnam era. Warren struggled, daily, hourly, to make sense of his son's death, trying to place it alongside those of his friends who had given their lives to stop fascism two decades earlier, but unable to convince himself that it was the same. The struggle continued in his mind. With each day his discomfort with delivering draft notices increased.

He had watched Thomas grow up, the shy, quiet boy on Tyler Street. Being the local postman, he heard plenty of gossip and he knew something of the boy's story. He had seen him playing in the yard as a child, had given him mint gumdrops or licorice sticks which he carried for the children along the way. In later years he had passed him on the street walking home alone from school for lunch. He had seen Thomas out running, training with the soccer team. He was friendly with Ellen, as he was with everyone on his route, though these days he couldn't think of charming or amusing things to say as had been his custom.

At the end of the driveway, he reached into the bag and pulled out the mail for the Wellington family. His stomach turned over. A year earlier he had delivered a draft-classification questionnaire. Thomas had completed the form and mailed it, and Warren had carried back the letter confirming his status: 2-S, full-time student. In the fall, four months after Thomas's graduation, a month after the law school deferral had been granted, and a month before his own son's death, Warren had handed Ellen the letter reclassifying Thomas as 1-A, eligible for the draft.

He paused now, steps from the door, pulled the induction notice from the stack of letters, bills, and Ellen's *McCall's* magazine, and held it in his hand. Fine droplets of water landed on it. The image of his son as a boy appeared before him, and then the image of the medals the military had sent after his death. He winced. Looking up at the house, he was relieved not to see Ellen at the door.

He stepped onto the porch, lifted the cover of the brass letterbox, and dropped the mail into it. Then he turned and hurried away.

Ellen was devastated to see the Selective Service System seal on the envelope when she retrieved the mail from the box later in the day, after returning from a visit to Ashley's school. She had trusted, irrationally she thought now, that Thomas's number wouldn't come up, that he would be spared, and the conflict would wind down and the threat disappear. An old pain rose up in her, raw and open, the pain she had suppressed for two decades, but never expunged. An unbearable loss that she felt she could not face again.

April 7, she thought. Maundy Thursday. Only three weeks away.

An hour later she called the office of Draft Board Sixteen in Arlington, the board with jurisdiction over Belmont. "He's going to school in September," she told the man who answered the phone. "He's already been accepted. He was supposed to start last fall but he deferred his matriculation for a year due to . . . an illness in the family. But he *is* committed to attending in the fall."

"Is he currently a full-time student making satisfactory progress towards a degree?" the man asked, not hiding his irritation, having fielded an increasing number of similar calls since the last round of notices was mailed.

"Well, not exactly, but as I said—"

"Then he's not 2-S. Is he married?"

"No."

"Does he have any handicaps, physical problems?"

"Uh, no."

"I'm sorry, ma'am. Make sure he brings enough clean clothes for three days and enough money to purchase a month's worth of personal items."

Ellen hung up the phone, dropping it slowly onto the cradle as if she might think of something else, something with possibility.

She closed her eyes and rubbed them with her fingers. Upstairs she could hear Ashley and a friend singing. The Beatles had recently released "We Can Work It Out" with "Day Tripper" on the B-side, and Ashley was wearing out the 45 on the record player she'd received for her fifteenth birthday.

Opening her eyes, she scanned the induction notice again. "Willful failure to report at the place and time named in the Order," the document concluded, "subjects the violator to fine and imprisonment."

She picked up the phone and dialed Angela's phone number.

Thomas said good-bye to his mother, after trying to assure her that everything would be all right in the end, and then set the phone down on the hook. He collected himself, and then went in to see his grandmother. "Nanna, I have some . . . bad news." Thomas hadn't told her about his previous correspondence with Draft Board Sixteen. She didn't even know that he was involved in the Selective Service System, much less that in choosing not to go to school to be with her, he had left himself unprotected from the draft—though in fairness, the rapid expansion of the draft had taken the country by surprise. He felt a strange distance from what was about to happen to him, upset more by having to leave than on where he might be going.

"What is it, Tomuzzu?" Angela asked, startled by his tone of voice.

Thomas tried not to sound cheerless. "I've been . . . drafted. I have to report on April 7 for induction into the Army." Angela had been dusting under photographs on the table by the front window. Her back was to Thomas. As he spoke, she froze. A long moment passed. Then he moved, hurrying to her side, afraid she would collapse.

"No." She turned to grip his arm with strength he did not know she had.

"No?" He noticed that she was holding his graduation photograph in her other hand.

"Why?" she demanded.

"Well, there's a ... situation in Asia, a kind of war, I guess, against Communism ... in Vietnam."

"No. They can't have you. Oh, my Jesus. This is going to kill me."

"Sit down, Nanna. Come." He led her to the sofa and settled down next to her. He put his arm around her shoulders. They were silent for a minute, each with thoughts rushing through their minds. Angela was wearing the housedress she always wore for cleaning, maroon with a faint black floral print. Her hair was pulled back, hanging down in a loose braid between her shoulder blades, where it escaped below the black ribbon into an unruly curl.

"That was your mother on the phone?" Angela asked, finally.

"Yes. The notice came in the mail today."

"And what does she say about it?"

"She's upset. She cried a bit ... on the phone. She said I should have stayed in school."

Angela turned to him, focused, intense. "Tomuzzu, people get out of this. People find ways out. There has to be a way out. Doesn't your family know anyone—someone? Please, God, please, go talk to your mother and to her husband. Beg them. *I'll* beg them. They can't let this happen. I won't let it happen if I have to ... Tomuzzu, please." She held his arm tightly. Her breath came short and fast, as though she'd been running. Thomas couldn't look at her. He stared past her at the pictures on the table where she'd been dusting: his grandfather, his father, himself. He wanted to reassure her, to promise her, to swear he would never leave her, but he knew he couldn't, that he no longer had the power to make such a promise.

"Tomuzzu, tell me you'll talk to your mother and her husband."
She always referred to Edmond as his mother's husband. "Please."
Thomas absorbed the despair in her voice. She sounded as though
she were pleading for her own life.

"Okay, Nanna. Okay. I'll go this weekend."

"Can't you call Henry Cabot Lodge?" Ellen suggested. They had
just come home from church, and Edmond was sorting through
the Sunday *Times*, pulling out the sections he intended to read.
Ellen had thought it best for Thomas not to be there.

"Call Henry Cabot Lodge? Are you joking?" Edmond looked
up at her with disbelief. "No. No. I say, let him serve. Frankly, I
think he should do the honorable thing and enlist. He should
enlist in the Navy or the Marines, officer corps. That way he won't
have to serve in the Army." He poured himself a Bloody Mary from
the pitcher Ellen had prepared, sat down at the kitchen table and
opened the front section of the newspaper.

"Can you see Thomas in the Marines?" Ellen asked.

"Honestly, dear, I couldn't have seen him as a fisherman, particularly after the education we provided him." Edmond smirked.
"Perhaps he could go into the Navy, with all that experience he has
now on the high seas. Seriously, Ellen, the military might be good
for him. Teach him a little discipline, get him back to his senses."
He raised the newspaper and held it in front of him to indicate that
the conversation as far as he was concerned was over.

"Edmond, please. Put down the paper. We need to talk about
this." Ellen stood across the table from him, still dressed in her
church clothes, navy skirt with a pale-blue blouse and floral scarf,
in muted tones because it was still winter, and Lent, arms folded
across her chest.

"What's to talk about? He's been drafted. Not surprising really.
He's a healthy young man with nothing much going on in his life

and his country needs to be protected. Now he's going to have to take responsibility for himself."

"Why can't you call Henry? Your parents know him well. He knows my parents too. There must be some reasonable way around this."

"Darling," he replied, in the aggravated inflection he had used to address the children when they were pestering him, "Henry Cabot Lodge is the United States Ambassador to Vietnam. How do you think it would look, from a public relations standpoint, if it were known that he was helping the grandchildren of his country club friends avoid the draft? I'm not sure the president, who, by the way, you voted for and I voted against, would appreciate that. The bottom line, Ellen, is that we're trying to stop an evil force from spreading across Asia and on to who-knows-where. You know as well as I do what those bastards are trying to do. They have to be stopped. We're all going to have to make sacrifices."

A sense of shock coursed through her. "Edmond, how can you talk like that? Good God. We're all going to have to make sacrifices? We're talking about our son's life. We're talking about Ashley's brother. Do you know what it would do to her if something happened to Thomas?"

"He hasn't been very keen on being my son for some time. Interesting that now he wants my help." He snatched the bottle of Tabasco sauce, shook a few drops into his drink and then stirred it aggressively.

"Edmond, you can't possibly be that cold hearted." Frightened, nearly desperate, as this was the only solution she had been able to imagine, her voice was rising. "Jesus Christ. Think about it. His father and his grandfather were both killed. Do you really think it's fair for him to go off to some jungle on the other side of the planet? Think about what his grandmother has already lost."

"Why shouldn't it be fair?" Edmond shot back. "His father and grandfather died fighting for something important. And don't even start with me about his grandmother and what she's had to endure.

She would have been better off starving to death in Italy? They came here for a reason, no? They could have stayed in Italy and died on the wrong side of both wars. Both wars. Instead they died as heroes on the right side. And, in the bargain, she's got a grandson who graduated from the greatest university in the world—lot of goddamned good it's done him."

Ellen shook her head. She wiped away a tear with the tip of her finger. "Please. I'm begging you . . ."

"Ellen, you're getting hysterical. Calm down. Thomas won't be going to Vietnam or anywhere else to fight. He'll do as I said and enlist in one of the other services. I'll take him to the recruiting center myself. He's a Harvard graduate, isn't he? They're not going to put a gun in his hands and send him into the jungle. He'll have a desk job over here somewhere. What the hell they'll do with a classics major I can't imagine, but it won't be combat. Besides—Ellen, please stop crying—this whole Vietnam situation is winding down. It's almost over. Everyone knows that. General Westmoreland says we're in the win phase. They're just teaching the Reds a lesson now, and our troops'll be home before Tom goes anywhere. I guarantee it."

Ellen stared out the window, considering his words, until she felt she could speak. "I don't know, Edmond. I still think you should—"

"I'm not contacting Lodge or anyone else, Ellen. That's final. He'll serve his country honorably like everyone else. Pull yourself together. Everything's going to be fine." He picked up his drink and took a sip. "Maybe he'll learn his damned lesson and go to school like he should have from the start."

"Pilate."

"Pilot?" He repeated. "I don't understand, Nanna."

"Pilate. *Pilatu.* Pontius Pilate."

"I'm afraid I still don't understand." Thomas had returned on Sunday evening from Belmont with the news that nothing could or would be done within the family to intervene with the Selective Service.

"Pilate. That's what we call someone at home who washes his hands and won't do anything, who refuses to act."

"That's sort of harsh, Nanna. I mean, he's not exactly—"

"Harsh?" She sprang to her feet and crossed the room to the table with the photographs. She pointed to the photograph of her husband, taken not long before he left. "Harsh is watching my husband go off to die." She tipped the picture on its face. It fell with a snap. Then, laying a finger on the photograph of his father, standing on the steps in front of the house, she hissed, through clenched teeth, "Harsh is watching my son go off to die." Again she pushed the photograph forward. It clattered on the tabletop. She picked up Thomas's graduation picture. "Harsh is watching my grandson take his turn to go off and die. That would be harsh." She shook her head. "I won't do it, Tomuzzu. I won't do it. *Basta!* Your mother's husband is a rich man. He's a powerful man. He knows people. He could stop this if he wanted to."

Thomas sighed, exhaling slowly. He was confused. Why did Edmond refuse to intervene? Was it a kind of punishment for finding his grandmother and working as a fisherman, or did he really believe Thomas should go? Was it his responsibility to fight for his country? Was it right that he could play the game and probably get a desk job instead of being sent like others to Southeast Asia? And was that even true, would he really get a desk job if he enlisted? And what about Angela? Hadn't she given enough? Did one from every generation have to die? And his mother? Why didn't she stand up to Edmond? Did she think it was right for him to go? His mind jumped from question to unanswerable question.

Angela, who had been brooding over her photographs, brought him back. "Harsh?" she muttered to herself, flicking her fingertips off her chin in a gesture of disdain.

"Nanna, it's not that simple. He's in an awkward position. Just because you know people doesn't mean . . ."

"Exactly. An awkward position. That's why we use the name: *Pilatu.*"

"Nanna, listen, Edmond thinks the war is almost over. A lot of people are saying so. By the time I get trained and so forth—"

"You sound exactly like your father and your grandfather before him, God have mercy on their souls. It's amazing how they can fool us, isn't it, Tomuzzu? Tell me this, Grandson: if the war is almost over, if they don't really need you, then why are they drafting you?"

Thomas had no answer.

Standing across Arlington Street in front of the statue of William Ellery Channing, Angela examined the church, following the spire 190 feet up into the sky. She kept her eyes fixed for a moment on scant, feathery clouds passing high overheard. She had learned early on never to enter a Protestant Church, and in fact she never once had. Perhaps under these circumstances, it would be admissible? Without words, she prayed for forgiveness in advance.

Cars sped past her down Arlington Street, racing to cross Boylston before the light changed. A driver blasted his horn, irked that the car in front of him had stopped for the yellow light. Angela shuddered. She hated the city. She had been to Boston few times over the years, rarely since Vittorio's death. Everything she disliked about it seemed worse now: it was bigger, louder, dirtier, faster. She gathered herself, smoothing her overcoat and adjusting her hat, the black one she wore when she had occasion to dress formally. Though she longed to get back on the train and go back to Gloucester, to admit that this endeavor had only the faintest hope of success, she knew, in her desperation, that it was the only hope she had been able to find, like someone spending her last dollar to buy a lottery ticket because her children were starving.

With the *Boston Globe* not being published due to a strike, Thomas, like many others, had begun to pick up the *Christian Science Monitor* in its place. Angela often read the headlines of the *Globe*, but rarely opened it further, finding it dense and inaccessible. The *Christian Science Monitor,* on the other hand, was readable, and it was there, the day before, that she had seen a small article on page seven about a protest march over the weekend.

On Friday, March 25, a young man named David Benson had destroyed his draft card at a gathering of protesters in front of the Boston Army Base. The protesters had also tried to disrupt traffic to interrupt the flow of draftees being bused in from local draft boards across the state for induction. Benson and eleven others were arrested. The following day, Noam Chomsky from MIT and Bradford Lyttle from the Committee for Non-Violent Action led two thousand marchers from Cambridge Common across the Harvard Bridge into Boston and on to the Arlington Street Church. Along the way they were heckled by counterprotesters and pelted with eggs and beer bottles. In recent months, anti-war activists and organizers had decided that the dramatic increase in the draft was the best way to build opposition to the war in Vietnam. The march was an effort to develop solidarity in the movement. Angela read the article with great interest and then later in the day decided: she would contact these people for help. The Arlington Street Church seemed the clearest place to begin.

Carefully, anxiously, she walked across the street and up the front steps of the church. Before entering, she crossed herself. Once inside, she was surprised to discover that it looked like a church: basilica style with a long nave; Renaissance arches copied from a church in Genova; stylized Corinthian columns bursting with acanthus; stained-glass windows depicting the Madonna of the Flowers, the Annunciation, the Good Shepherd, the Sermon on the Mount. No crucifixion to be seen, and no holy water with which to bless herself; but otherwise, it looked like a church. She paused for a moment, relieved to be in a quiet and seemingly holy place, out of the city's mania, and then moved forward. Hearing a shuffling of papers above her head she turned to see the back of a man sitting at the organ console in the balcony, below towering brass organ pipes which rose to the full height of the sixty-foot ceiling. "Excuse me, sir," she called up to him. He didn't answer. "Excuse me, sir," she tried again, conscious of her accent, "is there an office? Is there someone here I can speak to?"

"Down the right aisle, through the door, down the stairs," he responded without turning around. Angela thanked him and hurried away, pulling the door closed behind her just as the first deep tones of Handel boomed out into the sanctuary.

In the church office she found a woman close to her age sitting in front of a typewriter. Her hair was yellow white and pulled up in curls on top of her head. She wore horn-rimmed glasses on her substantial, round nose, and a pink cardigan sweater over a gray flannel dress. "May I help you?" she asked, sizing up Angela with vague curiosity.

Angela reached into the pocket of her coat and pulled out the article from the *Christian Science Monitor*, which she had carefully clipped. Unfolding it gingerly, as though it were an ancient treasure map, she handed it to the woman.

"Ah, yes," the secretary said, holding the article in one hand and tilting her bifocals with the other. Angela wasn't sure from her reaction that the woman entirely approved of the events the article described.

"Is there someone here who knows about this? Do you know how I can speak to Mr. Ch-, Mr. Cho—"

"Professor Chomsky?"

"Yes, thank you, or Mr. Lyttle?"

"What's your question regarding, if I may ask?"

"I'm sorry?"

"What do you need to know?"

"It's about my grandson and . . . the draft."

"I see. Why don't you have a seat? I'll be back in a moment." Angela sat down in front of the desk in a black college chair bearing the seal of Harvard Divinity School.

The secretary returned after a few minutes. "The senior minister suggests you go to Cambridge and speak to the people at the American Friends Service Committee. They might be able to help you. Good day." The woman sat down in front of her typewriter and returned to her work, looking over her glasses at her notes, at what she had already typed, and then back at her notes. Presently, she glanced back at Angela, who sat still in the chair, looking perplexed. They stared at each other for a moment.

"Cambridge?"

"You don't know how to get to Cambridge, do you?"

Angela shook her head.

"Do you have any money?"

Angela nodded.

"I'll call you a cab."

Angela clutched her rosary and prayed as the cab lurched through Boston, raced across the bridge, and then wove recklessly through traffic in Cambridge. Finally, when she was near to being sick, the driver stopped short in front of the address the church secretary had given him.

"This is it, lady. It'll be three bucks." Angela pulled her change purse from her pocket and drew three bills from it, passing them across the seat, her hands shaking noticeably. The driver, who wore a beaten leather cap over unkempt hair and a doughy, pockmarked face and chomped the stub of a once-sizeable cigar, looked at the money out of small, close-set gray eyes before plucking it from her hand. "In this country, it's customary to give the guy a friggin' tip," he muttered.

"Excuse me?"

"Never mind, lady. Never goddamned mind." Angela shrugged, opened the door and stepped out onto the curb. The cab screeched away, sped down Massachusetts Avenue, pulled a sudden U-turn at the next corner and shot back past her towards Boston.

I hate the city, she thought.

There was no sign in front of the building, just a dented steel door with the address on it. She went in and climbed the steep, dimly lit stairs, clinging to the railing. At the top there were doors on each side of the narrow landing, one of which bore a hand-written sign: AFSC. She knocked. A voice called for her to enter. Turning the knob she pushed the door, which squeaked on its hinges, startling her.

The door opened into a large, windowless square loft lit by fluorescent lights suspended from rough beams on the ceiling. Tall bookcases packed with books and binders interspersed with filing cabinets lined one wall, with more books piled on the floor. Along the wall next to the door was a table with four telephones on it, with a clipboard holding a thick packet of paper in front of each. A half-eaten sandwich and a mug of coffee sat next to the phone at the far end of the table. In the center of the room, an overfilled trashcan was surrounded by crumpled balls of paper, so that it looked like a fountain. Placards mounted on sticks of wood were stacked against the wall in a corner. The top one, in large, bold letters, read "STOP THE WAR!" Angela glanced around, full of doubt. It seemed unlikely that the solution to her problem was to be found here.

The voice answering her knock had come from a young man with a mottled yellow beard. He wore a faded baseball cap backwards, from which curls billowed on every side, a gray sweatshirt which said "BROWN" on it across the chest, and corduroys which were threadbare in the knees. He was sitting in front of a mimeograph machine, cranking off copies of a flyer by hand. It was warm in the room and sweat dripped down his face and into the beard. "How can I help ya, ma'am?" he asked.

"I have a question . . . about the draft and . . . my grandson." The young man stopped cranking the mimeograph machine.

It hiccupped, spitting out one more flyer, and then hissed and stopped.

"Has he been drafted?" The young man wiped his face on his sleeve and stood up. Angela nodded. "And you're trying to help him? That is so cool. Damn, I wish my grandmother would do something like that for me. So, where is he?"

"He's at work. He doesn't know I'm here."

"Hot shit. You are a far-out lady." Angela shook her head, befuddled.

Before today, she thought, I thought my English was not so bad.

"Let me introduce you to Larry. He's the one who knows about the draft."

Larry was sitting on the other side of a partition at a desk composed of two low file cabinets spanned by a piece of plywood. He was surrounded by papers and file folders stacked precariously, so that it seemed as though at any moment they might slide together into a single heap like a collapsing house of cards. On the walls of the partition were posted flyers announcing anti-war events across New England, along with newspaper articles reporting on protest activities. Larry was older, perhaps in his forties. His black hair was thin at the crown, with hints of gray at the temples. It was cut in the style of the early Beatles, with bangs straight across his forehead. He had long sideburns and a mustache, also dashed with gray. His shirt was of homespun cotton, dyed a watery blue, just deeper than his faded jeans. A cigarette, which had burned down to the filter without being smoked, smoldered in a pottery ashtray on top of a stack of papers on the desk. Larry was reading and making notes in the margin of a document, handwritten on yellow legal paper.

"Hey, Larry, this lovely lady has a question about the draft," the younger man announced, appearing with Angela at the opening of the cubicle. "You got a minute?" Larry turned and looked at Angela.

"They drafted her?" The two men laughed. "Jesus, it's worse than I thought."

"No, man. Her grandson. She's trying to help out her grandson. Ain't that sweet?"

"Gotcha. Yeah, that is sweet. Wow. Okay, here," he grabbed a pile of papers, a potential avalanche, off the seat of a folding chair. "Sit down, ma'am—please. Gimme the whole story." While Angela settled herself, Larry reached for his cigarette, noticed that it was burned down to the filter, the ash skeleton of it lying in the ashtray, stubbed it out and lit another. He dropped the pack on his desk, then picked it up again and offered it to Angela. She shook her head.

"So, your grandson got drafted?"

Angela nodded.

"He's 1-A?" Angela nodded again. "He's not a student? Not married? Not a father?" Angela shook her head to each question. "No handicaps—bad vision, bad back, bad ankles, nothing?" Angela shook her head.

"Okay. Well, tell me about him. Doesn't sound good so far, but maybe we can come up with something. He's not a Quaker by any chance?"

"No, he's healthy. He's a good boy."

"Oh no, a Quaker. I mean, his religion."

Angela blushed, embarrassed by her ignorance. "Uh, no. He's been raised in the . . . Episcopal Church." She had to think of the word. "The thing is, sir, I don't really understand very much about war. I don't understand about this Vietnam. Why—"

"Me either, honey," Larry scoffed, resting his foot on the edge of an open file drawer and pushing himself back to balance on the rear legs of his chair.

Angela's eyes filled with tears. "All I know is that my husband was killed in France in the first war, and my son was killed in Sicily in the second war, and it just doesn't seem right, or fair, or—"

"Hang on, now," Larry interrupted, dropping the front legs of his chair onto the floor with a thud. "Your husband, the boy's . . . grandfather, was killed in World War One? Fighting for the US?"

Angela nodded. "And your son, the boy's father?" Angela nodded again, quizzically, wondering why the man seemed so excited by her misfortune. "He was killed in World War Two, fighting for the United States?"

"That's right. In Italy."

"And is he—your grandson, by any chance, the only son of your son?"

"Yes. My son never even got to see him. He was born after Vittorio left."

"God bless America!" Larry exclaimed. "Jesus, I wish they were all this easy. You're absolutely right, lady. It's not fair. And believe it or not, even the government agrees with you. Let's see . . . surviving sons." He opened a file drawer to his left, studied it for a moment, chewing his thumbnail, then beamed and pulled out a file. "*Surviving Sons*," he announced. He opened the file. "Congress passed the law originally in forty-eight, right after the war. Back then it only protected the sole surviving son if one or more of his brothers had died in service. They just expanded it two years ago, though. How 'bout that? Now it applies to a sole surviving son where the father or a brother was killed in military service."

"I don't understand," Angela said. She continued to read the exultation on Larry's face and was ready to be happy too, but was not there yet.

"It means that because his father died in service, they can't draft him. It's an exemption for only sons. You're all set. Now, Congress can pull the exemption during wartime, but they haven't yet. So far they haven't even declared war on Vietnam. So . . . your grandson walks!" He raised his arms in the air like a referee signaling a touchdown.

"Is this true?" Angela's heart was beating fast.

"It's true, ma'am! It's all right here." He tapped his finger on the open file. "You may have saved the boy's rear end by coming here. No one at the draft board would ever offer this to you, but if you present your evidence, there's nothing they can do. He's exempt."

"I don't believe it. I don't believe it." She wasn't sure whether to trust this man and his excitement—it seemed too easy, ephemeral.

"Believe it. Like you say, it only seems fair, right?"

"What do I do now?"

Larry leafed through the file and handed her a piece of paper. At the top were typed the words: *Only sons and the draft.* "He should take this piece of paper, along with your son's death certificate. You have that, right?"

"Yes, of course. It tells where he's buried in Italy."

"When's your grandson's induction supposed to be?"

"April seventh. Next week."

"Have him take this paper, the death certificate, and his birth certificate. They should issue him a letter saying he's exempt under the 'sole surviving son' provision. And that's it. He goes on with his life. Man, I wish they were all that easy."

"I don't know how to thank you," Angela whispered. As it began to register that she had found a way out of the nightmare, she felt an urge to hug Larry, or to cook him a meal, to shower him with gifts.

"Now, now. You don't need to. That's why we're here." He jumped out of his chair. "Come here. Give me a hug." Angela stood and Larry embraced her.

"Now, buy some champagne on the way home and have a toast in honor of the AFSC."

Larry walked her to the door. The mimeograph machine had broken down, and the young man was attempting to fix it, squatting on the floor next to it with a wrench and an instruction manual and mumbling to himself. Larry closed the door behind Angela. "Jesus, I wish they were all that easy."

More than anything, Thomas was moved by his grandmother's courage. That she had discovered an exemption, a provision, a way out for him was a wonder. But it was as a sign of her love for him that her efforts had the greatest meaning. And with the awe at what she had done came an overwhelming sense of relief that he wouldn't have to leave her. He would care for her from now on, and make sure that she never lacked anything she needed.

He stopped in the harbor in the morning to tell the captain he wouldn't be at work. They were scheduled to spend the day repairing nets and scrubbing out the hold. He had planned to stop work at the end of the week in any case to spend his last few days preparing to leave. From there he drove to Belmont. As he had hoped, no one was home. It was Wednesday. Edmond was at work, Ashley at school, and his mother at bridge club.

Important family documents were stored in a fireproof box on a shelf behind some books in Edmond's study. The key was hidden on a hook under a blue-and-white Spode teacup in the china cabinet in the dining room. Thomas only knew this because at twenty-one, when he had come into control of his trust funds, his mother had shown him where the relevant documents were kept.

Setting the gray metal box on Edmond's desk, he took the small key and unlocked it. After a moment, he found an envelope marked, in his mother's handwriting, "Birth certificates: Thomas & Ashley." He opened the envelope. The first one he unfolded belonged to his sister. He put it back in the envelope and picked up a second piece of paper. This one was the certification of his legal adoption by Edmond. Folding it and sliding it back into the envelope, he took his birth certificate. It was on legal-size green paper, folded in half and then in half again. Carefully, he opened it. He began to read: "Registry Division of the City of Philadelphia . . ." When he reached the place where parents' names were listed, he froze. There, in the block designated for "name of father" was the single word his angry and embarrassed grandfather had written on the application in the hospital nearly twenty-three years earlier: UNKNOWN. Thomas stared at it with horror, his hands shaking.

"I don't think we should discuss this over the phone," Larry said, and then cleared his throat. "I think it would be best for you to come into the office."

Thomas hung up the phone.

"What did he say?" his grandmother asked anxiously.

"He said we can't talk about it on the phone. I think he's afraid someone could be listening in. He wants us to come to the office to talk about it."

"Fine. Let's go."

"Now?"

"Now? Yes, now, Tomuzzu. You're supposed to report a week from today. We're running out of time. You might have to go to Philadelphia to get your birth certificate fixed." She was tired, not having slept during the night. Thomas had come home late the previous afternoon after driving around trying to avoid telling her the news. She had been furious: "How could your mother have written '*Unknown*'? My son wasn't even dead yet." Thomas had no answers to her irate questions—the same questions he'd been asking himself, the same questions he wanted to ask his mother, demanding answers. Instead of sleeping, Angela had sat in bed much of the night reading the Bible and praying. Thomas was up late as well, working on his list of things he needed to do before his induction.

They drove into Cambridge, arriving before noon. Thomas parked in front of the AFSC office. "I can't believe you came here all by yourself," he said as he opened the door for her.

"Well, Tomuzzu, it may be nothing compared to what we have to do next."

Larry was in his usual place, poring over documents and making notes. He was tracking casualties in Vietnam for a report he planned to issue in time for an anti-war "read-in" at

Harvard in early May. With a red bandana tied on his head and a jean jacket on, he appeared to Angela younger than he had before.

"Do you have your birth certificate with you?" he asked Thomas once they had been introduced and an extra chair had been found. Thomas gave him the document. Larry read it and frowned. "This would be a long shot—no guarantee they'd accept it—but do you have a baptismal certificate of any kind?"

"I do, but my father's name isn't on there either."

"Hmm. Well, I'm sorry to say, if you can't prove this man—her son—was your father, then the 'sole-surviving-son' provision won't apply to you. Unfortunately, I don't think the draft board'll take your word for it." He frowned in sympathy. He handed the document back to Thomas, who held it open and looked at it as though hoping he might find something different on it. They were silent for a time.

"Now what do we do?" Angela asked, determined not to give up.

"Yes, good question." Larry settled back into his chair and reached for his cigarette. He took a long drag and let the smoke escape through the corner of his mouth. "Well, unless you think you could get married or, preferably these days, get married and have a baby in the next—"

"I have until Thursday. A week from today."

"Unless you could get married or have some kind of . . . accident before then, I hate to say it but I think you've only got one other option."

Thomas and Angela waited for him to continue. Leaning across his desk, Larry flipped on a transistor radio. The Beach Boys came on, singing their latest hit, "Sloop John B." Larry turned it up loud, then shifted forward in his chair, motioning for Thomas and Angela to come closer.

"It won't sound good at first, but it's a way out more and more guys are taking. You won't be alone, that's for sure. I predict it's going to become an exodus once people finally realize how stupid and destructive this so-called conflict is."

"So?" Angela prompted, impatient and worried.

"I think your only option is Canada."

"Tomuzzu, go get my Bible for me, please."

There had been few words between them on the way home. Larry's conclusion had created a vacuum between them, eliminating all the air and leaving them none for breathing, let alone to speak. Angela had gone into the house and cooked. They had eaten in near silence. She made coffee, and then sent him for her Bible.

When he returned, she was sitting on the couch. She signaled for him to sit down next to her. "I want you to read something to me."

"Yes, Nanna?"

"I want you to read to me about Abraham and Isaac. It's in Genesis. Chapter twenty-two. Start at the beginning of the chapter."

Thomas, uncomprehending but obedient, found the passage and began to read:

> And it came to pass after these things that God did tempt Abraham and said unto him, Abraham: and he said, Behold here I am. And he said, Take now thy son, thine only son Isaac, whom thou lovest, and get thee into the land of Moriah; and offer him there for a burnt offering upon one of the mountains which I will tell thee of. And Abraham rose up early in the morning, and saddled his ass, and took two of his young men with him, and Isaac his son, and clave the wood for the burnt offering, and rose up, and went unto the place of which God had told him. Then on the third day Abraham lifted up his eyes, and saw the place afar off. And Abraham said unto his young men, Abide ye here with the ass; and I and the lad will go yonder and worship, and come again

to you. And Abraham took the wood of the burnt offering and laid it upon Isaac his son; and he took the fire in his hand, and a knife; and they went both of them together. And Isaac spake unto Abraham his father, and said, My father: and he said, Here am I, my son. And he said, Behold the fire and the wood: but where is the lamb for a burnt offering? And Abraham said, My son, God will provide himself a lamb for a burnt offering: so they both of them went together. And they came to the place which God had told him of; and Abraham built an altar there, and laid the wood in order, and bound Isaac his son, and laid him on the altar upon the wood. And Abraham stretched forth his hand, and took the knife to slay his son . . .

"That's far enough. You can stop."

Thomas looked up from the Bible at his grandmother.

"There's something that's always bothered me about that story. Do you know what it is?"

Thomas thought for a moment. "That Abraham was willing to kill his son?"

"No, Tomuzzu. My question is, Where was Sarah, his mother? Where was Sarah when his fool-headed father was leading him off into the woods to kill him? All her life she waited for a son. She thought she was barren, and then, in her old age, God gave her a son. And she was going to look the other way while God took that son away? It's not believable. No mother could do that."

She took his chin in her hand and looked into his eyes. "I said this to you the day I met you, Tomuzzu, and I'll say it again, because I want to make sure you understand. After your father died, I wondered why I stayed here. I even asked myself why I continued to live. Why I got out of bed in the morning. My life seemed to have no purpose at all. For years I tried not to think and I just worked, until I couldn't work anymore, and I took care of Carlo, and I just waited for death to give me a gift. And then you appeared at my door and I understood why I had continued to go on all these years. At once it all made sense. I'd been waiting, without knowing it, in my old age—just like Sarah—for this beautiful boy, my son's son." She paused.

"Tomuzzu, I have to live with the fact that I stood by and let your grandfather and your father lay themselves down on that altar. Maybe by doing nothing to stop it I laid them on the altar myself, an altar to God or to man and war and power and madness, whatever unholy altar it was, I stood by. And they were taken. Both of them were taken. God tested Abraham's faith, but he didn't take Isaac. I went forward in faith. They convinced me to, and what was mine was taken away. Twice. And so now, I have no more of that kind of faith. I can't stand by, Tomuzzu, and let you be taken. I won't offer you on that altar. I won't."

She pulled an envelope from inside the front cover of the Bible and pressed it into his hands. In her eyes he saw her resolve.

"Please, please, leave, Tomuzzu. Go to Canada. Please."

April 5, 1966
Gloucester, Massachusetts

Dear Mother,

I hope this letter finds you, Edmond and Ashley well.

As you know, Thursday is the day I'm meant to report to the draft board for induction into the Army. I know this won't be easy for you and especially for Edmond to understand, but I've decided that I'm not going to report to the draft board and that I'm not going to serve. In fact, by the time you get this letter I'll be in Canada. I'm sorry that I can't tell you in person and say goodbye, but I've been advised not to tell anyone until after I've crossed the border. It's a crime what I'm doing, and no one is exactly sure what the government will do about people who leave the country to avoid the draft. I wouldn't want you to be implicated in any way, so this—telling you in a letter which you'll get after I'm gone—seems like the best way to proceed.

I imagine you're wondering why I've made this decision. You know of course that my grandfather and my father were killed while serving in the military. The only way I can assure my grandmother that the same won't happen to me and give her peace, is to go away. She begged me. I explained to her that I could join another branch of the service and probably get a desk job and offered other reassuring scenarios, but, understandably, she was unconvinced. It seems my father and my grandfather promised her similar things. So, I'm going. Depending on what happens I may never be able to see her again anyway, but she prefers that risk to the risk of my going to Vietnam.

My advisor tells me that you'll receive another notice or two in the mail demanding that I report to the draft board. You can disregard them. If anyone contacts you, just explain that you don't know where

I am. I guess that will essentially be true. Eventually my case will be turned over to the US Attorney. I may be tried and convicted in absentia, and that will be the end of it, or a warrant will be issued for my arrest if I ever return. So far it seems like the Canadian government isn't going to cooperate with the United States in tracking down draft evaders, so I should be safe there.

Ironically, I could have been exempt from the draft if my father's name—my real father's name—had been on my birth certificate. Turns out there's a law allowing that the sole surviving son of a soldier killed in a previous war is released from the obligation to serve. But there was no way for me to prove that I qualify for the exemption. Maybe someday you'll be able to explain to me why his name wasn't on my birth certificate.

I'll write again when I can. Don't worry—I'm okay.

Your son,
Thomas

April 8, 1966 (Good Friday)
Montreal, Canada

Cara Nanna,

I made it! Smile, Nanna—don't be sad. I'm here, I'm safe. I'll admit there were a couple of moments when I thought I wasn't going to get here. Not because of any problems at the border. The guards came on the bus to check our documents. One, who looked like he was younger than me—just a kid, really—shined a flashlight (it was late at night) on the front of my passport for a moment and kept right on going. I was prepared to explain that I was visiting Marie's family and I had the addresses she gave me ready to show him, but he wasn't interested. The reason I feared for my life was that I was convinced the bus driver was drunk! He kept swerving back and forth—worse and worse as we crossed into Vermont and it got dark outside. He would speed up and then slow down and then speed up again. We were all terrified. Plus, I think there was exhaust leaking into the passenger area. All of us on the bus felt sick. You'll be happy to know that I said the rosary about fifty times on the beads you gave me the other night. I kept thinking about how awful and perverse it would be if I died in a bus accident while trying to escape the war. Anyway, thank God that's all behind me and I'm here in one piece, out of the clutches of Uncle Sam.

We crossed the bridge into Montreal close to midnight. I got a cab at the bus station—told the driver I wanted a decent hotel. I'd say the one I ended up in is more than decent—very big and fancy on one of the main streets near the Cathédrale Marie-Reine-du-Monde. (Hopefully she's looking down on me!) It's above the train station and connected to a vast underground world—stores and restaurants and passageways. Seems fitting to be down there since I'm officially in hiding.

I'm not sure where to go from here, Nanna. I'm trying not to think about it too much, at least for a day or two. I don't plan to go to Marie's family's house in St. Faustin until I've had some more time to think. After all, I've got nothing but time now. Funny to think that everything I've ever known is behind me, out of reach. Including you. But I know we'll be together again soon, once this all gets sorted out.

I'll write again in a few days.

Your grandson with love, Thomas

―――――――――

April 17, 1966
London

Dear Nanna,

It was so good to talk to you on the phone on Easter! I'm glad I was able
to reach you. I was awfully lonely after we talked, thinking of you and
Marie having Easter dinner together without me. It was cold and rainy
in Montreal too, with even a few snowflakes, which didn't help.

Anyway, the good news is that everything went smoothly and I'm
here in London. I crossed the Atlantic in just eight hours! Didn't you
tell me it took you more than a month? The time difference threw me
off, though. I stumbled into this hotel—the Regent Palace—collapsed
into bed and slept for twelve hours. Still not sure my body's caught up. I
don't seem to feel hungry or tired at the right times. But it's better today
than it was yesterday.

I'm glad I decided to leave Canada and come here. I feel more like
a tourist and less like a fugitive. Try not to worry about me. I'm staying
safe and even eating okay. Missing you. More soon.

Your grandson,
Thomas

April 18, 1966
London

Dear Mother,

Surprise! I'm in London. Yes, London, England. I arrived two days ago (I think. I'm a bit confused by the time change) via BOAC from Montreal into Heathrow. I vaguely remember being here as a child with you and Edmond. Nothing specific stands out in my memory, though, except maybe Big Ben. In any case, on Easter Day I decided to come over here. Why not? I feel like a person who was just born at age 22. I've got no past and, as it turns out, no future other than what I create in the moment. Montreal just didn't feel like the right place to end up. I wasn't really comfortable with how a young American man was perceived in Canada. No one knows how to respond to a deserter. There's lots of suspicion about subversives, Communists, and so forth. I don't really fit in the hippie scene and, well, leaving the US was not exactly a great act of conscience. I don't even know how I feel about the war.

So, I'm staying in a hotel just off Piccadilly Circus. I've been strolling around a bit through the city—Covent Garden, Trafalgar Square, and even the West End. I saw the changing of the guard at Buckingham Palace. Planning to go to St. Paul's tomorrow.

I hope you're well and not worrying too much. Didn't you always tell me that things have a way of working themselves out? I'm trying to believe you.

Your son,
Thomas

April 25, 1966
London

Dear Nanna,

Just a quick note to let you know that I'm on the move again. A week has gone by quickly! I wake up in the morning with nothing to do and still the days seem to be racing along. I've enjoyed the sights here, from Parliament to Westminster Abbey to the Tower Bridge. I've gone for a couple of long runs up one side of the Thames and down the other. The weather has been lovely with only one rainy day. Yesterday I went to the National Gallery—a museum that is curiously full of Italian paintings. No one could explain to me exactly how all that Italian art ended up in a British Museum. I can only imagine what Carlo would have to say about that.

Anyway, I woke up this morning ready to go. I'm not sure how I know it's time to go, but I do. I'm trying to follow something. I can't explain it yet. Seems to come from deep inside, like maybe it's the same something that led me to you.

I'll write again when I get to Paris. I say a prayer for you in every church I visit!

Your grandson with love,
Thomas

April 30, 1966
Paris

Dear Mother,

I seem to keep getting further away, and I keep crossing things—the US-Canadian border, the Atlantic Ocean, and now the English Channel—each one a reminder that I can't go back. I'm a criminal. I'm in exile.

I'm lonely. Can you believe it? Me? For the first time in my life I can actually say that I'm lonely. Exhilarating in a weird way, really, considering all the time I've spent alone. Something has changed, though. Is changing. I miss my grandmother, and Ashley, and you.

I've been angry for a while, Mother—another emotion that was probably there all along but I couldn't find it. I've been angry at you ever since I met my grandmother. Angry that you lied to me—or at least chose not to tell me the truth my whole life. Angry that I missed all those years with her, and grew up not knowing who I really was, who I really am. And more recently, angry that I had to go to this extreme, that I had to leave her to be able to assure her that I wouldn't die like my father and my grandfather. I haven't known exactly how to handle all of the anger, so I stayed away these last months, afraid it would come out in ways I'd be sorry for later, or that Edmond and I would end up in a huge argument.

But I've had time to think—lots and lots of time to think. I don't want to be angry forever, especially knowing that we may never see each other again, you and I. So I've tried to see it the way you asked, to consider that you always did what you thought was best for me. I'm getting there, slowly.

I'm in Paris, now. It was an adventure getting here from London—the train to Dover and the boat across the Channel to Calais, and then back on the train to Paris. The crossing itself was magical—fog and sun and rainbows, the white cliffs leaving and my first sighting of the Continent arriving. Paris is glorious, though it seems strange to be here as I hadn't planned or expected the trip. Anyway, not sure how long I'll stay here in Paris. Days? Weeks? Not too sure of anything, really.

Have they come looking for me yet? The Army, that is? Just tell them you have no idea where I am.

I'll keep in touch.

Your son,
Thomas

April 30, 1966
Paris

Carissima Nanna,

I just finished a letter to Mother and was thinking about you and all that's happened since I saw you last. Are you sure this was a good idea? I know it was the only way to be certain nothing would happen to me in the military, but it seems crazy for us to be so far away from each other. Cruel and unfair—all those years you were so close by and I never knew it, and now I know just where you are but we can't be together. I'm 4,000 miles away. Sometimes I think it would be better to come home and face the consequences—go to jail if necessary. At least then we could see each other. You could visit and bring me good things to eat! I really miss you. I'm aimless and uprooted. Even a little scared. I'm just now able to admit that. Don't want to worry you, but I can't help wondering what the rest of my life will be. Wandering the world alone?

I hope you're well. I think about you all the time. You could write me back at the hotel, although I'm not sure how long I'll stay here. I have an itch to keep moving, as though there might be someone following me. Larry said they wouldn't. I hope he's right. I'm sure J. Edgar Hoover could find me if he wanted to!

Give Marie a kiss for me. I'll write again in a few days.

Suo nipote con affetto,
Tomuzzu

May 2, 1966
Paris

Cara Nanna,

I'm leaving Paris to go to Italy today. Just packed my bag and am getting ready to go to the train station—wanted to let you know. I'll be taking an overnight train to Bologna. I met some tourists from there yesterday. I heard people speaking Italian and after hesitating and trailing along behind them for a while finally dared myself to say something to them. They turned out to be university students who were on vacation after finishing their exams. I've never been very good at making friends, but it didn't seem so hard with them. We talked for a while at first on the street and then in a café and later at dinner. They hadn't met too many Americans before and had lots of questions—mostly about the Kennedy assassination, Bob Dylan and Vietnam. They were all opposed to the war and to "American imperialism." Carlo would have liked them! I didn't mention that I had left the country to escape the draft, though. I just told them I was a tourist. It was fun to try out my Italian, although I must say I often got left behind in the conversation. They tried out fragments of English on me, which was funny too. Last night they left to go home, and suggested—insisted, really—that I come visit.

Of course, I guess that's where I've been headed all along anyway—since I decided to leave Canada. Maybe I just needed God to put a signpost in front of me to show me the way? I'm excited, now. Hoping to sleep in my "couchette" on the train and wake up in the morning in Italia!

I'll write when I get there.

With love,
Thomas

———————————

May 5, 1966
Bologna, Italia

Cara Nanna,

Sono qui! I miei piedi stanno su terra Italiana. Che meraviglia!

The train ride was long. I didn't sleep much. There were several station stops, and we had to wait at the border of Switzerland and again at the Italian border while officers came aboard to check our passports. I was bleary but happy to see the sun glowing in the east after we crossed through the Alps—very exciting to see Italy for the first time!

A cab driver at the train station recommended a pensione that just happened to belong to his brother-in-law and very nicely delivered me here. I'm practicing my Italian, trying not to be shy, asking directions and ordering food in restaurants. Nanna, being here is amazing. I don't remember ever feeling this way before—open to the world around me in an exciting and sort of unexpected way. At night I've been sitting on the steps of San Petronio—the huge church in Piazza Maggiore—just watching people and listening. The friends I made in Paris said they'd be back in town on Monday to start studying for their next set of exams (they do things differently here), so I'm looking forward to seeing them. I wish you were here!

Con un bacione,
Tomuzzu

---

19 May 1966
Bologna, Italy

Dear Mother,

I realize it's been a long time since I last wrote. I apologize. As you can see, I'm now in Italy. I left Paris at the beginning of the month and came to Bologna (on a long overnight train ride) to visit some Italian friends I met in France. They insisted I come, and I really had no reason not to take them up on their invitation.

So, I'm fine—having a great time, actually. Who knew being a fugitive from the United States government could be so much fun? I've attended a couple of lectures, in the Facoltá di Scienze Politiche. Politics is the major topic of conversation here. Bologna is a communist city—imagine that? After a lecture the other afternoon a group of us went to an osteria (tavern) for a beer. Picking up on the prof's comments, they started to give me a hard time about American foreign policy, especially with regard to Vietnam. I made the mistake of mentioning that I had left the country to avoid the draft (previously I *had told them I was just a tourist, traveling for a while before starting law school). Well, you would have thought I was another Garibaldi! I thought they were going to have a parade for me they were so impressed. I didn't have the heart to tell them that it wasn't really about ideology.*

At first I felt very much like a foreigner—like I was wearing a sign around my neck that said "tourist" on it. But I bought some clothes and some shoes at a fashionable store in the center of town, and with my Italian improving, I can almost pretend that I belong here. I'm beginning to fool people. I like that.

I'm staying in a little pensione not far from the center and close to the university. It's very homey—I have a nice little room with a bed, a desk and an armoire. I like to sit in the big front window and watch the world go by down below on via San Vitale. Who knows? Maybe I'll stay a while—take a couple of courses when my Italian gets better. The law school is meant to be excellent, the best in Italy, they say. I could get my degree here. Anyway, I'll try to do a better job of letting you know where I am, but for now I'm here and I'm well.

Mother, I have a favor to ask. I know you probably don't feel like I have the right to ask a favor at this point, but I don't know who else I can turn to. Would you be willing to check on Angela? I worry about her, being all alone. I'll put her address and phone number below. Maybe you could give her a call and make sure she's okay? I would really appreciate it.

Love to you and everyone there.

Your son,
Thomas

May 29, 1966
Bologna

Dear Nanna,

I'm just back to my room in the pensione after attending Pentecost Mass at San Petronio. The Mass was beautiful—the clergy were all in red, with huge bouquets of red roses on the altar. After the service, the monsignore released a white dove, which flew across the piazza and landed on the head of King Neptune in his glorious fountain. We all watched from the steps of the church, and everyone cheered when he lit on Nettuno.

I've mostly been traveling since I wrote—day trips and a couple of overnights. I went to Venice, which I loved. It is the most amazing, enchanting place I've ever been. Last weekend I went home with my friend Massimo who lives in Genova and studies law in Bologna. His family lives in a modern apartment building in an industrial part of the city, but we saw the old harbor, including what they say is Christopher Columbus's house, and the duomo. I was surprised to see a large bomb set on a pedestal right in the sanctuary. Turns out it was dropped on the church by the Germans during the war—came right through a window and should have destroyed the whole place except that it failed to explode. They consider it a miracle.

I've lighted candles for you in churches all across central Italy. You're in my prayers.

Love,
Tomuzzu

June 1, 1966
Bologna

Dear Mother,

Just writing to tell you that I'm pushing on. I'm packed and getting ready to leave the pensione in Bologna later this morning for a train south. I've had a good time here and made some good friends. I've improved my Italian (my friend Stefano says I'm autosufficiente now) and traveled quite a bit to other cities and towns around Bologna, and even further, including Venice and Genova. Last night my friends took me out to Pizzeria La Mamma in via Zamboni in the university quarter to say goodbye. We were out until 3:00 am. It was fun. I drank too much beer! I could imagine myself staying here—permanently, I guess. I've already made good connections and I've begun to feel at home on the one hand. After all, I've got to end up somewhere, right?

But I keep bumping up against the same thing. People in the north of Italy really look down on the south. They say Sicily isn't really part of Italy. The sentiment runs very deep. It's like racism in the United States. So guess what? I stopped telling people that my family came from Sicily. I started saying that I was Italian, but I didn't know exactly from where. And then, the other day, I realized what I was doing. I was going right back to what I did my whole life. Pretending not to be something I am.

Bologna is known for its liberal, even radical politics, but in some ways it's like the Lincoln or Belmont or Weston of Italy. It's full of jewelry stores and fancy clothing stores and trendy bookshops and expensive restaurants. (It's called Bologna la rossa, but also Bologna la grossa—the fat.) The difference for me of course is that I can pass here. I don't stand out like I did at home, and my otherness as an American seems to be an okay thing, not a bad one—a novelty, at least. But the truth is that I'm not from here. I don't belong here, either.

I got closer to something, here in Bologna. But there's something else—more—further on. I'll admit I'm a little afraid that I'm after something that doesn't exist. Maybe we're all dis-located—out in the world on our own, and some people are just better at creating the illusion of connection than I am.

I'll write again when I can.

Your son,
Thomas

—————————

June 6, 1966
Roma!

Cara Nanna,

I hope you like this rosary. It was blessed by Pope Paul VI himself! I bought it yesterday at the Vatican after attending mass in St. Peter's Square. It was very exciting. I had chills even though I was sweating in the heat of a balmy spring day. I thought of you and how much you would have enjoyed seeing "il papa" in person. He has a warm presence—even from far away you can feel it. I understood most of his sermon, which was in Italian. I could hardly believe I was really standing in front of the Vatican listening to the Pope.

Rome is incredible. I have the sense that I could stay here for months and not begin to see everything. It's like London and Paris in that way, but somehow more alluring and dramatic. It feels different than Bologna too. Seems a bit more relaxed. People drive faster, but *life moves a little slower. The intervallo at midday lasts longer. Only tourists go to restaurants before about eight o'clock at night, too, when the Romans begin to come out. The weather is spectacular—warm and sunny. I hope it's the same where you are.*

More soon.

Your niputi with love,
Tomuzzu

June 9, 1966
Rome

Cara Nanna,

I don't know exactly how to tell you what I did today. Sorry if my handwriting is kind of shaky. I'm on the train back to Rome from Nettuno, thirty miles or so to the south. Nanna, I have been to the Sicily-Rome American Cemetery.

First let me tell you that it is a beautiful, tranquil place. I got a taxi from the small town of Nettuno to the gates of the cemetery—very impressive and official-looking bronze gates. Inside there's a visitors' center, which looks out on a reflecting pool, with the tomb of the Unknown Soldier on a little island, and then a long grassy mall. At the other end of the mall there's a very nice chapel and a museum which tells the history of the Sicily invasion and the battles on the mainland when the Allies fought the Germans back to Rome. The cemetery is laid out with ten plots, five on either side of the mall, divided by neatly kept hedges and paths. 7,861 military dead are buried here under white marble crosses. In the chapel, the names of 3,095 more whose bodies were never found are engraved on the walls. It really is a peaceful place, with cypress trees and pine trees and lots of flowers in bloom and all kinds of birds singing. It's jarring, though, to see the pictures in the museum of the ugliness of war, and to read the history of the fierceness of some of the fighting as it moved up toward the German's Gustav Line south of Rome, and then to wander through this lovely, orderly, calm and quiet, perfectly tended place where all the dead are buried. Does a pretty cemetery make the truth less awful or the pain of 10,000 families less real?

A very nice man—an American serviceman—in the office helped me find my father's grave. He told me that a priest was available if I wanted one, but I really just wanted to be alone. Vittorio Amorelli is buried in plot C (I remembered that much from the letter you showed me) closer to the reflecting pool than to the chapel. The guide—Henry his name was—walked me to the spot. I had flowers—a bunch for you and a bunch for me that I had brought from Rome, and I arranged them at the base of the headstone.

How can I describe what I felt, Nanna? There I was, as close to my father as I've ever been, or could ever be. I cried, hard. I'd never really cried before about the fact that my father died, that I never got to meet him. Seeing his name there on the cross, it felt real in a different way than it ever had that I did have a father, and that he was killed, as though I had just been told the news for the first time.

Then suddenly I had an urge to dig. I wanted to tear away the grass with my hands and dig down to his coffin. Crazy, I know. I wanted to see him and to be able to touch him. I'd come such a long way (literally and figuratively) and then to be separated from him by six impenetrable feet of dirt was unbearable.

I'm sorry if this is hard to read. I have tears in my eyes again as I write it, thinking about you and knowing how much you loved him and how devastating his death was for you and how much you've missed him. I saw his grave, Nanna. I was that close. Finally I sat down—sort of collapsed—on the ground. It was warm and I started to feel tired. I fell asleep there in the sun, lying on my father's grave. I wish I could say

I dreamed he was holding me in his arms, but I didn't. I'm afraid that's beyond where even my dreams could take me. But, I woke up feeling different, ready.

We're getting close to Rome, passing from the countryside into the outskirts of the city. Your son is resting in peace. I'll write again as soon as I can.

Ti voglio bene,
Tommaso

June 13, 1966
Naples, Italy

Dear Mother,

I think I last wrote from Bologna. Since then I've been to Rome and am now in Naples. Italy keeps changing as I move south. I guess I do too. I went to visit my father's grave in the American cemetery near Rome. As you can imagine, it was kind of overwhelming. I know so much more about him now than I did before I found my grandmother. I didn't really know anything before that. But I'll never know everything. I'll never know what kind of father he would have been, or how he smelled or what his voice or his laugh sounded like. I know from pictures what he looked like when he was twenty. It's hard to imagine what he would have looked like as he approached fifty.

Did you love him, Mother? I have to admit, I never thought much about that possibility until recently. I've always focused on what happened after—on what you did after he died—marrying Edmond and so forth. Did you love him? Would you have married him? I'm sorry I never considered what it must have been like for you when he left or when you found out he'd been killed. I think I haven't been totally fair. I do wish, though, that you had made it possible for me to have a relationship with my grandmother as a child. I understand that there were obstacles. I know it wouldn't have been easy or comfortable on either side, but still . . .

Have you called her? I worry about her.

I'm leaving here soon. I'll write when I can.

Your son with love,
Thomas

June 14, 1966
On a ferry in the Tyrrhenian Sea

Nanna,

A quick postcard to tell you that I'm on my way. I'm so excited I can hardly believe it. Naples just disappeared from view behind us. Now I'm watching the horizon for the first sight of land even though it will be a while. We should be in Palermo by this evening. I feel like you're with me, even though we're far apart.

With love,
Tommaso

June 28, 1966
Cefalú, Sicilia

Cara Nanna,

I'm home. I'm home! Let me tell you what happened. Maybe if I tell it in order I'll remember everything I wanted you to know.

I'll start when Sicily first came into view. I left Naples early one morning two weeks ago—feels like longer!—on a ferry. Didn't you take a ferry to Naples and then the ship to the US? I thought about that when I saw land in the distance. The first I saw of splendid Sicily was the last you ever saw of your home. The sun was shining and the coast was so beautiful—the green mountains sloping up from the gray-blue sea and the shimmering beach. I thought about you and Nannu leaving there, choosing to leave everything behind. I know you wanted something better for your children and grandchildren—which is me, of course. You left this amazing place—home, family, everything—for me.

I stayed overnight in Palermo in a hotel. I could barely sleep even though I was tired and left on the first Messina train I could get the next morning. I was actually trembling when the train began to slow down and the conductor called out the stop: "Cefalú!" I walked from the train station down through Piazza Cristoforo Colombo, past the crowded fish market and down to the beach. Cefalú is spectacular, just like you described it although the duomo and the rocca are even bigger and more impressive than I imagined. The duomo dwarfs the whole town, and then the hill above makes even the duomo look tiny. I stood on the beach for a while watching the fishermen in the harbor and just trying to absorb everything and to get myself to believe that I was really here.

Finally I walked into town through the Porta dell'Arena and onto via Vittorio Emmanuele. It was nearly noon and I hadn't eaten anything, so I stopped into a little cantina in a tiny piazza—the Cantina di Cicerone—do you remember it? I thought I would have something to eat and then check into a hotel so I could start exploring and trying to locate the family. As soon as I walked into the place, the host, an old but spry little man, started staring at me. Every time I looked up from the menu, I noticed him looking at me, studying my face. Then, he came over and stood right in front of me and declared, as though he had just solved a mystery: "Amorelli!" I couldn't believe it. He recognized me as an Amorelli! After I had taken a second to catch my breath and get over the surprise, I explained that I was indeed an Amorelli, but that I was a second-generation American just coming back to Sicily more than fifty years after my grandfather, Tommaso Amorelli, left. Before I could finish, he was taking off his apron, picking up my bag like it was empty and dragging me by the hand out the door.

I followed him down the street and then up via Botta. We went up to a door and he started ringing the bell and shouting to the window above. A woman appeared amid the wash that was hanging out to dry on the balcony and my new friend very excitedly explained who I was. Nanna, since that moment, I don't think anyone has gone to work or done much of anything except celebrate. I've been hugged and kissed and wept over more than I could ever begin to tell you. And fed—everyone wants a chance to feed me! I can't believe it, Nanna. I thought I would have to explain who I was and I really didn't know how they would receive me being an American and everything, coming back after so long. I don't think they could be happier or more generous and welcoming if Nannu himself or you came back.

I'm staying with Nannu's brother, Calogero. He can't stop crying. He and everyone else old enough to remember say I look exactly like my grandfather. I'm nearly the same age he was when he left, so it seems especially shocking, as though fifty years haven't passed. Zu Calogero has told me at least ten times that he begged Nannu not to leave. He says he told him that the promise of America wasn't real, that the ship owners were just trying to sell tickets, and that the factory owners in America were looking for cheap labor to exploit. "How could the streets be paved with gold? I knew it was a scam!" He says there have been hard times and they've never been rich, but they've survived and they've been together. I think it really hurt him that Nannu followed Carlo instead of listening to him, and it broke his heart when the family got your letter and learned that Nannu was dead. He says my arrival is like God giving him another chance. He and his wife Lorena are so kind. Everyone is. They said I can stay with them as long as I want.

I've met scores of cousins and neighbors and friends—on your side too. All of the older people remember you and they all send their love. I've seen the house where you were born and the church where you were baptized and married. And the duomo. I love the duomo. The mosaics are stunning, just like you said. The one of Jesus is maybe the most beautiful thing I've ever seen.

What else? Zu Calogero took me out on his boat. He was impressed that I knew a few things about fishing. And the kids—my little cousins, have taken me up the hill to see the ancient Temple of Diana and the castle at the top. The view is indescribable, looking through the crenellations on the wall of the fort and out across the sparkling sea. I can't believe this is where I'm from (where we're from)—this lovely, delightful place. It even smells wonderful. I can't imagine what you must have thought when you arrived in New York City—and the first time it snowed! Oh, Nanna. I'm sorry you had to leave this place. It seems like paradise to me.

There are a couple of cousins my age, too—Zu's grandchildren—two boys and a girl, and two more boys and two girls on your side—your sister's grandchildren. I've met all their friends. They're so proud of their American cousin, a novelty to show off, I guess. But they are so fun and their friends are great. I can only understand half of what they say (they try to remember to speak Italian instead of dialect) but I'm having a ball getting to know them.

I know I'm rambling on and on. It's just amazing to be here and to see this place and to meet these people. It's so ironic, Nanna, and it hurts my heart. You and Nannu left because you wanted a better life for your children and grandchildren, and here I am, back in Sicily, enjoying life more than I ever have before. Everything you went through—Nannu's death and my father's too. I know times were hard here and you did what you had to do, or what Nannu believed he had to do. I know I wouldn't be alive—never would have been born—if you hadn't left, but the price you paid seems way too high. I'm sorry, Nanna. I miss you.

I should go now. My cousin Sebastiano wants to take me to see the sights in Palermo today. I'll write and tell you more as soon as I have a chance.

With love,
Tommaso

June 30, 1966
Cefalù, Sicily

Dear Mother,

I arrived here in Cefalù a couple of weeks ago. I found my family quickly and easily. Someone actually recognized me as an Amorelli just a few minutes after my arrival and brought me here to the home of my grandfather's brother, Calogero. The whole family—both sides—has claimed me as their own. It's all been overwhelming. I've never been hugged and kissed so many times or with so much warmth and sincerity in my life. People argue over whose turn it is to have me over for dinner. And my cousins are so proud of their American relative. They've been showing me a good time.

Did my father tell you much about this place? Calogero is still here, and one of my grandmother's sisters is still alive. Calogero is retired officially from fishing, but he still has a small boat and loves to go out on the water. He's taken me with him a few times. Sitting in his little boat out on the water, listening to his stories about my grandfather, looking in at the beach and all the other brightly colored fishing boats in the harbor and at the town rising up from the edge of the sea to the hills, and up and down the coastline, I can almost imagine what it would be like to be from here.

So, that's all for now, Mother. Know that I'm fine. Don't worry about me. I don't know when or how we'll see each other next. I guess we'll have to wait and see what happens. I hope the military hasn't been breaking down your door. I know this can't be easy. I'm sorry. I wasn't sure what I was doing when I left. Now I know that I needed to come here. I don't imagine that's any comfort to you, though. Again, I'm sorry.

Give my love to everyone there.

Your son,
Thomas

July 2, 1966
Cefalú, Sicily

Dear Brother Andrew,

It's been a long time since we've seen each other, and a lot has happened since I left the monastery for the last time. I was angry that day. What you said confused and bothered me for a long time. But you were right.

I didn't know myself well enough then to understand what you were talking about.

I was aware that my mother's husband, the only father I knew, was not my biological father, but I didn't know any more than that. Through some detective work, I found my grandmother. Meeting her changed my life.

As fate (God?) would have it, I was drafted earlier this year. My grandmother, who had lost her husband in World War I and her son in World War II, begged me to leave the country rather than go into the military. I could not say no. I went to Canada, and then to England. And then, realizing where I was going only gradually, I traveled to Paris, and then to Italy. I visited my father's grave at the American cemetery near Rome and by then it was clear to me that I was on my way here.

So, I'm in Cefalù, my ancestral home. I've been warmly embraced (and embraced and embraced again) by my family. I can't help but think of the Prodigal Son when I consider the generosity and the feasting and the celebrations that have attended my "return." It is very good to be here.

My grandfather was a Sicilian in America. My father was a Sicilian-American. I'm now considering the possibility that, given time, I could be an American-Sicilian.

Thank you, Brother Andrew, for your friendship and for your insightfulness. I'm sorry I wasn't ready to receive it at the time, and I'm sorry I stormed out on you. I just want you to know that you made a difference. I might have found my way to my grandmother and to the truth on my own eventually, but you made it happen much more quickly and one might say, just in time.

I hope you and everyone at the monastery are well.

Yours,
Thomas Wellington

July 7, 1966
Cefalú

Cara Nanna,

I'm writing to you on my twenty-third birthday. Happy birthday to me! If only you were here it would be the most perfect birthday I could imagine. Your sister's daughter Alessia will be hosting a celebration tonight. Everyone is coming. It promises to be a great time. They started cooking yesterday!

What a year it's been. Last year I spent my birthday with you and Carlo and Marie. Do you remember? We had lobster and Marie made a chocolate cake. Carlo opened a bottle of wine which he'd been saving for a special occasion. That meant a lot to me. I was supposed to be getting ready to start law school. So much has happened.

Birthday aside, life here has nearly returned to normal. People finally went back to work. I'm still staying with Zu Calogero. I've settled in quite comfortably. During the day I help his son and grandson on their boats. At night I go out with my cousins and friends—eating and drinking and smoking cigarettes and laughing. I must start running again before I get any more out of shape.

Lately, Nanna, I've been having this feeling—when I'm awake and especially in dreams. I guess it started knocking around inside of me when I first got here, but it just keeps growing stronger. I feel like I've been here before. I know it sounds crazy, but I'm almost sure of it. Everything is familiar. I've walked these streets. My feet know the cobblestones and the little back alleys that cut down to the water. I've spoken this dialect. I've climbed the hill up to the fort and sat looking down at the coast before. I've swum in this water and fished in the harbor. I've sat through mass at San Nicola and lit candles in the duomo.

I've played soccer in the piazza with my friends. I've breathed the air, eaten the food. My face, my body, have been warmed by this sun before. I've been here before. It's impossible, but I know it's true. It's like my soul knows this place, even if my brain can't quite remember the details. Like I said, crazy.

Did you know I would come here when you told me to leave the United States? You never mentioned it, but did you know? I have the idea that you knew. I didn't know. It took time. I didn't know where I was going. At first I thought I'd stay in Canada and hope that one day I'd be able to come back to you in Gloucester. But I was being pulled to Sicily—magnetically pulled. By the time I got to the American cemetery—well, by then I felt silly because it was all so obvious. Maybe it's better you didn't tell me to come here, even if you were thinking it. I had to figure it out for myself.

We'll think of you tonight, Nanna. Light a candle for me. I know you probably already have today. I'll light one for you, and pray that you're well. Be happy, Nanna, knowing that I'm home.

Your grandson with love e un gran bacio,
Tommaso

———————

Thomas settled into life in Sicily. He adopted the rhythm of the day, the cycle of festivals and holy days, the climate, the food, the sense that the past was always present. His mannerisms shifted imperceptibly, so that he barely noticed. He dressed like his male cousins, combed his hair back like they did, learned to swear in dialect when they played soccer together in the evening. He shouted a greeting to his neighbors in the morning, and knew the names of the shopkeepers, waiters, gelato bar keepers, and newsboys he met in his daily circuits. At sea with his great-uncle Geru, he grew familiar with the progression of tides and currents in the harbor, and learned the best places to go to catch something for dinner. He even learned to ride a Vespa through the ungovernable maze of roads and alleyways.

If he thought about his old life, it was with an unsettled sense of fear and an unease akin to guilt. He was a criminal in the United States, a draft-dodging coward in the eyes of the law, a feeling that was mitigated only slightly by the growth of the protest movement which eventually led to the end of the war. If he went home, he would be put in jail. As much as he felt like he had shed a culture and an identity in the elite institutions of suburban Boston, which had never been a comfortable fit, his connection to his family had been real, and he had walked away from it without turning back. His mother, whose life had been marked by loss, and her steadfast effort to persevere and make a life for him. His sister. What was it like for her to lose her brother, whom she adored? Maybe, he reasoned, her life would be simpler without him, this awkward, mismatched half-sibling whose presence always required an explanation. Edmond and his grandparents, who had always tried, but had not always succeeded, to disguise their discomfort and treat him like he belonged. As he wrestled with these ambiguities, it seemed easier to let go of the uncomfortable emotions and questions than to engage them, to try to reconcile them, so that over time he thought about America as little as he could. He was no longer the same person, and it was no longer even the past—his life had started over again, and whatever came before had been all but erased. He remembered his grandmother talking about how the letters from family back home became more and more infrequent over the years, until finally they stopped. It didn't matter who had closed the door; the door was closed. His life was in Sicily, completely.

FOUR

THE BELL RANG, a high-pitched clanging from the arabesque sandstone tower above the courtyard, announcing the end of the school day. The teacher turned from the past subjunctive conjugation he'd been writing on the chalkboard, took off his glasses and placed the chalk on his desk. "*Basta così, ragazzi.* We'll continue from there tomorrow. Don't forget your homework assignment!" For a few moments there was a scramble: shuffling of papers, chairs being pushed back and then neatly tucked under desks, the chattering, laughing, and teasing of adolescents who've just been set free for the afternoon. Then as the students jostled out of the room the noise traveled away down the hall like a train pulling out of a quiet village, leaving the teacher alone. He smiled to himself. It was a fine group—one of his favorites in nine years of teaching at the school.

Loosening his tie, he took his tweed sport coat from the back of his chair and draped it over his arm. The day had warmed up after the sun erased clouds and an early morning chill. With his briefcase in hand, he walked out of the classroom, down the corridor, and out into the brightness of a perfect Sicilian spring day.

His daughter, seven-year-old Angela, was waiting for him on the steps of the elementary school next door, wearing her school uniform—blue jumper over a white shirt—and holding her book under her arm. A smile bloomed across her face when she saw her father. "*Papá!*" she called out, as though she had not seen him in many days, rather than just the few hours since he had dropped her off at the door to her classroom. She ran to him, grabbing him around the waist. He leaned over to kiss the top of her head, and then her forehead, and then her cheek.

"Hello, my sweetheart. I missed you!"

"I missed you, too, Papá."

He took her hand. "Shall we go, Angelina? Mamma and Elisa will be waiting. I have to drop something off on the way." They walked hand in hand down Corso Ruggero to the piazza, stopping in the municipal building across the sloping square from the *duomo*, perched in regal disproportion to the clutch of medieval buildings surrounding it. He had finished a translation project for the mayor, who was intent on increasing tourism by advertising in American and British newspapers and magazines. From there they continued down the hill to via Porto Salvo, chatting about the events of the day and trying to guess what Mariella might have prepared for dinner.

Reaching their door, from where they could just see through the ancient porta and out to the harbor and the glistening sea beyond, the little girl challenged her father to a race up the two winding flights of stairs to their apartment. Giggling, with him close behind, she charged up the steps and, panting, bounded through the door calling out, "Mamma, I won! I beat Papá!" Her father followed her, pretending to be exhausted and out of breath.

"It's not fair," he declared, bracing himself against the door posts. "She didn't run. She flew, like only little angels can. Floated right up the stairs." His wife stood in the doorway to the kitchen smiling, little Elisabetta clinging to the hem of her pale blue dress. Somewhere in Mariella's background there was a Norman ancestor; her complexion was fairer than her husband's. Her hair was streaked with auburn which lightened nearly to red during the summer, and her eyes were almost greenish, with a playful sparkle Thomas had noticed from the beginning. Angela resembled her father, with black hair and his olive skin tone and dark eyes, while Elisabetta, named for her maternal grandmother, took after her mother, a scattering of freckles decorating her round cheeks and upturned nose.

"I hope you two are hungry after all that racing," Mariella said, reaching down to pick up her daughter. "Come sit. Dinner's ready." She crossed the room to kiss him, and then to put the toddler in his arms before returning to the kitchen.

Mariella was a friend of his cousin Giuliana. He had fallen in love with her from a distance, unable to speak to her or even to be in her presence without blushing, forgetting how to speak Italian and feeling idiotic. She was lively and fun, popular, always with a young man or two attempting to woo her. She was charming, a good listener with warm, alluring eyes and an easy manner which drew people to her and made them feel liked and valued as friends.

In time, she noticed the shy American watching her. He was tall, handsome, but different, awkward but in an appealing way, refined but not snobbish. Guarded, but genuine. They moved towards each other slowly, over the course of a year, with her taking nearly all the initiative, to the point that she almost lost interest waiting for him to respond with something approaching enthusiasm, if not passion. For him it was a terrifying ordeal. He shook with fear the first time she kissed him, but he held on.

After eight years of marriage, they knew each other well. The barriers had fallen, which not only made room for a deep and enduring love, but for him to become himself. He was grateful to her for the patience and tenderness with which she had opened him, and she to him for taking her seriously as an intelligent human being.

Though they had an outwardly traditional marriage—she stayed home with the children and did the shopping and most of the cooking and cleaning while he earned a living for the family as a teacher—they treated each other as equals. They made decisions together. They read the same books and discussed them, along with politics and religion, subjects which fascinated both of them. She never hesitated to state her opinion, even if she thought he would disagree; and while they occasionally argued, they were guided by a true sense of respect for each other. Now he looked at her across the table wondering as he did essentially every day how he had managed to become something he could never have foreseen: happy.

After dinner, Mariella cleared the dishes from the table while he settled the girls in bed for their nap. As was their custom, they met back at the table for coffee and a chance to talk before they, too, would retire for the *sunnacchiata*. She set his espresso before him, and then, next to it, a letter.

He didn't need to look at the return address to see that the letter was from his mother, not his grandmother, who's occasional birthday cards and notes were addressed in her shaky, arthritic handwriting. Ellen wrote in her perfect, flowing cursive. They had corresponded regularly over the years since he left: birthdays and holidays, major life events. At times they had discussed plans for her to visit, but something always seemed to get in the way—the long illness and eventual death of Edmond's father, the birth of Ashley's first child, even the energy crisis which had limited international travel, and Edmond's insistence that she would be an "easy target" for criminals in Sicily. The years just went by. The frequency of her letters had increased recently, though, and with them a growing sense of urgency. This was the fifth letter in the three months since January 21. On that day, the day after his inauguration, to fulfill a campaign promise, President Jimmy Carter had issued Proclamation 4483, granting pardon and unconditional amnesty to those who had violated the Selective Service Act during the Vietnam era.

Thomas stirred sugar into his espresso, then picked up the letter, sealed in a red, white and blue airmail envelope, and opened it. Mariella watched his eyes scan across the page. He finished reading and passed it across the table. While he preferred to speak in Italian, she had learned enough English from him over the years to take in the main point of the letter: his grandmother was not well and asked for him almost constantly. She put the letter down on the table in front of her and smoothed it with her palm.

"What are you going to do, Tommaso?" He shrugged, picking up the demitasse. She leaned forward, resting her elbows on the table. "*Amuri*, it's time for you to go. She's asking for you. Begging for you. Why don't you go to the travel agency this evening and make plans to go?"

"I can't, Mariella. Not right now." Despite his mother's entreaties, he felt no desire to step back into what felt like ancient history, an alien world.

"Why not? They can't do anything to you now, Tommaso. The new president changed all that. You're not a criminal or a fugitive anymore. No more excuses. Go."

"It's just not a good time, my love. Okay? Let's drop it. I have to give exams soon. You know that. And there's another project to do for the mayor. Then I'll have papers to grade at the end of the term and then summer school." He turned and reached for the newspaper on the table behind him.

"Tommaso, don't you dare start reading that newspaper. We're having a conversation." He turned back, tilting his head to the side and raising his eyebrows. "And don't give me that look, either, my love. You and I both know that it's never going to feel like a good time. You're just going to have to explain it to the head of the school and to the mayor. They'll understand. It's a family emergency." She paused, her eyes searching his face. "What is it, darling? Why won't you go?"

Again, he shrugged. To her, it seemed like the shrug of a child trying to wiggle out of doing his chores, and she felt both pity and anger.

"I just . . . don't want to go back there. It's been a long time and I've put all that behind me. This is where I belong, with you and the girls. And . . . it's complicated. There are just too many ghosts."

The pity faded, anger beginning to win the struggle in her. "That's bullshit. Don't you see how selfish you're being? Would you be here if it wasn't for her? She saved your life. Do you ever think about that? Now, in her old age, all she wants is to see you again before she dies."

He pushed himself back from the table, folding his arms across his chest.

"It's been *eleven* years, Tommaso. The only ghosts are inside of you. I know you wanted to leave your old life behind, and from the way you've described it, I don't blame you. And you've done a damn good job of making a life here, with a little help from your wife. But you can't pretend that you didn't exist before you stepped off the boat in Palermo, and you can't deny your grandmother the one thing she wants, something she has every right to ask for, to demand. Now stop being such a stubborn mule and make some plans to go to her."

Later in the day, after he had lain awake next to her while she slept, Thomas took the girls down to the harbor and out in the small boat he had bought years earlier, used, from an old-timer no longer able to row it or care for it, whose sons had long ago left for America or to work in factories on the mainland. They floated out of the harbor and down the coastline, the *duomo* and then the *rocca* growing smaller and nearly fading from view before they turned back. The sun burned a white streak of fire across the water as he rowed the boat back east toward the harbor. The boat was his prize. He gave it a fresh coat of paint each spring and scrubbed it out thoroughly after fishing. The old-timer's gloom stayed with him though, and at times he imagined with a chill the day when he would be forced to pass the craft on to someone else for his brief turn. He loved fishing and delighted in bringing something home for Mariella to cook, or to bestow with a generous smile on the widow who lived downstairs. Yet even more than fishing, his greatest delight was to take the girls out on the sea. He loved to watch them, dangling their arms over the sides of the boat, dragging their fingers languidly across the gently rolling surface of the dark, deep water.

He pulled on the oars, keeping a steady, even rhythm. His wife's words passed again through his mind. Leaving the United States, he had been a person with no future. Arriving in Sicily, he was a person with no past. Mariella was right on that point. Even his closest friends knew only a cursory outline of his previous existence. Even to him after the years began to pass, his earlier life seemed shadowy and possibly not real at all. He had produced a copy of his Harvard diploma in applying for a teaching job at the school, but otherwise had given no other proof of his identity than the recognizable and indisputable characteristics of his face. He felt convinced that he was someone else now.

And, therefore, he was undone by the idea of going back "there." The fact that his grandmother had been asking for him was particularly unsettling, a phantasmic hand reaching out of the past to poke him in the back. He had imagined, convinced himself, that in making a life in Cefalú he had done as his grandmother had wished, and that she wouldn't fault him for giving himself completely to that new life. Returning had been impossible for so long.

He stopped rowing, crossed the oars, and rested them on his lap. He followed the ripples of a breeze as it blew across the water until it began to nudge the boat, turning the bow towards the shore. He stuck an oar in the water and pushed gently, to counteract it. Smiling to himself at the irony, he concluded: I've become the other half.

Ashley had fallen asleep, head on her mother's shoulder, sweater pulled around her neck like a blanket, not long after the delay was announced. Six months pregnant with her second child, she was tired from entertaining a busy two-year-old all day. It was nearly midnight, the terminal quiet and empty except for a scattering of friends and family members, many of them asleep, others pacing past the closed newsstand and fast-food counters, waiting for the overdue flight from New York.

Ellen was awake, watching the flight listing for updates and supporting her daughter's head and neck. She admired and appreciated Ashley, the daughter who had become her closest friend as an adult, the only one who understood the close relationship that Ellen had developed with Angela. Edmond had been angry, oppositional from the beginning, when Ellen first responded to Thomas's letter by going to see the mother of her first lover, and increasingly so when Ellen began to take responsibility for her in her infirmity. Indeed, it was Ashley who had mollified him, trying to bring him to a place of acceptance, if not understanding. Ellen often thought that their marriage would have collapsed if it had not been for Ashley's charm and diplomatic skills. She loved Edmond, but her sense of duty to Angela would likely have won if a choice had been forced, if he had ever demanded that she abandon the old woman, especially when that sense of duty developed into something much deeper: a friendship, and more than a friendship: a strong and ineffable bond built on the basis that they had both loved and lost the same two men.

She was anxious, glancing at her watch again and then again at the arrival information on the board. For months she had been writing to Thomas, encouraging him, imploring him in whatever words she could find to come back to the United States, afraid that Angela would die before he did. While she was concerned that Thomas would be filled with regret if his grandmother died, she was more concerned that Angela would die brokenhearted. Now, with his arrival imminent, her apprehension had become more pointed, locating itself in her chest, so that she felt she would not be able to breathe until Thomas and his grandmother were in the same room, face to face.

For eleven years now, they had seen each other regularly. At first Ellen visited on holidays, driving to Gloucester to take Angela to lunch. Then, she began to make the trip weekly, and sometimes more often. Both of them looked forward to their times together. The awkwardness of the connection, the fact that they had been brought together in such a strange and ultimately tragic way, soon faded. Ellen simply enjoyed her company, the stories she told, the warmth of her presence, the lack of pretense, her wit and insightfulness. She understood what had drawn Thomas so strongly to his grandmother, what she offered that had been missing from his life. At the beginning, visiting her was a favor to her son, the one he had asked for and one which she hoped might in some way be redemptive. Soon, though, the relationship stood on its own legs, unsupported by obligation or remorse.

For her part, Angela was grateful for the company and for the assistance which Ellen gave her, more and more over time. She was alone, frightened by her sense of vulnerability, and in need of help. Yet she, too—against any of the instincts which would have set her against a woman who had borne an illegitimate child to her son; a woman of a different class and religious background, from a different world, who had kept her grandson from her for twenty years—developed a sincere affection for her might-have-been daughter-in-law, and with it an appreciation of the love that her son must have had for her.

Two years earlier, after Angela had fallen while stepping out of the bathtub, Ellen had arranged for her to leave the apartment in Gloucester and to move into a nursing home. Marie, her best friend of more than fifty years, had died, and Angela was alone in Gloucester, stuck in the house except when Ellen could get there to take her out to shop and get her hair done, or to go to Mass. Because of her deteriorating health, she was no longer able to care for herself. Her arthritis in particular made cooking and cleaning painful, slow, and, above all, frustrating, because she could not do them to her own exacting standards, nor could any housekeeper

Ellen hired. Her heart was not strong either, weakened by coronary artery disease, which was Ellen's greatest concern. While she was more than willing to pay for nurses to care for Angela in the apartment, she wanted her closer, so she could see her more often and reach her quickly in an emergency. After suggesting the idea regularly for years, she had finally convinced Angela, reluctant to give up the house which contained the memories of her beloved Vittorio, to move. The nursing facility was a short drive from the Wellington's home in Belmont, and with nurses on staff and Mt. Auburn Hospital close by, Ellen's worries were at least partially alleviated.

From the loudspeaker, the arrival of the flight, the final one of the day, was announced by a hoarse, tired-sounding voice. Ashley stirred, along with others who were waiting. Ellen's heartbeat sped up. Again she imagined Thomas and Angela reunited, and she thought about the sad irony of how much more time she had spent with Angela than Thomas ever had, or ever would. Then, kissing the top of her daughter's head, she stood up and tried to take a deep breath. For the first time in more than a decade, she was about to see her son. A sudden surge of emotion took her by surprise.

The flight crew emerged from the gangway first, followed by a bedraggled parade of rumpled businessmen. Ellen and Ashley waited, Ellen standing on her toes in her espadrilles trying to see further down the line of passengers. Finally, he appeared. Spotting him, Ellen covered her mouth. Ashley let out a gasp which became the beginning of a sob. All at once, the subtle, mysterious, intangible passage of time was real. The twenty-two-year-old was thirty-four. His face, shadowed by a long day's growth of beard, was fuller, mature, with not even a hint of boyishness. To Ellen he seemed larger, more substantial. Ashley grabbed her mother's hand and squeezed.

Thomas recognized his mother and stopped walking. She was less changed than he had expected, as pretty as ever, with perhaps a few small lines on her forehead. A moment passed, however, before he realized that the pregnant woman next to her was his sister, who had been fifteen years old, lanky and with a short, pageboy hairstyle the last time he had seen her. He shook his head and grinned, shattering the immobilization that threatened to prevent the last twenty feet of the four-thousand-mile journey from being crossed. He dropped his satchel to the floor and opened his arms to receive the embrace of his mother.

Not having slept on any of the flights, to Rome, to New York, to Boston, or during the extended layover in New York, Thomas slumbered deeply for twelve hours, waking startled to find himself in the room of his childhood, the noonday sun glowing around the edges of the window shade. Coming to his senses, he was wrapped in melancholy, the source of which, he realized, was not the reminders of his youth in the room but rather the absence of his wife and daughters. He missed his family, never having left them before, and desired nothing more than to be back home. While he wanted to see his grandmother, he felt unprepared for the overwhelming emotional impact their reunion would surely have, and he was certainly not looking forward to his more imminent reunion with Edmond, who had been asleep when they arrived from the airport.

After unpacking his suitcase, showering and shaving, he braced himself and went downstairs. "It's the weary traveler!" his mother called cheerfully. She had come in from the garden, where the high June sun was already creating work for her, to see about lunch. Edmond had taken the day off and had played an early round of golf. He was on the telephone with his secretary, hanging up abruptly when he heard Thomas on the stairs. "Good morning, Tom," Ellen said, meeting him with a broad smile at the bottom of the stairs. "How'd you sleep?"

"Just fine, Mother, thank you. Took me a minute to figure out where I was just now, but aside from that—"

"Well, good. I'm glad you got some rest. That was quite a journey you had. Now . . . come say good morning to Edmond. He's waiting for you." Thomas rolled his eyes. "Come on, now. He's been looking forward to seeing you. Behave yourself."

She led him by the hand around the corner and into Edmond's office. "Look who finally rolled out of bed," she announced.

"Well, Thomas," Edmond said, turning from his desk. "Look at you. My God. What became of that little boy? All grown up. A man." Thomas crossed the room and extended a hand, which Edmond gripped and shook vigorously.

"Very good to see you, sir. It's been a long time, hasn't it? You're looking well." Sensing, after an awkward pause, that neither man knew what to say next, Ellen came to their aid.

"Tom, your sister and Drew and little Whitney will be here shortly for lunch. Why don't you give me a hand?"

The tautness slackened gradually over lunch. The presence of a child provided a catalyst, and young Whitney was as charming as the situation required. Before long he was bouncing in "Unco Tommy's" lap, giggling and singing. Thomas answered a series of questions about life in Sicily, his family, his work, his boat. He even managed to ask a few, catching up on the Lathrops, who spent winters in Palm Beach and summers on the Vineyard, and Mrs. Wellington, who, recently widowed, was preparing to sell the house and move to a retirement community.

Independently, Thomas and Edmond had decided to be cordial and to avoid substantive topics. Thomas asked him about his work, and about his new car, a Volvo. Edmond asked him about the weather in Sicily and about the food. He considered asking him his opinion about *The Godfather* and *The Godfather II* winning Oscars and about the accuracy of their portrayal of the mafia, or whether Corleone was a real town, but decided against it.

Soon Whitney began to show signs of needing a nap, and Ashley and her husband Drew said goodbye. He too had taken the day off from work at the brokerage office, but had scheduled a late afternoon meeting. Ellen, leaving the dishes in the kitchen for the maid, found Thomas on the patio where he was reading the newspaper and dozing. "Are you ready, Tom?" she asked, putting her hand on his shoulder.

"Mm. I don't know if I'm ready, but I guess we should go."

"Yes. It's time. She's expecting us."

The sun had vanished behind an advancing cloud bank, which brought with it the threat of an afternoon storm. Ellen turned into the driveway of the nursing facility, lined on both sides with blooming lilac bushes, slowing as she drove past the gatekeeper's booth. The guard, recognizing her, smiled and waved, putting a surprised look on his face.

"He's wondering why I'm here today," she explained. "I usually come on Wednesdays and Saturdays, and sometimes on Sunday afternoons too."

"Thank you for being so good to her, Mother. I'm really grateful to you, more than I could say." He felt the weight of the time that had passed, the years he had missed with his grandmother. His mother had taken his place, and he imagined the price she had paid to build a relationship with Angela.

"No need to thank me, Tom," she replied, pulling into a visitor parking space near the main entrance of the large brick building. "I think we've been very good for each other." He waited for her to say more, but she didn't. Instead, she reached into her purse, pulled out her lipstick, and used the rearview mirror to freshen her makeup. "If I don't have makeup on, she tells me I look pasty, and then she asks me if I'm eating right, and then, well, you know . . ."

Thomas laughed. "I guess she hasn't changed."

"Not so much."

Ellen greeted the receptionist at the desk, a woman older than her by at least ten years, whose white uniform bore her name on a blue pin: Betty. "Mrs. Wellington, you never told me your son was so good looking," Betty remarked.

"I'd almost forgotten myself." She patted the blushing Thomas on the shoulder. "Thank you, Betty. Now . . . do you think his grandmother is excited to see him?"

"I imagine so, Mrs. Wellington. She's been a bit . . . quiet, though. Hasn't had much to say the past couple of days. A lot on her mind, it seems. Hopefully this will cheer her up."

"I'm sure it will. Shall we?"

Thomas took a deep breath and let it out slowly. All of his efforts to prepare, to steel himself for whatever she might look like or however she might respond to him, collapsed. A cold sweat seeped out on his forehead.

"Don't worry, Tom," Ellen whispered, taking him by the arm. "It's going to be fine."

Betty picked up the phone and dialed. "Mrs. Amorelli, you have visitors." She listened for a moment. "Yes, of course. I'll tell them." She hung up. "She says she'll be ready in five minutes. She wants to get out of bed and into her chair." Angela's arthritis and osteoporosis, made worse by years of toiling over washtubs, sewing machines, cutting boards, and kitchen sinks, had made sitting painful, and her compromised heart left her tired, so that she stayed in bed and slept much of the time. She did not like television and, unable to knit or to sew, she preferred her dreams to the long, slow days with nothing to do.

After giving him a tour of the facility—dining room, activity room, health center, all in complementary shades of mauve, teal, and ecru—Ellen led her son to the door of his grandmother's room and then paused. "Why don't I just go in and make sure she's ready? Wait here, okay?" He nodded stiffly, imagining his grandmother's initial reaction to this place, the loss of her home and her independence, her community in Gloucester, her church, his own disappearance from her life.

"Hello, Mom," he heard her say. "You look wonderful today. How are you feeling?"

His grandmother's voice was clear and strong in response. "Fine, fine, Ellen. How are you, dear?" The hair on his arms and on the back of his neck bristled. "So, where is he?"

"He's here, darling. Are you ready? Fine. Tom?"

Clenching his fists, he stepped into the room, bowing forward as though he were afraid of hitting his head on the door frame, or of disturbing someone. Her room was small, furnished with a bed, a bureau, and an armchair. Ellen had replaced the nursing home's mauve bedspread and curtains with a bright print Angela had chosen from among the samples Ellen showed her. The photographs she had kept in her parlor in Gloucester were on the bureau: his grandfather, their wedding photo, his father, his own graduation picture, along with a bouquet of flowers, which was delivered to her fresh weekly at Ellen's instruction. On a small bedside stand, Angela kept her old, worn Bible, the rosary Thomas had sent her years before from Rome, and a small statue of the Madonna.

Seeing his grandmother sitting in her chair, Thomas was even more surprised that the voice he'd just heard had come for this small, frail-looking elderly person. She wore the same kind of flowered housedress he remembered, but it seemed to hang from her thin shoulders as if it were on a wire hanger. She was hunched forward, her white hair pinned up in a bun. She had aged more than he expected someone would in eleven years, as the vagaries of a hard life had accelerated the process. He felt ashamed, knowing that he had contributed to the suffering she had endured.

Grasping her walker for leverage, and with a supportive hand from Ellen, she raised herself up out of the chair, wincing at the pain in her back, hips, and knees. Then, pushing the walker to the side and opening her arms, she motioned with her fingertips for Thomas to come to her.

No one was capable of speaking for a time, including Betty, who watched from the doorway, a handkerchief pressed to her eyes. Thomas and Angela held on to each other until he felt her knees wobbling. His mind flashed back to their first embrace, the day they met, when she had slowly come to understand who he was, and they had first started to love each other. He and Ellen helped her ease back into her chair. "I think I need to take a nitro," she whispered to Ellen, who calmly went to the dresser and took a tiny pill out of a small brown bottle. Nitroglycerin was the only medication she would take, and only because the symptoms it relieved frightened her.

"Stick it under your tongue, darling." She reached down to check her pulse at her wrist. "It's just the excitement," she explained to Thomas. "She'll be fine, right, Mom?" Angela forced a smile, color noticeably returning to her face.

"Sit, Tomuzzu," Angela ordered once she stabilized. "Sit. We have many things to discuss."

They talked for hours, with a short break while Angela took a needed "*durmitina*," giving Thomas a chance to go into the bathroom and weep, the reality of the years that had passed overcoming him. Angela asked detailed questions about his life in Sicily, listening to his responses, trying to picture everything he described. They talked about old times in Gloucester. Angela told him how much Ellen had done for her, while Ellen insisted that Angela had done far more for her. Thomas had brought photographs, which he took from an envelope.

"Here we are on our wedding day," he began, giving her a picture of himself and Mariella in front of the altar in San Nicola, her lace train cascading down the marble steps of the altar. He handed the photos to her one at a time: a family picnic on the beach; Thomas and Sebastiano in front of the Cathedral in Monreale; he and Mariella in Agrigento at the Temple of Concord;

Thomas in Enna, where he had gone to see the place where his father died; Angela's and Elisa's baptisms, in front of the same altar in San Nicola; the girls in the doorway of the ancient Temple of Diana, wearing matching sundresses, surrounded by wild flowers and sky; his boat: blue, yellow, and red on the beach in the harbor. Angela held each one in her swollen, crippled fingers. He watched her eyes as she studied each one, taking in the details of the life she had made possible for him. At one point, he handed her the next snapshot before she was ready. She stopped him, holding his hand in hers until she had finished with the previous one, and then squeezed his hand to indicate that he could continue.

Late in the day, Ellen excused herself to call Edmond, as they were going to be late for dinner. "It's good you're here, Tomuzzu," Angela murmured. "Thank you for coming." She was tired, but she fixed him with an intense gaze.

"Of course, of course. I'm so glad to see you too, Nanna," he replied. He cleared his throat, leaning closer to her. "Nanna, I'm sorry I haven't . . ." She held up a hand to stop him.

"Shh. *Basta*." She began to speak in dialect. "Don't apologize, *Niputi*. You did right. You've done well. Your mother gives me all the reports. I'm proud of you. It's given me peace to know that you're happy."

"Thank you, Nanna." He responded in dialect, which he had worked hard to master over the years. "You gave me a gift greater than I could have imagined when you sent me away. I never knew I could have what I have in Cefalú. I never would have found it without you."

"God is good, Tomuzzu. God is good." He was moved by her faith, surprised that she could say those words. He tried to smile in agreement. "Now, Tomuzzu . . ." she whispered, staring into his face, "I need you to do something for me."

"Of course. Anything, Nanna." He took her hand.

"I want to go home."

"Home?" He was taken aback, then saddened. "Oh, Nanna . . . you can't go home. Someone else lives there now. Mother brought you here because you need people to look after you. You can't . . ." Again, she stopped him, raising her index finger to her lips.

"Tomuzzu, you know what I mean." Even as he was trying to talk her out of it, he knew what she was really saying. Home meant only one thing.

To Angela, Sicily was less a real place now than a tenuous, possibly false memory, with sights and aromas, sounds, an atmosphere, a character just beyond the edge of what her memory could recall or her imagination could recreate. As though in retribution, Sicily had left her, just as she had once left Sicily.

He knew, now, why she had sent for him.

"Tomuzzu, *Niputi*. Please. Take me home."

Her doctor, an unsmiling, youngish man whom Ellen had recently engaged after Angela's previous gerontologist retired, opposed the idea adamantly, to the point that he insisted on expressing his opposition in writing a formal letter in her medical file. She was not strong enough in his opinion to withstand the journey to Sicily, a journey which would consist of three airplane flights and nearly twenty-four hours of travel. Her heart was functioning at a fraction of its capacity, and the episodes she experienced were life threatening. Her nitroglycerin tablets had stabilized her in the past, but there was no guarantee that they always would, especially under stressful circumstances.

Thomas, sitting in the doctor's office the day after seeing Angela, emphasized his grandmother's desire to travel back to Sicily. "She's stronger than she appears, Doctor, believe me. And when she makes up her mind about something, well . . ." The doctor listened, hands folded under his chin. Rain had been falling all morning. Thomas paused, watching it through the window behind the doctor's desk.

He was tired, not having been able to sleep again, with the weight of his grandmother's request heavy on his mind, and the doctor's contrariness was eroding what remained of his composure. Even if the doctor was right, how could he possibly say no to her? But if the doctor was right, how could he responsibly say yes?

"I appreciate the motivations, Mr. Wellington," the doctor interrupted, standing to indicate that the meeting was over, "and you must do as you deem appropriate. I simply need to make clear my unequivocal determination that she is not in the kind of physical condition that would make such a trip advisable."

Edmond drove them to the airport. They would fly from Boston to New York and then overnight from New York to Rome, where they would take a day to rest before the final leg to Palermo and on to Cefalú.

Climbing out of the car at the curb, Thomas disappeared into the terminal to arrange for a wheelchair. Ellen took the opportunity to thank Edmond for understanding. "Of course, dear," he replied, smiling, though he had long ago given up trying to understand. "It's about time you met those grandchildren of yours." She nodded, then kissed him on the cheek before opening the door to assist Angela.

They traveled first class to increase the chance that Angela would be able to sleep comfortably. She had reluctantly agreed to take the pain medication her doctor had prescribed, which made it possible for her to withstand the transfers from car to wheelchair to airplane seat, and then through the process again onto the flight to Rome. She said little, seeming to withdraw into herself to conserve her strength. Thomas and Ellen exchanged worried glances whenever she seemed especially weak or pale, or when she grimaced in pain, as when she had to be helped into and out of the cramped airplane bathroom. Both of them, though they never spoke of it, were terrified that she would have an episode there in their arms, seven miles above the Atlantic Ocean where they were helpless to do anything to save her. Though they tried, neither of them rested, feeling the need to watch Angela almost constantly.

All three were relieved to arrive in Rome midmorning. They checked into a hotel close to the airport. Angela went to bed and slept until evening. Thomas and his mother slept as well, though uneasily. In his adjoining room, Thomas turned on the television, pleased to hear Italian being spoken. He'd made it there and back, though he hadn't expected to have company on the return.

They ordered room service. Angela had little appetite but was encouraged to eat. "You're going to need strength, Mom," Ellen pleaded. "Tomorrow is a very big day."

The plane took off under overcast skies, swallowed up by the dense, gray cloudbank within a few seconds of leaving the ground. An hour to the south, however, the cloud cover broke up and cleared, revealing the shimmering sea below, the coast of Sardinia just visible in the distance. Angela had fallen asleep shortly after the stewardess served coffee and a brioche. She snored softly, mouth open, holding her grandson's hand. When the plane began to descend, Thomas woke her.

"Look, Nanna. Can you see, down below? Home." He wasn't sure if she could see the island growing closer off the left side of the plane as the pilot banked to make his approach, until he saw a single tear drip out of each of his grandmother's eyes.

"*E bella, Sicilia, no?*"

"*Sí, Nanna. E bellissima.*"

Sebastiano met them at the baggage claim, greeting Thomas with a hug and a kiss on each cheek. Thomas introduced his mother.

"Mother, this is my cousin, the best man at my wedding, and my daughter Angela's godfather." He repeated himself in Italian for Sebastiano. "And, of course, this is my grandmother." Sebastiano knelt down next to the wheelchair and took her hand. "Welcome home," he said, smiling. "I hope you're ready, because there are a lot of people very excited to see you." Angela reached out to touch the young man on the cheek.

After another difficult transfer from wheelchair to car, they set off across Palermo to pick up the A19 east towards Cefalú. As they passed through Bagheria and the sea came into view, Angela seemed to awaken, as though she had been in a state of hibernation. Life returned to her face, which had seemed pallid and sickly to Thomas and Ellen when she had woken up in the morning, and she began to talk. She spoke slowly at first, unprompted by the others, telling the story of the day she left Sicily.

"My mother begged me, one last time before I got on the train to Palermo, to change my mind. 'I know he's your husband,' she said, 'but don't go. Write to him again. Tell him to come back.' I remember the way she cried. I watched her out the train window. She was sobbing, holding onto my father. It was awful. I didn't cry, though. I felt bad for hurting her. My God, I was so young. I don't think I knew what it all meant. I wasn't thinking that I would never see them again."

In the back seat, Thomas translated in a hushed tone for his mother, not wanting to interrupt.

"It's as beautiful as I remember," Angela continued. "The sea and the sky, the flowers . . ."

She fell silent as they entered the industrial zone around Termine Imerese, giant power plants and factories spewing black smoke into the pristine blue. Sebastiano read the surprise on her face. "Yes. Sicily has changed, hasn't it? For good or bad, who knows? We have jobs—some jobs at least. But we've given something up to get them."

Then Angela saw the mountains, green and brown, smoothly peaked, one rolling into the next, and she knew that they were almost there. They reached the outskirts of Cefalú just as the town was quieting down for the *intervallo*. Sebastiano steered expertly through the tight streets and parked his Fiat as close to the door of Thomas's apartment as he could. At once Mariella and the girls charged out the door into the street. "*Papá!*" the girls cried in unison. He opened his door and they clambered onto his lap, covering his face with kisses.

The next few minutes were a confusion of introductions, embraces, kisses and tears. Ellen understood nothing of what was being said but received the enthusiastic welcome of her daughter-in-law and granddaughters with a profound happiness, even a sense of relieved satisfaction that stayed with her and increased in the coming days, to see that her son, despite everything she feared she had done wrong, had made for himself a good life.

As word of Angela's arrival began to spread, Thomas and Sebastiano nearly carried her up the stairs to the apartment. Mariella had dinner waiting. They ate, with Thomas giving an account of the trip and all that had taken place. The girls waited anxiously, dancing about, to tell him about all the important things that had transpired during his ten days' absence.

Family members and friends waited respectfully until five o'clock so that Angela could rest. Then Ellen and Mariella settled her into a comfortable chair in the living room and the onslaught began. Thomas introduced each of them, explaining the connection and waiting for it to register with his grandmother, who would then pull the niece or nephew or cousin or neighbor close to her and bestow a kiss on the cheek. Seeing the joy as she received each person, Thomas was proud, knowing he had done something right.

For four days there was feasting and celebration. Each morning, Thomas took his grandmother and his mother to see the sights: the *duomo*, the beach and the harbor, the church of San Nicola. Angela delighted in all of it, her seemingly impossible wish being fulfilled. At night, after she napped, there were festivities. She was given the honors of a celebrity, even by those who had never known her, born years after her departure from Sicily. Her husband's brother, the last of her generation still living, and his family threw the biggest party of all, sparing nothing to show her a generous welcome. The outpouring of affection quickly erased the significance of the decades that had passed. She felt in some way redeemed, at peace, whole. She received all the attention with humility and grace, thanking everyone repeatedly and giving particular thanks to Thomas and Ellen for making the trip possible. "I'm so thankful God let me live long enough to come home." Thomas had become accustomed to the generosity and warmth of his family and of people in Sicily generally, the consistent outpouring of hospitality, but it struck him anew now, seeing the genuineness of the love being extended to his grandmother, and to his mother as well, who tried, bewilderingly out of her element, to accept it.

By evening on the fourth day, Angela was exhausted. She walked with hesitation, holding tightly to whomever was closest, as though she were walking on ice. They arrived back at the apartment from dinner at her niece's house at eleven o'clock. Mariella had left the party earlier to put the girls to bed. She met them at the door and helped them get Angela up the stairs and into bed. The color had left her again, and she seemed weaker, frailer. Still, though, she smiled, kissing everyone goodnight before lying down to go to sleep.

"Maybe we should find a doctor tomorrow," Ellen said before turning in herself. "It might be good to have her blood pressure checked. I have all of her records, Tom, and her prescriptions. You'll need to translate them. She's going to need a doctor here. I'd feel better if we took care of that before I leave."

Angela was conscious when her heart went into fibrillation. Lying there, breathing the sweet springtime air of her home, she felt calm, despite the crisis that was taking place inside of her. The blood began to back up, damage spreading quickly through the muscle tissue like a stain.

She tried to imagine her husband's face but couldn't bring it into focus. Instead, she saw Tomuzzu, or then again, maybe it was Vito, but as a boy. Or was it Tommaso, as she had known him in his youth? She tried harder, as her extremities went tingly, and then numb. She wanted to see Tommaso, wanted to hold his image in her mind, his expressions: triumph when he walked in the door after being away on a fishing trip . . . satisfaction when he finished eating a holiday dinner . . . the look in his eyes when he wanted to make love to her. But the images would not congeal. Frustrated, she gave up and tried to imagine the face of Christ as he appeared in the golden mosaic in the *duomo*: serene, welcoming.

And then, her mind clouded over and she went to sleep.

ABOVE THE TOWN there is a hillside of extraordinary beauty, even for Sicily. The sun arrives early in the morning, and lounges about comfortably all day. Wild grasses offer miniature flowers, lavender and yellow, to the sky. Lone cypress trees pierce the ground, fixing the unruly terrain to earth. The landscape undulates a time or two before carrying warm, fragrant breezes gently down across meticulously tended ochre fields of grape vines, olives, and citrus trees, and on to the sea.

Long ago, an unremembered ancestor, drawn by the sublime peacefulness of the place, chose it as a burial ground. The rich, red-black soil shelters the remains of generations: here an old man who nearly reached one hundred years; there a boy who drowned in the harbor; and just beyond, a woman who died giving birth to her fourth child. Many of the graves, long since forgotten, have returned to their natural, grassy state. Others, more recent, are marked with whitewashed wooden crosses, and lovingly adorned with roses, hyacinth and gladiolus.

A young man wades through the knee-high grass, wiping sweat from his forehead with a handkerchief as he reaches the top of the hill. He walks pensively, reverently, to the newest grave, where the soil is freshly dug, untouched even by rain. Here is buried a woman who left Sicily as a young bride to follow her husband to the land of promise, only to return more than half a century later to die in her native land. Flowers cover the site like a blanket to protect the deceased. The man bends to place his own token among the others: a bouquet of white lilies.

"It's me, Nanna," he whispers, "Tomuzzu," and adds a prayer, asking God to smile upon her, concluding with the *Padre Nostro*, and then he turns to face the sun and looks out over the water in the distance, watching enormous lazy clouds drift languorously from west to east. Images of his grandmother, in life and in death, tie his emotions in a knot, just below his voice box, and release a shiver through his body.

She was lost to him before birth, and then, restored. And, once again, by the power of fate, lost, only to be given back just in time. Three times she had ceded the one she loved most, twice to death, and once, finally, to life. Indeed, she was the one who had given him life, the life he had now. And, while his father had not lived long enough to be his father, she had given him Sicily, which became a father to him, claiming him as a son. Her death leaves him . . . empty, though he is consoled by the knowledge that he fulfilled her final wish.

After a time, he readies himself to leave. Kissing the tips of his fingers, he touches the white cross bearing her name. "Goodbye, Nanna." He mouths the words, for no sound can break the knot in his throat. He turns to go.

Concludiamo all'inizio

(We end at the beginning)

THE CHURCH DOMINATES THE PIAZZA, rising in elegance above the nondescript municipal building, a café, a pharmacy, and a few other establishments arranged along the cobblestone streets that cut across the square. The church is beautiful, with a simple bell tower and an alabaster statue of the Madonna wearing a golden crown. I know that my great-grandfather lived in this town when the church was being built. He was a young man then, and I can imagine him, along with the other faithful people in the parish, getting up early in the morning to work on the church before going off to his job as a *carbonaio*, or leaving work to spend a few hours laying bricks or spreading plaster or painting before going home to his wife and three children, my great-uncles and aunt.

I have been looking forward to seeing this church. I have had this well-developed vision in my mind of how it would play out. I would go into the church, light a candle in memory of my great-grandparents, who had left this land in search of a better life for their children and their children's children. I would wander into the sacristy and find the priest, who would pull out old leather-bound parish registers, and we would find the records of my family—baptisms, weddings, funerals. This history that had been out of reach would be right there in front of me, factual and clear in the fancy cursive writing of ecclesiastical officialdom.

But the church is closed. Boarded up. Towering scaffolding stabilizes the belltower. Cracks in the façade and missing chunks of stucco give evidence to the earthquake that had shaken the town— part of life on the slope of the most active volcano in Europe. I stare at the closed door. I turn back to the rental car, parked in front of the pharmacy, where my wife and my four-year-old son sit looking at me, registering the disappointment on my face.

It's a warm May afternoon. I'm writing a book, a novel, about being Sicilian-American. I realized months earlier that I couldn't write any more without going to Sicily, and I planned this trip. We've been here for a week, arriving on a bright morning at the tiny, outdated airport in Catania. I drove from Catania to the house we had rented in a small village on the water, adjusting to the driving culture that made our infamous Boston drivers look polite and overly cautious. Tears filled my eyes when we came up over the rise above Acireale and I saw the coast, stretching all the way up to Taormina, and looked out across the sea to Calabria to my right, and then at the lemon groves and the villages, church domes and watchtowers, cast up the side of the mountain until they faded out and the red and black volcanic wasteland rose up to meet the still snowy peak, where smoke poured out of the cone and tumbled down from ten thousand feet of elevation. My great-grandparents left this warm, textured, gritty and atmospheric place for me.

We met my cousins, descendants of my great-grandmother's sister, and had dinner at their home in the city. My grandfather had maintained the family connection and had made trips to Sicily, decades after his father had left, traveling to Naples and then on a steamship for weeks to Ellis Island, and then to cold and wintry upstate New York, where he found work in a match factory, eventually after two years saving the money to send for his wife and three children. My grandfather, as he would explain with a sly grin, was born exactly nine months after his mother arrived, followed soon after by two younger sisters. We travelled across the island to meet my grandmother's family in Agrigento, who also welcomed us with warmth and generosity, and took us out for a dinner with so many courses of fish and pasta and desserts, and conversation about Sicily and America, Berlusconi and Bush and World Cup soccer. I began to have a new sense of how deep family is, and how these lost decades meant nothing when we happened into each other's presence, an airplane erasing in a short time all that had transpired—wars, inventions, movements, careers, tragedies, celebrations.

This village, Santa Venerina, is the missing piece. Somehow, my grandfather had lost the link with his father's family. We had driven up from the fishing village where we were staying in search of the connection. The church, I was sure, would be the key that would open the door. I was wrong. Across the piazza, a group of men stands, chatting and gesticulating, smoking cigarettes and laughing. I look at my wife. She gestures in their direction. "Go ask about the church." I approach slowly. I hear the banter, but none of it registers. My Italian is good. I had taken four semesters of intensive Italian and then spent my junior year studying at the University of Bologna, where the purest and most correct Italian is said to be found. What I hear in Sicily is dialect, dialects—not regional accents of Italian but whole other languages, infused with sounds and emphases not heard in Italian, rooted in the island's past—Phoenician and Arabic, Greek and Spanish and Norse and French. It's the language of resistance—resistance to Latin and textbook Italian forced on the populace by outsiders, Romans and "Italians," when Italy finally came into being in the 1860s. Italian is what you speak when you must—in a government office or at school. Sicilian is your true language, though you can switch back and forth without thinking about it.

The men see me coming towards them, and they look surprised. This is not a tourist town. I'm not the twentieth person today to ask them why the church is closed. "Terremoto," one man answers when I ask. I look at his face. He resembles my grandfather. When he realizes I speak Italian, we begin to chat, and the other men break off and go to sit on a bench in the shade of a clump of palm trees by the town hall, smoking and laughing.

"My great grandfather was from this town," I explain. "I wanted to see the church, and to speak to someone about family records. Do you know if there's anyone around? *Il Padre*?"

"No, no one there. The records have been moved to Acireale. Work hasn't even begun on the church yet. These things take time. But your great grandfather—he was born here?"

"Yes. He left here as a young man to go to America."

"What was his name?"

"Murabito. Salvatore." A look comes across the man's kind face. Suddenly he seems suspicious, like I'm playing a game.

"Murabito? Salvatore?"

"Yes, sir. That was his name. He was born here."

"My name," he says, "is Murabito, Salvatore." We stare at each other, both having the same thought. Is he joking?

"The family was in the charcoal business," I explain.

"My family was in the charcoal business!"

"My great-grandfather left, in 1907. His charcoal warehouse burned, and the mule died. He took it as a sign that he should go to America."

"I know this story," he tells me. "My aunt used to tell this story, about the brother who left after the fire."

We stare at each other for another long moment. Suddenly, he throws his arms around me. We stand there in the piazza, in front of the church which our ancestors built together, on these cobblestones which our ancestors may have laid together, holding on to each other. A hundred years disappear. He's my uncle, my godfather, my family. I could have grown up helping him in his workshop, where he made furniture, and then the wooden blinds that cover every shop door and window in town. I could have run around with his children, who are my age, speaking their dialect, understanding their jokes, knowing every alleyway and corner of this little town, familiar with the aromas of food, of crops being burned in the fields in the spring, of lemons, the call of the man selling fennel and eggplants and blood oranges out of the back of his truck. I could have been an altar boy in the church, and played soccer on the dusty field by the elementary school with a scrappy group of kids, my friends. Of course, I know it doesn't work this way, but I can't help thinking about how an accidental fire in a charcoal shed and the death of a mule shaped my destiny.

Years later, I will have made many trips to Sicily. My cousins—third, fourth, whatever they are—will be among the people I'm closest to. My son will have grown up with their children, and they will use Snapchat and WhatsApp to send each other photos and memes on almost a daily basis. In their world, the letters that used to take months to cross the ocean, maintaining the family connections like a thread spun out and frayed, have been replaced by bytes that fly around the globe in milliseconds. I will have attended many Sunday masses and weddings, baptisms and feast days in this church, which was restored and reopened and then damaged and closed and restored and reopened again, the cycle of life on the flank of this timeless and dynamic landscape. I won't have learned to speak dialect, but I will have come to treasure this connection, the blessing of being welcomed as part of this family. My family. I will marvel at the way this chance encounter in the piazza has healed something that felt broken, filled in what had always seemed to be missing or lost, and changed everything.

The author with Salvatore Murabito,
Santa Venerina, Sicily, May 2005.

Ringraziamenti

(Acknowledgments)

W HEN PEOPLE ASK ME how long it took to write *The Land of the Living*, I usually say, "about thirty years." This story lived in my imagination, insisting that I tell it, until finally, I sat down one night after our son went to bed and wrote a page, a description of a hillside in Sicily and a young man visiting his grandmother's grave. When I had revised that page and felt okay about it, I read it to my wife. "That's good," she said. "Write some more." It was the beginning of a journey that meandered and diverged through the demands of work, parenting, life, as I wrote, revised, did research, traveled to Sicily, wrote more, traveled to Sicily again, and again. A completed manuscript sat for years, until one night, down with a visit from the global pandemic, I pulled out the jump drive where it had been stuck and re-engaged with Angela and her remarkable life.

Along the way I received help from librarians and archivists, and feedback from family and friends. When I finished a full revision in 2023, I kept Keith and the print team at the Gardner Staples busy making copies of the manuscript, which were then read by generous people who offered their encouragement and support. There are too many to name, but special thanks to my family and to Bishop Doug Fisher, Chuck Collins, James Rutenbeck, Cam Roberts, Lynne Potts, Cathy George, Brother Curtis Almquist and quite a few of my parishioners at St. Paul's Church. Their support gave me the confidence to explore publication.

Which led me eventually to the creative and strategic people at Green Writers Press, Dede Cummings's mighty publishing company located in Brattleboro, Vermont. From the start, I felt a strong sense of collaboration, and I have been accompanied throughout the process and also challenged to make the book better. I'm filled with gratitude especially for Dede, Rose Alexandre-Leach, Britt Lange, Helen Horner, Justin Bigos, and Ferne Johansson. Without this dynamic team, *The Land of the Living* would not be what it is.

And then, like any person with a dream and a goal that seems like a stretch, I'm deeply indebted to the people who believed in me. My parents have never wavered in their support for me and this book. Handing them the first draft years ago was the most gratifying moment of the whole process. The two people who were closest throughout, my companions on this journey, Jenny and Adam, made it all feel like an adventure to savor together, so that it never felt like work. Love and thanks to both.

The author is an Episcopal priest. He climbs Mt. Monadnock every week and visits his cousins in Sicily as often as possible.